WATCH HIM DIE

CRAIG ROBERTSON

**SIMON &
SCHUSTER**

London · New York · Sydney · Toronto · New Delhi

A CBS COMPANY

First published in Great Britain by Simon & Schuster UK Ltd, 2020

3 5 7 9 10 8 6 4 2

Simon & Schuster UK Ltd
1st Floor
222 Gray's Inn Road
London WC1X 8HB

Simon & Schuster Australia, Sydney
Simon & Schuster India, New Delhi

www.simonandschuster.co.uk
www.simonandschuster.com.au
www.simonandschuster.co.in

A CIP catalogue record for this book
is available from the British Library

Paperback ISBN: 978-1-4711-6536-8
eBook ISBN: 978-1-4711-6538-2
Audio ISBN: 978-1-4711-9393-4

Typeset in the UK by M Rules

Printed and bound in Great Britain by CPI Group (UK) Ltd, Croydon, CR0 4YY

To Ezrah, aged two, who slowed down this book's arrival but made it all worthwhile.

CHAPTER 1

Los Feliz was hip, that's what they said. Happening. Caleb guessed he knew what that meant, probably. It was a white kind of hip; not cool exactly, but nice, definitely one of the better places to live in Los Angeles. Better than Culver City, that was for sure. It was laid-back and busy, always new places opening but still had the old joints that had been around for ever, like the Dresden and the Vintage film theatre. Is that what they meant? Whoever *they* were.

Los Feliz was immediately below Griffith Park and just east of Hollywood in central LA. It was a neighbourhood where people actually walked. Not like Beverly Hills Gateway or Trousdale, where Caleb would most likely get arrested for walking. Or like Westmont or Chesterfield Square, where he might get shot. It was okay. Safe. Nice. *Hip.*

The big bonus was that it was the kind of neighbourhood where he could actually walk onto someone's lawn without the cops getting called or a dog getting set on him. That was important because lawns were his business.

It wasn't exactly a career and he didn't plan on doing

1

it for ever, but for now it meant cash to put him through school. It meant enough green that he could help out his mom and, on a good week, still spring for burgers for two on a Saturday night at HiHo if Lacey could get the night off.

He was saving the planet too. One lawn at a time.

Caleb's job was simple. And hot and hard and dull. He'd cycle around in search of front yards where the owners were respecting the drought and not watering their lawns. He thanked them for it by way of a patronising little sign that was supposed to encourage the neighbours to do the same. Every sign meant money.

Los Feliz was one of the areas that could be relied on to give a damn, so it was good pickings most weeks. Liberal lawns, that was what was really making America great again. He'd spend five days working every street within the Los Feliz boundaries, North Western Avenue to Hyperion, Loz Feliz Boulevard to Fountain. The next week, he'd cross the freeway and tour Atwater Village. The next two weeks it would be the sprawl of Silverlake. Just him and his second-hand Schwinn and as many signs as he could get into his backpack.

Loz Feliz was his favourite of the three neighbourhoods. No hassle, traffic okay by LA standards, good people and the bonus option of an occasional lunch break in the shade of Griffith Observatory when he had the time to make the trek up.

He wasn't sure he'd want to live here even supposing he ever had the money, and that wasn't too likely. Sure it was nice and all, big houses, a cool place to hang out, but it just didn't seem like a place he'd live. It was too quiet and that would drive him crazy. He'd need to hear folks yelling at each other or it wouldn't seem like home at all. Still, all Caleb cared was that it was good for his wallet and most weeks it was.

He was on Finley Avenue now, going east to west towards the bars and restaurants on North Vermont. He'd walk, cycle, walk, whatever it took. Most times he could tell from the saddle if the selfish assholes had soaked their lawns, seeing them lush and cursing them. The section between Hillhurst and Vermont was usually good for a couple of stakes though, so he was on foot, pushing the Schwinn and with Drake banging out into his headphones.

Watered. Soaked. Hosed. Wait, *there*. Dry and bare. Nice.

The house was just back off the street, dark wooden timber and white sills, with a square of parched lawn gasping in the heat of the afternoon sun. There was no sign of anyone around, no gate, no fence, just an easy two strides from the sidewalk to the grass. Caleb laid down his bike and slipped the pack off his back.

He positioned the small stake on the faded turf and drove it into the baked earth with two blows of his mallet. The sign was forced grudgingly through what was left of the grass, its message displayed to the neighbourhood.

Job done, Caleb paused for a moment to admire his work. He didn't really care all that much about the message. It was a good thing, he guessed, but he was more interested in the fact that twenty signs, all verified by photographs from his phone, meant sixty dollars. The message meant money.

He slipped his phone from his back pocket, stepped back to get the house into full view and took the photograph. The lawn was suitably dry, a bleached shade of grass that he liked to call dollar green.

He knew the wording on the sign by heart and could even recite it backwards if called upon to do so.

You're awesome. Your neighbourhood thanks you for not watering your lawn during this drought. You're saving everyone else, not just water.

Caleb took another photograph, making sure he got the house number in clearly this time. It was slightly shabby for this part of town, a millionaire dressed like a tramp, curtains drawn and a set of shutters closed. It could have done with a lick of paint too. Still, at least the owner was helping save water by letting his lawn go to seed.

Caleb could tell how long it had been since a lawn had been watered, it was like his own science. Even under a September sun, it didn't take long at all for the blades to turn towards yellow and the moisture to be sucked from the earth. Five days this had been, that was his best guess. Six at the most.

Maybe that doesn't sound long, but in Sprinklerville it was an age. For the grass, it was a lifetime. For Caleb it was three bucks.

'You're awesome.'

Yeah, awesome. Fool couldn't even find the time to open the curtains properly and let some light inside.

Caleb bent to pick up his bag of signs and was on the

rise when, from the corner of his eye, he saw someone move between the slight gap in the curtains. This could be bad – people weren't always best pleased to have something stuck in their lawn unasked. It might even mean losing the three bucks.

He froze, mid-rise, and tried to wait it out, hoping he hadn't been seen. Not that he was doing anything wrong, but he hadn't exactly asked permission either and didn't want some crazy with a shotgun rushing out and yelling at him to get off his lawn. It seemed okay, the door didn't open and no one banged on the window.

When he stood fully, he couldn't see anyone. Maybe he'd imagined it. *No. Wait.* There it was again, movement, definitely. He held up a hand in apology or greeting or something, he wasn't quite sure what. No one waved back.

He took half a step away but was drawn back immediately as he saw a dark shape dance in the shard of light that split the drawn curtains. It wasn't a person, but what the hell was it? He edged closer, seeing the shape sway and change direction. Caleb strode warily across the lawn until he was just a few feet from the window and could make out the shape. It was flies, a business of them, flitting across the window pane as one.

He couldn't say quite why, but they freaked him. So many of them and so agitated. He moved till he was right at the window and saw them close up through the glass. Eight, no nine, of them were on the pane, their spindly legs scratching at the surface. At least another twenty of their brothers and sisters fogged the air.

Caleb slowly removed his headphones and could hear

them clearly, buzzing like an army of tiny electric saws. This was wrong. Weird. His skin bristled and his heart pumped faster.

He pressed himself up against the glass, making an angle so he could see more of the room through the gap. He saw nothing but furniture and paintings, nothing until he followed his eyes and his instincts, seeing where the flies were thickest.

There was something on the floor below him, a shape immediately recognisable yet unbelievable. Caleb's breath exploded onto the window pane in shock.

There was a body lying on the floor.

Face up. Mouth open. Skin grey and purple. Flies everywhere.

CHAPTER 2

It was one of those rare and unpleasant September nights in Glasgow when it was warm as well as wet. Humid. *Close*, as the vernacular would have it. Cool and cold rain they were used to, *very* used to. Warm rain might have sounded better but it wasn't.

People were splashing along Paisley Road West trying to avoid the worst of it but stewing under raincoats, brows slick with sweat as well as the downpour. Detective Inspector Rachel Narey sat in her car yards from the corner of Lorne Street and watched them scurry. People covered up for the rain wasn't helping. She wanted, needed, to see them – heads and all. It was the only way it could possibly work. If it could work at all.

Her husband and daughter were home and dry, a few miles across the river on the other side of the city. She glanced at the dashboard clock, guessing that Tony might be reading Allana a bedtime story and felt a familiar pang of guilt at missing out. Sure, it came with the job, but this time was worse because it was voluntary.

No one was making her sit listening to the rain bounce

off the car roof, and no one was paying her to do it. This was unpaid overtime of her own choosing.

Tony, to his credit, didn't mind. Or if he did, he made a good job of not showing it. God knows if anyone knew what she was like, it was him. Dogs with bones didn't have a look in.

She'd never been one for giving up on a case even when she was told, ordered even, to leave it alone. Not if it got under her skin.

There. The figure lurching out of the Grapes. He was about the right height and build, collar up, head down, bald head shining under the streetlight. Surely. But no, just as she convinced herself it was him, the man lifted his head and she saw that it wasn't. The adrenalin left her like a disappointed lover.

As the man neared her car, he caught her gaze and mouthed a clear 'what the fuck you looking at' as he passed. He took a further couple of unsteady steps, still glaring back over his shoulders, before feeling he'd made his point and stomping towards home and the waiting arms of his loved ones.

This wasn't going to work. She had to be sure and be unseen. And she'd have to be quick.

The puddle splashers came and went. A steady stream of them to and from the Grapes and the Bellrock across the way, and in and out of the takeaways. They came in ones and twos and bigger groups that she didn't much like the look of at all. If he was in one of those then she'd have a decision to make.

This time of night was always a feeding frenzy in

Glasgow. No self-respecting Weegie could go home without filling his or her stomach with salt, grease and congealed fats. The city's eating habits had undergone a massive overhaul – you could get deep-fried quinoa and avocado these days – but it was back to the tried and tested after shutting time.

Narey was parked just a few yards from Chicken Choice, purveyor of late-night fried poultry for the discerning inebriate. You didn't have to be drunk to eat there but it helped.

Crucially, her few yards' dash through the rain would be considerably shorter than the walk from the Grapes. As long as she saw him in good time then she'd be inside comfortably before he was. She just had to recognise him.

As she thought it, two men emerged from the pub. One short and slim, swaying under the streetlight, the other much more like what she was looking for. Tall, broad and bullet-headed. It could be him.

The two men parted company with an attempted hug that turned into waves goodbye. The smaller man headed towards town but the larger one had chicken on his mind. Narey was sure it was him.

In one movement, she got out of the car, head down, swung the door closed and clicked it shut as she walked away. She was in Chicken Choice and shaking off the rain before the big guy had got halfway there. She turned away from the door and made a show of looking up at the menu. When she heard the heavy footsteps in the doorway, she knew he'd only be able to see the back of her head. She listened to the sound of his coat flapping and the raindrops falling from it.

'What can I get you?' The server was an older man, sparse grey hair on his head.

'I'll have the peri-peri chicken for two, salad with one of them.'

She wondered if the newcomer at the door would recognise her voice. She certainly liked to think so, hoped he was looking at the back of her head right now with a sinking heart. She made him wait, listening for the sound of his footsteps in case he decided to leave. She heard none.

Narey turned as casually as she could, just straightening up after surveying the menu board. She even feigned slight surprise at seeing him standing in the queue. He didn't look at all happy to see her.

Tam Harkness had an odd but not unusual shape, not for Glasgow anyway. Fat from the food and muscly from the gym, his body bulged in podiness and in tone. He was all belly and biceps, topped by a neck last seen on a gorilla and a shaved head punctured with a prominent, throbbing vein. She couldn't see the tattoos on his forearms but knew they proclaimed his love for his football team and his mother. She must have been very proud.

'This is harassment. I'm phoning my lawyer first thing in the morning. This is fucking harassment.'

'Harassment? Buying chicken is harassment? Let me give you a bit of advice, Tam. Save yourself the hassle and the money. Your lawyer will be laughing up his sleeve as he bills you. I'm buying chicken.'

'You're following me!"

'I was here before you were. That's not following.'

He took a step forward, his bulky frame towering over her.

'You knew I was going to be here.'

'You're sounding very paranoid. Is that the result of a guilty conscience?'

'Bullshit!'

Narey could see the look of concern on the face of the man behind the counter. She hoped he wasn't thinking of calling the police. That wouldn't help things at all.

'I don't think it's bullshit, Tam. It's only natural you'd have a guilty conscience after harming your girlfriend.'

His eyes widened and his cheeks flared red. The vein on the side of his temple throbbed louder than before.

'I've told you. I've told you a fucking hundred times, I don't know where she is! I had nothing to do with her disappearing!'

He was rattled, angry and losing control. Just as she'd wanted.

'Did you think I was talking about Eloise? Oh, I'm sorry. I was talking about Alison Dodds. You remember, you broke her arm and two of her fingers. You left her with a black eye and bruised cheekbone. I was talking about your other ex-girlfriend. Unless you'd rather talk about Eloise?'

'Get tae fuck!'

'Please!' The man behind the counter was scared now. 'I don't want any trouble. Please, sir. Go now.'

'I'm no fucking going anywhere,' Harkness bellowed. 'I've not done nothing. I'm staying. She can get the fuck out.'

'Please, sir. I'm going to call the police.'

Narey was ready for that and had her warrant card held high for him to see. 'I *am* the police, sir. As this gentleman knows very well. There won't be any trouble, I can assure you.' She turned to face Harkness again. 'So, seeing as you brought up Eloise, let's talk about her.'

'Fuck off.'

'We *will* find out what happened to her, Tam. You know that, don't you?'

He stood taller, his mouth twitching. 'Well, I hope so.'

'Do you?'

He was breathing harder, talking through gritted teeth. ''Course I do.'

Narey turned her head back to the counter, where the shop worker stood open-mouthed. 'Do you know the name Eloise Gray? Young woman from Cardonald who went missing five months back? It was all over the papers and television. Her blood found next to her parked car. You remember?'

The older man nodded warily, his eyes switching between Narey and Harkness.

'You'll have seen all the searches that were done, the door-to-door interviews, the appeals and the reconstruction. You maybe read how we ran checks, but her bank account had never been touched, her emails never read, her phone never used or found. Maybe you heard how a man was pulled in for questioning, a prime suspect, no less. But how we had to let him go.'

The shopworker shrugged, scared.

'You see, this gentleman here is Thomas Harkness.

12

Tam used to be Eloise's boyfriend. She broke up with him after he slapped her around, chipped one of her teeth with a backhander. Isn't that right, Tam?'

He just glared, trapped by the conversation.

'Tam here didn't take it too well when she ended it. Sent her threatening texts, said he'd hit her harder. Said he'd make her sorry she'd treated him like that. Then she disappeared. All that was left was her blood and her abandoned car. Doesn't look good, does it?'

The older man looked at Harkness, clearly intimidated by his size and belligerence, deliberating before making the slightest shrug of his shoulders that he could get away with.

'Oh it doesn't. Trust me. I've been doing this job a long time. Someone who does what Tam did to a woman, he's done it before and he'll do it again. And again. Can't help themselves, men like Tam. And they can't take the rejection. Their poor little egos can't handle it. They build themselves up into such a rage that they can't do anything else except explode. I'm betting you practised screaming at the mirror, didn't you Tam?'

Harkness moved closer, eyes bulging, his neck red as the blood pulsed, his face contorted into a picture of hate. She felt his breath on her face, smelling beer, cigarettes and bile.

'You don't know me.'

'Oh yes I do. I know you and I know your type. Coward. Bully. Thug. Those steroids you take for the gym won't be helping with the rage either. I bet you're just busting to lash out right now, aren't you? Aren't you, Tam?'

He clearly was but settled for leaning further forward again to snarl in her face, flecks of spittle landing on her cheek. 'I wouldn't give you the satisfaction of hitting you.'

'But you want to.'

'Aye, but that's no a crime. Not wanting to. *You* want it so you can arrest me and save you the bother of fitting me up like you've been trying to do. I'm no that stupid.'

She whispered. 'I think maybe you are.'

He took a step back to give himself some room and seemed on the verge of proving her right. She steeled herself but the blow didn't come. Instead he grabbed his right forearm with his left hand and held on.

'What happened to Eloise, Tam? Is she dead?'

'How do I know? So there was blood but that doesn't mean anything. She could have just cut herself. She's just done a runner. Probably off with her new fancy man. Or if something's happened to her then it's him.'

The fancy man. The mystery beau. The unknown stranger who was the unseen witness for the defence. Eloise had told friends how she'd met someone, a schoolteacher named Jamie. She hadn't dated him but was keen to. He seemed lovely, kind and caring and liked all the things she did. Dogs, hill-climbing, old movies and Oasis. The fancy man had ticked all the boxes. Harkness's lawyers were, of course, all over this.

The only problem was that no one could find Jamie. Narey's team had asked for a surname but none of her friends knew it. They contacted every school in the central belt and there wasn't one teacher named Jamie. There were nine named James in its various forms but none of them admitted to going by Jamie, none of them claimed a passion for classic movies or fitted the fair-haired, six-foot, blue-eyed description.

Jamie was their main lead other than Harkness but it got them nowhere. Some suggested that Eloise had just made him up, that she was trying to convince her friends that things were better for her than they were. Her friends insisted she wouldn't have done that.

Some of the squad latched onto Jamie, drawing comparisons with the Suzy Lamplugh case from the mid-1980s in London. The young estate agent disappeared after going to show a house to a client she'd referred to as Mr Kipper and was later declared dead, presumed murdered. Jamie was their Mr Kipper, that was the way many saw it.

Narey didn't rule it out but she was focused on the devil she knew. Harkness had previous, Harkness had motive, Harkness had threatened her. Harkness was someone she could go after.

'It's him you should be looking for,' he was telling her. 'Find that Jamie character and you'll find her. She's run off with this guy.'

Narey snorted. 'No chance and you know it. Eloise's mum was in hospital. Treatment for blood cancer. There's no way Eloise would have disappeared and left her like that. She and her mum were really close. She visited twice a day every day. You really expect us to believe she'd leave her?'

'I don't know. He's killed her then. Whatever, it's nothing to do with me.'

She pursed her lips as if considering that. 'And of

course, nothing to do with you that her mother took a turn for the worse, sick from worry, and that she ended up in intensive care.'

'No, nothing. And she pulled through.'

'Yes, she did. And now she lives every day in the knowledge that someone *murdered* her daughter.'

She'd held the word back deliberately, saving it for maximum impact. He reacted as if it were a red-hot poker and she'd just rammed it up his arse.

'You can't . . . I didn't. I liked Eloise. I really liked her.'

'Yeah. That's why you smashed her in the mouth. That's why you threatened her. That's why you told her you'd make her sorry. Is that how much you liked her, Tam?'

The man's mouth started making words that he couldn't finish, managing just guttural sounds instead. He jabbed his finger at her repeatedly, backing towards the door as he did so. His eyes were reddening and, for a moment, she thought he was going to cry.

Job done. Sort of.

She turned back to the man at the counter, who was standing with his hands spread wide.

'Sorry about that. It looks like I've just cost you a customer. I guess you never know who you're going to bump into when you're buying supper.'

'It's okay,' he told her graciously. 'I'm thinking maybe he wasn't a good customer anyway.'

'No,' she agreed. 'Not good at all.'

Narey drove for a few minutes until she spotted a figure sheltering from the rain in a shop doorway. One glance was enough to know he was intending to bed down there for the night. She parked and got out of the car, striding quickly through the rain.

He saw her coming, just a kid, probably no more than seventeen, grey skin and panda patches around wary eyes. She'd no doubt that his street radar had pegged her immediately as a cop.

'It's okay. I'm not here to hassle you. Nothing like that.'

He was still cautious, ready to spring up and grab the handful of belongings that were stuffed into a scruffy backpack, but he didn't run. She walked with the plastic carrier bag in front of her and he eyed it up, doubtless able to smell the contents.

'Want this? From the chicken place up the road. Just made and still hot.'

The boy's brows furrowed. 'What's wrong with it?'

'Well, it's high in trans fats and saturates, has far too much sugar and salt and it will play havoc with your blood cholesterol. But it will probably taste good.'

He was still confused. 'Why did you buy it if you don't want it?'

She smiled. 'I just lost my appetite.'

CHAPTER 3

The kid was still in the garden of the house on Finley when the cop car rolled in. He stood where he'd called from, pale and scared, a set of headphones around his neck, obeying the emergency operator's orders not to move.

The uniforms eased their way out of the car like it was a Sunday morning.

'You Caleb?'

The boy nodded then thought better of it. 'Yes, sir.'

Kovacic made for the kid while Rojo headed to the window.

'What were you doing here?' It sounded like an accusation because it was.

'Working.'

'Working for the homeowner?'

'No.'

Kovacic – broad, bulky and close-cropped – furrowed his brows and stared. 'Then who you working for?'

'A company – nViron. They pay me to check folk's lawns. I look for ones that don't use too much water and put up a thank-you sign.' He gestured over the cop's shoulder to the back of the sign he'd staked earlier.

The cop shook his head, sighed heavily and produced a notebook. 'Spell it. The company.'

'Small n, capital v, iron.'

Kovacic looked up from his pad. 'That's not a word. You don't spell like that. I hope you got a number for them so I can check your story.'

Caleb held up one of the signs from his bag: nViron, the company's number below it. Kovacic scowled and jotted it down. 'What's your full name?'

'Caleb Ashton Washington.'

'You got a real job?'

'Just this.'

Kovacic stared hard. 'Address.'

Caleb gave it and the cop called it in. 'You don't go anywhere till that comes back exactly as you say it is. Understand?'

'I just found the guy,' Caleb protested. 'I saw him lying there and called the cops. What else should I have done?'

'You go around looking in people's windows?' Kovacic shouted. 'Casing the joint or are you some kind of creep? Maybe something worse.'

Scared, Caleb began to stammer out denials, cut off only by the other cop striding over and pushing himself between Caleb and Kovacic. Rojo walked his partner a few yards away.

'What are you doing, Mario? The kid's shitting himself.'

Kovacic grinned. 'Just busting his balls. Because I can. And because I was waiting on you.'

'Not because he's black?'

'Fuck you. What's going on inside?'

'One dead guy. No sign of foul play. I'm guessing he's been deceased a few days. Neighbours say the homeowner is an Ethan Garland. Late fifties, lives alone, keeps himself to himself. They don't know much about him. Say he's lived here ten years, works from home, something to do with online magazines.'

'We going in?'

'CSI are on their way but they could easy be a couple of hours. No reason to wait. Don't want to deprive you of the chance to break a door down.'

Kovacic smiled. 'Let me at it.'

It took just seconds for the burly cop to smash through the lock and the door to fly back on its hinges. They stepped inside, cutting through a haze of dust motes swirling in the sudden burst of sunlight. They smelled death immediately.

'Man . . .' Kovacic groaned. 'The stink. A stiff in near a hundred degrees. We don't get paid enough for this. Annie's making black risotto tonight and this is killing my appetite.'

'Mario, it's *why* we get paid,' Rojo reminded him. 'Let's just get on with it.'

They moved from the hallway to the backlit murkiness of the room facing the street. Standing in the doorway, they saw that the curtains screened the strong daylight rather than shut it out. A shard of sunlight cut through the middle of the gloom like a laser, showing dust and flies dancing together. Rojo flicked a light switch to avoid tripping over anything but they could have found their way to the body blindfolded.

The neighbours had described Ethan Garland as being in his late fifties, stocky, broad-shouldered build with receding fair hair and glasses. The bloated corpse on the floor was either Garland or someone impersonating him.

'Jesus, I hate it when they've been unattended,' Kovacic moaned. 'We don't get paid—'

'You said.'

Rojo couldn't argue with the sentiment. The stench of the putrefaction was almost overwhelming and the trail where foam-filled blood had leaked from the mouth and nose was enough to turn even a strong stomach, and his partner didn't have one of those. Kovacic backed off, leaving Rojo to examine the body.

He knelt, a handkerchief covering his mouth, and examined the body without disturbing it. He'd seen enough corpses that he could do his job but not so many that it didn't still affect him. When that day came, he figured it would be his cue to quit and work mall security.

There was no sign of trauma, no visible injuries or wounds. There had been no indication of a break-in. Nothing suspicious at all. The man was dressed in light brown chinos, now stained darker round the groin, and a white short-sleeved shirt hanging loose at the waist. His spectacles lay halfway off his face.

'Heart attack,' Rojo conjectured aloud. 'Most likely. Maybe a brain haemorrhage or a blood clot. Heart attack most likely though.'

'Charlie,' Kovacic called to his partner. 'Take a look at this.'

Carlos Rojo looked up, irritated at the interruption. 'What?' He followed the other cop's gaze, seeing a number of framed pieces on the wall. 'Art? Didn't think that was your thing.'

'It's not. But this ain't art. Like I said, take a look.'

Rojo caught the tone in the other cop's voice this time and huffed his way to his feet. Kovacic was standing before a thick black frame. Behind the glass, a black Jack Daniel's T-shirt was pinned to the canvas.

'Who'd frame that?'

'Read the plaque,' Kovacic told him, before taking a couple of paces to his right where the next frame hung.

Rojo read the engraved gold plaque screwed to the wall as if they were in some art gallery.

'*Shirt worn by Richard Ramirez aka the Night Stalker.*'

There was a black and white photograph in the bottom right-hand corner of the frame. Ramirez, flinty cheekbones and piercing stare under the tangle of dark hair, being led into court with a detective on each arm. He was wearing a Jack Daniel's T-shirt. White lettering reading: *Old Time. Old No. 7 brand. Tennessee Sour Mash Whiskey.*

Rojo hadn't gotten close to getting his head around the T-shirt when Kovacic's voice pulled him away.

'And there's this. Christ, Charlie, check this out.'

Rojo moved towards him while still looking back at the worn T-shirt under glass. He nearly walked into Kovacic, who was standing in front of another object hung on the wall.

The square frame was black ash, in stark contrast with the pure white canvas behind. It took Rojo a moment to work out what he was looking at, just a curl of dark on a second, raised white mount in the middle of the piece. It was a curl of hair. The attached plaque told him whose.

'*Charles Manson.*'

'The fuck?'

'Right?' Kovacic felt vindicated. 'There's more. Check out the clown.'

Rojo did. The painting was garish, heavy-handed daubs of red, white and blue. A heavyweight clown in red stripes, the white podgy face swathed in blue at the eyes and red at the mouth. There was no plaque on this one, just the artist's signature at bottom left. *J. W. GACY.*

'Gacy. John Wayne fucking Gacy. What is this, Charlie?'

Rojo lifted his shoulders. 'He's a collector, I guess.'

'A collector? What's wrong with fucking stamps or baseball cards?'

'Damned if I know, but today it's going to be someone else's problem.'

Kovacic turned to him. 'You're not calling this in? Are you kidding me? You said yourself it's a heart attack. We don't need help with this.'

'This . . .' Rojo waved an arm at the wall. '*This* changes it and you know it. This is weird shit, Mario. And given we have a body, it gets to be someone else's weird shit.'

It was half an hour before Detectives Bryan Salgado and Cally O'Neill got to the property on Finley. That was partly down to the inevitable LA traffic, officially the world's worst, but also because Salgado and O'Neill weren't exactly busting a gut to get to a heart attack victim.

Rojo met them at the front door.

'This better be good, Carlos. Forensics say it's natural causes.'

Salgado was long and lean, well dressed in a blue suit and tie over a white shirt, a pair of Gucci aviators over his eyes. At six four, he towered over O'Neill and contrasted with her pale skin and red hair pulled tightly back on her head, just as his tailored clothes contrasted with her functional black trouser suit and blouse.

'Yeah, well, I'm sure forensics is right,' Rojo told him. 'It's the other stuff.'

'What *other* stuff? The message I got was there was some weird shit on the walls. Unless the weird shit killed him, I'm not sure why we're here.'

'Tell us the weird shit killed him, Carlos,' O'Neill chimed in. 'Please tell us it was the weird shit. Is today going to go all *X-Files*?'

Rojo closed his eyes and slowly shook his head. 'Why didn't they send someone else? As if the smell isn't bad enough, I have to listen to you two play Mulder and Scully. Come inside, I'll show you.'

The detectives followed him through the front door and into the lounge where Garland lay. The room now held two crime scene investigators and they'd taken charge of the remains. Rojo guided Salgado and O'Neill past the body, all three cops now wearing protective masks, to where Garland's collection hung.

They moved from piece to piece in silence, Salgado

and O'Neill sharing the kind of unspoken conversation that only long-term partners can fully understand. Raised eyebrows, stolen sideways glances, murmured noises.

'What the hell is this stuff?' Salgado asked finally.

'Murderabilia,' O'Neill answered before Rojo could. 'Collectibles. These freaks buy artefacts connected to serial killers. It's big business.'

'You're shitting me.'

'I shit you not. There's serious money in it. This painting by Gacy? There's a ton of them out there but this would still cost a few grand. Maybe five.'

Salgado and Rojo looked at her. 'How do you know this stuff?'

'Same way I know anything. I read. I learn. You should try it.'

Salgado laughed. 'I'll stick to getting by on Puerto Rican good looks and charm. So, who collects this stuff and what does it tell us about the dead guy?'

'About him?' she shrugged. 'Maybe not much. I'd wonder about the psychology of anyone who collected this shit but it wouldn't mean a lot. The theory goes that many of them are just fascinated by serial killers, like half the population, but they go a step further and buy stuff that gives them a kind of connection to the killer.'

'Sick fucks.'

'Well, yeah, but the world's full of them. It's what keeps us in a job. Does it mean the dead guy, Garland, was up to no good? Not necessarily. But I'd say it warranted a look around.'

'Some of us have already had a look.' Kovacic

announced his return to the room in his usual sensitive manner. 'There's more. Much more. This guy was a complete psycho.'

Salgado and O'Neill swapped glances. 'Show us.'

Kovacic gave them a guided tour of Garland's home, pointing out all stops of interest. The Manson piece of art hanging above the bed; a bible belonging to 'Son of Sam' David Berkowitz in the hallway below framed prison letters from Ed Kemper, Gary Ridgway and Arthur Shawcross; as well as a weights bench and dumbbells, the second bedroom even had a bed cover with a white prison label sewn onto the other side declaring it *Property of Ellis Unit, Texas Department of Corrections* and the initials *HLL* scrawled on it.

'Henry Lee Lucas,' Kovacic informed them before reluctantly admitting he'd had to google it.

The collection was a who's who of American serial killers. Art, clothing and letters once owned by Ted Bundy, Albert DeSalvo, Joel Rifkin, Aileen Wuornos, Edward Wayne Edwards, Ottis Toole and Dennis Rader.

Every room ramped up the unspoken sense of alarm. It was sometimes called 'blue sense', cop intuition, knowing, just *knowing* when the shit was going to hit. Salgado was a big believer in it. O'Neill not so much, thinking it lay somewhere between seeing the obvious, and believing you were right even when you were wrong.

They both knew the house screamed trouble – whether it was down to instinct or common sense, there was no ignoring it.

Kovacic led them into the kitchen and stopped in the

middle of the floor, well aware that he was holding court and clearly enjoying the moment.

'This is my favourite,' The cop wore a twisted grin that made O'Neill want to slap him. She didn't like that the only thing stopping her was the desire to see what he was going to show them. The uniform moved next to the refrigerator and she dreaded what might be inside as he tapped a gloved hand on the front of it. All three cops held their breath as he slowly inched the door open.

Kovacic was eying them all with glee, waiting for their reaction. When the door swung open, he laughed loudly at seeing the mild disappointment when it only revealed milk, juices, vegetables, two wrapped portions of meat in brown paper and a couple of cans of beer.

'Very funny,' Salgado snapped at him. 'You wasting our time, wise guy?'

'Nope,' Kovacic's grin widened. 'You're all staring right at it.' He slapped a hand on the side of the old fridge.

'This is Jeffrey Dahmer's refrigerator. Can you believe that? Dahmer's actual fridge!'

He pointed to a plaque stuck on the side of the machine. *Formerly the property of Jeffrey Lionel Dahmer. Bought at auction 1996.*

'Dahmer kept the severed heads of his victims in his fridge.' O'Neill's reminder was short and to the point. Kovacic slid the door closed again.

'Yeah, right. Kinda my point. Anyway, I say this is my favourite but I think there's more. And worse.'

'Worse?' Salgado sounded sceptical. 'What else have you found?"

Kovacic grinned again. 'Nothing yet. That's what you smart guys get paid for. But there's a room downstairs. A cellar, I guess.'

'And?'

'And it's locked. With a keypad lock. So . . .'

Salgado looked at O'Neill before answering for all of them. 'So, if he was happy to hang all that freaky shit on the walls, what the hell down there is so bad that he felt the need to hide it?'

CHAPTER 4

They bypassed the cellar's number entry system by a more old-fashioned method – Kovacic on the battering end of a metal enforcer. The heavy wooden door groaned and swung till it slapped against the wall inside. The cop had his body camera on so the whole thing was videoed. Behind him, a crime scene investigator was doing the same with a handheld device.

O'Neill led the way down the short staircase, Salgado and Rojo following along with Kovacic and two criminal-ists from the Field Investigation Unit. It was cool and quiet inside, the impression reinforced by the clinical white walls. Windowless and still, it felt like an underground bunker or a laboratory.

Except it was more than that. They all felt it the moment they stepped inside.

There were more framed pieces, perhaps a dozen of them, white wood against the white walls, hiding in plain sight. Two large white cabinets stood against one wall like ghostly sentries. In the middle of the room was a large black glass desk and on top of that sat a single black Anglepoise lamp and a black computer monitor and keyboard.

They moved silently from frame to frame, like respectful patrons at the opening of a new exhibition, nodding and assessing, all reluctant to be the first to say it was good or bad. Even though they all knew it was bad.

The names on the items didn't jump out at them the same way those upstairs had. But it was their job and the cases came back to them. Rodney Alcala. Lawrence Bittaker. Randy Steven Kraft. Lonnie Franklin Jr. William Bonin.

'California's finest,' Salgado announced dryly.

'This is where he keeps the good stuff,' O'Neill announced.

Salgado couldn't quite agree. 'I'm not sure "good" is the word I'd use.'

'You know what I mean. These are the highlights of his collection. Things that mean more to him. The ones upstairs, everyone knows their names. They are the headliners, your Golden Age serial killers, if you like. This stuff is more niche, more insider knowledge, more . . . on the edge.'

'More personal?'

'Yeah, maybe,' she conceded. 'Maybe. And . . . there's this.'

She pulled at the three handles on one of the white cabinets. They didn't budge.

'A locked cabinet inside a locked room? I'm pretty sure I want to know what's in there.'

One of the forensics, a short and stocky hipster known

to all as Elvis, stepped forward. He produced a long, thin-bladed knife. 'Let me.'

They were all aware of Elvis's reputation, of a misspent youth that brought transferable skills and street smarts to his job. If you needed an angle, Elvis was your man.

He studied the lock from a couple of positions, deliberated, then slid the blade into the space with the precision of a surgeon. Or a burglar. The room reverberated to the sound of a quiet, satisfying click. Elvis stepped back, job done.

Salgado pulled back the upper drawer to reveal a glass display case, a larger version of those that hung on the walls. Everyone in the room crowded around to see what it held but Salgado stretched his arms wide to push them back. 'Let's do this properly.'

He reached under the unit, lifted it clear of the drawer and placed it on the black glass desk. The case itself was floored with red velvet. On top of that sat a women's hand-bag, about twelve inches by eight. Made of black plastic, it had two leather handles, a large metal clasp, and a large V-shape was formed in the centre by metal studs.

A black business card with white print seemed to give it ownership. *Elizabeth Short. 15 January 1947.*

Next to that, a white card had a single name printed in black. *Frankie Wynn.*

'Bullshit.'

'No fucking way.'

O'Neill wasn't as sure as Salgado or Kovacic but she thought she knew the name. 'Elizabeth Short was the Black Dahlia, right?'

'Right. How the fuck could he get this?'

'He couldn't,' Salgado insisted. 'Could he? I mean, if this was the bag she was carrying when she was murdered . . .'

'Who's this Frankie Wynn character?'

'Beats me. Never heard of him. But if the other cards and plaques are anything to go by, he's the guy. And no one knows who the guy was.'

Salgado shook his head and turned back to the white cabinet, sliding out the lower drawer and letting out a gasp of surprise that he immediately cursed himself for. The others crowded round again, seeing that the drawer, like the case above, was lined in red velvet and contained a closed black leather display case.

'Can this shit get any weirder?' O'Neill asked the question but they were all thinking it. It turned out the answer was yes.

Salgado flipped the catch on the case and propped up the lid. Inside were six velvet bags that matched the drawer's red lining.

'Jesus. Make sure you get this on film. Everyone else give them room to shoot it.'

Salgado grimaced as he felt the first bag while picking it up. He slowly, carefully slid the contents onto the velvet floor of the case. It was a finger. A finger, raggedly severed at the end and bloodlessly pale.

'Shit.' O'Neill screwed up her face.

'Elvis, bag this before I open the next one,' Salgado instructed. 'We don't need cross-contamination, right?'

'Nope. Which is why nothing else can go onto this velvet.'

'Yeah, okay. Just do it.'

Salgado picked up the second pouch, aware that he was playing a game of guess the contents as he did so. His guess proved wrong when an ear tumbled noiselessly onto a plastic sheet.

'Different victim.' O'Neill's voice held no doubt.

'What?' Salgado and the others were a step behind.

'Different skin tone, different victim. I'd say neither are Caucasian, but the ear is a few tones darker than the finger.'

Elvis bagged it before being asked and Salgado reached for the third one. 'Any guesses?'

'I say toe,' Kovacic replied, even though he knew the question wasn't meant for him, or truly needed a reply.

It wasn't. Instead, the third pouch produced a thumb. The fourth *was* a toe and the fifth a human scalp.

They now lay side by side on the top of the cabinet, each encased in a transparent plastic bag.

'Are we all thinking the same thing here?' O'Neill asked them.

'Try us.'

'Okay, the house is full of murderabilia. Creepy and weird but not in itself a crime. Everything is labelled though. Every item has the name of the killer. It's part of his thing, right? Showing off. Displaying it, shouting it.'

'Right. But in here, presumably the prized pieces of his collection, nothing.' Salgado continued thinking. 'All unmarked, no sick plaques of honour. No mention of who killed these people, assuming they are actually dead.'

'I think that's a fair fucking assumption.'

'So, the question is, what's different about the person that killed these people? Why'd he not want to put the killer's name to them?'

'Because it would be admitting guilt. Because these are his *own* collection. Garland is a serial killer.'

'In that case, yeah, we're thinking the same thing.'

The four cops, uniforms and detectives, stood and looked at the array of body parts in silence.

'Anyone remember that episode from *The Wire*?' Salgado asked eventually. 'The one where Bunk and McNulty go to the scene of a shooting. They see more and more bullet holes and all they say is "fuck". Over and over. "Fuck. Fuck. Fuck."'

'Yeah.'

'Well, that.'

CHAPTER 5

Dark clouds scudded low over Police Scotland's west HQ on French Street as Narey drove into the car park, the building's wide glass front shining bluer than the sky above or the Clyde below. It had been four years since they'd upped sticks and moved to Dalmarnock in the East End from the old red-brick monstrosity on Pitt Street, but she still thought of it as new. And she still didn't like it much.

Sure, the parking was so much easier, the building was clean, fit for purpose and free of asbestos, but it had no bloody soul. Pitt Street had the ghosts of five thousand coppers and the stale stench of their cigarettes in the bones of the place. On a night shift, you could hear them swapping war stories and grumbling about reorganisation and overtime and where it had all gone wrong. She missed it.

She knew it was the inevitable result of modernisation but all it did was make her feel old and she wasn't a fan of that at all. Bringing up a three-year-old and a husband while holding down a more-than full-time job was already accelerating the ageing process and she didn't need nostalgia finishing the job.

She was inside and halfway to her office when DC Davie Corrigan stepped across her path with the apologetic look of someone about to spoil her day before it even began. Her heart sank. Could they not even wait until she took her coat off?

'Detective Superintendent McTeer is looking for you. Says you've to go straight to his office once you get in.'

'Does he know that I'm in?'

'Shouldn't think so.'

'Then I'll get a coffee first.'

Corrigan's face screwed up. 'I'm not sure that's a great idea. If you don't mind me saying. He was pretty insistent.'

Narey sighed. 'Okay, okay. Did he say what it was about?'

'He just said that you'd know.'

Shit. Tam Harkness. It had to be. He'd made a complaint about her harassing him in the chicken joint. It wouldn't stick but the brass wouldn't be happy. The last thing she needed was for them to tell her to back off. *Damn it.*

McTeer's office was on the top floor, the fifth. She opened the door as soon as he replied to her knock, her plan being to go in with momentum and get her retaliation in first.

He had his back to her, fishing through files in the cabinet that stood near his desk.

'Take a seat, Rachel. I'll be with you as soon as I find this. Do you remember when they promised we'd be a paperless office? Fat chance.'

The superintendent was known to be a reluctant administrator, a man who joined the force to catch crooks not to file reports but got too good at what he did so kept getting promoted despite his protests. It was the kind of career history that always endeared itself to those still working cases. He'd earned respect from his work as well as his rank.

He turned, dropping a folder on his desk and finding Narey still standing.

'If you're standing up because you're going to argue with me then at least let me say what I've got to say first. Sit down, please.'

She slid reluctantly into the seat, her intended momentum taken from her by the more experienced player. He watched her sit then exhaled heavily, his eyes never leaving hers.

'Let's start with a guessing game, Inspector. I'll go first. Why do you think I've asked you to my office this morning?'

Oh shit. If McTeer was playing the guessing game, then he was mightily pissed off. She couldn't win the game, she just had to make sure she didn't lose too badly.

'Sir, I was only in Chicken Choice getting some food to take home. How was I supposed to know Harkness would be there?'

McTeer stared at her, unblinking.

'Detective Inspector Narey – firstly, wouldn't that just be the silliest bloody answer if my question wasn't about Thomas fucking Harkness? And secondly, don't kid a kidder. You're talking to me, not preparing your answers for Professional Standards. Not yet, anyway. Am I understood?'

'Yes, sir.'

'So, once more, why do you think I've asked you to my office this morning?'

Her only chance of getting out of it relatively unscathed was to front up. It was the only thing McTeer was going to tolerate.

'I'm guessing I'm here because Tam Harkness, or more likely his lawyer, has been complaining that I've been harassing him. Which, if I'm not talking to Professional Standards, then I'll admit I did. A little bit.'

'A little bit?'

'I wanted a reaction. I wanted him to know that I've not gone away, that I'm still on his case. In every sense. I can't let this go, sir.'

'Yeah? Well maybe you'll have to. As you rightly guessed, I've spent a fair bit of this morning getting my ear chewed by a very angry lawyer. That's not something I enjoy. Nor is making concessions to a lawyer, nor is apologising to a lawyer. I've never liked bloody lawyers. This one is a poisonous little toerag who was obviously loving every frigging minute of it.'

'I'm sorry, sir. I'll speak to him myself if—'

'No. Oh no you won't. I've persuaded him not to make an official complaint and not to go chapping at the chief's door and there's no need for you changing his mind on that. Agreed?'

'Agreed, sir.'

McTeer shook his head wearily and blew out hard. 'Rachel, how sure are you that Harkness is guilty of this?'

He was asking her straight. Cop to cop.

'Honestly? I can't be sure. I've got no evidence, that's

for sure, or else he'd be in a cell. Everything circumstantial says it's him and everything about *him* says it's him.' She sighed heavily. 'Sir, I'll admit my judgement might be skewed by him having a history of violence against partners and having threatened her. I want it to be him, I know that. But from the start I've shoved that as far to the side as I could and been as objective as I could. And I think Harkness is guilty.'

'You *think*?' McTeer ducked his head and scratched the top of it. 'Rachel, if you were sure – or if I was sure – that Harkness had killed her, then I'd tell his lawyer to do one and back you every inch of the way. But as it stands, I have to tell you to back off. Or at least back far enough off that he can't see you. You understand?'

'Yes, sir.'

'I'm not expecting you to like it. I just need you to act on it.'

'Yes, sir.'

'Okay, good. What about this Jamie character? The supposed new man in Eloise Gray's life. Where are we with him? Do you believe there's mileage in him yet?'

'I think there's more in Harkness but yes, of course, I'm not ruling him out of anything. But we've hit a dead end in every direction with him. There's no Jamie the teacher. He lied or she lied, or she was wrong.'

'If he did lie to her about who he was then doesn't that make him more interesting to us?'

She sighed internally. 'Yes sir, it does. No argument. But we've nothing to tell us who or where he is.'

'Then I suggest you find something. I'm not saying he's

a better lead than Harkness but he's not throwing lawyers at us. You don't have to get off his case, just get out of his face.'

'You're a natural poet, sir.'

'I knew I had to be good at something. You hear me though, right?'

She hesitated but had nowhere else to go. 'Yes, sir.'

'Rachel, take a bit of advice from a bitter old man. When they offer you DCI, think about it carefully, then take it. Then a few years later when they offer you Superintendent, think about it, then politely tell them to ram it. Unless you're within a year of your pension, in which case think of the money and your grandkids. Otherwise it's a pain in the arse and not the job you're good at or meant to be doing. You're good at what you do. Go do it.'

CHAPTER 6

Ethan Garland's next of kin was listed as his wife. Ex-wife, to be more accurate. He and Marianne Ziegler had been divorced for five years, separated for two more, but he'd still listed her as his go-to in emergencies. And emergencies didn't get much bigger than death.

Salgado and O'Neill quickly learned that she'd moved out to Thousand Oaks, forty miles west of downtown LA. She was a teacher in a local grade school and her address was listed as Brossard Drive. The detectives were having to wait for DNA results to come back on the body parts and for Kurt Geisler, the best of their tech guys, to work his magic on the computer in Finley Street. That meant they had time for a drive.

Marianne had reverted to her maiden name, seemingly having dropped the Garland tag as soon as she possibly could, which didn't sit well with the idea that they might still be on close terms. Records showed she'd moved to Thousand Oaks in 2012, previous known address the marital home in Los Feliz. Despite being just forty miles from the city, her new home was a torturous hour-plus drive along Highway 101. For better or worse, it gave them time to talk.

The two of them had worked together for three years and usually rubbed along pretty well. O'Neill was the brains of the partnership, logical and clear-headed, they both knew that. She was considered where he was impulsive, calm where he'd rage. Salgado worked on instinct, trusted his gut and his partner. More often than not, both were right.

She was originally from the East Coast, about sixty miles from Boston, moving to the Golden State to go to college and staying. He'd occasionally rib her when her old accent resurfaced, usually in a few vowels when she was angry or drunk. Not that either happened often.

Salgado was an Angeleno from Boyle Heights and got a nosebleed if he went west of La Cienega. Son of a cop who was the son of an immigrant. Being a cop was an inevitability for him, he'd known it since the day he first watched his old man pull on his uniform and broke his mom's heart by telling her he'd be doing the same. She'd done her best to talk him into studying law but he'd never had either the smarts or the stomach for being on that side of it. It was always going to be 'the job'. No one was more surprised than him when he ended up in a suit, but he liked it. Hell, he loved it.

She had a partner, an architect named Ash, who she didn't talk about much, and he'd learned to stop asking. He had a wife and two daughters and talked about them non-stop.

*

42

'Cally, you know that if we don't tie this up soon then we're going to get heat to drop it, right? The guy's dead and the DA's office isn't going to win any prizes for prosecuting a corpse.'

She shook her head from the driver's seat. 'You don't believe that dropping this is right any more than I do.'

'Hell no, I don't. My gut tells me there's something big here and I want us to have a part of it. But other people might see it differently and you know that too.'

She didn't reply for a full five minutes but he could hear her thinking as she steered them towards Thousand Oaks.

'Did I ever tell you about my first DB?' she asked. He knew she was talking as if the intervening gap had never existed.

'Just my second day on the job working out of Metro and we got a call to an apartment off Beverly Boulevard. Neighbours called the cops because of a bad smell coming from the place. We break the door down and sure enough there's a decomposing corpse. A young woman named Sara Zamorano.

'She had a broken neck and had been lying there on her bedroom floor for maybe a month. There was no sign of a break-in, the body was obviously in bad shape, but it was screaming out foul play to me. She was young, late twenties, no reason she'd have fallen, nothing for her to have tripped over. My partner said accidental causes, straight off the bat. Everything that happened after that, he used to back up his thinking.

'He was a guy named Jack Megson. In his forties, paunchy, jaundiced, misogynist, casual racist, quick to go for his nightstick, but hey, he loved his mother. You know the type. We had to do door to door in the building and Megson made every interview go the same way. No one heard anything, no one thought anyone would harm Sara, no one had any reason to think it wasn't a terrible accident.

'It wasn't that Megson didn't want to work the case, not that he didn't care exactly, more that he didn't care enough. More that he wasn't remotely fucking moved by any of it. He was just pissed that it meant paperwork and he didn't need there to be any more. She was dead, right? Nothing would change that, right?

'And nothing did. No thanks to Jack Megson, no thanks to me. So, I made two promises to myself. First, that I'd never forget Sara Zamorano. And I haven't. There's not a week goes by that something doesn't remind me of her and that apartment. Second, that the day I became like Megson would be the day I quit. That if I stopped caring, if all I worried about was paperwork, if all the bodies became the same then I'd be out.'

They drove in a silence for a full minute before Salgado replied.

'Do you remember every victim on every case you've been called to?'

She considered it. 'No. But I remember that they were all different and I remember that I cared every single time.'

Thousand Oaks wasn't just an hour's drive from LA, it was also a world away. For a start, whoever named the place couldn't count. There were far more than a thousand of the trees. It was an oasis of rolling hills, close to both beaches and mountains, without quite the scalding heat of the deserts and the valleys. There were wide boulevards and an absence of high-rises. It was LA's wet dream, but not all the Angelinos voiced approval.

'What's with all the space and white people?' Salgado complained as they hit downtown. 'And the sky. How can they have so much sky? And it's far too quiet.'

'Fourth safest city in America,' she reminded him.

'This ain't a proper city. And if it is, it's the fourth dullest. We'd be out of a job in a month. Give me bangers and drive-bys any day of the week.'

'Yeah? Careful what you wish for, Salgado. I get the feeling we're going to have all the bad shit we can handle.'

They both fell silent for a while at that, both tasting the truth of it.

Brossard was just a couple of minutes north of Thousand Oaks Boulevard, pretty one and two-storey properties, many with lawns and yards that would cost a film star's divorce in the city.

'This is some pricey real estate for a schoolteacher, ain't it?' Salgado questioned.

'Looks that way. We're not talking LA prices, but some of these got to be three quarters of a million for sure.'

It turned out the answer was in the address. The half added to the number indicated not the impressive, well-tended house facing the street but a much more modest garden building to the rear. It was nice enough, but so tightly squeezed in between its neighbours that you had to wonder if they realised it was there.

O'Neill knocked on the door with Salgado standing a few feet behind her. They had no reason to think of the ex-wife as a suspect and were better off not frightening her into silence. Anyway, despite what they knew and feared about Garland, this was still a death notification and there was policy to work by.

The woman who opened the door was a little over five feet tall with long auburn hair pulled behind her and seemingly held in place by the spectacles on top of her head. In her mid-fifties, she was slim in a sleeveless hippie dress of summer colours. She smiled as brightly as her dress.

'Hi. How can I help you?'

'Ms Ziegler? I'm Detective O'Neill from the Los Angeles Police Department. This is my partner, Detective Salgado. May we come in?'

The smile faded like a setting sun. 'Um, sure, of course. Please, follow me.'

She led them into a small, busy room that screamed love, peace and happiness. A huge mandala tapestry stretched across one wall while the others were a patchwork of prints, dreamcatchers and Hindu symbols, all held together by strings of lights. A calico cat was curled up in an armchair, one black eye opening to appraise them while the ginger eye still slept.

The woman scooped the cat up into her arms and took its place on the chair, cradling it on her lap while offering the two-seater sofa to the detectives. They opted to stand and that did nothing for her peace of mind.

'Ms Ziegler, we—'

46

'Marianne. Please. It's Marianne.'

'I'm afraid we're here with some bad news, Marianne. It's about your ex-husband, Ethan Garland.'

Whatever Marianne had been expecting, it hadn't been that. She seemed puzzled, as if not sure what would constitute bad news. She leaned forward, smothering the cat with her body.

'Ethan? Why would you . . .'

'You're listed as his next of kin.'

'*I am?* Why would he . . . That man. Still, I guess there's no one else. His mother has been dead since he was young, his father too. Ethan has cousins in Nevada but he hasn't had contact with them for years. But still, he says it's *me*?'

The significance of it finally dawned on her. 'So, wait. Why are you here?'

'I'm sorry, Marianne,' O'Neill continued. 'I have to tell you that Ethan died at his home in Los Feliz. He suffered what seems to have been a heart attack.'

They watched her closely, seeing her eyes follow the words as if she were reading a music score, the resulting thoughts peppering her forehead.

'Oh.'

It was all she could manage. A single syllable of surprise. She sat in uncertain silence, looking from one cop to the other, thinking of a response.

'I loved him enough to marry him once but that seems a long time ago now. I just –' she looked at them apologetically – 'I just don't know how I'm supposed to feel right now. I *need* to feel, I *should* feel, but I don't know what it should be.'

47

'There's no rules,' O'Neill reassured her. 'No should or shouldn'ts. I take it things didn't end well with Mr Garland?'

'You could say that. You could say it didn't end well at all.'

There was no mistaking the anger. It might have been dulled by shock or sentiment but both detectives could hear it loud and clear. Before they could question that, Marianne sat taller in her chair, the cat stirring as her grasp tightened.

'Wait. You're detectives, right? I don't understand. All I know of police work is what I see on TV, but I thought it would be uniformed officers who did this. You said Ethan died from a heart attack.'

Her eyes narrowed further and her voice sharpened. '*What has he done?*'

Salgado and O'Neill liked the sound of that. Liked the sound of there being *more*.

'Why do you say that, Marianne? You think it's likely he'd done something? Is that the kind of person Ethan was?'

She held Salgado's gaze for an age, a debate erupting behind her eyes.

'Yes. Yes, it is the kind of person he was.'

Her voice tripped over its own guilt, stumbling over the bad taste it left in her mouth. Marianne didn't like talking bad about the dead. Even Ethan Garland.

'Is this why you're here? Not to tell me but to question me? I'm *not* Ethan's next of kin, I can't be after this length of time. Detectives, *what has he done?*'

The cops exchanged glances, a silent discussion on how much to say. Salgado settled it.

'We're not yet sure he's done anything. We do have reason to think something else might have happened but we're not in a position to discuss that right now.'

She stared again. Harder. Longer.

'What do you want to know?'

They breathed out. 'Tell us about Ethan. How did you meet him, what was he like, why did the marriage break down?' O'Neill paused. 'Tell us what we need to know, Marianne.'

She blinked back tears and swallowed hard, composing herself. And she begun.

She'd spent years dating other kinds of guys, got promised the moon and got let down time after time after time. Ethan had been different and that's what she'd liked about him. He had a quiet kind of confidence: sure of himself, but not a braggard. It was like he knew who he was and was okay with it.

They'd met in a diner where they both went for breakfast. It was weeks before they nodded at each other and another before they smiled and said hello. A week later, she asked if she could sit beside him and they chatted most days after that. She had to do all the running and liked that Ethan didn't just want to drag her into the sack.

She stopped long enough to gulp down some air and stroke the cat behind an ear.

They got married six months after that first date. It was a small wedding. Ethan just had the few cousins in Nevada as family and only one of them showed up, a guy named

Mike Durrant. Marianne's mom and dad were there, her brother, a bunch of people from school, some friends. Her dad and brother didn't like Ethan right from the get-go but she figured that was because he wasn't their kind of guy, the jock or whatever.

'I thought I knew better. Even when the wedding night didn't go the way I expected, I still thought it was all okay. Or would be.'

'Not as you expected?'

'Nope.'

'Can I ask why that was?'

'Well it wasn't down to me, Detective. The only thing I'd liked about the football guys and that type was the sex. They were pigs and they were all about them and they couldn't form a coherent sentence, but they knew how to use their bodies. Let's just say I liked that. Ethan and I'd never had sex before we got married and I guess I thought that was how he was. Religious or whatever. Waiting till it was right. But that wasn't it at all.'

They were married six months and beyond some kissing, he barely touched her. She tried to talk to him about it, but he didn't want to know. She was sure that he masturbated, but not enough to call him on it. She hoped he'd change, or she'd change him, but every time she tried to touch him, to *encourage* him, he'd get mad, shout at her, storm out of the room or throw things. It got so she just stopped trying.

She stopped, rubbing at reddening eyes, and having to look away from them. She resumed, telling them that Ethan had always been odd but that she just hadn't seen it at first. He was cold, never really loving or caring, just cold. He just didn't care enough about people and he certainly didn't care enough about Marianne, spending hours on end working in his office in the cellar, never explaining what he was doing or why.

'I wanted to know though, so I kept at him. I nagged at him till he snapped. He was across the room and had his hands around my throat before I knew it. He was strong, much stronger than me. I remember his fingers digging into my neck, squeezing my windpipe, choking the life out of me. I was sure I was going to die.

'I can't say exactly why he stopped except that I saw something change in his eyes. It was like he woke up, suddenly realised what he was doing and quit. He looked at me for a few moments as if he didn't know who I was then let me go.'

Marianne closed her eyes, screwed them tight shut. Her head bobbed up and down.

For the first time in their marriage, for the first time since they met, Ethan wanted sex. Right there and then. She didn't, but she didn't have any say in it. When it was over, he just got up and left the room. Hours later he said he was sorry but that she shouldn't have pushed him. She somehow convinced herself he hadn't raped her, that it was all her fault.

Two months later, she was reading when he emerged from the cellar in a vile mood. He barged into the kitchen and came back out demanding to know why there was nothing to eat. She said she'd made food earlier but that he'd been in his office and she'd make him something else. He grabbed her by the arm and dragged her to the stairs, saying he'd show her his office if she was that desperate to see it. She got no further than the door. He pulled it back as if to let her inside but forced her arm into the gap and slammed the door closed on it. Repeatedly. Only the noise of the bone breaking made him stop.

There was a hush in the room. O'Neill bristled with anger while Salgado did his best not to breathe.

When there were items on the news about something terrible, a murder maybe or a school shooting, Ethan would just sit very quietly and intently and not take his eyes off the screen. Marianne learned not to interrupt and just let him watch. If there was a multiple pile-up with fatalities or maybe a natural disaster, then he'd go from channel to channel devouring it all.

'Did he ever talk about any murders in particular?' Salgado asked.

Marianne's eyes widened. 'Oh my God.'

'We're not assuming anything here,' O'Neill rushed in to reassure her. 'We're at a very early stage of the investigation.'

'But that's what you think, isn't it? You think Ethan killed someone.'

'We think it is possible that he has. Or at the very least that he was involved in something connected to a killing. Marianne, do you think that is something he was capable of?'

No hesitation. '*Yes.*'

In the end, Marianne ran.

*

Ethan was watching a news item on TV, a murder story. She talked over the show and he went crazy. He threw things around, told her how the victim on television had had his throat and wrists cut and was left to bleed to death. He asked if she wanted the same. She said she wanted a divorce and he backhanded her hard till she fell to her knees. He stormed out of the room towards the kitchen and she *knew* he was going for a knife. As soon as he was out of the room she made for the front door and ran. She didn't stop running till she got to Thousand Oaks.

'Marianne, do you remember that news story on TV? The one Ethan had been watching when you interrupted.' Salgado held his breath. 'Do you remember who it was that had been killed?'

She looked up at him, momentarily surprised.

'No. I'm sorry.' She looked distraught. 'I hadn't been watching it, I only saw a headline about a man's body being found.'

Salgado and O'Neill felt the lead slip through their fingers.

'But I do remember the date that I ran from that house,' Marianne added. 'Like it's engraved on my heart. Would that help?'

'That would help a lot.'

The one cousin of Ethan Garland's that had turned up at his wedding to Marianne Ziegler, Mike Durrant, turned out to be a retired mechanic living outside Carson City. O'Neill got his address from Marianne and had the Carson City sheriff's department call on him.

A few hours later, Sheriff's Deputy Thomas Kearney phoned her back with a report on the conversation. Durrant had been surprised and upset by the news of Garland's death but said he hadn't seen his cousin in six years and hadn't spoken to him in four. He'd explained that although his mother and Ethan Garland's father had been brother and sister, an eleven-year age gap meant the two cousins weren't particularly close.

'He says that his family went down to LA every summer for a few years and he regularly got stuck with Ethan. He remembers him as a slightly strange kid, dark and brooding is how he describes him, a bit of a loner. He says that Ethan wasn't the kind of kid who would sit around and chat about sports or movies, but if you found a dead bird he'd want to poke it with a stick and see what was inside.

'He says the last time they met was in 2016 when Mr Durrant was in LA for a funeral. He gave Ethan Garland a call and they met up for a beer. His memory is that Ethan was very distracted and regularly drifting out of the conversation. Mr Durrant finally challenged him on it and Garland said it was because he'd got involved in some new partnership and it was playing on his mind a lot.'

'A partnership?'

'Mr Durrant asked him about it and says Garland was very vague. He said something about how he'd met some guy and they were exploring ways of working together. He got the impression Garland regretted bringing it up and tried to change the subject. The last time they spoke was on the phone. Mr Durrant says he asked how the partnership was going and Garland said that he couldn't talk about it. That was the last he heard from him.'

'Anything else?'

'Mr Durrant says the trips to LA were often cut short because his father, Len Durrant, and Ethan's father, Zachary Garland, didn't get on. Mr Durrant says his dad warned his kids to steer clear of Zac Garland because he was trouble.'

'Did he say what he meant by that?'

'He was reluctant but said that Zac Garland was the black sheep of the family. He said that his Aunt Veronica, Ethan Garland's mother, had committed suicide when Ethan was young and everyone blamed Zac for driving her to it. He pretty much said that Zac was always screwing around – women would call the Garland house looking for this guy or that guy. The names varied but Veronica was sure Zac was just giving them aliases. And he was violent. He says everyone was kind of scared of the guy and that one night, when Len Durrant was drunk, he told Mike that he was sure Zac had done something terrible but had gotten away with it.

'Zac had been in insurance, made plenty of money from it but was always on the move from one firm to another, one customer to the next.'

'Did he say anything about how Ethan was when his mother killed herself?'

'Yes. He says Ethan blamed his mom. That he'd always blamed her for his dad not being home and then he blamed her for committing suicide. Mr Durrant says Ethan and his father were very close and Ethan would never hear a bad word said about him. I asked him if he would be surprised if Ethan had gotten himself into any serious trouble. Right away, he said he would but then he stopped and corrected himself.

'He says that Ethan had a temper and he was Zac Garland's son. So, nothing would surprise him.'

Oh, I think it would, O'Neill thought. *I think it would.*

CHAPTER 7

The house on Finley Street had been in lockdown since Garland's body was found, everything being photographed and documented. Salgado and O'Neill switched back and forth between the house and LAPD headquarters on West Street where they'd bagged an office that they were sharing with computer techs, principally Kurt Geisler, and had regular visits from the criminalists. They'd also picked up a hitchhiker from CCSS, the cold case section of Robbery Homicide. Charlie Randall had been stationed with them on the likelihood that some of the body parts might belong to old investigations and he'd bring what knowledge he could.

They'd begun to put together an investigation board, or a 'crazy wall', as Salgado preferred to call it. It didn't have anywhere near as much on it as any of them would have liked. A head shot of Garland, pics of the more gruesome parts of his collection. It needed to grow or else it would be shut down, as would their case. There were resources for a potential serial killer but not much for a weirdo who collected freaky shit. They had to prove they were after the former.

Which meant that Elvis was greeted like a hero home from the war when he came through the office door. The fact he was carrying a bag of doughnuts and a four-cup tray of coffees helped too.

'I got Ms Donut's finest dough-and-sugar in a variety of flavours. I got a latte macchiato, an americano, a flat white and a doppio. If you want sugar in that, you got doughnuts. And I got DNA results. If you want to nominate someone for a pay raise or a Nobel Prize then my name's Elvis and I'm here all week. Questions?'

'Is the americano a blonde roast like I asked?'

'Salgado, can it.' O'Neill got on the case. 'Elvis, what's the results?'

'Nothing final.' He began handing over coffees as he talked. 'But I know how impatient you investigating types get so I come bearing information that you may find useful. Tests aren't complete on the body parts, but I can tell you one thing.'

Elvis paused to hand out doughnuts, and for dramatic effect.

'The five body parts come from five different people. I can confirm that you have five different victims. All unrelated.'

Salgado pumped a fist and didn't care if anyone noticed. He wanted this to be big.

'You have four male victims and one female. We are *not* at a stage where we can try for matches but we will be very soon. When that happens, you will be the first to know. And before anyone asks, no we don't know how old they were, we don't know if they had an Irish grandmother or if they're directly descended from either Africa or George Washington. We should have full results by late this evening.'

'Five victims,' Salgado repeated.

'Don't try to sound so happy about it,' O'Neill cautioned. 'I don't think the mayor is going to declare a public holiday to celebrate.'

'You know what I mean. Garland is our guy. He's done this. Five of them. What else have you got for us, Elvis?'

The criminalist held his arms wide, as if offended. 'Coffee, doughnuts and DNA aren't enough for you? Tough crowd. Okay, I also have the autopsy report on Garland. Full and official results to follow, but I have the headlines. Basically, as expected. He had a massive coronary, didn't stand a chance. No suspicious circumstances.'

He paused to let that sink in. 'He'd had no history of treatment, nothing picked up on previous physicals. There was chronic heart disease, but it was never likely to show except on the table after he'd been cut open. The pathologist said he had a ticking time bomb inside him and didn't know it. No way he was dodging this one.'

'Fuck him,' Salgado muttered. 'Respectfully.'

'Nice, Detective. Nice. Unless you need me for anything else then I'm going to have myself a doughnut then I will have left the building. That DNA won't test itself.'

'Good work, Elvis. And thanks for the doughnuts and coffee. I'll write to the Nobel committee. Sweden, right?'

'Right. Don't forget the stamp.'

As Elvis turned away, Salgado saw the IT tech twitching to get into the conversation, sheets of paper in his hand.

'Okay, Geisler, what you got? Elvis has set the bar pretty high.'

'Well, I ain't got doughnuts.'

'You lose.'

'I figured. What I've got is an update on Garland's PC and not much of it is good news. All I have in the way of search history is a very limited session but even that means we caught a break. I've printed out everything from that and I've emailed copies to you both too.'

'A limited session doesn't sound like a break,' Salgado complained.

'Yes, I know,' Geisler replied patiently. 'But it's way better than nothing, which is what we were supposed to get. My guess is he habitually locked this room behind him when he went upstairs into the house so as to safeguard whatever he was viewing or searching. Where we got the break was that he never made it back down so couldn't log off.'

'How would the computer wipe his history?'

'It looks like he used a Tor connection. You know what that is?'

'I know the word,' O'Neill admitted, 'but basically, no, I don't know.'

'It's an anonymity network. Tor lets you do whatever you do, and no one knows who you are, your internet business isn't monitored by anyone.'

Salgado leaned forward in his chair. 'But it's monitored by us, right?'

'Not by *anyone*,' Geisler repeated. 'It uses relays, over seven thousand of them, to disguise the source IP address. Each relay only decrypts enough to reveal the next relay.'

'So, it works like a mafia cell.'

'Exactly. It's all on a need to know, no need to tell basis.'

'And it's not going to tell us?'

'Right. At least not quickly. Given time, I can get some of it. Given for ever, I might be able to get all of it. But that's time we clearly don't have. I'll need to talk to the service provider, get a warrant, yada yada yada. And I'll almost certainly need help from the Feds. If they'll give it.'

'Oh great.' Salgado sighed theatrically. 'So, what *do* we have?'

The sigh was matched by one of exasperation from the tech. He was pretty sure he'd explained this already.

'We have the search history from that one session. It's all in the doc I emailed you but if you need it summarised, I can do that.'

'Please do.'

'Okay. It runs to just a three-hour period, but he was busy. There was quite a bit of time spent on Facebook, a few articles viewed on there and I've listed them all. He was also on a number of news sites, some mainstream but others are on the alt-right. InfoWars, Breitbart, World Net Daily, Townhall. He spent a short time on Gab and 4chan but short enough that I don't think he could have done anything more than looked in either and left again. Apart from that, there were some general searches on Google and they're all listed in the doc. Which I emailed to you and which I am now also handing to you.'

Salgado began to retort but Geisler cut him off.

'I also have this.' He held four sheets of paper. 'The

bad news is he seems to have done a lot of regular house-keeping on this machine. He wasn't a hoarder, that's for sure, and has gone out of his way to protect himself. But I did find one file that he had, presumably for easy, probably regular, access. This is the printout of it. It's definitely interesting.'

Interesting was a word they liked.

'Again, I've emailed it to you both, but I thought you'd want to read it immediately. There was no useful title on the file, it was labelled "Christmas Card List" so I almost went past it but then I thought it might give you known associates. But it's not that at all. Not unless his cards were weirdly detailed.'

O'Neill took the printout and began to read it.

'It's a list of names with biographies for each,' Geisler explained. 'It lists age, appearance, job title and description, likes and dislikes. A mix of male and female.'

'A list of victims?' O'Neill couldn't hide the excitement in her voice.

'Well . . .' Geisler's tone didn't offer the hope she wanted.

'Kurt, don't tell us it's Christmas in one breath then Santa's dead in the other,' Salgado warned.

'It might be Christmas,' Geisler shrugged, 'but I don't have anything that says it's snowing. I've only had the chance to run a few of the names but no hits so far.'

'So, what are these?' Salgado sounded like he was ready to shoot the messenger.

'That's your job,' Geisler smiled. 'It's why you get paid the big bucks.'

'You really should stop hacking my bank account and

hack this fucker's computer instead. We need everything you can screw out of it.'

'I'm on it.'

O'Neill and Salgado began studying the list. It was broken down into sections, all under individual names.

Alice Reid: Age 29. Five foot two. Blue eyes. Long dark hair. Slim. Best feature, eyes.
Single. Mother of one. Graphic designer. Monday to Friday. Been in same job three years.
Ambition: manager or run own art gallery.
Likes: Cats. Modern art. Running. Dance. Cake. Rain.
TV shows: Mad Men. Better Call Saul. Love Island. RuPaul's Drag Race.
Favorite movie: La La Land.
Music: Nina Simone. Adele. Beyoncé. Amy Winehouse.
Dislikes: Pushy guys. Mondays. Traffic jams. Smoking. Pigeons.

'What the hell is this?' Salgado asked aloud.

Greg Hurst: Age 32. Six foot one. Fair hair. Blue eyes. Athletic build. Optician. Formerly worked in retail. Current job two years.
Ambition: own own business.
Likes: Sports, particularly running. Cars. Travel, particularly cities. Partying. Dogs.
TV shows: Big Bang Theory. Curb Your Enthusiasm. Black Mirror.
Favourite movie: The Hangover.

Music: Nirvana. Kings of Leon. Foo Fighters.
Dislikes: Mornings. Carrots. Decaf.

Brianna Holden: Age 27. Five foot four. Green eyes. Long
blond hair. Slim. Best feature, thinks it's her smile but
it's her legs.
Married. Mother of two. Shop worker. Been in same job
three years.
Ambition: to create own clothing brand.

The list went on. Steve McLennan. Kris Perera. Ellen
Lambert. Jamie Stark. Danny Cook. Stefan Kalinowksi.

Chrissie Ramsay: Age 32. Five foot four. Dark brown
hair. Green eyes. Curvy. Married. Student. Studying
politics and philosophy.
Ambition: Wants to be a policy advisor.
Likes: Activism. Equality. Buddhism. Craft
beer. Cooking.
TV shows: Chef's Table. The West Wing. House of
Cards. Breaking Bad.
Favourite movie: The Shawshank Redemption.
Music: Joni Mitchell. Wyclef Jean. Springsteen. Rage
Against the Machine.
Dislikes: Poverty. War. Misogyny. Climate
change deniers.

And the list went on.

O'Neill called over to the cold case cop. 'Hey, Charlie,
any of these names mean anything to you?'

Randall was a long streak of a man, as slim as he was tall with a mournful face that nurtured a perpetual grievance. He took the printout from Salgado and scanned it. They watched his eyes go from top to bottom and then repeat the process.

'Nope. Not one of them is familiar. I wish I could say different.'

'How many outstandings do you have, Charlie?' she asked.

'Too many. This is southern California. If you want to add missing persons to unidentified bodies to unidentifiable bodies then double it and add the number you first thought of. Ask me tomorrow and it will be more.'

'CCSS must be a laugh a minute,' Salgado teased.

'It has its moments. Can't all be car chases and press conferences.'

'Yeah. We're all about the glamour.'

'You notice that about half of this list is in italics and half in a plain font?' he pointed out. 'That mean something?

'Detectives!'

The shout was from their left, but they let it wash over them.

'*Detectives!*' Geisler's voice was urgent. 'You better see this. *Now.*'

They turned to where the tech was sitting, fingers above the keyboard of the computer they'd moved from Garland's cellar, and looking at a pop-up box which was open and flashing on the screen.

'What's that?'

'A chat function. I took the chance of opening it and we have a visitor. They came on almost as soon as I opened it.'

Inside the chat box, the name of the caller was listed at the top. Matthew Marr. Below was his opening line.

Where the hell have you been, Ethan? It should be done by now. He should be dead.

They froze. Cops. Forensics. IT techs. None of them trusted their eyes to read it only once. It demanded to be checked.

He should be dead.

In the absence of a response, the screen flashed again.

Ethan?

Salgado motioned Geisler out of the chair and took his place. With a final look at O'Neill, he began typing.

I'm here.

The pause seemed huge but was probably no more than ten seconds. No one in the cellar dared breathe until they saw the icon shift and knew the person on the other end was typing. In a heartbeat, the reply appeared on the screen.

Goodbye.

CHAPTER 8

Sinky worked in the Blue Lagoon in Gordon Street, serving fish suppers to the masses. The chippy was right next to Central Station and within staggering distance of a hundred pubs and clubs, so the place was always rocking and likely queuing out the door any time after 11 p.m. at the weekend. And it was Glasgow, so the weekend ran four or five days long. Sure you had to deal with your share of bams, but most of them were civil enough. Even the junkies were polite.

Sinky's superpower was knowing who was going to order a deep-fried Mars Bar with chips. He could spot them a mile off. First off, chances are they were tourists. Hear an English accent in the queue and it was a good bet they'd be eying up the DFMB. Liverpudlians were the worst for it. You'd see them nudging their mates – *Go on, dare you.*

Chip shop hours weren't exactly nine to five, even in Glasgow, so when he got the chance of a night off, he grabbed it. Most free nights he'd head out for a few beers with his best mate Titch, and then anything could happen.

Titch was the kind of guy that could get Mother Teresa into trouble. As long as she'd had a few pints of Best.

So it was that they were walking in Springburn at half one in the morning. They'd got a taxi from town and Titch had insisted the driver dropped them a quarter of a mile from where they going. Just in case.

Titch wasn't small. He was a good six foot, but his first name was Richard so it was the law that he be called Titch. He was a student. Sort of. He was doing a course in social sciences at Glasgow Caley. Sort of. He'd dropped in and out and was always spinning them some line as to why he had to defer another year before he picked it up again. He was a year shy of thirty now and still going strong with the studying. Sinky had never quite worked out what social sciences actually was and he couldn't ask anymore.

Titch was the one that was always coming up with plans for them. Sinky figured it was because he had plenty of time on his hands to do it. So it was this night. Titch had been reading on some forum about how the old Highland Fling pub on Cowlairs Road was haunted. The bar had been abandoned for years and was supposed to be in a hell of a mess inside but, of course, Titch being Titch, he was dismissive of any suggestion of spirits other than whisky, vodka or rum.

If Sinky's superpower was detecting potential pur-chasers of deep-fried confectionery, Titch's was pubs. He quite literally knew them inside out, including knowledge passed on lovingly by his dad and grandad, and his mis-sion this night was to prove that the Highland Fling was haunted by nothing more than neglect.

'Ghosts my arse,' he said for the umpteenth time as they staggered up Millarbank Street. 'Some wee neds fucking about maybe. But ghosts my arse. We're going to see some genuine Glasgow history, Sinky. And we're going to prove that shitehawk on the forum is talking through his hole.'

Sinky had given up arguing. When Titch was on one it was best just to let him get on with it. Anyway, Sinky was rubbered.

'My granda says the old Highland Fling was a great night out. Live music all weekend. Thursday, Friday and Saturday. There was a house band but the talent was the locals. Sandie Shaw impersonators. Maurice Chevalier too, whoever he was, and some guy called Wee George who could do every hit of the day in a Donald Duck voice. Can't buy that stuff, Sinky.'

Sinky nodded even though Titch wasn't looking.

'My da was in the Fling one morning, seven o'clock it was. Cops had been tipped off it had been opened to serve booze to boys over from Ireland for the Walk. Lifted gey near the whole pub. Never got to court though. Half the Springburn polis were in there having a bevvy with the boys so they had to let them all go.'

They neared the corner of Cowlairs Road, a glazier's on their left, and Titch saw what they were looking for. 'There you go, wee man. The Highland Fling. Or what's left of it.'

All Sinky saw was a whitewashed wall and a boarded-up window, a shutter down over the door and a red sign above that had faded to a poorly pink. They turned the corner and saw the whitewash, not so white anymore, stretch fifty yards down the street. It was a single-storey concrete block with little in the way of windows, a sure sign of a pub to be avoided, according to Sinky's dad. Above the wash, in white lettering on red, you could just about make out the words 'The Highland Fling'. As long as you knew what they were.

'Mon, wee man. We go in here.'

The opening was just about wide enough to let one of them walk through at a time. Neither it or the thought of what was inside made Sinky feel very good about the adventure. Titch, on the other hand, was full of lager and vodka and had the confidence of a social scientist.

He led the way and Sinky followed. They put on the torches on their phones and picked their way across broken glass and strewn rubbish: chair legs and crates, ashtrays and coils of wiring. The light picked out a pool table with a strange white crust that turned out to be fallen plaster. It was an island in an ocean of plastic tumblers, beer cans, empty bottles and carrier bags.

'Wee vandal bastards,' Titch complained.

They moved into another room, one ringed with a sweeping arc of leather seating that hugged the wall. It, like everything else in the abandoned Highland Fling, had seen better days. It might have been dark green or black under the dirt. If Sinky didn't know better he'd have sworn it was covered in pigeon shit. The smell suggested he didn't know better.

There were chunks out of the walls and furniture trashed for the fun of it. Graffiti named the culprits but they'd never face justice. The old pub looked like a bomb had gone off.

They were looking round the room seeing torn leather, cracked and blackened mirrors, all under the thin stream of mobile phone light. From the corner of the room, or maybe somewhere beyond, Sinky heard a scurry that confirmed his worst fears. He stepped to the side and a polystyrene cup cracked under his foot, sending the sound round the room and his pulse rate soaring.

'The ghost,' Titch made exaggerated bunny ears with his fingers, 'was supposedly seen in the cellar. So that's where we're going, my man.'

Great, Sinky thought. What could possibly go wrong, tripping around in the dark in a shithole like this?

They passed another room, a second bar by the look of it, that defied walking through as the floor was swamped by plaster, breeze blocks and strip lighting. Titch led the way down to the cellar, singing 'My Way' in a Donald Duck voice as he went.

They were aware of a difference as soon as they entered the room. The chill was instant and obvious. The cellar smelled too, big time. Sinky wasn't sure if it was either or both of those that made him suddenly uneasy or the fact that they were tripping into the bowels of this hellhole.

The ceiling was lower, the floor no less of an obstacle course. The torch from Titch's phone picked out five beer barrels dotted round the floor.

'Don't suppose there's actually gonna be beer in those? I could go another drink right now.'

'Nae chance, Sinky. They'd have disappeared long ago

if there was. Okay, ghosties. Come out, ya bams, wherever you are.'

Sinky didn't appreciate the daring of unknown demons as he ducked low to avoid a strip of something hanging loose from the low ceiling. They were venturing further into the corner, the walls whitewashed and exposed under torchlight. As he lowered his head, he saw something pass through the sweep of his own phone's beam – his brain immediately told him it shouldn't be there. A brief flash of limb and flesh that made his sphincter twitch and his heart hit the concrete floor.

'Holy fuck!'

'Calm down, Sinky. There's no such . . .'

Titch saw it too and dropped his phone in shock. He fell to his knees and scrambled around to pick it up. Together they shone their lights into the corner.

There, on the cellar floor, next to a beer barrel, lay a body.

Naked. Discoloured. Female. Dark hair falling onto purpled shoulders.

Titch took two steps backwards and fell on his arse. Sinky moved back and offered a hand to help him up, never taking his eyes off the body even though he desperately wanted to.

'Ghosts, you said, Titch.'

'No, no. I said no ghosts. And that's no a ghost.'

'Too right it's not. Although if it starts to fucking move and wail, I'm running right through that wall.'

Titch was back on his feet and they edged closer. It wasn't courage, or even alcohol that took them forward, it was something neither could quite explain. They just wanted to see.

Whatever they'd expected, whatever they'd feared seeing the body from the other side of the cellar, the close-up reality was worse. The two men stopped and stared, not believing what they saw.

The body had been cut in half just above the waist. Like a magic trick. Like a horror movie. Like a nightmare.

'Holy fuck.'

'Aye.'

'We phone the cops, Titch?'

'Oh fuck aye. But let's get the fuck out of here first.'

CHAPTER 9

When the phone rang, Narey sat straight up in bed and grabbed it before it could ring again. The clock said it was 4.07. She'd done this long enough to know that good news never rang in the middle of the night.

Tony stirred next to her but he just pulled the cover over his head rather than ask what was going on. His own experience told him it was something he didn't need to know about.

'Yes?'

'DI Narey? Sergeant Iain Finnie at Barloch Street.'

'Yes, Sergeant?'

'I'm told you're the person to talk to about the Eloise Gray case.'

If she'd still been half asleep, that had changed in those two words. 'Yes. What's happened?'

'Two men had been crawling about in the old Highland Fling pub in Springburn earlier this morning. We took the call. They were exploring the place for some daft reason. Anyway, they found a body in the cellar.'

'Eloise?'

'Certainly looks that way. One of our boys, Kevin Waddle, he made the connection and pulled up her mispers sheet. Everything fits. Height, build, hair colour. Clothes and shoes that she was last seen in.'

'Any jewellery?'

'Yes. Silver ring on her right index finger. Moon necklace.'

'It's her.'

'We think so, ma'am. SOCO is there now and they will take DNA. But we're sure it's her.'

'I'll be right there. Where's the pub?'

'Cowlairs Road. But, DI Narey ... there's something you need to know about the body.'

The corner of Cowlairs Road was cordoned off. An abandoned pub in an abandoned corner of the city, looking even smaller and more desolate under the early morning streetlight. Despite the hour, a few shadowy figures kept watch from the underpass a hundred yards away. Going out or going home, or having no home at all, they'd been drawn by the cop cars and the ambulance. But for that activity, the entrance to the pub would be completely overlooked and easy to enter unnoticed.

Narey showed her warrant card to the uniform on the door, standing tall in the falling rain like an unlikely bouncer on a long-shut pub. He moved aside to let her in and she saw the interior of the old bar in all its vandalised glory under the temporary spotlights.

A call like this always made for mixed emotions. She'd wanted to find Eloise from the first day of the investigation and that had become a desire to find her come what may. When you know you can't do anything to change what's happened, it becomes easier to accept, even hope for, the unwanted option of finding her dead. That at least offers the chance of going after the bastard who did it. Still, for all that, this wasn't what she wanted. Not here, not now.

A constable led her through the ruins of the pub to the cellar. As soon as she stepped inside, she saw the white-washed walls bathed in light and a huddle of blue-suited SOCOs near the corner of the room. As they moved, she caught glimpses of purple-hued flesh. Eloise. *Oh Jesus, Eloise.*

The forensics became aware of her arrival and parted to make way for her. For a brief moment, she wished they hadn't. The disfigurement, the decomposition, was awful, but it was clearly Eloise. She forced herself to look longer than she wanted, making sure, taking what she could from it.

The body had been posed. Her arms were positioned above her head, the elbows bent at right angles. Her legs spread apart.

'Was she killed here?'

'No.' The crime scene manager was Campbell 'Two Soups' Baxter, his bearded jowls evident behind his mask. He was abrasive at the best of times, and this wasn't one of those. 'She has been moved here post-mortem, possibly quite considerably so. You will have been appraised of the dissection. It's a technique called a hemicorporectomy. In this case, done somewhat inexpertly. Her body has been drained of blood but there's no evidence of it within the cellar.'

'Cause of death?'

He sighed and wobbled his head from side to side. 'Let's wait and see, but the cuts you can see at her wrists, relatively small as they are, may have been designed to have her bleed out. There are contusions above her wrists consistent with tie marks, so I'd suggest she was restrained and left to die slowly.'

It was unlike Baxter to make any kind of speculative offering, particularly without being asked. Narey knew this kind of savagery, particularly against a young woman, was the weak spot that allowed his humanity to show.

'You're saying that her death was deliberately prolonged?'

He didn't look her in the eye but cast his head down, seemingly quite literally chewing on the answer, finally nodding reluctantly but firmly.

Shit. Shit. Shit.

'Have you found anything else?'

'We have. A piece of clothing snagged on a loose nail. It isn't covered in dust or dirt like the rest of the place so we believe it to be recent. It doesn't come from either of the gentlemen who discovered the body. We'll tape-lift from it and hopefully get skin cells for matching.'

'Can I see it, please?'

Two Soups held up an evidence bag. Inside was a scrap of black cotton, perhaps an inch square in size.

'You'd think he'd have noticed leaving that behind.'

'I can only imagine that he had his hands full, Detective Inspector. Quite literally.'

'I guess so. This is ripped from a T-shirt, maybe?' Tam Harkness habitually wore black T-shirts.

Baxter demurred, 'It's possible.'

Narey hesitated. The one question that she really wanted to ask had been stuck in her throat.

'How long, Mr Baxter? How long has she been dead?'

That question could as easily have been rephrased as, 'Was she alive when I was searching for her? Or had she been murdered before I even heard her name?'

Baxter reverted to type and refused to answer either spoken or inferred questions.

'I wouldn't care to speculate, Detective Inspector. We have science for that. You will have results as soon as it is humanly possible to get them to you.'

He left her to it, his parting gift a look that suggested he'd be grateful for her getting out of the way before too long. She was in no hurry to oblige him.

Why here? Why did he bring you here, Eloise? Somewhere you would inevitably be found. And why place you next to the beer barrel rather than hiding you behind it? And why take you at all?

She was still lost in her own thoughts when DS Rico Giannandrea made his way through the cellar minefield to stand at her shoulder.

'I'm sorry, Rachel. I know this wasn't how you wanted it to end.'

She answered without taking her eyes of Eloise. 'Ah, but I did want it to end, Rico. That's my sin. I'd got to that stage that I wanted to find her. Dead or alive. Be careful what you wish for, that's what they say.'

'Yes, but *they* don't know what they're talking about. I know how you meant it and so do you. You couldn't have done more to find her, and you couldn't have done anything to stop this from happening.'

'Yeah, maybe. Okay, you stay here and oversee this, Rico. I've got a visit to make.'

'Eloise's mother?'

'Yes. I should maybe wait until they confirm it but it's her, I know it is. And I don't want her finding out from anyone other than me.'

'You don't want me to go with you?'

'No. I need to do this myself. But I'll be paying another visit later today and I'll need you with me for that one. Just to make sure I don't do anything I shouldn't.'

'Tam Harkness.'

'Yes.'

CHAPTER 10

When the caller named Matthew Marr signed off there had been stunned silence in the room. For an instant. It broke, almost immediately, into a cacophony of recrimination, anger and confusion.

'Shit, Salgado what the hell have you done?'

The detective turned open-mouthed to face O'Neill's accusing stare. 'Well at least I did something. Everyone else just wanted to sit and look at it.'

'Yes, you did something. You blew it.'

'We don't know that.'

'It sure as shit looks that way.' O'Neill was furious. 'Geisler, is there any way of knowing who the hell that was and where he is? How do we get back in touch with him?'

'Of knowing who he is or where? No. To get back in touch we can just do what we did. But we can't make him play. He'd have to want to talk to us and it don't seem like he does right now.'

'Dammit.'

The caller's opening line was still on the screen, screaming at them.

**Where the hell have you been, Ethan? It should
be done by now. He should be dead.**

'*He should be dead*,' Salgado repeated. 'What the
hell is this?'

'We need that guy back on the line,' O'Neill insisted.
'We do whatever we need to get him to talk to us. Fuck.
Geisler, we're going to need everything you can find on
this damn computer. Everything. If someone – what
the hell have we got here – if someone is dying then we
need it fast.'

'I'm on it. Our first problem is doing two things at once
that will get in the way of each other. We need that line
open for you to communicate with your guy, but I also
need the elbow room to get into the guts of this machine.
Can I make a suggestion?'

'Go on.' Salgado was grudging.

'We spend five, ten minutes now trying to talk him out
into the light. Chances are that will fail, but we should try.
After that I suggest we send him a message every hour on
the hour. Establish a routine, let him know when we'll be
here if and when he wants to talk. In between, I do my
thing and squeeze this bird like it's a lemon.'

O'Neill and Salgado looked at each other over the tech's
head, both shrugging.

'Okay, Kurt, it's good,' O'Neill told him. 'Apart from
the weird mixed metaphor about the bird and the lemon,
that's as good a plan as we've got for now. We need to
work out a wording to use with him. Treat him like a
jumper standing on a ledge. Lure him back inside.'

'So that we can kill him,' Salgado added.

'Yeah, just don't tell him that. So, what do we say?'

'We've already missed something that we should have said,' Geisler told them. 'There was clearly some kind of codeword that this guy expected, and we didn't deliver. He knew immediately that it wasn't Garland on the other end of the chat. There's no point in trying to pretend otherwise. I say we tell him we just want to talk and reassure him it's safe to do so.'

'We tell him that we're cops?'

'Not until we have to. I'd go for honest up to the point of stupid.'

'You could be describing Salgado.' O'Neill grinned. 'Okay, let's do it. Message this creep then we go to the hourly plan.'

> We should talk. You've nothing to lose by having the conversation.

It wasn't going to win a Pulitzer, but it did the job. Short, to the point, open-ended, non-threatening. They alternated it with variations of, Are you there? I just want to talk.

As they'd discussed, Geisler and Salgado tried it for ten minutes, but they could see that the messages hadn't been read, never mind responded to. They signed off with, I'm here if you change your mind. Will be here on the hour, every hour.

The room seemed colder and brighter in the cool of the evening when Geisler called Salgado back. The tech's last message – Let's talk, Matthew – was front and centre on the computer screen. Timed at 7 p.m. precisely. Below it, a single word and time notified that it had been viewed almost immediately. *Read 19.01.*

Salgado drew breath and tried to make sense of it.

'Would he have had to click on your message for us to know he'd read it?'

'Yes. The indicator initially reads as "delivered" until it's clicked, then it changes to "read".'

'But he could have seen it without having to click on it?'

Geisler nodded. 'As long as the chat box was open, yes. And the fact that it was viewed so quickly suggests it almost certainly was.'

'So, he's making a point. Letting us know he's seen it. Letting us know he's still there. Why?'

'Not my area of expertise, Detective. But I'd say he might want to talk but he's making you sweat for it.'

Salgado pulled out his cell and called. O'Neill answered immediately.

'Why is this guy Marr talking to us when all he's doing is putting himself at risk? Why is he taking the chance of communicating with us?'

'He replied?'

'No, but he read it. Let us know he did too.'

The line went quiet while she thought it through. 'He wants something from us. Something only we, or Garland's computer, can give him.'

He let it percolate. 'Yes. Yes, that's it. You're a genius, O'Neill.'

Salgado ended the call and reached for the keyboard.

Who are you, motherfucker? Who should be dead
and what the fuck do you want?

He stared at the line for a while, aware of Geisler standing anxiously over his left shoulder. His finger hovered above the enter button but didn't press it. 'Don't worry. I'm not that stupid. Not quite. Anyway, even if he's there, I want to make him wait. It's twenty-five minutes till he expects us to message him again. Let's wait till then.'

His poised finger switched to the delete button, stripping the line away a letter at a time. He hesitated when only the last three words were left, *Who are you*, then punched those too into oblivion.

They dragged their feet. Salgado looked from the keyboard to the screen and back, playing out conversations and strategies in his head. It was all the more real now, knowing that Marr would be coming back.

The moment the clock reached the top of the hour, Salgado typed and sent.

I'm here, Matthew. Let's talk.

His eyes were on the status. Delivered. He watched and waited, aware of his own nervousness, unsure if he was the cat or the mouse, still not sure what he'd type or do. Was the man even there ... Yes, yes, he was. *Delivered* became *Read* and a surge of adrenalin made Salgado sit up and draw in breath.

He waited again, giving Marr the chance to reply. Two minutes and that still hadn't happened. He typed again, giving up an element of his knowledge but sure that Marr already knew anyway.

I know you're there, Matthew.

Read. No reply.

And I know you want to talk.

Read. No reply.

So what are you waiting for? Scared?

Read. No reply.

Maybe I got it wrong. I guess you don't want to talk after all.

Read. Replied.

Okay. Let's talk.

Salgado jumped. Hesitated. Answered.

Goodbye!

The gap was long and Salgado imagined the confusion. Marr typed again.

No. I said I'll talk.

Read. No reply.

You're playing games. Fuck you.

Read. No reply.

The tech looked at Salgado like he was crazy. And maybe he was.

It was a huge gamble and one he was going to find difficult to justify or explain to his bosses if this blew up in his face and Marr never came back to him. Hell, he was going to have enough trouble explaining it to O'Neill.

Marr hadn't messaged again after saying fuck you. It was enough to make Salgado worry. Had he overplayed the poor hand that he had? If he had managed to make his only point of contact so mad that he'd walked away, then he'd be out on his ass.

The countdown to the next hour crawled even slower than the previous one. He'd sent Geisler home, seeing no point in them both missing out on a night's sleep. The empty office echoed to his thoughts and he had to get up and walk around the room, circling the chair, talking to himself.

'Asshole. *Asshole*. Always got to take the risk.'

He walked and talked and watched the clock inch over towards nine.

'Always sure you're right. You had him and kicked him loose. You blew it.'

He wound himself up further by wandering around the perimeter of the room, then back to stand in front of the investigation board, staring at the photographs that were pinned to it. His mind drew lines from Garland's photographs to the images of the body parts they'd found in the locked cabinet. He slammed the doors shut to hear the noise bounce off the walls. He saw nothing and the clock turned over like sludge.

Five minutes till nine and Salgado slid back into the chair, eyeballing the computer as if he might be able to jump-start it with the power of his mind. The machine stared back, refusing to bend.

When the clock showed one minute to go, he could feel his veins knot at the wrist, pulse quickening, but it was like it was all dressed up with nowhere to go. It showed nine. Nothing. Not immediately. But he hadn't expected there to be, just hoped. Marr would be doing the same thing. Sitting, waiting, not wanting to be the one to go first, not sure if the other would go at all.

9.01.

9.02.

9.03 and it was Marr who folded first.

Okay, you made your point. Talk.

Salgado held his nerve for as long as he dared, wanting to puncture the other guy's sense of certainty but not prepared to take another chance of losing him.

I'm here. And I'm listening.

Where is Ethan? Is he dead?

Yes.

How did he die and who are you?

He had a heart attack.

**I asked who you were. If he'd been murdered,
then I'd think you were the person that killed
him. If he did die of natural causes, then there's
one answer most likely as to who you are.**

Salgado didn't see any need or practical way to hide it.

I'm the police.

There was a considered pause, but not a long one.

Who am I speaking to?

Detective Bryan Salgado, LAPD. And
who are you?

**You can see the name on the screen. And
I'm guessing LA cops can read.**

So, you're Matthew Marr?

**Maybe. But it's good to have it confirmed
that that's what you're seeing. Ethan never
knew my name. Who am I? Go fuck yourself,
that's who I am.**

Salgado swore under his breath.

Let's get real here, Matthew. Why don't you
tell me what it is you want?

They batted it back and forth for a few minutes, neither giving way, until Salgado heard the door open behind him. O'Neill and Geisler slipped through it, the cop pulling up a chair while the tech hovered behind.

'He's talking? Let me read what he's said. Delay him till I catch up.'

'Delay is easy. He's dicking me around. I'm gonna push him.'

'Be careful.'

Salgado linked his fingers as he thought, then released them to type.

> Matthew, if there isn't a reason for you to talk to me then maybe there isn't a reason for me to talk to you. Get to it. Let me take a wild guess. It's something to do with the man who should be dead. Am I right?

There was another, much longer, pause.

> **Right. And if we don't talk then you don't find him. You don't find him, he dies.**

Salgado swore loudly. O'Neill did it quietly.

'And he's still dicking you around,' she told him. 'Still not telling us what he wants. Trouble is, I think whatever he wants . . . I'm not sure I want to hear it.'

'You think it's something worse than this guy dying?'

'Yeah. That's what scares me.'

Salgado nodded soberly. 'Well, let's find out.'

Okay, Matthew. I believe you. But I need
something to work with. Who's going to die if
we don't talk?

**Oh, he's probably going to die even if
we do talk. You see, I don't know who he
is or where he is. Only my friend Ethan
knew those things. But if we don't talk?
It's definite.**

The man's words caused the room to slip into silence. Both
Salgado and O'Neill felt the walls close in on them as the
air disappeared from the room.

Get to the point you piece of shit. What
do you want?

**That's easy, you arse. I want to
watch him die.**

CHAPTER 11

Salgado had got out of the chair and kicked violently at it with the sole of his shoe, causing it to slide across the room until it hit the far wall.

'What the hell is this, Cally?' he shouted.

She was calmer. Angry and shocked, but in control. She stood at the desk, taking Salgado's place and typing.

How can you watch him? You need to tell me more.

Seems I need to tell you everything, Detective.

This is why you came back to talk. Because there's something in the hard drive in this computer that you need to let you see whatever it is you've orchestrated with Garland. Right?

Right. Gold star. Top of the class. A cop with half a brain. Whatever next?

So how do we do it, Matthew? How do we let
you see whatever it is?

**There is a mechanism hidden on the
computer that it seems you haven't found
yet. It's inside a couple of other things for
security and it's disguised as something
else. You won't find it unless you're looking
for it. I can tell you where it is, and you just
have to flick the switch.**

Salgado nodded at her. 'So, we do it, right?'

O'Neill turned to Geisler, eyebrows raised in question.

'This could be a bomb,' he cautioned. 'Not literally, but
a self-destruct that could delete anything we might find
in the computer.'

'You think?'

'I don't know, and it's up to you whether we take
the chance.'

'Shit.'

She typed. Okay, Matthew. Talk us through it.

The instructions might as well have been in Swahili for
all that they made sense to either of the cops, but Geisler
did as he was told and in moments, a small box popped
up in the top right-hand corner of the screen. Its buttons
were all self-explanatory. Power. Play. Stop. Share.

'It's a video feed. It's controlled from this computer.
We can give him access to view it, but we retain control. We can let him see it, but we can turn it off any
time we want.'

'And will he know that?'
'I'd say probably, yes. But if not, you can demonstrate.'
Salgado smiled tightly. 'That I like.'
Geisler typed.

> Share will make it available to how
> many people?

Just me.

'Is he telling the truth?'
'I can't be sure. Most probably yes, though.'
'And this won't fuck over the whole computer?'
'No. Probably.'
'Shit. Okay, do it.'
Geisler clicked 'Power' then 'Play'. A box appeared that filled half the screen with an option to fill it all. As they watched anxiously, it wavered, buffered and came to life, a sharp black and white image forming in front of them. They struggled to take it all in at once.

The camera was pointed directly at a young man, sitting slumped and tied against a metal radiator. His jaw was slack, his mouth catching flies. One arm was handcuffed to the radiator, the other was free but lay still at his side. There were a few days of growth on his chin but that in itself told them little. There was little sign of life.

'Oh Jesus ...'
'Fuck. Fuck. *Fuck* ...'
Was he dead? Was it even live film or a photograph? The clock in the bottom corner ticked over in real time, suggesting the former, but the man was as still as any

corpse. O'Neill looked to his chest in the vain hope of seeing it beat.

Just within reach was a glass. She had to look twice to see if there was water in the bottom of it. There wasn't.

None of them said anything more. They just burned with anger at what they saw, at what they were being forced to watch. O'Neill saw Salgado's fists bunch and the vein on his neck tighten.

Abruptly, the imprisoned man's head moved, jerking from left to right then falling back into place. A tremor followed through his right leg as it kicked limply then fell still again. Either he was dreaming, or his body was rebelling against whatever agonies it was going through.

He was alive. Barely.

CHAPTER 12

'We need a doctor to see this,' O'Neill announced. 'Someone that can give us an idea of his condition. We need a clock on him so we know how long we've got.'

They both searched the visuals of the room for clues. The radiator was old school, thick and heavy, suggesting an older property. The wall behind the radiator was papered in an odd design, a mottled background that could have been mosaic or leopard skin, overlaid with geometric shapes that formed what looked like hanging lanterns. The carpet was thick and brown, hiding all sorts of crumbs and bugs and secrets.

The man was maybe early twenties. Maybe late twenties. His hair was thick and dark but lay tousled and oily across his forehead, stuck by sweat or fever. He looked at first glance like a messy drunk, slumped eight beers down on a sidewalk. They'd both seen enough of those to know this was different though.

There was a wildness about his eyes when they briefly slipped open, unfocused but searching. His mouth jammering without words or energy. Once they'd looked long enough, they could see his stomach contracting, convulsing, agonising. His body was reaching out, whether he was aware of it or not.

They'd both seen dead bodies and they'd both seen dying. This was the latter.

Salgado tapped Geisler on the shoulder and motioned him out of the seat. He slid into his place and typed.

This is what you wanted to see?

Yes.

Tell me why.

I don't have to explain myself to you.

No? Oh I think you do.

Salgado nodded and Geisler leaned in past him and cut the video feed. Marr's response was immediate and frenzied.

**What the fuck have you done? Put that back on!
Put it on now!**

Salgado breathed. Waited.

**You're condemning him to death unless you
put it back on.**

No, you're the one who's doing that. You and
your friend Garland. You want to see it that

96

badly then you talk to me and you answer my
questions.

A long delay then an answer.

Put it back up and I'll talk to you.

And you'll answer my questions?

**I'll answer some of them. I guess we'll both
have to work out how much I want to watch
this. And you need to work out how much
you want an answer to any question that
might make me quit.**

I guess we do.

Salgado looked to Geisler and jerked a thumb towards the
video. The feed resumed.

But here's my line, unless you're here talking
to us, every hour on the hour, this feed is
turned off. And you should know, we're
coming after you. Hard.

**Good luck with that. You don't know who
I am. You don't know where I am. Neither
did Ethan. I'll talk to you. As long as it
suits me. As long as he is alive. When he's
dead, I'm gone.**

You're a sick piece of shit.

**We're all different, Detective Salgado.
Different wiring, that's all. Maybe I'll find
out how you're set up. That could be
interesting.**

Salgado slammed his hand against the keyboard, twice.
He then banged it hard a third time before deleting the
resultant letters one by one. O'Neill pretended not to
notice, staring ahead at the screen and waiting for the
sentence he'd actually send.

We have a different view of what's
interesting, Matthew.

**Seems that way. But I think maybe people
aren't as different as some would like to
make out. What I do, what you do. Different
sides of the same coin. Maybe you're not
so much better than me as you like to think,
Detective.**

Salgado raised his hand again, flat above the keyboard
ready to smash it down, before O'Neill cautioned him.
'Don't rise to him. Going to do none of us any good.'
'I won't. Okay, I am. But I won't.'
'Want me to talk to him?'
'No.'
'Then type. Ask him straight out where the hell this kid
is. He must know something.'

Where is this, Matthew? Where is this guy
being held?

**I wouldn't know. And I wouldn't tell
you if I did.**

'He's lying. No way Garland hasn't told him at least the
kind of dump spots he uses.'

Come on, Matthew. I could just switch it off.
Might have to if you're no use to us.

A pause. They could see him begin to type then it went
blank again. Finally, he answered.

**I don't know where he is. Telling you and ending
this would make it completely pointless for me to
talk to you. But I have no idea where he is. This
one is Ethan's.**

O'Neill reached for Salgado's shoulder and began to talk,
but he'd caught it too.

This one? That means there's more? And if
this is his, does that mean some are yours?

There was a long break. Perhaps Marr regretting a hasty
use of words.

Let's pass over that for now.

99

Maybe we don't want to.

We?

I've been joined by my partner. Detective Cally O'Neill.

Quite the party. Anyone else there I should know about?

Oh, there are lots of us. Might as well be an army as far as you're concerned. Are there more like this guy on the video? And are some of them yours?

It was Ethan's turn. That's all I'm telling you. For now, at least.

His *turn.*

Salgado pounded the keyboard as he tried again.

You must know something about where this guy is. The kind of places Garland would use.

What I can tell you is that no one else will know where this guy is. No one else will have fed him or given him water. Only Ethan. It's very unlikely anyone will stumble across him. Ethan will have made sure of that. Wherever he is, he won't be easy to find.

Shit. Shit. Shit.

How long has he been there, Matthew? How
long has he been without food?

**I think four days now. That was the plan.
And now he's almost out of water. I'm not
sure he's got the strength to pick up what's
left even if there is any.**

'Fuck this shit!' Salgado shouted as he typed.

So, tell me why I should let you keep watching
this. What am I going to gain from it if you
have no idea where this man is?

**I don't know where he is, Detective. But I
know other things. Lots of other things.**

Salgado turned to O'Neill, mouth half open. 'You think
that's a good thing or a bad thing?'
She exhaled hard. 'I'm almost sure it's both.'

CHAPTER 13

Narey and Giannandrea were parked outside the tenements in Midlock Street for forty-five minutes before Harkness turned up. Giannandrea saw him first – black jeans and T-shirt, leather jacket – turning the corner at the whitewashed cafe, and nudged her.

He hadn't noticed them in the car and had got to the door entry system before he heard their footsteps approaching. He looked warily over his shoulder, his face crumpling angrily when he saw who it was.

'Can we have a word please, Mr Harkness? Inside would be best.'

'What the hell do you lot want now? You've been told to stay away. My lawyer has spoken to your boss and you've been *told*. Just fuck off. You're getting nowhere and you're getting nothing from me.'

He turned away from them and punched numbers into the security panel before reaching for the door handle.

'There's been a development, Mr Harkness,' she told him. 'The rules have changed.'

She regretted not being able to see his face, but it had

been the only way to stop him. She could still see the effect it had. He froze on the handle, his shoulders tensing then slumping. He slowly shifted round till he was facing them, his face set to neutral but the eyes giving away the anger.

'What development?'

'I think we should talk inside. The street isn't the place for it.'

'Fuck this. I'm phoning my lawyer. He says this is harassment. I've not to say a word to you unless he's present.'

They tag-teamed him.

'Really? Are you worried you'll incriminate yourself, Tam? Or is he?'

'If you haven't done anything then you've nothing to worry about. No reason not to talk to us.'

Harkness looked from one to the other, the heat rising in his cheeks, his brow tightening.

'What development?' he repeated.

She held his stare, trying to work out if he knew or he'd guessed. He was angry and scared but that might be the case whether he knew they'd found Eloise or not. She wasn't for giving him any clues just yet.

'We need to talk to you. It can be here or it can be at the station. Make your choice now.'

At that, she felt the same vibe she'd got from the man a few times before. A barely suppressed rage that was on the point of snapping. His arms were crossed over his chest and he gripped his own biceps as if to hold them in place.

'My lawyer said you had to back off.'

'Things have changed. Your flat or the station?'

'Neither without my lawyer.'

She'd had enough. 'Then phone him. You can make the call from the interview room. Sergeant.'

Giannandrea moved to the man's side. 'Let's go, Mr Harkness. And let's not make this unpleasant.'

'This is out of order.' He weighed up his options and found them lacking. 'Okay, I'll talk to you but only here and not till my lawyer gets here.'

'Too late,' Narey told him. 'We're taking you in. We need your assistance with our enquiries into the disappearance of Eloise Gray. Move.'

He moved, fists bunched, eyes wild, but he moved. They put him into the back seat of the car and drove.

It was two hours before the lawyer, Gareth Stein, turned up. In that time, Harkness simmered, refusing all attempts to convince him to start without Stein being present. Narey tried to read his thinking but the end result of all the possible scenarios was that the angry man became more angry. Whether he knew they'd found her or not, even whether he'd killed her or not, the only possible eventuality was that this short-tempered thug would be as he was.

Stein was a criminal defence lawyer at a well-established Glasgow practice, Henderson and Park, but had only been there a couple of years. He was in his late twenties, all youthful vigour but without the usual baggage of moral righteousness. He came dressed in an expensive pinstripe but still managed to carry an air of street fighter.

Narey despised him immediately.

'This is outrageous, Detective Inspector. Your superiors

are already aware of my client's treatment at your hands, as you well know. You have been told to back off and been warned of the consequences of not doing so. If this doesn't end today then I will have no option but to present a formal complaint against yourself and to initiate proceedings leading towards financial compensation for my client for emotional distress.'

'Have you finished, Mr Stein? Good, then we can get on.'

The lawyer was momentarily taken aback by her complete dismissal of his opening rant. He recovered enough to speak but she'd already moved on, leaving him behind.

'Mr Harkness, I'd like to thank you for voluntarily agreeing to this interview. For the purposes of the tape, also present are Detective Sergeant Rico Giannandrea and Mr Gareth Stein, solicitor for Mr Harkness.'

She paused just long enough to let Stein think he could interject but spoke before he could actually do so.

'Mr Harkness, can you tell me when you last saw Eloise Gray?'

'How many times? I've been through this. I don't know where she is.'

'That's not what I asked you. When did you last see her?'

'A few days before she was supposed to have disappeared.'

'*Supposed to have?* You don't think she disappeared?'

Harkness screwed his eyes up. 'You know what I mean.'

'No, I'm sorry. I don't.'

'My client simply means that he can't know whether or not Ms Gray disappeared because he had no involvement with it or knowledge of it. Inspector, you told my client that there was a development with your investigation that somehow necessitated his presence here. Would you please tell us what that is so we can make an informed decision as to whether his assistance to your enquiries will continue?'

'Of course, Mr Stein. And thank you for your patience.'

She faced Harkness, studying him, waiting for his reaction.

'Mr Harkness, Eloise Gray's body was found in the early hours of this morning.'

His mouth fell open. He hadn't expected that.

She steamed over him. Telling him more and telling him nothing. Not giving him time to adjust to one slap before slapping him again.

'She'd been murdered.'

'Detective Inspector—' the solicitor tried and failed to stop her.

'The extent and manner of her injuries leave no doubt that this was an extremely brutal attack and in no way could they possibly have been the result of an accident.'

'*Inspector—*'

'You were once romantically involved with Eloise, Mr Harkness, so it's only fair that you hear what happened to her. I hope that you can now see your way clear to helping us with our investigation.'

'Yes. Yes. Of course. I—'

'My client isn't prepared to say anything at this time.'

'I haven't accused him of anything. I have simply updated him on the latest development in the investigation. Why would he *not* be saying anything at this time?'

She'd watched Harkness go from nervous to shocked

to disorientated. He'd managed to disguise either nothing or everything and she really doubted it was the latter. He was completely thrown and wasn't a good enough actor to hide it.

The lawyer was talking, protesting and excusing, but no one in the room was listening. She wasn't sure that Harkness was hearing anything at all. His head slumped forward, mouth open, eyes unfocused. He'd left them.

Narey felt her mobile vibrating in her pocket but let it ring. The call stopped and almost immediately Giannandrea's phone rang instead. When he looked at the screen and nodded at her, she called a temporary suspension to the interview and left the room. She returned Campbell Baxter's call, knowing it to be urgent.

'Detective Inspector, I've got some news for you that I suspect you're going to like to hear.

'We have a probable match on the piece of clothing found at the Highland Fling this morning.'

'Already?'

'I prioritised it. And we had the benefit of having a potential match at hand.'

Her breath caught and made time stand still. He'd said little but it was more than enough to make her thought process race ahead of what he was saying. She had to pull herself back into the conversation.

'I urge some caution as the results are not complete. However, I am breaking the habit of a lifetime to let you know that the sample of clothing collected from the scene is a probable match to one Thomas Harkness.'

The breath left her slowly, much like a sigh of relief. She

wasn't elated, not jubilant or triumphant. Sometimes the journey exhausts you enough that you don't have the energy to celebrate getting there. Sometimes it just seems wrong.

Once back in the interview room, she pretended to study the notes in front of her. She wanted time to compose herself and time for the solicitor to stew and wonder. His client had finally looked up, seemingly aware of the change of atmosphere in the room.

'Interview recommenced at 12.37. Those present as before. Thomas Harkness, I am arresting you under Section 1 of the Criminal Justice (Scotland) Act 2016 on suspicion of the murder of Eloise Gray. The reason for your arrest is that I suspect that you have committed an offence and I believe that keeping you in custody is necessary and proportionate for the purposes of bringing you before a court or otherwise dealing with you in accordance with the law. You are not obliged to say anything but anything you do say will be noted and may be used in evidence. Do you understand?'

Harkness was stunned and his lawyer's eyes widened. 'What's going on here? My client came here voluntarily and not—'

She snapped at him. 'Things have changed. Your client has been cautioned and his change of status will be recorded in the custody suite. Mr Harkness, you will be taken there now and will have the opportunity of consulting with your lawyer.'

Harkness jumped to his feet, red-faced and shaking. Stein was indignant.

*

Less than an hour later. Different room. Different game. Narey was determined not to let Harkness have the chance to settle.

'Have you ever been to Springburn?

He was surprised at the question. 'Yes, sure. Quite often, I guess.'

'Have you ever been in the Highland Fling pub?'

She looked for the reaction in his eyes, saw something but wasn't sure what it was.

He looked to his lawyer as if expecting him to know what to say. 'What is this about, Inspector?' Stein demanded.

'It's a simple question. Has your client ever been to the Highland Fling pub? Yes or no, Mr Harkness?'

'Maybe. I'm not sure.'

Harkness was hedging and it clearly worried his solicitor.

'Okay, let me try to help you. It's on Cowlairs Road at the corner of Millarbank Street. Have you been there recently? Say, since Eloise disappeared.'

Harkness looked from her to his lawyer and back, searching for the right answer. He settled on, 'No.'

'Are you sure?'

'Yes.' It sounded very unsure.

'In that case, I'm confused. Because we have evidence to place you inside the Highland Fling.'

'It's a pub, Inspector,' Stein interjected. 'By the nature of pubs, people don't always remember being in them. And being in a pub is neither a crime nor evidence of guilt.'

'Oh, I think your client would remember being in this one. It's been shut for a number of years. And it's where Eloise Gray's body was found.'

She pulled the pin on that grenade and dropped it in Harkness's lap to watch it explode.

He got out of his seat, standing there stupidly, unsure what to do or say. A tug on his sleeve from his lawyer sat him down again.

'What evidence do you have, Detective Inspector?' Stein struggled to gain a semblance of control. 'You said you had forensic evidence for my client's arrest.'

'We have DNA.'

Stein's face fell, as did his client's. She wanted to stick the knife in deeper.

'There was a torn piece of clothing found at the scene. We extracted DNA and it has tested as a probable match for Mr Harkness. We can place him at the scene where the body was discovered.'

Harkness looked round at them as he said it. 'Eloise. I mean . . . I really liked her.'

He sounded punch drunk. Narey had heard it before, the voice stunned and surprised, not sure if he was up or down, not trusting his own head.

'So why did you hit her? Why did you threaten her?'

Harkness shrugged in shame. 'I didn't mean to. It just happened.'

'Why did you kill her?'

'I didn't.'

Narey reached into the folder in front of her and took out four A4-sized photographs. She placed them face down on the table between her and Harkness. His eyes went to them immediately and she left him time to wonder.

'These photographs,' she tapped the top one with her

index finger, 'are of Eloise. They show her as she was found in the Highland Fling.'

Harkness stared hard at the back of the prints.

'Do you want to see them?'

His head nearly swung off his neck as he shook it, mouth tight and eyes fixed.

'Are you sure?'

He was. And so was his lawyer. 'My client said he didn't . . .'

She tapped two fingers on the back of the photographs. Her mind's eye seeing what was there. Eloise lit up by the harsh light of the flash gun. The shadows that she cast against the whitewashed walls behind. Her skin yellow and purple and fat and torn.

She wouldn't, couldn't, turn over the prints and let Harkness see them. Revealing specialist knowledge that he could only know by being involved would weaken the likelihood of a conviction. Stein surely knew that. Harkness didn't. He sat as far back as his chair would allow, his eyes stretched wide.

'I'll ask you again. Why did you kill her?'

The voice was small. Weak. 'I told you. I didn't.'

'Do you really think a jury is going to believe that? I'm not sure even your own solicitor believes that.'

It was a cheap shot and Stein reacted angrily.

'That's out of order, Inspector. Don't assume any view of my relationship with my client other than his presumed innocence. I want to speak to him alone. Nothing more will be said until I do.'

'You do that, Mr Stein. And perhaps you should advise

him of his best course of action. Co-operating with us would be in his best interest.'

'I'll be the judge of that, Inspector.'

'I'm sure you will.'

Narey and Giannandrea stopped the recording and got up from the table. She paused halfway across the room, looking back to see Harkness with his head on the desk.

When they stood on the other side of the door, the claustrophobia of the interview room slipping away, Giannandrea turned to her with a tight, satisfied smile. 'Tam Harkness. After all this time. That's got to feel good.'

'Yes, but there's only one problem.'

'What's that?'

'I don't think he killed her.'

CHAPTER 14

Their shift was meant to start at eight but Salgado pushed through the doors of the giant glass cube that was LAPD headquarters on West 1st Street just after six. The three hours' sleep he'd had was full of thoughts of Ethan Garland and of a kid dying of thirst and starvation.

His nerves were jangling with the growing certainty that they were on to something bigger. It excited him, scared him, energised him. Sleep wasn't an option. Sure, they'd need to put their hands up soon and get more people on the case, but he wanted it for them as long as possible, to get as deep into it before it had to become part of something they couldn't handle alone.

This day had to get started and he wanted to get a jump on it before anyone else did. Except that when he got to his desk, O'Neill was already there.

'You'd think you might want to make an early start on something like this,' she chastised him without even turning to see who it was.

'It ain't even . . .' He gave it up. She'd probably been there half the night.

'How's the kid doing?'

The monitor to her right was running the video feed. The now familiar sight of the young man slumped against the wall. It was less than twenty-four hours since they'd first set eyes on him, caged and abandoned, but they both burned with frustration at not being able to get to him.

'Nothing much has changed from what I can see. He's sleeping a lot, then gets restless, then frustrated and tugs at the chains till he wears himself out. Then he sleeps and repeats. He might be getting weaker, but I could just be seeing what I'm expecting to see.'

They watched the screen together, helplessly mesmerised by the lack of action, waiting for his head or hands to move, waiting for proof of life.

'There's a report on my desk from one of the docs, Dorothy Sinclair, and not surprisingly the prognosis isn't good,' she told him. 'She says that putting a definitive timetable on it isn't possible as there are too many unknowns. We don't know when he last had water and how much of it he had. His body weight and level of hydration at the start of the deprivation would also be a factor, plus alcohol intake prior to the deprivation would hasten the process. However, she has listed the symptoms and progression of continued dehydration. In progression, they are darkened urine, thirst, visual disturbance, rapid heartbeat, confusion, weakness, disorientation, and finally organ failure. She says the kidneys will probably go first but progressing to heart and liver.'

'What's our move, Cally? We've got to find this kid fast.'

'We wait for Elvis and the DNA. Until then, I'm

working my way through missing persons, looking for anyone that might fit this guy.'

'Then let's split it. I need to do something or I'll go crazy.'

They'd been at it an hour when Charlie Randall, the cold case assignee from CCSS, pushed through the door and headed straight for Salgado's desk. With his long frame, lugubrious features and time spent chasing the long dead, he'd been christened the Undertaker. Salgado saw him coming and knew that he brought news but couldn't read whether it was good or bad by the man's perennially gloomy features.

'What's up, Charlie?'

Randall perched himself on the edge of the desk, looking happy to have a rest.

'I've been chasing down the provenance of the purse that was locked away in Garland's cabinet. The one said to belong to the Black Dahlia. Case is still open so we had to keep them in the loop anyway, but I hoped we could get a line on the bag, maybe get an idea where Garland could have got it from. I spoke to them last night.'

The murder of Elizabeth Short was possibly the most infamous murder in a city awash with them. In January 1947, a woman walking on the west side of South Norton in Leimert Park saw what she thought was a store mannequin dumped on an empty lot. When she looked closer, she realised it was the body of a young woman, completely severed at the waist, drained of blood and washed. Her face had been slashed from the corners of her mouth to her ears.

Beth Short, just twenty-two, had been strung up by her wrists, her corpse posed. A rose tattoo on her thigh had been cut off and inserted in her vagina.

The press labelled her the Black Dahlia and it stuck. Men were arrested, men confessed, but no one was ever convicted of her murder. Her story became legend, laced with sex, corruption and tales of gangsters and crooked cops. Books were written, movies made, and Elizabeth Short never rested in peace.

The case had never been solved, so had never been closed. Responsibility for it had been passed down through generations of detectives whose main responsibility was to talk to the press any time some new claim hit the media.

'Who's in charge of that now?'

'Howard Kelsey. You know him?'

'Howie? Yeah, I know him. He's one of the good guys. So, what did you get?'

'Well . . .' Randall's drawl suggested there was good news and bad. 'First thing is the purse. A black bag, same shape as the one in Garland's collection, and a single black shoe were found on top of a trash can at a restaurant, Delmonico's, in the 1100 block of Crenshaw Boulevard. A guy named Robert "Red" Manley identified the bag as belonging to Beth Short. Manly was the last person known to have seen her alive but that was six days before she was killed.'

'Was this Manley a suspect?'

'Yep. He was their number one guy. But they interviewed him, put him through two lie detector tests and he aced them. But ... well, there's a couple of buts. First, the bag that Manley said belonged to Short is still in the case file in archives. I got Howie to check and he says it's still there. Or at least there's a bag and no reason to think it's the wrong one.'

'And?'

'And Frankie Wynn, the name that was tagged with the purse. You know Howie, so you know he's not the kind who's just going to take ownership of a case like that and sit on it. He knows the file. In the initial investigation, around sixty people came forward to confess that they killed Elizabeth Short. Since then, it's something crazy like five hundred people who've come forward and said they did it. But of those sixty or so immediately following the killing? One of them was a man named Frankie Wynn.'

'Shit.'

'Uh huh. Now, this guy's statement was taken but he was quickly dismissed as either crazy or an attention seeker. He couldn't give them anything to show he knew more than what was in the papers, so they kicked him to the kerb. The guy had said he worked at a restaurant, wait for it, Delmonico's on Crenshaw, but when they followed up, the owner had never heard of anyone named Frankie Wynn.'

'That's wild. So, he's given a fake name or a fake job, and that fake job just happens to be where the victim's bag and shoe were found. Like what, three miles from the scene? How can this make sense?'

'How the hell do I know? But I do know that Howie

Kelsey is going to want that purse and anything we get on Garland's collection.'

'This is our case, Charlie.'

'It's an unsolved homicide, Salgado. Probably the number one unsolved in the history of the LAPD. Good luck holding on to it.'

'Bullshit. Anyway, how the hell could Garland have known who killed the Black Dahlia when the LAPD doesn't? He was guessing.'

Randall shrugged lazily. 'His collection doesn't suggest a man who would be guessing about something like that.'

Salgado stared back, not sure what to say or think. The telephone rang and saved him the trouble for a while. 'Salgado.'

'Detective, I have a result for you. The first DNA back from one of the body parts we found in the cellar.'

He could hear the tone underlying Elvis's bland statement. If excitement could ever truly be described as laid-back, then this was it. Elvis wanted to be asked. Elvis knew it was good.

'Which part?'

'It's the finger, and it's a match to a known victim.' Elvis paused for effect. 'High profile.'

Salgado felt the hairs on the back his neck prickle and pay attention. 'Are you going to tell me who?'

'Walker Wright.'

'Walker fucking Wright? Are you shitting me?'

The look on Charlie Randall's face suggested he was equally surprised at hearing the name.

'Nope.'

Salgado was now sitting upright in his chair, waving an arm as non-frantically as he could towards O'Neill.

'You're a sonofabitch, Elvis. No doubt?'

'One chance in a billion that it isn't.'

Walker Wright had been as high profile as it got in the summer of 2019. He dominated front pages, news bulletins, political speeches and LAPD man hours. There had even been overtime.

He was a TV weatherman for one of the local cable affiliates. That made him a very minor celebrity by Tinseltown standards, but it did mean people knew his face.

So, there was some coverage when he didn't show for his shift and couldn't be found anywhere. His mother didn't know where he was, nor his girlfriend or neighbours. Walker Wright had just vanished.

It didn't raise too much hoopla at first. He was a grown man, entitled to throw away his career by enjoying a couple of days of no-show. The company's view was simple. If he turned up safe and well then they'd fire his ass. If he didn't, they'd mourn the loss of a great talent in the entertainment news industry.

Walker did turn up. A little at a time.

A severed finger was sent to a rival news station along with a note saying it was his. His mother was called to examine it and said, yes, it was her son's. A long white scar that he got after falling from his bike as a kid. It was Walker's, she was sure.

CBS Los Angeles got the next package. Two fingers.

Like the first one, they had been cut, seemingly, from the same right hand.

There was chatter that it was all a big publicity stunt, that the station was in on it. If that really was what it was all about then it worked better than they could have hoped. Walker was soon the most talked about weatherman in America. It left LAPD on the pointed end of a very sharp stick that was rammed up their asses and they could do nothing about. They had nothing.

They knew the last known sighting of Walker was on the 210 heading east towards San Bernardino. The cameras couldn't find him again after that and it was thought that maybe he'd turned off somewhere near Rancho Cucamonga. And that was all they had. No credit card use, no phone use. Nothing.

Eventually, Walker faded from first item up to second to fifth to the slot before the goofy 'and finally' piece. The conspiracy nuts kept it alive online for a while longer until they too got bored.

They never did find the rest of Walker Wright. Just three fingers and a man missing, presumed murdered.

'Walker Wright? *Seriously?*'

O'Neill was as surprised and disbelieving as Salgado had been.

'Yep. Garland has a severed finger. So, either he's somehow bought it, same way he bought some of that other shit on his walls or . . .'

'Or he's killed him himself. Even if he didn't kill him, it follows that he might have known who did.'

'He killed him,' Salgado said.

'Your gut?'

Salgado shrugged. 'My gut. Your brains. Everything we know about it and him. You doubt it?'

'No.' She turned away from him, still talking. 'I used to watch his mother on TV. Walker Wright's mother. A strong woman getting broken bit by bit. Made me feel bad that we couldn't find her boy, couldn't give her some kind of peace. Even though *we* never worked the case, I felt like *we'd* let her down. The LAPD, you know what I mean?'

'Nature of what we do. We're always letting people down.'

She shook her head. 'Not true and you know it. But we did let that woman down. Till now. We've got a chance to do something about it.'

Salgado stood, arms crossed across his chest.

'I'm listening and I'm all for finding what's left of this guy, but how do you figure we're going to find him when a squad couldn't find him before?'

O'Neill tipped her head to the side and looked at him like she couldn't believe he was quite so dumb.

'Because we have an advantage they didn't have. We know who killed him.'

CHAPTER 15

Narey fell through the door of their house on Belhaven Terrace, a bag of shopping in each hand, and closed the world out with a shove of her backside. The door shut out the tumult of rush hour traffic on Great Western Road and all the problems on the other side of it, if only temporarily. She enjoyed the silence while it lasted, closing her eyes over and enjoying a couple of moments of stand-up snoozing.

It lasted as long as it took for her daughter to realise she was home. An excited howl of 'Mummy, mummy' floated through from another room, swiftly followed by little feet running over wooden floors and rugs. Alanna swung round the corner at impressive speed and ploughed straight at her. Narey didn't have time to put the shopping down and instead had to settle for hugging both the bags and her daughter as a mop of fair hair buried itself at her waist. It felt good. Better than anything had done all day.

'Hey, sweet pea. How are you? I've missed you!'

Alanna didn't answer, not in words, but buried her head deeper before she finally emerged, eyes shut and grinning maniacally.

'Did you miss me?'

'Yeah!'

Yeah was her favourite word. A bit ahead of cheese and just in front of *Bing*, her favourite TV show. None of those words made Narey particularly proud of her parenting skills but needs must. If the price to be paid for catching bad guys while raising a child was that her daughter ate a bit too much dairy and was fascinated by a whiny anthropomorphic bunny rabbit then she could live with that.

'Yeah? Good. Because I really missed you.'

Other footsteps came into the room, skin slapping against the floorboards. 'Hey, I missed you too so I'm hoping I get a hug as well.'

'I think I've just about got energy for that. Come on, sweet pea, let's go hug Daddy. Mummy could do with it.'

'That bad?' Tony Winter strode across the room and took the bags of shopping from her, stooping to kiss her full on the lips.

Narey allowed herself a sigh. 'Not that bad. Long day. Confusing day. Nothing a hug and glass of wine won't cure.'

'Why confusing?' Tony was barefoot in jeans and a T-shirt. He put an arm round his wife, her holding their daughter, and the three of them shuffled together towards the living room.

'Well, I don't want to talk about it. Obviously.'

'Obviously.'

'But . . .'

Winter looked at her over Alanna's head, the surprise obvious on his face. He looked down at the child. 'Come on, darling, let's get your mum a glass of wine. I don't think she's feeling well. She actually wants to talk to us about her job. About one of her cases. Remember this when you're older, the day mummy let us into her world.'

Narey mouthed a reply that no three-year-old should hear but accompanied it with a grin. 'Let's call it a one-off. And after this one is asleep.'

'No sleep. No sleep.'

'What? No, of course not. Come on, sweet pea. Mummy wants to hear all about your day. Did Daddy sing "Wind the Bobbin Up" for you?'

'Yeah!'

'Ah, never mind. We can always report him to social work.'

'Oi! Daddy heard that.'

'Daddy was supposed to. Daddy's got a voice like an electric drill.'

Alanna finally fell asleep while still murmuring demands for one more story. Narey and Winter turned her light off and sighed in unison before taking their tiredness to the sofa with a couple of glasses of Rioja. He took the corner and let her stretch out on her back with her head on his lap, letting slip a sigh that was somewhere between relief and exhaustion.

It was a full minute before she spoke and even then it was no more than a warm-up.

'Have you heard from Uncle Danny?'

Winter nodded, mid-mouthful. 'I got a text from him this morning. He and Pauline are in Naples and going on to Rome tomorrow. He says he hates cruises and is bored out of his mind, but the old bugger is obviously loving it.'

'That woman is the best thing that could have happened to him. If he'd stayed single much longer, he'd have turned feral.'

'Turned? Danny was born feral. But you're right, she's just what he needed, even if he'd never have admitted it.'

She went quiet again. He waited.

'So, there's this case I've been working on.'

'Thomas Harkness.'

'I didn't say that.'

'You didn't have to. There hasn't been another case in months that has affected you like this one has. Your mouth twitches every time his name or Eloise Gray's is mentioned. It's Harkness, right?'

'Right. Or at least, maybe it is. We've got firm evidence tying him to her killing and we're going to charge him.'

'And yet the tone of your voice tells me this doesn't make you happy. *Wait*. Do you have a body? Have you found Eloise?'

She blanked him. Tony was a journalist, a reporter for the *Scottish Standard*, and she insisted on strict demarcation lines between his job and hers.

'No comment. Not till tomorrow at the earliest.'

He sat up straighter, shifting her from where she lay. 'You've *found* her? Christ. Where?'

'I'm saying nothing. You know I'm not giving you a heads-up on this. And it's not what I want to talk about. It's Harkness.'

He huffed, knowing she wouldn't be shifted. And he got it. If he started turning up exclusive after exclusive from her cases, then she'd be facing a disciplinary panel in no time.

'Okay, tell me about him. Although this is killing me. What's the deal with Harkness? You've always been sure he killed her.'

'Yeah. I was sure. Until today. We have evidence, very firm, stand-up-in-court type evidence that would put him away for Eloise's murder. And yet I don't believe he did it. It's like everything I thought is upside down. Now I'm not sure what to think or what to do.'

'Jesus. And you thinking he didn't do it is based on what?'

She managed to look embarrassed. 'Instinct. Experience. Something like that. The evidence being too good to be true and just turning up now when a certain location has probably been visited a number of times and nothing found.'

'Okay . . . so this evidence . . .'

'That I'm *not* going to talk about tonight.'

'Yeah, I get that. But this evidence. You think it's been planted to frame Harkness?'

'Maybe. It would explain it but there's so much that I don't know.'

'So, you accept that planting evidence could happen?'

'Well it always . . . wait. Whoa. Christ, you're not going to start on that Keith Hardie stuff again, are you?'

'It's not *stuff*. It's an investigation. It's a miscarriage of justice.'

'He was caught bang to rights.'

'Most of that was circumstantial. You know that.'

'Apart from the bloody evidence? Apart from the DNA that actually convicted him?'

'Apart from *one* piece of evidence. One highly disputed piece of evidence. You take that away and there was precious little holding that case together. Sound familiar?'

'Keith Hardie killed a fifty-six-year-old woman. He left her to bleed to death. Stevie Crichton might be a bit of a bellend, but he's a solid detective. He made that case and the jury agreed with him. You really sure you want to spend so much of your time trying to prove this guy innocent? I can get you the scene of crime photos if you want. We both know you like that sort of thing.'

It was a low blow and she regretted it immediately but there was no taking it back, not least because it was true. It was enough to send Winter into a rage.

'Bullshit! The jury agreed with him. Aye, because judges and juries always get it right. Keith Hardie was at home with his partner. Two other people, with no motivation to lie, saw him go in. No one saw him leave. His neighbour, who was a nosey old cow, swears she'd have known if he'd left and come home again. He had no motive to kill Irene Dow. He had no knowledge of *how* to kill Irene Dow the way she was killed. He had no history of violence or any other criminal activity. The *one* bit of evidence was lapped up by the cops and the prosecution and the jury. But it was some bullshit plant. Take that away and there was fuck all. He didn't do it.'

She took a breath. It was a long-established working practice that if one of them got mad, the other had to stay calm. If they both lost it then the walls of the house might come tumbling down.

'Tony, you can't just discard the biggest piece of evidence in the case as if it never existed. It existed. It still exists. Hardie's DNA was on her. A note written by him was in her coat pocket.'

'Yet you can discard it when it suits you? You're telling me you have evidence to put Harkness away and you're going to ignore it?'

'That's different. I—'

'No. I'm not seeing it as different at all. Listen, I was with Keith's mother this morning and you want to go and tell her he's bang to rights. Helen knows her son. She knows his partner and knows she's telling the truth. That woman is in bits because of the injustice that's been done. She's going to keep at this whether the cops like it or not. And I'm with her. I'm writing stories on this until the truth is there for everyone to see.'

She stared back at him, saying nothing but refusing to blink.

'You're pretty sexy when you go full-on *All the President's Men*, you know that? The fearless reporter seeking truth, justice and the West Highland Way.'

'Piss off, I'm serious.'

'I know you are. Still sexy though.'

'How sexy?'

'Let's go to bed and I'll tell you.'

'Okay, but I'm still serious. Keith Hardie is innocent and I'm not giving up on that.'

'I know. I know. Keep talking.'

CHAPTER 16

O'Neill and Salgado watched the young man talking to himself, seeing his tongue loll out of his mouth like a dog in the middle of the afternoon. He was speaking too low and sat too far from the camera for them to hear what he was saying but they could guess.

His body language shouted where he couldn't. He was dying of thirst and the agony of it was tormenting both his physical being and his mind. His head shifted drunkenly from side to side like he was arguing with himself or the world. Occasionally he convulsed in a desperate kicking, lunging motion as if his body were shrivelling before them and rebelling against it.

'I can't bear to watch him,' O'Neill admitted. 'He's dying in front of us. We can maybe track down Walker Wright but there's no guarantee it's going to bring us any closer to finding this guy.'

'It's all we can do, Cally. We do our job, we follow the case, we make progress, and we *do* get closer.'

'I know it, I know it. It's just . . .' she waved a hand at the screen by way of unnecessary explanation.

A knock on the outside of the open door interrupted their tortured viewing.

'Detectives?'

O'Neill looked up to see a tall, slim man approaching the desk alongside Charlie Randall. He was dressed in dark suit pants and a pale-blue open-neck shirt, his head dusted in fair hair.

'Howie Kelsey!' From behind her, Salgado was out of his seat and shaking the newcomer's hand. 'How you doing, man? Not seen you in a while.'

'I'm good, I'm good. I hear you're trying to steal one of my cases.'

Salgado laughed dryly. 'That's the last thing we need. We've got plenty to do without taking on anything else. Howie, this is my partner, Cally O'Neill.'

Kelsey smiled and they shook hands. 'Good to meet you, Cally. I—' He stopped mid-thought. 'Shit, this is your guy?'

He nodded at the screen that they'd been unable to tear themselves away from.

O'Neill nodded, unwilling or unable to discuss it further. Kelsey took the hint.

'Listen, from what I've heard, and what I can see, you guys have your hands full. I just wanted to give you a heads-up that I'm looking into this purse that you guys got hold of that supposedly belonged to Elizabeth Short. I'm not intending to step on your toes or get in the way of the search for this kid, but it might happen. I promise I'll do my best to make sure it doesn't.'

'Can't ask for fairer than that,' Salgado nodded. 'We

don't know how Garland got hold of this purse or even if it's what he says it is, but if you can find that out then we'll be all ears. Right, Cally?'

'Of course. We'll take any help we can get. Not sure we can offer much back though. All we can concentrate on is finding our guy. You think the purse might be genuine?'

Kelsey spread his arms wide. 'Well, it might be. Here's what I know. After the Short killing, a purse and a shoe were found on a trash can out back of a restaurant called Delmonico's on Crenshaw – I think Charlie filled you in on that part. The cops were called but trash collectors beat them to it and took them to the dump. A detective named Ralph Asdel went to the dump, rescued several purses, several pairs of shoes and took them to the station. A lead's a lead, right? He then talked a boyfriend of Elizabeth Short, guy named Red Manley, into coming down to try to identify them and Manley picked out a shoe and the purse.

'But here's where it gets complicated. Manley was a very stressed, mixed-up guy. He got sectioned by his wife just seven years later after suffering nervous breakdowns and hearing voices. So, you make your mind up on how reliable his memory was. I checked the archive and the purse that Manley ID'd is still there. It's similar to the one in your guy's collection but it's not the same. Given that Manley was unreliable, maybe your guy had the real deal. But I've turned up a couple of things to make me think it might be.

'Next thing, Asdel picks up on a witness statement from a guy in Leimert Park who says he'd driven to Norton about nine on the night before the body was found, to dump a load of shrub cuttings. As he drives past the spot where the body was later found, he sees a 1935 light-coloured sedan with its rear door open. Standing next to the car is a slim man, about five foot eight, with a dark hat pulled down low. This slim guy strains to look inside the shrub cuttings guy's car. The witness drives off, circles and comes back. This time, the sedan's door is closed and the slim man is behind the wheel. As soon as he sees the witness's car, he drives off fast as he can.

'Asdel plugged away trying to trace the light-coloured sedan, traced down all the 1935s he could, solid spade-work stuff. He traces one that belongs to a guy named Tony Giordano. Now Giordano is a waiter and guess where he works? Delmonico's.'

'You're kidding?'

'Nope. Asdel interviews the guy but can't pin anything on him. He's clean. Solid alibi for the night of the murder. Plus, he's six foot tall and not particularly slim. But Asdel sees that this guy's car was recently painted black. Asks him why. Giordano says he just wanted a change. Asdel files the report but no one is particularly interested.'

'But *you're* interested, right?'

'Oh, you bet. And there's more. The Frankie Wynn character who confessed gave his place of employment. Want to take a guess where?'

'Delmonico's – Charlie mentioned that part too.'

'Right. So, yeah, there's reason to think the purse your guy had is the genuine article. And plenty of reason for me to wade back into the Dahlia file and see if there's anything that's been missed, anything that can tie this together. If there's something I think might be of use to you, maybe give you an idea how your guy got hold of the purse, then I'll come back and let you know. If there's not, then I'll stay clear and wish you guys luck. That work for you?'

'Thanks, Howie. We'll take whatever you got. The Black Dahlia, man? It's like the Holy Grail. You should go ahead and order yourself a silver bar because you'll make lieutenant if you can crack that.'

Kelsey grinned. 'Thought never crossed my mind.'

'Of course it didn't. But seriously, man, anything you turn up here could help. And God knows we need something. And fast.'

They'd requested all the available data they could get on Garland. The information turned up shortly after Kelsey left, and they jumped into it. Some of it came in a thick sheaf of printouts, the rest was delivered on screen.

After around twenty minutes of searching, O'Neill waved to Salgado and the urgency of the movement had him on his feet.

'What you got?'

'Garland's bank records, going back five years.'

He pulled up a chair, seeing scrolls of numbers and dates on the screen, immediately drawn in.

'Interesting?'

'Very. There's so much of it and it's going to take days to go through it all. But I've concentrated on one day.'

'The day that Walker Wright went missing.'

'Yes. June twenty-first, 2019. These are his transactions

from that day.' The screen changed and highlighted a dozen or so items. 'A couple of them are monthly debits and don't mean much, certainly not to that day. But these,' she tapped the screen with a pen, 'these are the ones I'm interested in.'

'Talk numbers to me, O'Neill.'

'Okay, $49.75. Cost of filling his car at a Shell gas station just north of Barstow on the 15.'

'Mojave Freeway? He buy anything else?'

'He bought the gas at 8.24 in the evening. The next time he used his card was at 6.46 the following morning when he ate breakfast at Peggy Sue's, a retro diner also on the 15. Just four miles from the Shell station.'

'So, what did he do in between? Drive to Vegas and play the tables?'

'With a body in the trunk? Without taking out cash or using his credit card? Doesn't seem very likely. Also, he didn't buy gas again until two days later in LA. He'd need to have filled up way before then if he'd driven all the way to Vegas. I don't think he left the area, but he didn't pay for a hotel or motel unless he paid cash.'

'Okay, so what are we thinking?'

She shrugged. 'I don't know what you're thinking, Salgado. But I'm thinking we need to go to Peggy Sue's.'

'What about Marr? That's a five-hour round trip if we're lucky. You think we can spare that time when we still don't know where the kid is?'

'I've spoken to Geisler. He's at Garland's computer. He'll talk to Marr if he comes online. So far, he's been quiet, but Geisler is going to feed anything to us soon as it happens. I say we've nothing to gain by sitting here waiting.'

'Okay. I guess we're going on a road trip.'

Peggy Sue's was in the Mojave Desert, a jukebox-shaped mirage in the shadow of the Calico Mountains. Its rainbow livery was a surreal interruption to the myriad shades of desert brown that had accompanied them since before Hesperia.

They rolled into the car park and drank in the sight. What it lacked in subtlety it made up for in joyful tackiness, resplendent in candy pinks, blues and greens, its entrance fashioned like a giant 1950s Wurlitzer.

'I like it,' Salgado announced. O'Neill just blew out air and said nothing.

Inside, they were greeted by a massive ice cream sundae, a life-size statue of a dinner-suited butler and a fortune teller machine containing Elvis Presley in his late Vegas period. Salgado grinned and O'Neill raised her eyebrows. They followed the highly polished black and white check-board floor and took a seat in a booth as far from the maddening crowd as they could.

Their waitress was Patty. With her retro uniform and thick layer of ghostly make-up, she might have worked in the joint since Buddy Holly was in the charts.

'Hey, folks. Welcome to Peggy Sue's. What can I get you?'

'Just coffee, thanks.'

'No breakfast?' Patty looked slightly disappointed under the cake.

'Yeah, maybe we should,' O'Neill relented. 'What's good?'

Patty brightened. 'I like the Rita Hayworth Cheese Omelette. It's got cheddar and American. Or if you're ready for lunch then the Buddy Holly Bacon Cheeseburger is always good.'

'I'll have the Rita Hayworth.'

'You got it. Curly fries with that?'

'No, just the omelette and coffee.'

'You got it. What about you, cutie?'

Salgado looked up from the menu and smiled. 'I'll take a bowl of the Jailhouse Rock then a King Kong Monster Burger.'

'Curly fries?'

'They're famous, right?'

Patty smiled right back at him. 'Says so right there, honey. And I'd never lie to you.'

'I'm counting on it.'

The waitress lost ten years on the spot and whirled away in a swish of uniform to fetch their coffees.

'You just can't help yourself, can you?'

'I just like making people happy. Do you know this place was built in 1954 from railroad ties and mortar from the nearby Union Pacific Railyard? The owners took it over in 1987 and worked to restore it to its original state, filling it with their extensive collection of TV and movie memorabilia. Says so right here, just like Patty said.'

'Great.'

The coffee arrived steaming hot, placed carefully between them by a contented waitress.

'Breakfast will be coming right up. Can I get you guys anything else right now?'

'Patty, we were wondering if you could help us.' O'Neill showed her badge. 'We're passing through from LA and we're trying to find someone who's missing. Would you mind taking a look at this photograph?'

Patty's contentment faded visibly.

'Do you know how many folks we get in here of a day? Darling, I'm not sure I'd remember Buddy Holly himself if he'd sat where you're sitting and ordered a Rock Around the Clock with curly fries. Although,' she smiled sweetly at Salgado, '*him* I'd remember. He's cute.'

'It's important. Could you at least look?'

Patty took the edge of the photograph as if it were contaminated but deigned to study it. They saw a wrinkle of surprise crease her face. She let the thought simmer.

'You know ... actually maybe. Yeah, this guy. If it's the one I'm thinking of, he was real mean to Elly. He cussed at her, said there'd be no tip, just cos his breakfast took two minutes longer than he'd thought it should. Let me get her.'

Elly was of a similar vintage to Patty, another ghost of diners past. She picked up the photograph of Garland and jabbed a finger at it accusingly.

'Yeah. Yeah. This guy. I remember him.' She leaned in conspiratorially and whispered. 'A real son of a bitch. Pardon my French.'

'What do you remember about him, Elly?'

'Well, we open at six and this guy barged in right on the dot as if he'd been waiting all night for us to open the doors.'

'He was definitely alone?'

'Yes. Made out as if he'd never want to be around people. I remember thinking he looked like he hadn't slept. Five o'clock shadow and kinda grimy. Not like a hobo or nothing, just like he'd been working.'

'Did he say anything? Maybe about where he'd been?' Salgado asked.

'Nothing like that,' Elly shook her head. 'He wasn't one for small talk. I wouldn't have remembered him at all except he cussed me out when his food wasn't on the table as quick as he'd have liked. He shouted at me. In front of other customers too.'

'You say you thought he'd been working. Did he maybe have dirt under his fingernails? Dirt on his face, anything like that?'

Elly shrugged. 'Sorry. I don't remember. He was just . . . a bit grubby. Kinda sweaty.'

Marianne Ziegler, formerly Garland, answered the phone breezily, but the wind dropped as soon as Salgado introduced himself. 'Oh. Hi. Is there more news, Detective?'

'Nothing yet, Marianne. I had just a couple of questions and hoped you could help us out.'

'Okay. Sure.' The tone was much more reluctant than the words.

'My partner and I are over in the Mojave Desert. A bit north of Barstow. We wondered if maybe Ethan had ever talked about anything up this way. Maybe some place in the desert, maybe a town nearby he used to visit.'

'Barstow? I don't remember him ever talking much

about Barstow. Although he did used to drive the old Route 66 with his dad when he was a kid.'

'Can you think of anywhere else around this area that he might have known? We're trying to trace his movements and need a place to start. What about Peggy Sue's Diner, that mean anything to you?'

There was silence on the other end of the line, Marianne thinking.

'Yes. That name is familiar. An old-school diner, right? He used to stop there with his dad when they went on trips. He went there and a waterpark. Talked about the park a lot. Happiest days of his life and all that.'

'Do you remember what the waterpark was called?'

'Oh, it was a long time ago. It was like a woman's name. Uh ... no, sorry. It'll come to me. Can I call you back?'

'Sure, Marianne, thank you.'

Patty arrived with the cheque and Salgado shoved six ten-dollar bills across the table. 'Keep the change, Patty.'

'Why thank you, honey. Y'all have a good day now.'

When Salgado didn't reciprocate, she hesitated. 'You got some more questions, cutie? You don't need to tip that much to ask me anything.'

He grinned. 'Just the one. Do you know of a waterpark anywhere between here and Vegas, or maybe between here and Baker? I don't know what it's called but it might have a woman's name.'

Patty made a face. 'A woman's name? Can't rightly say I know where that might be.'

'Lake Dolores.' Elly had been serving at a nearby table and obviously listening in. 'It's Lake Dolores.

139

Rock-A-Hoola Waterpark was originally called Lake Dolores, after the wife of the man who built it.'

'So it was!' Patty exclaimed. 'Lake Dolores. I haven't heard that name in years. That place used to have kids coming from all over in the sixties. First waterpark in America, you know. Shame it closed down.'

'It's closed?'

'Oh hell yes. That's why I didn't think of it right off. It's been closed for, man, must be fifteen years. It's been another twenty years since it was called Lake Dolores. Nothing but a ghost park now. The buildings are all still standing but nothing but cockroaches there these days.'

'Is it far?'

'Far? Honey, it's less than twenty miles away straight along the 15. You can't miss it.'

CHAPTER 17

It was right there off the freeway, just a deserted desert block in full view of every car and truck that thundered east to Baker and Vegas or west to Barstow and LA.

Lake Dolores. Rock-A-Hoola Waterpark.

'I must have driven past this place a dozen times, maybe twenty, and never stopped to wonder what it was,' Salgado admitted.

'Hiding in plain sight,' O'Neill told him.

'Guess so.'

They'd turned off the freeway onto Yermo Road, a dusty two-way that ran alongside the rail track. A half-mile long freight train paced beside them for a bit then disappeared into the distance as they slowed to turn left, crossing above the freeway then left again onto Hacienda Road and the old entrance to the abandoned park. Salgado pulled into the dirt and parked.

The desert sun hit them as soon as they got out of the car, standing either side of it and staring at the faded signs and multicoloured buildings they could see through the palms and across the sand.

Salgado looked doubtfully to the ground and O'Neill could see the thoughts see-sawing through his head.

'You worried about those shoes?' She pointed at the brown Italian leather brogues on her partner's feet. 'They look good with that expensive suit but there's a chance they might not be the best choice for the desert.'

'No,' he replied defensively. 'I'm worried about snakes. I don't like snakes.'

She tried to hide a grin. 'There's bound to be rattle-snakes round here. It's their territory, not ours. But you'll hear them. They rattle real loud.'

'They all look like sticks, right?'

'Right. And all sticks look like rattlers.'

'Great.'

Two great palms stretched to the sky right in front of them. Behind, on the hill to the right, a huge white cylindrical water tower dominated the vista. To the left, the faded remains of the waterpark sprawled beyond the sand with the Calico Mountains in the distance. Salgado sighed then led the way.

Patty had told them the park was built up water ride by water ride by the first owner, a guy named Bob Byers, intending it just to be for his own kids and their cousins, until it grew big enough that the obvious thing was to open it for business.

It was now a weather-worn graffiti palace. Every available inch was spray-painted in slogans and art, much of it suitably sinister. The old water tower on the hill had a giant Coca-Cola bottle etched on it, while the billboard a hundred yards in front of it proclaimed itself to be the property of Shie47.

Dry sticks cracked under their feet and O'Neill hid a smile each time Salgado jumped. The slick city boy wasn't enjoying this much.

As they neared the park entrance, they saw there were a number of buildings that would easily serve as a body dump. Even if Walker Wright was here, he wasn't going to be easy to find. It could have been the pink stucco block to the right with the art deco frontage, or maybe the long block behind the four stocky palms. That was before they even passed through the gates.

Salgado stepped over a fallen palm, sidestepped a piece of rock and made his way inside the first building, O'Neill at his heels. They were greeted by a riot of decay and destruction. The ceiling had been pulled down, insulation strewn on the floor and dangling from exposed beams. An air duct drooped in mid-air like an elephant trunk while another sprouted copper wiring like a steampunk haircut. The walls and thick central pillars were covered in art, leading them deeper into the room in search of hidden corners. They advanced warily, Salgado not the only one giving thought to what might be sleeping under the rubble that littered the floor. Every step offered the chance of disturbing a sleeping rattler or stumbling across the weatherman's decaying corpse.

The first building didn't give them anything other than chills, the second one the same. They passed through the official gate, defaced with the uplifting message that *Life*

Is Bittersweet, but with the consolation that *Jesus Loves You* from John 3:16.

A kids' stroller stood abandoned on the baked tarmac, daubed in paint and long forgotten.

'This place is creepy as hell, O'Neill.'

'You think? Is it the ghosts of long-lost childhoods or the bones that might be bleaching in the sun? Or the snakes?'

'Fuck you.'

'I'm just asking.'

Salgado stomped off to the right, reclaiming his machismo by barrelling straight into the next building, a low-slung white concrete oblong that was sprayed in green and red. As soon as he was inside, he slowed his pace, seeing it was a minefield of potential missteps.

'Shit.' She was right behind him. 'If we thought the rest was creepy . . .'

'Yeah.'

The white walls screamed with graffiti, the ceiling falling towards them as polystyrene tiles booby-trapped the floor. Air ducts and wiring, broken doors, dark corners and half-open closets. It was in half darkness, punctured by blinding laser beams of light as the sun broke in through holes in the plasterboard.

Outside again, the sun felt even harsher. It was over ninety with not a whisper of wind. They had to manoeuvre their way through a twisting section that looked like it once held water, across a now unnecessary bridge to another, bigger building.

As soon as they were inside they saw it used to be a

concession stand, a long counter facing out to the public, the floor behind it a mess of tiles, panels and spurs of wood. Two metal panels that might have been the back of control boxes glinted in the sun. Beyond them, a human-shaped hole had been broken through plasterboard. Salgado shrugged and ducked through it, finding a maze of rooms. Some dark, some light, all junked with boxes, cabling, metal spikes, ceiling tiles and pieces of wood.

They emerged once more into the broiling heat and climbed a steep hill behind the dried-out concrete river, where concrete steps led to a series of concrete crossbar-like structures at the top. It was a concrete Parthenon. From there the barren park spread out before them, the highway and train track beyond.

Salgado did a 360, seeing a dust devil spiralling maybe halfway to the Calicos in the west. The wind blew, muffling the cars on the 15 and increasing the sense of isolation.

'So, we were wrong?'

He puffed out his cheeks and grimaced. 'I don't think so. Garland's bank record says it. The diner says it. His ex-wife says it. And . . .'

'Don't tell me. Your gut says it.'

'Yes, it does. It surely does.' He finished his slow spin, ending up staring east at the white water tower a thousand feet away on the hill.

'In there,' he told her. 'He's got to be.'

It seemed taller once they stood at the foot of it and looked up, blinking, into the sun. The white cylinder was occasionally daubed in red to the top, black and blue graffiti at the bottom. The exterior was warm to the touch.

A large round hole, maybe three feet in diameter, was carved into the shell. It presumably was covered by some kind of hatch back in the day but now offered a porthole into the tower, albeit guarded by four thick black metal slats that were bolted horizontally across the gap.

'Shit, it's huge.'

'People have obviously been able to get in. There's graffiti all over the lower walls.'

'What the hell are those chains for?'

Maybe fifteen links of metal were drawn through the arc of the tower's floor into the middle. It was most likely part of the working machinery of the place, but it gave off a ritualistic vibe that screamed of pagan sacrifice.

'And what the fuck is that?'

Salgado's voice spiralled up the tower, bouncing back at them from the metal as it climbed.

There was a darker circle where the chains met in the centre of the floor. Their eyes strained to make out what it was, seeing it slightly raised and not quite a circle at all.

'It's a blanket,' O'Neill replied. 'Or a small tarpaulin.'

'Yeah. And what's it covering?'

'Shit.'

O'Neill backed off the tower wall and considered it, shielding her eyes from the blinding afternoon sun.

'If we had the equipment, which we don't, then we could cut these spars off and climb in. But, like I say, we don't. So, either we call for backup to cut our way in, or . . .'

They both looked at the white metal ladder running

up the side of the tower, encased in a white metal cage. According to the measure that ran from the tower's top to the desert floor, the lowest rung of the ladder was seven feet from the ground and the tower itself was forty-eight feet high.

She heard Salgado breathe out hard before he turned to look at her. 'You know I'm shit with heights, right?'

She smiled tightly. 'I know.'

'It's vertigo. I mean, I'll do it but—'

O'Neill cut him off. 'I can't take the chance of you falling off this thing. I'll do it.'

'You're going to make me look bad.'

'Yeah? Well I can live with that if you can.'

'I can as long as you don't tell anyone. You are going to be able to get out again, right?'

O'Neill shrugged. 'Probably.'

She took her jacket off, turning it inside out before placing it on the ground, acutely aware that her blouse was damp even before she attempted the climb.

Salgado boosted her up till she was able to grab a hold of the lowest rung then hoisted her further until she was able to pull herself up, struggle into the ladder's metal cage and catch her breath.

From there, she hauled herself up, the desert floor and Salgado shrinking below her as she climbed towards the sun. The temperature rose with every inch she got closer to it, her blouse sticking to her back, her brow glistening and her throat crying out for water.

She pushed on, hand over hand, step over step until she got to the top. There, the cage opened out onto the flat roof of the tower, divided into scuffed white slices of pie that converged in the middle where an opening let sunlight filter into the tower. Immediately in front of her was a second opening, a dark square that seemed likely to be her way inside.

She ventured one leg into the hole, hoping it would land on something solid. When it did, she stamped hard to make sure it wasn't going to move under her, then stepped her other leg in too.

The heat inside the tower was stifling and she felt like she was in a giant kettle heading towards boiling point. Her back was soaked and sweat dripped from her forehead, stinging her eyes. She wiped at them and settled for staring straight ahead at the inside wall as she descended, rung by rung. When her right foot stepped on fresh air it was time to look down.

There was still seven feet to the tower floor, just as there had been outside. She let both legs step off, glad of the time spent on pull ups and weights, dropping rung to rung by hand until she let go and hit the bottom.

The landing was maybe an eight point two, nothing for flair or artistic ability, but right on the money for safety. As she stood again she saw that the bottom rung was way out of her reach and there was no way she was climbing out of there again.

'You okay?' Salgado had his face pressed to the slatted opening.

'I'm fine. You might want to crack a window on the drive back to LA, but I'm fine.'

She wiped a sleeve across her forehead and eyes, trying

to adjust to the odd light at floor level, semi-darkness slashed with rays of sun from the opening above. Closer to it now, she could more clearly see the object in the middle of the tank, its dark shape gaining more definition. She walked around it, putting off the inevitable as she wasted time guessing rather than just getting on with the doing. The covering was a dark brown blanket, a heavy woollen type that might have been used for camping.

When she was on the far side of it, the shape between her and the anxious Salgado, she crouched, took the edge of the blanket, and cast a final look up at him before she began to lift it. Her nostrils were already telling her and so was her cop sense. Every sense that she had. Lifting the covering confirmed it beyond any doubt.

Salgado caught the look on her face. 'Is it him?'

She stared longer than she wanted to, unable to tear her eyes from what was left of the corpse.

'It's been three months. In over a hundred degrees heat. There's nothing much more than bones and dust. But there's fingers missing from the right hand. If it isn't Walker Wright, it's one hell of a coincidence.'

She glanced back up at the ladder that was out of her reach, then back down at the corpse.

'Call Barstow sheriff's station. And tell them to hurry.'

CHAPTER 18

Salgado and O'Neill were back in the city, the broken corpse of Walker Wright left in the care of the Barstow sheriffs, when they got a call from Kurt Geisler. He was brief and to the point but there had been no disguising the excitement in his voice. He had something.

Ethan Garland's computer had finally been removed from the house on Finley Street and Geisler had been picking it apart in a room in headquarters.

'How far away are you?' he asked O'Neill.

'Ten minutes, I'd say. What have you got, Kurt?'

'If you're ten minutes away then it will wait. It's easier shown than explained. But I think you'll be interested.'

O'Neill relayed the message and Salgado flipped the blue light, speeding through the last couple of miles. Once in the building, they raced to the IT room, barely stopping themselves from running along the corridor like school-kids. Geisler was hunched over the PC with his back to them and swung round on the chair as soon as he heard their footsteps. They tried to get a read on his face but all they saw was tiredness.

'Yeah,' Geisler nodded wearily in answer to the unasked question. 'It's been like chipping away at a coalface with a toothpick, but yes, I've dug some stuff out of this.'

'Good stuff?'

The tech blew out some air and shrugged. 'I think so. Nothing major like where the kid is, but I'd say gems. Little sparkly ones. Pull up a chair.'

Salgado grabbed a chair from the nearest desk and pulled it a few feet in front of Geisler, but O'Neill remained standing, her arms crossed in front of her.

'Like I say, it's been digging away to get out whatever I can. Partial search results, sites visited. Very, very slow going but it's been worth it. Everything is in a file that I'm going to email to you both but here are the highlights. First, I've got a search he made within Facebook, looking for another user.'

'Anyone we know?' Salgado was edging forward in his chair like a kid hearing a story.

Geisler nodded. 'Yes, it's a match to one of the names in the file that Garland had hidden as a Christmas card list. Stefan Kalinowksi.'

'Good work, Kurt.' The tension in O'Neill's voice was unmistakable. 'Can we be sure it's the same person?'

'Yes. There were a bunch of matches to what was written in the profile in Garland's file. According to his Facebook page, Stefan likes Echo and the Bunnymen, A Flock of Seagulls, Greenpeace and Quentin Tarantino movies. It's far too much of a stretch for it not to be the same one. But then there's the surprise.'

'Spill.'

'Stefan Kalinowksi isn't in LA. He isn't in California. Stefan Kalinowksi lives in Glasgow, Scotland.'

'*Scotland?*'

'Yep. And it gets better. Or stranger. Take your pick. A lot of the random search engine stuff points to the same place.'

Geisler handed a printed sheet to Salgado. 'A bar named Blackfriars. Another named Brel. A restaurant called Café Andaluz. A restaurant called Cail Bruich. A cab company. A museum named Kelvingrove. A music venue called O2 Academy. All searched for by Garland. All in Glasgow, Scotland.'

'The fuck?'

The tech smiled ruefully. 'That's pretty much what I thought. I went back to the search history we had from the time Garland was online before he died. There's a search for something in Glasgow there too. A look for the nearest subway station to somewhere named the Hillhead Bookclub – another bar.'

Salgado whistled and tilted his head to show surprise.

'Once I saw all the Glasgow references, I took the liberty of running a couple of the other names from Garland's profile list through a simple internet search with Glasgow thrown in. I got two solid hits.'

'*Scotland?*' Salgado continued to wonder.

'There was a girl from Belfast that I went to college with,' O'Neill was thinking out loud. 'Okay, I *know* that's not Scotland, but bear with me. She used to say "arse" where any of us would say "ass". I'd never heard anyone else say that, but Marr did. Check the transcript, but I'm certain he said something like "you're an arse" when you challenged him about the live stream. It didn't occur to me until now, but I'm sure he said it.'

'I'll check it,' Geisler confirmed. His hands moved across the keyboard, searching the transcript of the talks with Marr. 'Yep. Pretty much exactly what you said. He called Salgado an "arse". I think maybe we were too busy agreeing to notice the language.'

Salgado cracked a smile and pointed at the tech. 'Lucky you're a genius, Geisler. But that's nice work.'

'Okay, we need to contact the local force.' O'Neill finally uncrossed her arms, some of the strain easing from her. 'Glasgow PD or whatever it is. Ask them to run the names through their database and get back to us.'

Geisler handed over another sheet of paper. 'It's called Police Scotland. There's a phone number and an email address on there.'

Salgado nodded. 'Thanks, but I say we don't wait. I want to talk to that freak Marr now. He knows what this is all about and I want him to tell us. Kurt, seeing as you're on a roll, get him online. I'm going to talk to him. In fact, wait – I've got a better idea. Let's make sure he comes on.'

It took all of two minutes.

What the hell's going on? Why have you turned that video stream off?

This is Detective Salgado. I wanted to get your attention, Matthew.

**Well you've fucking got it. Now put
it back on.**

When I'm ready.

Now.

Not now, Matthew. I want to ask you
something first.

What?

How's the weather in Glasgow, tonight?
Still raining?

The message was read. No reply.

Don't go all shy on me, Matthew. None of us
have time for that.

It was a gamble. The same risk they ran every time they
pushed the guy. Everyone in the tech room held their
breath until the cursor flashed to show typing.

I want the stream turned back on.

Then you have to give me something. You
tell me how you'll talk to me if you get to see
the video. So talk. No talk, no video. Are you
in Glasgow?

The pause was lengthy. The cursor showed typing. Then
stopped as it was scrubbed. Then began again.

**So poor old Ethan was careless. Arsehole.
I should have known better than to trust
someone else. Yes, I'm in Glasgow. Now put that
video back on.**

Salgado and O'Neill looked at each other. He blew out
hard and dragged two hands through his hair.

> Prove it. And quickly. I need to know you're
> not just saying that. Tell me things about
> Glasgow. Now. Before you'd have time to
> look it up.

This time the response was immediate.

**Okay fucker. Best city in the world. Main river is
the Clyde but there's also the River Kelvin, the
Molendinar Burn, the Black Cart and the White
Hart. Oh, and the Levern Water. That do you,
fucker? Any more tests?**

Salgado waited and moments later got a thumbs up from
Geisler after a Google search.

> So, you're Scottish?

Can't you tell by my accent?

I can't ... Salgado deleted his initial response when he
realised he was being made fun of.

I'm in Glasgow. That's all you need to know
and all you're going to know. It's also all
Ethan ever knew so you can search his
computer all you want, or whatever you're
doing, because he didn't know who I was or
where I was other than Glasgow. It's pretty
small compared to Los Angeles but it's
plenty big enough to hide in.

He didn't know who you were? Your name
isn't Matthew Marr?

Don't be such an arse. Of course it's not.
Ethan never asked because he knew better.
Now put that video back on.

I need to know more.

I'm sure you do, big man. But you're not
getting it. Not tonight anyway. Video. Now.

He looked at O'Neill, who shrugged then nodded. 'We got
something. Much more than we had. Let's not push him hard
enough that he walks away. Because then that kid is dead.'

Salgado's eyes slid shut, hating it. He opened them
again and turned to Geisler. 'Do it.'

The tech made it happen and the response from the man
calling himself Matthew Marr was instant.

☺ That's the way. You know it makes sense,
big man. Now go fuck yourself and let me watch
this in peace.

Salgado got out of the chair and kicked it across the room again.

'We catch this guy. Nothing else to be done here. We catch this fuck.'

CHAPTER 19

Narey was at her desk, chasing wild geese through the internet. She'd been wading through both the Criminal History System and the Police National Computer for over an hour in the vain hope of stumbling over something that she could work with on the Eloise Gray case. She might have called it looking for a needle in a haystack, but she couldn't even be sure it was a needle she was looking for.

The landline rang, an internal call. She ignored it and continued to scroll through the database looking for something, anything that might give her an in. The caller refused to give up and Narey had to relent. She regretted her lack of urgency two seconds after she recognised Detective Superintendent McTeer's voice. This was all she bloody needed.

'DI Narey. I can only assume you were a long way from the phone. Can you report to my office, please? Now, if you could.'

'Sir, can I ask—'

'No. And I said, now.'

This was becoming a well-trodden path and she wasn't liking it much. She found herself wondering if someone was monitoring her searches on the CHS and the PNC. If McTeer had somehow got wind of the fact that she was doubting that Tam Harkness was guilty, then she might be facing a bollocking for pretty much the opposite of her last visit. Someone had to make their mind up round here.

She knocked on his door and, after a brief pause, he shouted for her to enter. The super was on the phone, his head resting on his hand, and saying 'uh huh' a lot. His face was not a happy one. 'Okay, okay. Leave that with me. Yes, I'll get back to you.' He hung up the phone. 'Or maybe I won't. You ever get one of those days when you wish you were still walking the streets in the pishing rain?'

'All the time, sir.'

'Yeah, me too. Okay, so what's the latest with your man Harkness? You still trusting your instinct?'

Damn it. She really hoped it wasn't Rico Giannandrea that had said anything. She wasn't ready to explain any of this until she got her hands on something resembling evidence. If it had been Rico, she'd throttle him.

'It's not just instinct, sir. It's ... experience. I've seen people react the way Harkness did, and I don't believe he was faking it. Look, I know this goes against everything I'd said before, but I need more time to try to get a handle on this.'

McTeer looked confused and she realised he'd had no idea she was doubting the man's guilt.

'Are we talking at cross purposes here, Rachel? I'm not sure that I want to know.'

'I'm not sure I want you to know either,' she conceded. 'Maybe we should start again. Shall I go back out and knock?'

'That won't be necessary, Rachel. Sit down, please.'

She settled herself in the seat opposite McTeer's desk, only now picking up on the look of consternation on his face. She sensed a worry from him that she didn't much like. He was building up to something and she felt a familiar rush of adrenalin that she didn't know was good or bad.

'We've had a call from the United States, from the LAPD. They—'

'*Sir?* This is about Eloise Gray?'

McTeer lifted his head from the printouts in his hand just long enough to look at her admonishingly over his spectacles. She stayed silent.

'It's an odd one, to say the least. They were called to what seems to have been a non-suspicious death; a man named Ethan Garland had a massive heart attack. However, there were items in the house that raised suspicion. They searched the premises and found body parts seemingly held as trophies. The evidence suggests this Garland was a serial killer and they just stumbled across him.'

He held a hand up without taking his eyes off the sheet, shutting off the questions he knew she was burning to ask.

'Their IT people went to work on his computer and among the few things they were able to dig out was a file of names with potted biographies. Age, job, physical descriptions, hobbies, things like that. They ran them against mispers and anyone with a record, but they got nothing. It was as if these people didn't exist. And yes, I know you're bursting to ask what this has got to do with us and are wishing I'd get to the point. So, it's this. Garland had done internet searches for places in Glasgow, so one of the LA detectives got in touch and ran the list of names they had past us.'

He paused just long enough that she couldn't help but fill the gap.

'And?'

'And —' McTeer took a breath — 'one of the biographies on the list was a divorced father of one. A six-foot, fair-haired primary school teacher who loved hill-climbing, old movies, cooking and dogs. His name was—'

'No way.'

'Yes, I'm afraid so. His name was Jamie Stark. It's either a very odd coincidence or he's the one we've been calling our Mr Kipper.'

Narey could only stare back at him as she tried to make sense of it. 'How the hell is that even possible?'

McTeer tossed the printout across the desk so that the clipped papers landed in front of her, sat back in his chair and slipped his reading glasses from his head. 'Rachel, I have no bloody idea. But it gets worse. Or at least stranger. Read the other names on the list.'

She snatched it from the table and skimmed through the names. Seconds later, she lowered the paper and looked up at him, her mouth open.

CHAPTER 20

Narey and Giannandrea were in a media suite inside HQ at Dalmarnock, sitting in front of a large screen waiting for Los Angeles to wake up. The eight-hour time difference was proving hugely frustrating but at least it had allowed them to do some work on the list that McTeer had provided. The fruits of that work had only made the time crawl slower as they became desperate for the Americans to get to their desks.

'So, what's the time over there now? Surely the lazy bastards are at work by this time?' DCI Derek Addison was in attendance on the orders of McTeer and making no pretence of hiding the fact he was none too happy about it.

Giannandrea checked his watch. 'It's five to six in the morning Pacific Time.'

'Which is five minutes later than the last time you asked, sir,' Narey added wearily. Addison had been a pain in the rear since the moment he joined them.

'Specific Time? Of course I wanted the specific time. And less of your cheek, DI Narey. You're not running the team yet.'

'Oh, give us—'

'Wait a minute.' Giannandrea broke up the sparring. 'Looks like we're on.'

The icon next to the LAPD connection had turned green. They were good to go.

'About bloody time,' Addison moaned.

Giannandrea made the call and it was accepted instantly. The link buffered for a few moments, showing just two slightly blurry figures on the screen, until it settled, and they saw two cops looking at two cops looking at two cops.

The male was in his early thirties, tanned and handsome in a sharp suit. She was pale and pretty with long red hair, looking as Irish as sweet Molly Malone, and she made the introductions.

'Good morning, Detectives. Or is it . . . afternoon? I'm Detective Cally O'Neill and this is my partner, Detective Bryan Salgado. Thank you for taking the time to talk to us today.'

'It's afternoon for us. I'm Detective Inspector Rachel Narey and this is Detective Sergeant Rico Giannandrea. Also in the room is Detective Chief Inspector Derek Addison, although he's here—'

'Under protest,' came the voice from the side of the room. 'Just ignore me and do your jobs. These two don't need me babysitting them and I'm sure you don't either. I'm only here because I have to be, so only refer to me if you really have to.'

O'Neill seemed taken aback by the interruption, but shrugged it off.

'Okay, sure thing, sir. Listen, I don't know how much

you guys know about what we've been working on or why we need your help, so I thought it would make sense to run through it, so we all know where we are. That work?'

'It works for me,' Narey told her. 'We have your list and have some answers to that but some more context would definitely help.'

She saw O'Neill and Salgado swap glances at that, sensing their anxiety to know what she had for them. They'd made their offer though and would have to stick to it.

'Okay, Detective, I'll make it quick.' Salgado took over. 'A couple of minutes ago, we emailed a full report on everything we have, but here's the highlights. We are investigating the activities of a fifty-eight-year-old white male named Ethan Garland. He was found dead in his home here in Los Angeles two days ago. Death was natural causes, but it's opened up a major investigation. We believe Garland was a serial killer, active over a number of years and responsible for a large number of murders. We're working those of course but, crazy as it sounds, that's not our priority. Garland left one unfinished.'

'*Unfinished?*'

'Officers, why don't we show you what we're dealing with?'

It was O'Neill's tone rather than what she said. The tone of someone who knew she held the winning argument. She turned the camera on whatever computer they were using until it pointed at another screen.

'The quality won't be great, because of not coming to

you direct, but we'll fix that and get you a feed you can use. This will let you see what we're dealing with, though.'

She adjusted the angle again until the second screen filled the one in Glasgow. It flickered once then snapped into focus.

It took Narey and Giannandrea a few moments to fully realise what they were seeing. It was a room, barely lit, an object in the middle, something else behind it. It took closer inspection and a little deduction to reveal it to be a person, the humanity initially disguised by the head slumped forward and dark hair obscuring the face. The chinos, the shirt and the build told them it was a man.

As they watched, his right arm shook briefly, perhaps uncontrollably, and the tremor ran through his body to his right foot and it too moved.

'He's alive?'

'Yes. Just. We can't be sure when he last ate or last had water, so medics can't give us a time on how long he'll survive if we don't find him. He wakes occasionally but he seems to be sleeping more and more in the time we've had access to the feed. We think a lot of the movement is the body reacting to the changes. How much cognitive brain activity is still going on is anyone's guess.'

The man's body shook again, this time his head falling to the side, held in place only by the chain that Narey could now see attached to the old iron radiator behind him. *Christ, his face.* The skin was a deathly shade of yellow, the cheeks hollowed and eye sockets like craters. A large blister was obvious on his left cheek.

His eyes were open, staring blankly at the floor. His

mouth was open too, perhaps more by gravity than choice, slackly yawning at the wooden floorboards.

'We think he's in his early to mid-twenties,' Salgado said. 'We've run the description against missing persons and have around a dozen possible hits. None of them give us a whole lot of hope, though. It may be he hasn't been reported missing yet. Our bosses are making a decision as to whether we release a photograph of him. A positive ID might narrow down search areas but LA is a big city and he could be anywhere. We're racing the clock here.'

The two Scots stared at the young man on the screen, five thousand miles away, seeing him die before their eyes and aware that they, somehow, had to play their part in saving him. It was surreal and a little unnerving.

'Okay, whatever help we can be, you've got it,' Narey told them. 'But where do we fit into this? We've worked our way through your list, so we know there's a link, but we don't know how or why.'

One of the Americans swung the camera back away from the young man and back onto them, their faces awash with tension.

'We need to get to this,' Salgado insisted. 'We're dancing when we need to be running.'

'You start,' Narey shot back. 'We'll do our best to keep up.'

'Do that. Garland used a Tor connection that hid his internet history and his general computer usage. Our tech guys are chipping away at that as we speak but all we have for now is a very limited search history. Most of it is general – news sites, some alt-right sites, plus Facebook,

Twitter and some general Google searches. Almost all of those searches were focused on Glasgow.'

'This gets weirder and weirder. What were the searches?'

'He looked for bars, restaurants, places of interest, local transit. We don't think he was planning any kind of trip to Scotland, since he'd no flights booked and he didn't have a passport. We know he had an accomplice of sorts, a man known to us as Matthew Marr. He is the Glasgow connection. That's about all we know, and we need you guys to help us change that.'

'Which brings us to your list.'

'I was really hoping it would. The suspense is killing me here, Detective Narey.'

She smiled. 'I'm not trying to piss you off, Detective Salgado, or to delay this. We are all wondering what the hell we're in the middle of and I needed a clear picture. Okay, the reason that I personally am sitting here is that one of the names on your list is the victim in a case that I'm actively working on. Eloise Gray. She disappeared five months ago, and her body was found this week. Given that happened just a couple of days before your list was sent to us, it's a coincidence I'm not very comfortable with. A fragment of clothing was found beside the body and DNA tests showed a match to our prime suspect. However,' she breathed deep, 'I don't believe our suspect is guilty and this list just convinces me of it.'

'What? Oh for fuck's sake, Rachel,' Addison exploded from stage right. 'Why the fuck am I just hearing this now? Why am I hearing it at all?'

She grimaced, eyebrows raised to the Americans away from Addison's view, and directed her response to them. 'I think he's been set up. I've no idea by whom or why but I'm guessing the answer to that will answer some of your other questions too.'

Salgado and O'Neill nodded at her from the other side of the Atlantic. 'We're hoping so. What about the other names on the list?'

'Okay. There's plenty. First of all though, the list is split into two. Roughly half in italics and half not. Was that your marking or his?'

'His. All his.'

'That makes sense. I have information on all the non-italic names but only have something on one on the other half of the list. Again, that's a direct link to my own case.'

She watched the two Americans look at each other and instinctively knew what they were feeling and thinking. She knew the rush of excitement tinged with fear, knew their pulses would be quickening, their minds racing. She felt the same.

'Brianna Holden was a twenty-seven-year-old mother of two from Shawlands on Glasgow's south side. She was murdered three years ago, found strangled on the outskirts of Pollok Park. A man, Kevin Monteith, went to trial, but the defence came up with a cast-iron alibi. Next—'

'Sorry. How did you say she was killed?'

'Strangled. My accent?'

'Right. Yeah, sorry.'

'Next, Stuart McLennan. Thirty-three years old. Drowned after falling in the River Clyde while heavily intoxicated. No witnesses. Ruled as accidental death. There was discussion of the possibility of suicide, as he'd been having marital problems, but nothing more to support that. Ellen Lambert was a name I knew. She was killed in her home in Kilmarnock – a town about twenty-five miles south of here – early last year, severe blunt force trauma courtesy of a poker from a fireplace set.'

'Nice. Who else do you have?'

'Kris Perera. Sri Lankan doctor, lived in Scotland for five years after graduating here. Murdered in what was seen as a racially motivated attack. His presumed attacker, a Barry Leitch, was found not guilty at the high court. Leitch was a member of right-wing groups and became a bit of a tabloid villain, but always swore he had nothing to do with the killing. We also have Chrissie Ramsay from Hamilton, thirty-two years old, drowned in the bath by her husband after he discovered she was having an affair.'

She looked up from the sheet of paper in front of her and saw the Americans staring back at her, tight-lipped, intense, knowing that they were secretly jumping for twisted joy inside. From the corner of her eye she was aware of Addison edging closer, leaning as far forward in his seat as he could.

'So, bottom line, all the names on the non-italicised side of your list are dead. All murdered or the victim of misadventure. All except two.'

'And those two?'

'Emily Dornan from the East End of Glasgow. Attacked while walking home from a night out with friends. She matches the description in the profile, so little doubt it's her. She was being strangled after being assaulted from behind, only survived because two guys were passing and chased off the attacker. One of them ran after the guy but he was never caught. The one left is Stefan Kalinowksi. Luckily for us, if not for him, it's a pretty unusual name. We've tracked down one person of that name and we're set to question him later today. I'm obviously going to speak to Emily Dornan too.'

Cally O'Neill had one arm propped up by her elbow, her hand covering her mouth and her eyes on the desk in front of her. When she looked up, she took her hand from her face and pulled it through her long auburn hair. 'Well . . . it looks like we came to the right place.'

Narey liked her. 'It looks that way. But it's about the only thing I'm sure of. The other half of the list, the names in italics . . . as best as we can work out, they don't exist. Any of them.'

Salgado shot forward in his chair. 'They don't exist?'

'Nope. I don't think they're real. We've chased down the list – Danny Cook, Greg Hurst, Ben Greaves, Alice Harper, Kelly Stein, Jamie Stark – and while we've found a few matching the names, none of them match the descriptions from the profiles. Not even close. Not the jobs, not the physical descriptions. Certainly, none of them are victims in the way that the others were. But . . . there's one of the names, real or not, that we know very well.'

'Go on.'

'Eloise Gray had told friends that she'd met someone she really liked. A schoolteacher named Jamie. We never knew a surname, but she'd told people he was six foot, blue eyes, fair-haired, thirty-two years old. He liked dogs, hill-climbing, old movies and Oasis.'

'Fuck.' Salgado spat the word out.

'Yeah. Fuck. Your Jamie is our Jamie. He was Eloise's Jamie and he is probably the person that killed her. And he doesn't seem to exist.'

'Sweet mother of mine,' Salgado was sitting back in his chair, his hands behind his head. 'What the hell is this?'

'A mess,' Narey replied. 'Your guy Garland didn't have a passport so presumably didn't leave the US, so he can't physically have been involved in Eloise's murder. What can you tell us about this Matthew Marr?'

'Not a lot yet,' O'Neill chipped in. 'We're in conversation with him and trying to get whatever we can. He says he's in Glasgow and we have to believe him till we know otherwise.'

'How is this conversation happening? And why? Why is he even talking to you?'

'We're using the same secure chat system he used to talk to Garland. And he's talking to us because he's getting a kick from it. And because we've agreed to run the video feed of the kid and let him see it.'

Narey couldn't believe her ears. 'You're letting him watch this guy die?'

'It's the price we're having to pay to keep him on the line. We're not happy about it but if we switch it off, he disappears, and we've got nothing.'

'Right. Okay, I see that. Can I get transcripts of the conversations? See if there's anything I can pick up on.'

O'Neill smiled. 'We've included transcripts in the

report we emailed to you. But we'd like to go a step further and have you talk to him directly. We figure you might get more from him, being local. Maybe trip him up and get us some kind of breakthrough. You up for that, Rachel? I can call you Rachel, right?'

'Of course you can. And I'm definitely up for that. Whatever it takes.'

'Good. For one thing we won't have to get up in the middle of the night to talk to the guy. Not that we're getting much sleep. Matthew Marr is our best hope, maybe our only hope of finding this kid before it's too late. Our tech guy is working on the router and he figures he can let you access it within a couple of hours.'

'Okay, good. That will give me time to read through what he's said so far.' She hesitated, filling the gap with a heavy sigh. 'You're sure your guy has killed five people?'

'At least five, yes. We've already found one of his victims and we're working on the others. Rachel, I know what you're thinking and the thing you need to know is that the first line we had from Marr, who thought he was talking to Garland, was that the kidnapped male ought to be dead by now. Marr also said it was Ethan's turn. Those were his very words. His *turn*.'

Narey's stomach flipped.

'Jesus. If they were taking turns . . .'

'Yeah.' O'Neill let the thought sink in. 'We think your guy is doing the same as ours. We think Garland and Marr are two of a kind. We'd been working on that basis but what you've told us about the names on that list kinda seals it. This isn't two cases, it's one.'

'I'm going to have to take this higher,' Narey told them. 'There are seemingly solid convictions against some of those names and there's a lot of people going to be very unhappy when I tell them they might have been done by someone that I can't identify.'

'Join the club.' Salgado laughed. 'We ain't too popular in some circles either right now. We're chasing Garland's victims in the hope they show us a pattern and give us a lead on possible dump sites so that we might find this kid alive. Your guy Marr is a different problem – he's still on the loose.'

'And he knows we're on to him.' O'Neill piled on the unnecessary pressure. 'He's going to go one of two ways. He'll either—'

'Shut it down, meaning there's a very good chance we'll never find him. Or he'll step it up while he still can.'

'These guys can't shut it down,' Salgado said firmly. 'It's who they are. If Marr, or whoever he is, has killed as many times as we think he has then he'll kill again. And chances are he's going to do it as quickly as he can.'

CHAPTER 21

Marianne Ziegler told them that she fled from Ethan Garland on 14 April 2012. She'd no doubt at all that was the date. *Engraved on her heart.*

Salgado had a contact at KABC-TV, a buddy from college, and a quick phone call had them en route to the studios in Glendale at GC3, Disney's Grand Central Creative Campus. Everything was digitally stored and Salgado's contact said he'd get them access.

Marianne hadn't been sure which show Garland had been watching so intently when he exploded at her but she said his favourite was Channel 7's *Eyewitness News*. Even if he'd been viewing another channel, *Eyewitness* was likely to have covered the same event.

The tech had left them the remote and the tape was good to go. They made themselves comfortable and got it started.

'Coming up on *Eyewitness News* tonight . . .'

A slightly younger Marc Brown was anchoring the show, promising forest fires, a double homicide, a father–child abduction, a multi-vehicle collision and video of a robbery of a taco truck.

'The double 187 sounds promising,' Salgado suggested.

'Really, Columbo? You think the homicide rather than the taco truck heist?'

'Will you ever cut me a break?'

'Never. And you know it.'

The schedule kicked off with an early season fire that was raging in the San Jacinto Mountains, burning its way through twenty thousand acres on the back of a dry winter. From there it trailed the double murder before hitting an ad break.

'I can't stand the sound of commercials,' O'Neill moaned. 'Can you fast-forward it?'

'I'm looking for a new grill, one with a built-in smoker. I don't want to miss the chance of a bargain. And I don't trust this remote not to miss part of the show once it kicks off again.'

'Sweet Jesus. Kill me now.'

When Marc Brown re-emerged from safety after the commercials, he didn't go to the promised murders but to some breaking news instead. A car chase was underway in Santa Monica and Channel 7 had an eye in the sky following it.

'You gotta be kidding me!' Salgado shouted. 'What the hell is this obsession with chases? They could fill an hour with this shit every night. It just lets some asshole get his fifteen minutes and a few traffic cops get to tell their kids they're on the news.'

It was the world's slowest car chase. A drunk driver in a red Nissan being tailed at distance by one black and white and then another, all being filmed live from the helicopter.

The Nissan was swerving, driving on the other side of the road, ignoring red lights and stop signs as it sped best it could along Lincoln. The cops had to stay back and play it safe, just blasting out lights and sirens to try to keep the civilians safe. It was oddly addictive while also being mind-numbingly boring.

'Now can we fast forward?'

'It might end at any minute. I don't want to scroll beyond it and miss anything we need.'

It didn't end at any minute. It ended after thirty-five minutes with a bunch of commercial breaks in between. The car got out of Santa Monica and onto PCH making for Malibu, doing no more than forty or fifty, on towards Topanga Canyon Boulevard and Woodland Hills.

'Come on suckers, spike strip,' Salgado implored. 'This is killing me. Time for a spike strip.'

Sure enough, just before the Nissan got to Ventura Boulevard, two cops were seen by the side of the road and moments later, the car ground to a halt, at least one of its tyres shredded. There was a further five minutes of half-hearted drama while the drunk got out of the car and finally got himself arrested. The news anchor reappeared, clearly as bored by the chase as anyone else.

'Next up, neighbours shocked by a double homicide in Culver City. Back after this.'

'Finally.' O'Neill was so ready to hear about the killings she was prepared to overlook the commercials this time.

'*Chilling screams. Police sirens. A double murder. All of it rocked La Salle Avenue in Culver City this morning. Authorities have a man in custody accused of murdering homeowners Bill and Janetta Coulson in the early hours. Eyewitness News reporter Andrea Wills joins us now live outside the Coulsons' home, where those murders took place. Andrea?'*

'Feel right?' O'Neill asked.

'Nope. Not yet anyhow.'

'Nor me.'

'Marc, I spoke to a neighbour just across the street and they told me they heard two gunshots around five this morning.'

'Gunshots? Not our guy. Shit. Shit.'

'Unless he cut them after shooting them?'

He hadn't. The Culver City killings were a robbery gone wrong. Two shots, two dead, no cutting. Cut to commercials.

They'd been watching for nearly an hour, sitting through an amber alert after a father from Inglewood had abducted his son, two deaths and four injured in a pile-up on the 110, and the long-awaited taco truck robbery in Park Mesa Heights. They were close to giving up when Marc Brown changed the narrative.

'Just in on Eyewitness News tonight, a twenty-five-year-old man from Reseda is given a life sentence for the brutal murder of a doctor's son in North Hills. Phil Reid is at Van Nuys Courthouse East where he has been covering the trial for us. Phil, tell us about this case.'

Both detectives sat upright and inched closer to the screen. This was much more promising.

'Marc, this has been a harrowing trial for the twelve jurors who had to endure it. For the Los Angeles Police

Department it represents the end of a particularly difficult investigation. For the parents of twenty-three-year-old Adrian Mercado it means justice for their son. For twenty-five-year-old Jamarco Freeman it means life in prison.'

'You remember this?' Salgado interrupted.

'Vaguely. Kid's body was found in a dumpster behind a cinema. Mutilated.'

'I'm interested.'

'Me too.'

The reporter told how an early morning garbage truck found the young man in the alley behind the Vista Theater on Sunset. Phil made great play of how the truck's crew were horrified and traumatised by what they found. He suggested that the sight of what had been done to the victim's body was so distressing that at least one of them vomited at the scene.

The key word, the one that the reporter treasured and used more than any other, was mutilated. He threw in a few variations too. Lacerated, disfigured, butchered, but mutilated was his favourite.

'This is it.'

'No question. Garland's trigger.'

Homicide Special Section– the unit that investigates serial, high-profile and arson-related homicides – had picked it up because the victim's father was a well-known doctor in the area and made the case high-profile enough to warrant them taking it. They didn't get a break for two weeks until an anonymous letter suggested Jamarco Freeman as the killer and that he'd used a Ford Transit to move the body. The letter even told them where to find the abandoned vehicle. Cops made a dawn raid on the Freeman house and discovered items of Adrian Mercado's clothing hidden under the house. They found more in the Transit along with the victim's blood and a shirt with Jamarco Freeman's DNA all over it. Freeman said the truck had been stolen and then returned.

The report closed with a final reminder about mutilation and a solemn *back to you in the studio.*

'Nice neat find in the house and the van,' Salgado suggested.

'When Ethan blew up at Marianne, he said the victim in the news story had had his throat and wrists cut, had bled to death, and that he'd do the same to her. You hear any mention anywhere in the report of those injuries?'

'Nope.'

The detective in charge of the investigation had been named as Dave Norrgord. Salgado already had his cell phone out and the number called up on his screen.

'Dave? It's Salgado. You got a minute?'

O'Neill could only hear one side of the conversation but read Salgado's face for clues as to the answers he was getting.

'It's about a case you worked back in 2012 ... Yeah, seriously. A kid named Adrian Mercado was found dead and naked in a lane behind the Vista ... Yeah ... Mutilated, yeah ...Yeah, that's the one. You put away a kid named Jamarco Freeman for it ... Uh huh ... No, just listen. Can you remember the details of the killing? Anything.'

O'Neill saw Salgado listen, no doubt having to hear Norrgord grumbling. She saw pictures being drawn in his mind then, abruptly, saw his eyes widen.

'Yeah? You sure? . . . Okay, okay. No, that's good. Just what I wanted to hear. Listen, I'll fill you in later, okay . . . No, later Dave. I gotta run.'

Salgado ended the call and breathed out hard.

'Mercado had his throat and wrists slashed and was left to bleed to death. The details of that were never released to the press and weren't disclosed in open court.'

'Yet Ethan Garland knew all about it?'

'Right. And the Vista is on Sunset, less than a mile from Garland's home.'

CHAPTER 22

Narey made sure she was in the incident room at Dalmarnock before anyone else. She wanted to have time to compose herself, work through what she was going to say and have answers for the questions that she knew would be coming her way.

She wanted the room as she wanted it. Her at the front, screen behind her, electric pointer, a seat for Detective Chief Superintendent Tom Crosbie, the lead for the Major Investigation Team, at her side, a dozen chairs ready in front. Printed handouts ready.

She crossed her arms over her chest and looked at it all. There were some heavy hitters on their way in and most of them were not going to be at all happy with what she was about to tell them. More than anything, she wanted to establish control, and she needed them to know she was running the show. If they didn't like it, and they sure as hell wouldn't, then they could do one. This was hers.

She swore under her breath and, with a glance at the door, she advanced on the chairs, shoving each of them back another three feet.

She stood back again. Deep breath. Nerves puffed out. Ready.

They shuffled in and they strode. Indifference taking a seat between bristling machismo and overflowing resentment. She knew all the faces, even the ones twisted with bitterness, and had known most of them for years. Friends, foes and fellow travellers. None of them had been told the reason for their requested attendance beyond the case that it related to, and that a potentially major development was to be discussed.

DCI Jim McMurray looked particularly pissed off, like there was a bad smell under his nose and it got worse every time he looked at her. The Ellen Lambert case had been his and he'd got promoted from DI largely on the back of it. He'd held out for the neighbour from the off and took his entire team down the pub when they nailed David McLean on the strength of a shirt that was smeared with Lambert's blood and local gossip that he'd been having an affair with her. McMurray wasn't the sort to like losing face.

Another DCI, Denny Kelbie, sat two chairs to McMurray's right and was just about the last person she would have wanted to be there. Kelbie was a nasty little shit, the kind who carried grudges against people he'd never met but saved special hatred for those who he felt had crossed him. That included almost everyone but most certainly included Narey. Kelbie had arrested the white supremacist Barry Leitch for the murder of Kris Perera and had taken it personally when Leitch got off with it. She could see the snarl already forming in the corner of his mouth and took some small satisfaction in knowing she was going to ruin his day.

Others didn't arrive displaying their prejudices so obviously, and that gave her hope. DS Mo Darwish was there for the McLennan case, the supposed drunk who'd fallen into the Clyde near the Broomielaw. He looked interested rather than aggrieved, and the same seemed true of DI Kathy Tait, who'd headed up the investigation into the murder of Brianna Holden without success.

Rico Giannandrea was there too, as was her old boss DCI Derek Addison. Superintendent Jason Williams and Chief Inspector Tom Cowie were both from uniform, and there were representatives from Scenes of Crime, including Campbell Baxter. The gang was all there. It was, potentially, exactly the sort of case that the Major Investigation Team was set up to handle. All she had to do was convince them all of that.

She reached for the PowerPoint clicker and brought up the main image. Holden. Lambert. McLennan. Perera. Gray. It was enough to bring the assembled mob to a reluctant, staggered silence.

DCS Crosbie took his cue from the five photographs and got to his feet. The man had all the charisma of an iron lung but his rank was enough to ensure everyone listened.

'Thank you all for coming at such short notice. Time is very much of the essence in the matter we're about to discuss and we're grateful you all managed to arrange your undoubtedly busy schedules to accommodate it. I can assure you it is of the utmost importance. I am here in a supervisory capacity and am going to hand you over to DI Narey who is leading on the matter at hand. For those of you who have rank issues, put them aside. Your cases are still your own but there is something new at play here that requires a cumulative effort. DI Narey, if you please.'

She saw it. The widening of eyes and the shifting of mouths when Crosbie said she'd be leading. That didn't please most of them, but it amused a few – Kathy Tait and Addison mostly.

'Thank you, DCS Crosbie. Thanks to everyone for coming along and apologies for the lack of information beforehand. This is extremely time-sensitive, plus we want to limit the number of people knowing about this for as long as is possible.'

She saw that the perfunctory introduction had told them nothing and served only to put a heat under simmering preconceptions of resentment and curiosity. There were a couple of sighs and some restless shifting in seats.

'These five people represent four distinct murder investigations and a case of accidental death. At least that was how they were perceived until this morning. New information that has come to light leads us to believe that they may all be the work of one previously unknown perpetrator.'

She had their attention now and laid it all out before them.

Speaking for just under ten minutes, she told them about Garland, about Salgado and O'Neill, about the kidnap victim, and about the list of names that had led the Americans to Glasgow. She then went through each case for those that weren't familiar with them.

'There may be more, but these are the victims we can be confident are linked to the unknown associate of Ethan

Garland. We're going to revise everything we have on all five of these cases. As the investigating officers, you need to talk to each other, flag up anything of interest and see where the connections are.'

'Bullshit!'

It was Denny Kelbie, perhaps inevitably, that led the resistance. 'I don't see it. Barry Leitch murdered Kris Perera whether that jury said so or not. He was guilty. You don't know anything about the case.'

Narey resisted the temptation. 'That's why I'm here. To learn about your case. That's why we're all here. To learn from each other.'

'Well I'm listening, even if no one else is.' Kathy Tait was on her feet, looking around daring anyone to challenge her. 'If your minds aren't open to what she's saying then maybe you shouldn't be here. If there's anything at all here that gives me an in on the Brianna Holden case, then I'm all ears.'

Jim McMurray scowled. 'Of course *you're* going to want to hear what she says, Kathy. You've got nothing. But I've got someone doing life in Peterhead for killing his neighbour. Case closed. Why the hell are we hearing about this now?'

'*Because now is when it's happening.*' Narey heard her own voice, louder than before, but didn't care. She saw Crosbie glancing up at her and couldn't be sure if he was approving or not. 'No one is doing this to *you*, Jim. This isn't about your case. Or Kelbie's or Kathy's. It's about all of them.'

'Mostly about yours though, right?' Kelbie could never

let it go. 'We're told you're leading this because it's your case that it's come out of, right? And it's *DCI* Kelbie to you.'

'No, it's not mostly about my case. It's mostly about a young man in Los Angeles who is going to die unless you and everyone else in this room, me included, puts their egos aside and accepts that maybe we haven't always got everything right and some sick bastard has been playing us like a fiddle. *All of us.*'

Kelbie readied himself to speak but she talked over him. 'And if someone dying in another country isn't enough for any of you then we have to face the prospect that this guy calling himself Matthew Marr has killed *here* and is going to kill here again. We've got a serial killer on *our* patch. He knows we're on to him, he knows he's running out of time and that's going to make him desperate. But he's not running out of time as fast as we are. Listen, the Americans have been talking to the guy in Glasgow and he's practically admitted that he and Garland have been working this together. They've been taking turns to identify potential victims and then somehow sharing in the thrill of the kill. It's sick, it's twisted, it's outrageous. And it stops now.'

Tom Crosbie stood. He waited until the hubbub from the front row had dissipated and spoke quietly but firmly. 'What DI Narey wants, she gets. Get this done and get it done quickly.'

This time, no one argued.

CHAPTER 23

Narey had one computer screen in front of her and one a couple of feet away to her right. She moved her gaze from one to the other and breathed out slowly. She'd been there for five minutes, thinking through what she was going to say and readying herself as best she could.

The screen in front of her was the one that she was going to have to deal with but the other kept drawing her away. The young man. The chains. The radiator. The inescapable sense that she was watching him die.

His head had lolled forward so that his face was hidden by his dark hair. Occasionally, the head would lift slightly, as if trying for umpteenth time that day to give a reminder to himself, and anyone that might be watching, that he was clinging to life.

She blinked and turned her head away, back to the screen lit only by the green dot that showed the man she needed to talk to was online.

She realised she was nervous, a state that confounded and bothered her, and that she wasn't used to at all. She'd spoken to murderers before, sometimes knowingly and sometimes not; that was the nature of her job. But this, this was different. Preparing to talk with someone she knew to be a murderer yet whose real identity was unknown to her was something she was struggling to get her head around.

Sitting to her left, and riding shotgun on the conversation to come, was Lennie Dakers, a criminal psychologist employed by Police Scotland. Tom Crosbie hadn't given her any choice in the matter but Narey was glad of the support, even if Dakers' presence only added to her unaccustomed bout of nerves. A legion of others had wanted to sit in with them but Narey had insisted they kept the numbers in the room to the bare minimum. This wasn't a spectator sport.

'Strange one, Inspector. Don't you think?' Dakers asked mischievously. 'It's like waiting for Christmas dinner but knowing the turkey is laced with cyanide and your gran has already licked all the Brussels sprouts.'

Narey smiled despite herself. 'I can't stand sprouts anyway, Lennie, so that wouldn't make any difference to me.'

Lennie Dakers was in his late fifties, casually dressed as always in jeans, canvas shoes with no socks, and a shirt that hung loose over his waist, wearing a single silver earring that matched his hair and designer stubble. Narey had little doubt that he had a joint or two in his jacket pocket but was hoping he'd resist the temptation until he left the station. Dakers was there to glean whatever he could from the man they were about to talk to, to read between the lines and produce a profile that might help them catch him.

'Okay, just remember that you're not interrogating him. You're talking to him. You're primarily trying to get him to speak about himself rather than admit to something. He is going to lie to us. And he's going to tell the truth. It's our job to work out which is which.'

Narey shook her head. 'Oh, I think that's *your* job.'

'Let's call it teamwork. You get him talking and I'll try to make some sense out of what he says, and what he doesn't say.'

'So, you have a plan?'

Dakers shrugged. 'Sort of. This is *not* how I'd normally go about getting a read on a suspect. Ninety-nine times out of a hundred it's done on crime scene behaviour. But other than the photographs from the Highland Fling, I don't have that to work with. Nor can I see him to look for physical tells. So, I need a language-based strategy and am going to use something called SCAN, which is scientific content analysis, or statement analysis.'

'And that's going to tell you whether he's lying or not?'

'Hopefully. It's not universally accepted, simply because there's not been enough empirical research done on it. But a lot of practitioners swear by it. The underlying principle is that the instinctive human reaction is not to lie.'

Scepticism spread large across Narey's face. 'You need to get out more. I could introduce you to a few that lie for a living. And I don't just mean lawyers.'

Dakers shook his head. 'No, that's just it. When most people are guilty of something, they don't tell you the truth, but that's not the same as lying. They will talk round it in circles, they will avoid talking about it, they will leave out crucial details that incriminate them, they say they don't remember or they're not sure. They don't want to lie in case it sounds like a lie, in case they say something that can be disproven.

'I'll spare you the technical stuff but I'm looking for inconsistencies in what this guy says and how he says it. I'm looking for pauses, for details, for qualifying phrases, avoidance, all indicators of deception. But I'm also looking for things that can be judged to be true.

'Also, as this is effectively a written statement, we must look at the response times, judge whether he's planning what he says, or perhaps editing. It might be simply that he's choosing what and what not to reveal, But they're all potential indicators of truth or deception,'

'And this works?'

He smiled. 'Some call it pseudoscience. I call it the best chance we've got.'

'Fair enough. What about for now though? You've seen the Highland Fling photos and you've read the transcripts of the conversations with the Americans. So, what can you tell me about this guy, Lennie? Otherwise, I'm going in here unarmed.'

'My initial feeling is that he's a compulsive narcissist. More than that, he's a vulnerable narcissist. He's willing to put himself at risk to get this experience. He came back online to talk rather than doing what you and I might think is the sensible thing and disappearing back into whatever hole he came from. That makes him more dangerous, but it might also make him easier to bait.'

'So how do we make that work for us?'

'Well, being a compulsive narcissist means he likes to

feel superior, so you should play dumb, be obtuse, misunderstand him. We need to look for inconsistencies, gaps, changes in tense, vagueness, things like that. But let him think that the power differential advantage is on his side, because then he'll let down his predatory guard. The idea is to get him to think he's safe because he's smarter, and then get him to lose control. That will most likely happen through anger or with him thinking he can take potshots at you. You're going to need a thick skin.'

'I'm a cop. In Glasgow. They issue thick skins first day in primary school.'

'Fair enough. You ready for this?'

'No. So let's do it.'

She breathed deep one last time and began to type.

> I'm Detective Inspector Rachel Narey of Police Scotland. We need to talk.

She saw that her opening line had been read but had to wait for a reply. She guessed he'd been taken by surprise.

Where are the Americans?

> In America. You're talking to me now.

Only if I want to.

> No. Only if you want to continue viewing the video feed. The deal's the same. The person on the other end of the line has changed but nothing else has. Talk or it gets switched off.

Okay. What do you want to know?

I assume you know why I want to talk to you.
There was a list of names found in Ethan
Garland's computer. Many of those names
had connections to Scotland, to the west
of Scotland in particular. Do you know why
Garland had those names?

I might.

Do you know the names I'm talking about?

Maybe

Let's say that you do. Do you know why
Garland had that list?

**Ethan was very interested in people. Maybe
that's why he had it.**

Did you know the names of the people on
the list? Do you now know the names of the
people on the list?

**I think some of the names might be
familiar to me.**

I haven't told you them yet.

Maybe I know more than you do.

Narey swore, already frustrated at the responses. Dakers
stepped in, sensing her growing anger.

'It's okay. This is good. He's using equivocation to

avoid directly answering an open-ended question. *Maybe*. *Might*. *I think*. That strongly suggests he's trying to deceive us. Ask him something direct.'

She typed.

> I'm sure you know more than I do. That's why I want to talk to you. But I need you to give me something. Call it in good faith for you being able to watch the video feed. Tell me something about one of the names on the list. Will you do that?

A pause.

> **Okay.**

> Who would you like to tell me about?

Another pause. Thinking. Perhaps calculating.

> **Brianna Holden. I will talk to you about Brianna Holden. Are you sure you want to hear it?**

She did. And she didn't. Of course.

> Yes. What happened to her?

> **She died. You know that.**

> Did you kill her?

> **I'm innocent.**

Narey looked to Dakers.

'He's denying his guilt, not denying the act,' he told her. 'Keep going. Perhaps ask how he knew her.'

She asked.

> I don't remember how we met. I think maybe we spoke online. I believe that's what happened.

'He's consistently using negation here,' Dakers said from her left. 'He's lying. Or lying by omission.'

> We got on very well. She liked me and I liked her. So, we arranged to meet.

> Did you know Brianna was married?

> She didn't tell me she was married.

> Where did you arrange to meet her?

> Pollok Park.

> Why there?

> I don't know. I don't remember.

> And what happened?

> Brianna acted very badly. As if she didn't like me anymore. I didn't start the argument. She did.

> Did you fight with her?

> She fought with me.

Did you kill her?

**Do you want me to just brush over the
details, Inspector? Would that make it easier
for you? Because that's not how it works. If
you want to hear it, you will have to hear it all.**

Her stomach tightened and her head turned to the other
screen where the young man was slumped motionless.

Go on.

**She smelled of vanilla and flowers. It was
on her skin. She smelled sweet and spicy
but when I tasted it, there was only the acid
burn of the spice.**

**Her skin tightened and flushed scarlet. She
wriggled and fought. She just made it worse
for herself. She died.**

**The colour of her face. A red I'd never seen
before. It blew up like a balloon as the life
squeezed out of her drop by drop. She died.**

Narey had to steel herself to reply. Dakers sombrely
nodded at her in confirmation. It was horrific but it was
useful. She typed.

Did you kill her?

I'm not guilty.

Do you know a man named Kevin Monteith?

I don't know. I'm not sure.

He was put on trial for Brianna's murder. Do
you remember his name?

No. I don't know. Maybe.

Did he kill Brianna?

No.

She was aware of Dakers scribbling furiously to her
right and moments later, he thrust a piece of paper
under her nose. She read it, her brow knotting in
confusion.

'Just ask him,' the psychologist encouraged her. 'I'll
explain later.'

Narey huffed heavily and began typing.

Does anyone else know all of you? All the
sides that you have?

The screen showed that the question had been read but
Narey wasn't sure that it would be understood. Yet she'd
barely turned her head to look questioningly again at
Dakers when the response arrived.

No. No one knows all of me. Do you think you do?

Narey turned to Dakers, looking for the answer.

'Tell him that no, you don't. But that you know he's
more than one person. No, make that – you know there's

more than one side of him. And ask which side you're talking to now.'

'You sure?'

'Yes.'

She typed and waited.

> There are different sides to me. That's true. And right now? I think you're talking to the person you're looking for.

'You know where you're going now?' Dakers asked her.

'I think so. Stop me if I'm going wrong.' She typed again.

> So, you're a different person to different people? And some of those close to you would have no idea you'd be capable of the things you've done?

A short pause.

> Yes. Is that unusual though? I don't think most people would want to show everything to everyone. Most people wouldn't dare to.

> Maybe. But what you're not showing is very different from other people.

> Is it? I don't really know. Anyway, I've talked enough. I'm going now. I have a video feed to watch. And all that stuff I told you about Brianna Holden? None of it is true.

CHAPTER 24

'He killed her.'

Narey was taken aback by the certainty in Dakers' voice. 'You said he was lying at other parts. How can you be sure?'

'Well, I can't be sure. But I'm as sure as I can be. The whole basis of SCAN is deception detection. Now, I'm no expert on it but I've been rereading what I can, and I hope I've got a decent handle on it. At the beginning, he was using a lot of equivocation, the *maybes* and the *mights*, one of the main deception techniques. When he spoke about how he met Brianna, he used a lot of negation and was almost certainly lying or trying to keep the truth from us. He also indulged in what is known as statement partitioning, meaning he broke down his telling of the meeting with Brianna and her murder into prologue, incident and epilogue. He rushed over both the prologue and the epilogue in order to omit things but luxuriated in the incident.

'More than that, when he talked about the crime, the act that led to Brianna's death, he revealed unique sensory details, things we didn't ask for and it's unlikely he made up on the spot. So, he talked about the smell of her perfume, the taste of her skin, the way her face changed colour. These were *experienced* memories. These were truths.'

Narey held his gaze for a while, accepting the sense that it made.

'Remind me never to play poker with you.'

'Oh, I'm terrible at poker. I spend more time looking for tells from the other players than I do at my own hand.'

She breathed out hard. Exhausted from the effort of concentration. 'So, what else have we learned?'

'Well, it's difficult just reading his words and not hearing them, but there's a calmness, a matter-of-factness about what he says, that leads me to think that he's capable of switching on and off the personality we spoke to. That's why I got you to ask the question about there being more than one side to him. It's likely, as you suggested to him, that he functions as a seemingly normal person, not outwardly displaying the characteristics that we'd expect from a serial killer. You've met the type before.'

Narey nodded. 'Of course I have. But I'm not sure I've ever fully grasped how they're able to do it.'

'Well, often they have an ability to disassociate, to save themselves from having to deal with difficult feelings, and to compartmentalise so that they can act as different people in different situations as needed.'

'Okay, I get that. But *how*?'

Dakers nodded. 'There's an American criminal psychologist, a friend of mine, named Katherine Ramsland, one of the very best in the business. She spent five years corresponding with Dennis Rader, the BTK killer. She says that people like Rader, like our man Marr, do what Rader called *cubing*.'

'Cubing?'

'Yeah. It was Rader who introduced her to the phrase, and it might be the best way of explaining how their minds work in terms of being able to function in society. Rader was a family man, he had a wife and two children. He graduated from university, had a good job, was president of the church council and a Cub Scout leader. And he tortured and murdered ten people across a seventeen-year period. How was he able to be all those things to different people? He likened it to being a cube, and showing whatever face he needed to.'

'Is that not just self-serving bullshit?'

'In one sense, yes. But it's more than that. We all do it to some extent. You have to be a different person at home with your daughter than you are when you're interviewing a suspect. You have to be a different person with your husband than your daughter. But, with killers who can function in this way, the skill set required is way beyond what most people could achieve. It's off the scale.'

'And you think that's how it is with Marr? That he cubes? He can display a seemingly normal persona to the rest of the world, then switch to someone that can murder five, six or more people?'

'I've not exactly got a lot to go on, but yes.'

'So how much more difficult does that make it for us to catch him? Or don't I want to know the answer to that?'

Dakers smiled ruefully. 'You don't. But there's something else. I'd say he's a compulsive narcissist. A risk taker.'

'Okay. So, the more risks he takes, the greater our chance of catching him.'

The psychologist blew out hard. 'That's one way of looking at it.'

'And the other?'

'He knows you're on to him and that the net, however slowly, is closing in. But he's a risk taker. He's going to kill again while the going is good. For the moment, I'd say watching the guy die is fulfilling whatever need he has. But that's not going to last. He'll kill again.'

CHAPTER 25

Kayleigh McGrath was small, slim and with a deep tan that suggested Shawlands must have a rare microclimate. Her dyed-blonde hair and heavy make-up completed the look. It was all but impossible for Narey to tell what the woman was thinking under the foundation, the eyeliner, the blusher and the fake tan.

Her sister was Brianna Holden, the twenty-seven-year-old wife and mother of two who was found strangled on the outskirts of Pollok Park three years earlier. Kayleigh reluctantly agreed to be interviewed after a few half-hearted attempts to say that she'd been through this often enough already.

'It's not that I don't want to talk about it,' she explained while drawing on a cigarette next to an open window in her flat, 'and obviously I want the guy caught. Obviously. I'd do anything to get the bastard that done it. It's just hard. You know?'

Narey nodded. She knew.

'I mean, I'm not stupid, I know I look like I'm all hard and dolled up for a night out but that's just the way I make

202

myself. There's not a day I don't think about Brianna. She's still my sister. And after that guy Monteith getting off, I've not been able to rest. Know what I mean?'

'I do. And I'm sorry for making you go through all this again but we're hoping a fresh pair of eyes might come up with something that wasn't noticed first time round. Can you talk to me about the night Brianna was killed?'

Kayleigh sighed heavily. 'Aye, sure. Why not? I was watching her kids because her man was at work. Brianna went out about seven and I had the kids in bed by nine thirty. That was it until we got the calls from your lot just after midnight.'

'Was she meeting another man?'

'Sorry?'

'Was Brianna meeting someone else the night she was murdered? She was dressed as if she might have been on a date.'

'No.'

'Are you sure. What did she tell you she was doing?'

'She didn't. And I didn't ask. She just said she needed me to watch the weans because she was going out.'

'Okay, what did you *think* she might be doing?'

Kayleigh looked away and Narey was sure she was right. 'How did Brianna meet this guy, Kayleigh?'

'I didn't say she met a guy. And I'm not—'

'Did she use a dating site?'

McGrath reddened under the make-up, clearly flustered. 'Brianna was married.'

'That's not what I asked you, Kayleigh. Did your sister use a dating site?'

Kayleigh McGrath crossed her arms across her chest. 'My sister was a good person. I'm not having her name—'

Narey had had enough. 'Kayleigh, let me stop you right there. This isn't about judging Brianna. It's not about who she was or what she did. I couldn't care less if she was unfaithful to her husband, except where it might be a factor in making sure we know who killed her. *Did she use a dating site?*'

'She should never have got married.' McGrath barged through Narey's attempt to interrupt, holding a hand up, pleading with her to wait. 'It was a huge mistake. Graeme Holden was a huge mistake. That guy was never right for her. He was a waste of space, but Brianna found that out too late. She hated being married to him. And yes . . .' She heaved out a breath. 'Yes, she started looking around. And yes, she went on a dating site.'

Narey felt her gut tighten.

'Do you know which site?'

McGrath pursed her lips and shook her head. 'No. She never said. She just told me that she was looking online. "Window shopping", was how she described it. At first anyway. Then she got a bit coy on me and I suppose I knew she'd got talking to someone she liked.'

'Why didn't you tell this to the police?'

'I didn't know if she was meeting anyone that night. I really didn't. And anyway, your people had no doubt that guy Monteith had killed her after they found her bag in his car. Except he was on CCTV on the other side of the city. Once he got off, I didn't want to go back and say. It seemed too late.'

'And you didn't want people to think badly of her.'

Eyes closed, head nodding, McGrath admitted it.

Stefan Kalinowski lived in the West End, in a flat on Highburgh Road, just a few hundred yards from where Narey used to live before she and Tony finally bought a place together. She looked up at the long line of old red tenements and got briefly sentimental for days when she was young, free and more or less single. She wouldn't swap though.

Kalinowski worked as an electrician during the day and played gigs in local pubs at night. He couldn't understand why they wanted to talk to him, but he was home between six and seven and she and DC Kerri Wells were welcome to visit.

He was in his early thirties, pushing six foot, dark-eyed and good-looking, with fair hair that he kept pushing back on his head. He was barefoot, mid-change of clothes Narey guessed, and seemingly anxious to get moving. He sat on the edge of a large, green armchair, a Greenpeace poster on the wall behind him.

'I'm singing in the Ben Nevis in an hour so I don't have too long, sorry. And I don't understand, what is it I can help you with?'

'Do you have any friends or family in America, Mr Kalinowksi?'

'*America?* Not that I know of. Why?'

'We're working on a joint investigation with police in Los Angeles. They have provided us with a list of names connected to that investigation. Your name appears on it.'

Kalinowski laughed but the smile quickly disappeared as he realised Narey was being serious. 'My name? That doesn't make any sense. But how do you know it's me? Mine maybe isn't a common name in Glasgow but I'm sure there's more than one in the US. Why me?'

'The name on the list we were given had information about the person. We were wondering if it fitted you.'

'Okay . . .' he sounded very wary. 'Try me.'

'Okay, let's start with music. Are you a fan of Echo and the Bunnymen? Maybe A Flock of Seagulls?'

'Yes . . . both. But . . .'

'And I see the Greenpeace campaign poster on the wall. What about Quentin Tarantino movies?'

'I loved his early stuff but lately he's disappeared up his own arse. I'm sorry, but this is just weird. It's freaking me out a bit. How do you know this stuff?'

'Has anyone from the US contacted you? Maybe through Facebook or online somewhere?'

'No. I'd remember. No one. Is this some sort of phishing scam? Do I need to change my bank cards or my passwords?'

'It might be something like that, but we've no reason to think anyone is after your bank details. What about online dating? Do you use that sort of thing?'

Kalinowski's mouth dropped open, confusion creasing him. 'What? No. What would I need to do that for?'

'There's nothing wrong with it,' Narey assured him. 'We're not judging you.'

He scoffed. 'Judge all you want. I don't do internet dating. I'm not being big-headed, but I don't have to. I've no idea what you people are talking about here.'

'Some of the other people on the list we've been given have been harmed, some very seriously. I don't mean to alarm you, Mr Kalinowski, but you may be at risk.'

'From what?'

'From attack by an associate of the person who held the list in Los Angeles.'

'This is nuts. So, some freak had got some stuff about me online. These people never leave home so I can't say I'm too worried. I can look after myself.'

'Stefan, this is serious, and you could potentially be in danger. I need to ask you again. Do you use a dating site?'

'I've told you, I don't. I really don't know what this is about but I don't use a dating site, have never used a dating site, don't think I ever would use a dating site, don't need to use a dating site. Does that answer your question?'

'I guess it does. I need to ask you to be careful. Watch where you're going, don't go anywhere alone, don't take any risks.'

'I'm not a child, Inspector. Like I say, I know how to look after myself. I'll be fine.'

Emily Dornan was surprised to find the police at her door. It had been two years since she'd been attacked and she'd assumed the case had been forgotten, if not closed. Somewhat bemused, she invited Narey and Wells into her house in Dennistoun.

She was in her late twenties, long blonde hair parted in the centre. Just as the profile in Ethan Garland's notes had suggested. She told them how she'd got off a train at

Alexandra Parade and realised someone was following her. She was punched and being strangled when she heard voices shouting. Her attacker let her go and ran off.

'And you'd no idea who it might have been that attacked you? Anyone that might have threatened you or held a grudge? An ex-boyfriend, maybe?'

Emily shook her head. 'I'm sure it was just some random. Either he'd followed me or saw me walking.'

'And you hadn't had any other plans that night? No date arranged, anything like that?'

Emily looked confused. 'No. Why?'

'It would fit into our enquiry, with what we know of the other incidents. Did you have a boyfriend at the time?'

'No. I was single. I'm seeing someone now but not back then.'

'And thinking back, were you happy being single or were you looking to date?'

'Looking to date. I've never liked being single much.'

'And were you maybe using a dating site? Looking online for someone?'

Emily laughed. 'Yeah, I was. Jeez, I'm glad I don't have to go through that anymore. That was a jungle, full of freaks and phonies. Some nice guys too but finding them among the creeps was the hard bit.'

'What site did you use?'

Emily's brows knotted. 'You think that's connected to the guy who attacked me? Really?'

'It might be.'

The woman blanched. Stripped of the odd comfort of being attacked by a complete stranger, disturbed by the possibility of it being someone she might have known or spoken with.

'I used a couple of sites. Igloo was one. And another called Amber. Oh God. That's what you think?'

'It's a possibility. Did you date anyone from it, anyone in particular you remember? Perhaps someone you had a lot in common with.'

'It was a long time ago. I dated one guy from Igloo, we went out twice. But the cops checked him out at the time, and he wasn't even in the country. He was in Dublin with pals.'

'Can you remember anyone else you chatted with? Maybe someone you turned down a date with?'

'Not really. It probably sounds terrible, but I just wouldn't remember. I wouldn't go on there again, even if I was single. Just too many nutters.'

Narey had one more call to make before she was sure. This was one interview she had to do on her own and the one she was least looking forward to. Her husband.

They'd got Alanna to bed surprisingly early and easily. Just two stories and one clamber out of bed was possibly a new record.

It didn't quite qualify as date night, as she was still on the clock, but it was just them, it was cosy and relaxed and she was just about to throw a hand grenade into the middle of it.

'You're still working.'

'What?'

He repeated his assertion. 'You're still working a case. You're not really here with us, your mind is somewhere else. And that's okay, but Alanna is in bed and you don't have to pretend with me.'

'I want to talk to you about Irene Dow.'

He froze just before he bit into his food, slowly looking up at her with his mouth open. 'You what?'

'Let's not make this any harder than it needs to be. I want to talk with you about Irene Dow and Keith Hardie. If that's okay with you.'

'Well, it's certainly okay with me but I'm wondering where my wife is and who you are. You know, the one that never talks about her cases and has zero interest when I want to talk about Keith Hardie.'

'Okay, do it the hard way if it makes you feel better,' she sighed. 'Yes, I want to talk about cases when it suits me, and it suits me now. If you feel the need to take the moral high ground, go ahead. But ... I need your help. And this is serious. And it might give you some of the answers you're looking for to help Keith Hardie's mother.'

He held her gaze for a moment. 'You didn't need to throw the last bit in. I'd have talked to you about it because you need it. Whatever it was. You know that. But, yes, can't deny I'd be interested in anything that helps prove Keith didn't kill her.'

'Okay then. So, let's talk. Usual rules apply. I'll tell you as much as I want, won't tell you anything I don't want to, and you'll just have to like it or lump it. Okay?'

He shook his head ruefully. 'Is it any wonder I love you?'

'No. Now, I told you that I had doubts about the

210

evidence in the Eloise Gray case. That I had doubts about the evidence implicating Harkness. I'm now looking at other cases that may be connected, where evidence may have been planted and the accused framed. This should make you happy.'

'It does.'

'Now, I don't know that Irene Dow's case *is* connected, but it might be. It doesn't fit the main criteria, which I'm *not* telling you about for now, but it might fit another part of it. And that's what I need to know from you.'

'Is this the bit where you get to the point?'

'Yes. I need to know more about Irene Dow. I need to know about her social life, her relationships, if she was dating anyone. That kind of thing.'

'Okay ... let's see. She had a group of friends that she'd lunch with, go out for drinks or to a musical, that sort of thing. There were five of them and they met at least once a week on a Saturday night in a local hotel. I spoke to all of them to get an idea about Irene and who she was. Maybe to get an idea of who else might have killed her.

'She was divorced, had been for I think ten years, maybe slightly longer. She was single, had been for four years. She'd had a bunch of dates in that time but none of them had gone anywhere. She was lonely though and was trying to find a partner.'

Narey said a silent prayer.

'One of the friends, a woman named Carol, was particularly close to Irene. She said she was doing online dating, trying to find a guy she could settle down with.

Said she'd been using it for a few months but hadn't found anyone.'

She reached forward with both hands and grabbed Tony by the collar and hauled him to her, kissing him forcefully on the lips.

'Okay . . . I guess you got the answer you wanted.'

'Yes, and you'll get a reward you'll really like. Soon.'

She had little doubt now. And she was sure of two things. First, Stefan Kalinowksi had been lying when he'd said he hadn't used online dating. And second, she had to go back to the office and make a call.

CHAPTER 26

Narey and Giannandrea were on one side of the screen. Salgado and O'Neill were five thousand miles away on the other. It was a rainy midnight in Glasgow, a scorching four in the afternoon in LA.

It was three hours after Narey's chat with Tony, three hours since she knew she had to speak to the Americans. She'd got a taxi to the station, picking up Giannandrea en route. If they waited till morning, then it would be halfway through the night in the US. And time wasn't something they had much off.

'Evening, Rachel. Or is it morning?'

'It's evening, Cally. Very very late evening.'

'You've got something?

'I think so. I've spoken to the sister of one of the victims on Garland's list. Brianna Holden's sister. She admitted to me that Brianna was meeting another man the night she was killed. Someone she'd met through online dating. The woman who survived the attack, Emily Dornan, had been using a dating site at the time. Another case that could be connected, the murder of

213

a woman named Irene Dow, she too was using inter-net dating.'

'Okay, this wouldn't be miles away from what we're thinking but it's good to get flesh on the bones. Go on, Rachel.'

'He's catfishing. Marr and Garland are catfishing.'

'Fake online identities?'

'It's the only thing that makes any sense. We've always suspected something like that. We knew Jamie wasn't real. We knew his connection with Eloise was too good to be true. So many coincidences in what she liked and he liked. He had to be scamming her. He was a catfish and she jumped on the hook.'

'Okay, hold on,' Salgado interrupted. 'I'm not saying I disagree with any of this, but I can't say I really know what the whole catfishing thing is. I know the phrase, but someone explain to me, please. Slowly.'

'Catfishing is where someone creates a false online presence,' O'Neill informed him. 'Fake name, fake photo-graph, fake age, maybe a fake job. Any and all of those. The object of the game is to scam someone. Sometimes for money, sometimes for sex, sometimes to make themselves feel good, sometimes just to be a troll, sometimes just to be hateful.

'So, you're online. Maybe in a chat room, maybe on a dating site. You get talking to someone, think they're a good-looking, blonde, twenty-five-year-old nurse with a figure like Beyoncé. Turns out she is a pot-bellied bald guy in his vest, dreaming about when he was forty.

'Maybe you tell her things you wouldn't tell her if she

wasn't so hot. Maybe you send her money. Maybe you send compromising photos of you that could get you into trouble with your wife or your boss.'

'And maybe you arrange to meet them.'

'Exactly.'

Salgado huffed. 'Come on, surely most people aren't stupid enough to fall for a scam like that?'

Narey flinched as she saw O'Neill turn to face her partner, eyes blazing and her expression twisted.

'It's not about being stupid. It's about being human.' Her voice sounded like a different person, as if it were coming from a different place. 'People – ordinary, decent people – make the mistake of thinking everyone's as honest and open as they are. It's their curse and what trips them every single time. Not everyone is as lucky as you, Salgado. You're married and you love your wife, you're content in your job and your relationships. You don't want for much in life other than more flash suits and the Lakers to win the finals. Not everyone's that lucky.'

'Now wait—'

'No, you wait. You need to hear this. Other people have gaps in their lives. The way the world is today, they don't always have time to find those things other than by looking online. So, they might be looking for love or friends, just someone to talk to or someone who'll listen. What they find is someone looking to take advantage of them. They go in with their hearts open and their eyes closed. Should they be more careful? Of course. Is it their fault? No way.'

Narey noticed Salgado had the sense not to interrupt again and got the distinct impression he'd been bitten before. O'Neill on a crusade was, clearly, a fierce warrior.

'A friend of mine made the mistake of going online looking for someone to talk to, maybe someone she could be with. After a while, after some nasty experiences, she got talking to someone who seemed to understand, someone *nice*. She opened up, told this person who she really was and who she wanted to be. She spilled her guts and it felt good. Until it didn't. Until the other person revealed herself as a fake, as a man rather than the woman he'd pretended to be. This guy, this sad excuse for a man, posted all over her Facebook, her Twitter and her Instagram that she was a lesbian. She'd barely come to this conclusion herself and hadn't acted on it, yet here was the world finding out, including her parents. She was humiliated, frightened, embarrassed, furious and briefly suicidal. The guy thought it was funny. He'd caught a fish and nothing else mattered.'

Salgado opened his mouth, but she shut it again with a wave of her hand.

'People aren't stupid, Salgado. They're human. When they are victims of this sort of thing, it crushes them. It makes them *feel* stupid, used, violated and humiliated. It makes them doubt anyone is real and trust evaporates.'

She finally let him speak.

'I have two daughters. This terrifies me.'

'Good. It should. Pull the plug on their computers and never let them talk to anyone.'

'Done. It starts today.'

O'Neill breathed and turned to face the screen again.

'You sure this is what Garland and Marr have been doing, Rachel?'

'Yes. The names and profiles on the list that are in italics – Danny Cook, Greg Hurst, Ben Greaves, Alice Harper, Kelly Stein, Jamie Stark – they are the fake profiles used to chat to potential victims. Marr and Garland have all the details of each written down so they can stay in character and fool whoever they're talking to. The profiles probably change on likes and dislikes to match the target. And that's what the people they talk to are. Targets.'

'So how do you think they do it?'

'It's pretty simple. Far too simple. I'm sure what they do is find someone to go after then scour other social media sites to scrape up all the information they can about them. They look until they find their likes and dislikes and mimic them. They start talking to them with a profile and photograph that fits what the target wants, tell them exactly what they want to hear and they're in under their skin.'

'It's that easy to find what people like?' asked Salgado.

'Unfortunately, yes. What are you on online? Twitter, Facebook? Instagram?'

'All three,' Salgado replied.

'And what do you say about yourself in your profiles?'

'Nothing. Name and that's it. And I never accept requests from anyone I don't know in real life.'

'And that's how it should be, but most people aren't that smart or that careful. Eloise Gray wasn't. Her Facebook profile listed favourite bands, favourite movies, that she liked hillwalking, liked dogs, everything. Jamie – whether it was Marr or Garland – has seen this, used it and presented himself to her as the perfect man, the perfect match. She fell for it and fell for him. And it cost her her life.'

A momentary quiet filled the room. Salgado broke it when he could no longer take the weight of the silence.

'Okay, you say it could have been Marr or Garland. I buy your theory. Absolutely I do. But that still doesn't quite explain why Garland was searching in Scotland. Why didn't Marr do that?'

'To cover themselves,' O'Neill suggested. 'No trail, electronic or otherwise.'

'Yes. I've no doubt it's that,' Narey agreed. 'If and when we get Marr, I'll bet we find some interesting LA searches on his computer. Somehow, these two bastards met someone as bad as they are. Garland probably couldn't believe his luck when he met someone just like him.'

CHAPTER 27

Narey and Marr. He trying to clamber into her head and she manoeuvring for a further glimpse into his. It wasn't a game, more a battle of wills. A fight to the death.

Lennie Dakers was her corner man, taping up cuts, willing her on, cautioning her not to drop her guard.

> When we last spoke, you told me about Brianna Holden dying. Then you said that none of what you told me was true. Which was it?

You decide.

> No. How about you tell me? The video feed that you're salivating over comes at a price. And that price is conversation and information.

I am not salivating. I'm watching. But I'll talk. I said I would.

> Thank you. How do I know you're telling the

truth about any of this? You could just be
making it all up.

I could be. I'm not.

Prove it. Because I'm not sure I can believe
any one person could be responsible for the
number of killings that you're hinting at.

Of course she could believe it. She'd seen it too often.
But she wanted him to believe he was special, and to
boast about it.

I can tell you things that no one else could know.

That made her breath catch and her pulse quicken.

Then tell me. Don't indulge your sad little
fantasies though. No bullshit. Just tell me
something only the person who killed them
could know.

**You know that's not how it works. I'll tell
you what I want. If you want to hear it,
you'll listen.**

The sour taste in her mouth made her want to spit. She
knew she'd listen. She had no choice.

**I phoned the police the day after Ellen Lambert
was killed. I can remember pretty much word**

for word what I told them. You can check that, right?

Right.

I phoned at 2 in the afternoon. I told them I lived on the street but didn't want to get involved. I said that I knew that a neighbour named David McLean had regularly been going in and out of Ellen Lambert's house. That they had been having an affair and that lots of people in the street knew. I told them I'd heard that Ellen was going to tell McLean's wife. After that, I hung up and left them to it.

Narey already knew that had been the substance of the anonymous phone call that had put Jim McMurray onto McLean's trail. The contents of the call had never been made public.

How did you meet Ellen Lambert? How did you find her?

'Flatter him,' Dakers advised from her left.

How could you possibly have persuaded her to let you into her life or her home?

It was easy. It is when you know how.

Did you find her on a dating site? On Igloo or Amber or something?

I might have. Or Ethan might have.

So, he did it? How could he charm her
enough that she trusted him? We know
Ellen didn't go out much after being hurt
in the past.

**Maybe we do our homework. Maybe we're
just charming. She was lonely and needy.
Ethan complimented her. He was nice to her.
Sometimes that's all people need.**

What sort of homework?

**She was on Facebook and on Instagram.
Her life was on there. An open book. So,
we liked what she liked. We hated what
she hated. We made her laugh. Ethan even
learned lyrics to Take That songs so he
could slip them casually into conversation.
She loved that.**

And she just invited you to her home?

**It took a lot of work. We had to earn it.
It took three weeks to make her trust us
enough to invite me over. She was wary and
we'd nearly given up but she weakened. She
was desperate, you see.**

Why do you say she was desperate?

**She'd been on her own for four years since
she was last cheated on. Ethan consoled**

222

her for that and expressed his astonishment
that anyone could do that to her.

> While you were planning something
> much worse?

I suppose so. She invited us over. Just
for a coffee and a chat. She trusted me to
behave, she said. I told her when I'd arrive.
To the minute. She opened her door and by
the time she realised I wasn't who we'd said
I was, it was too late. She was so surprised
when she saw me that she couldn't work
it out. She got stuck mid-sentence and by
then I was inside.

> Didn't she scream?

She couldn't. I made sure she couldn't.
When I took my hand off her throat, she told
me she was expecting someone. That he'd
be there any minute. I had to laugh. Was it
Danny Cook? I asked her. I laughed at the
look on her face. 'I'm Danny. Aren't you
pleased to see me?' She wasn't. Then she
did start to scream so I grabbed the fireside
poker and hit her with it.

That hadn't been the plan. I'd intended
to string it out. Make it last. See how she
coped with it. It was over far too quickly.
One smash. Job done. And when I hit her,

223

her face changed. She didn't look like the
same person anymore. In that split second,
I lost all interest in her. I made sure no one
was around, and I left.

Weren't you worried you'd be seen going in?

No. I don't worry. And she was trying to
make sure her neighbours didn't see me, so
she told me to use the side door.

How can you do this, Matthew? How can
you kill people and make it sound like it
barely matters?

It doesn't make any difference to me.
They're only victims.

They are people.

Not to me.

You don't like people?

No. I don't think I ever have.

There must have been someone. A wife, your
parents, children?

Doesn't mean I liked them. Not really. Not
like they meant something. They were just
there. Like furniture.

How could you marry someone if you didn't
feel anything for them?

**People are different. I feel differently,
doesn't make it wrong.**

Did your wife know that you didn't like her?

Pause.

I didn't say I was married.

But you were. You pretty much said that.

Pause.

**I didn't say it. I have people in my life. Everyone
has. That's all I meant. They are fittings
and fixtures.**

She made a note on the pad in front of her. *Was married.*

Matthew, why did you lose interest in her after
she didn't look as she had before?

It had been minutes since Marr had typed the line and
the delay in answering perhaps suggested it took him
by surprise.

What?

You said she didn't look like the same person.

**I don't remember saying that. You must have
got it wrong.**

225

I've just reread it. That's what you said.

**She just looked different. From what she
had before.**

I don't believe you. Who didn't she look
like anymore?

**Her. She didn't look like herself.
Ellen Lambert.**

Who did she look like?

Goodbye.

And he was gone. The green light went out, the line went dead, and her potential lead disappeared.

CHAPTER 28

Narey and Dakers sat back in their chairs, rubbing at their bruises. The man knew where to land his punches, jabbing at their consciences, throwing right hooks at their sense of morality, each one leaving a mark.

They sat in silence for a few minutes until Narey pushed herself out of her seat, distancing herself from the computer, and paced the room.

'Talk to me about this guy, Lennie. Tell me who he is. What he is. And try using words I can understand.'

Dakers grinned lazily. 'I'll try to keep it simple. And remember, I'm still guessing.'

'Aren't you always?'

The psychologist stopped and tilted his head to the side as he considered. 'Yes. Of course I am. But my guesses are better than most people's because I've studied and practised for over thirty years. It's like the golfer says … the more I practise, the luckier I get.'

'Get lucky, Lennie. Please. We need to nail this guy.'

'I'll try. Okay, so my best guess is that Marr wanted us to find Eloise Gray's body. We know he killed her

227

somewhere else. Somewhere he'd said that we'd never find, and so, presumably, where no one would find the body. Instead, he placed her in a building on a public street. Sure, it's abandoned, but it's known that kids go in there and mess with the place. He *wanted* Eloise to be found. So, the question is why.'

'And?'

'And I think our Mr Marr is a guy who's into power and into being in control. He has no doubt that he's smarter than us, superior to us. His twisted morality is right; our understanding of how things should be is wrong. He's an arrogant dick but his weakness is that he needs us to recognise it. There's no point in having all that power, no point in being control, unless other people know that you are.'

'If he's so superior, why does he feel the need to prove it? Why does he need us to tell him how smart he is?'

'He needs the confirmation of others. He knows he's the emperor but he needs us to bow before him.'

'We're missing something, Lennie. We must be. It's been bugging me for a while now. There are answers in what he's told us, or not told us, and we haven't seen them. I can feel it.'

Dakers nodded. 'Okay, I can buy that. So, what do we do?'

'We read it all again. His conversations with the Americans, and the interviews we've done. All of it. It's in there somewhere.'

Dakers huffed only slightly. 'Then let's do it.'

Everything had been transcribed and printed in

multiple copies. It was all there to be read on screen, but they were both of an age that they absorbed more of what they were reading if they were holding it in their hands.

Narey noticed that Dakers had three blank sheets next to the transcripts. He headed one Truths, one as Deceptions, and the third was topped by a large question mark. As he read, he stopped every few moments and jotted down a couple of lines on one or other of the sheets. She had to force herself not to look to see what was going where, and to concentrate on what she was reading.

She waded her way through Marr's boasts and the gratuitous details that were designed to sicken her, through the denials and the evasion, the truth and lies. It went on and on, every word pored over, every phrase and nuance examined. For two hours she trawled through it all, a second time and a third.

Every phrase made her think of another that she'd read earlier and previously. Each connection made her wonder and made her doubt herself. The words became a snowstorm, the sentences a whiteout. Eventually, she couldn't see letters for looking at them.

Before she knew it, she'd pushed herself out of her chair and pushed out of the room, the door hitting the wall as she sought fresh air and fresh ideas. She was aware of Dakers calmly looking on, a bemused smile on his face, as she charged by him. She kept pushing, past people and around people, until the cold of the night kissed her cheeks.

She paced and breathed and briefly wished that she

smoked. Instead, she strode round the car park until she had stored up enough oxygen to fuel her brain for another round. She stubbed out an imaginary cigarette with the ball of her foot, crushing it into the tarmac, and spun on her heel.

'Better?' Dakers asked without looking up as she re-entered the room.

'Let's find out.'

She settled herself again, renewed if not refreshed, and began reading through the transcripts of each interview for a fourth time. Like before, her gaze kept drifting occasionally to Dakers' lists, as if they might be the map to the treasure she sought. She managed to stay in the chair for all of ten minutes before she got out of it again and stood behind Dakers, reading over his shoulder and seeing the three lists full, from the top of each page to the bottom. *Truth. Deception. Question mark.* It was all there. She just had to see it.

She saw his shoulders sink and heard him let a soft sigh escape, exasperated by her standing there. He slowly turned until he was looking at her.

'Okay, so tell me, what are we missing?'

Narey began to answer but stopped herself, a different response forming in her brain. She held up a single finger, a plea for a moment to think. She then wagged it a few times and turned, moving quickly to the other side of the room.

Dakers watched her go to another file and pull out sheets of paper. He crossed his arms and let her work, knowing when to talk and when to shut up. He remained silent as she came back across the room, slower now, and stood in front of him with the paper in her right hand. With her left, she pushed her hair back as if giving her head more room to think. She closed her eyes and grimaced.

'Okay,' she began slowly. 'Talk this through with me. I need to know I'm making sense.'

'Go for it.'

'On your lists,' she nodded towards the sheets of paper, her eyes still closed, 'tell me where you've placed the conversation where Marr explained how he met Brianna Holden.'

Dakers didn't have to look. 'Deception.'

'Tell me why.'

'He employed negation and equivocation; he skirted the subject. I'd no doubt he wasn't telling us the truth, or at least not the whole truth.'

'And what was your understanding of *why* he was doing that?'

The question made Dakers pause. 'That he was trying to deflect from admitting he used the online dating sites to target his victims.'

'Yes, that was what I'd thought too.'

'And now you don't? We know that the mystery man her sister spoke of, this *Greg Hurst*, met her online. We know he ticked all the boxes, just the way Garland and Marr operated.'

Narey nodded. 'Sure. That's not in doubt and it's *not* what he was hiding. We know that Marr has admitted to doing that with the others, so why be so coy this time?

He'd nothing to gain from it. So, that suggests to me that he was hiding something else instead.'

Dakers looked thoughtful. 'Okay. It makes sense so far. Go on.'

'You asked what we were missing, right? Well, I think it's all about omission. And not just in what he didn't tell us during that interview.' She held up the sheets of printout that were in her right hand. 'So, these are the lists of names, profiles, likes and dislikes that they found in Garland's computer.' She placed the sheets of paper in front of him. 'There's the names of Marr and Garland's targets in Scotland, along with the names of the pseudonyms they used while they were catfishing them. Including Brianna Holden and Greg Hurst. And there's the various personal preferences that Marr and Garland had mined from social media. Tell me what you see.'

Dakers looked confused and Narey sighed impatiently. 'Okay, let me make it easier. It's about omission. Tell me what you don't see.'

He looked again and almost immediately let out a short gasp of irritation. 'There's no list of likes and dislikes against Brianna Holden's name the way there is with the others.'

'Correct. Which leads me to one conclusion, but I don't want to lead you to it in case I'm wrong. I want to hear it from you.'

Dakers stared at her, exhaling hard. 'Marr already knew her. He pursued her online but he didn't meet her there. He already fucking knew her.'

She nodded slowly. 'Yes. I'm sure of it. There was no need to make a list of Brianna's preferences. No need to list what she did or where she worked. He already knew it all.'

CHAPTER 29

'So, you think you know the guy she chatted to online. Greg. But that he wasn't Greg. He was someone she already knew. From *before*? Like an ex-boyfriend or something?'

Narey hadn't wanted to tell Kayleigh McGrath much more than she had to. However, the invitation to remember Brianna's former boyfriends led to an obvious conclusion. One that freaked the hell out of her sister.

'That's sick. That's creepy as fuck. Oh my God. Imagine . . .'

She saw the sister's own demons hurl themselves at her, seeing the horror of it etched on her face, turning pale under her fake tan as she imagined Brianna's secrets being used by the last person that she'd hope would have them.

When she was finally ready to talk, Kayleigh wanted to scream out the name of every guy that Brianna had ever dated or anyone that had asked her out or showed an interest. Yet part of her shied away from it, defending her sister's memory and making sure Narey knew Brianna wasn't some kind of slut.

'I know,' she assured her. 'I'm not judging, believe me. We've all had exes from before we were married, we all had to kiss some frogs. None of that matters. All I need to know is *who* is in Brianna's past, not why. Let's go through it. Tell me anyone you remember. Leave no one out.'

It was a slow process. Names known, names forgotten, names never known. Boyfriends, neighbours, work colleagues. Brianna was an attractive, outgoing young woman and so had more than her share of what Narey's granny would have called suitors. *Predators*, Narey thought. Potential predators at the very least.

Kayleigh did most of her talking, most of her remembering, perched on the other end of a series of cigarettes. She inhaled like she was sucking on life before nervously blowing it out the open window of the flat.

'There was a guy named Bruce Devlin. This is going back years though. Just after high school. Braw-looking guy and he knew it. Bit of a ladies' man. Brianna fancied him much more than she ever told him. Kept him dangling, you know? They went out for about six months on and off until Bri got drunk one Saturday night and got off with some guy whose name I can't remember. Devlin found out and that was that. His ego couldn't handle it.'

'Where's this Devlin now, do you know?'

Kayleigh frowned. 'I think he joined the army, but that was ten years ago. More, probably.'

'Did she ever date or know anyone by the name of Tam Harkness?' It was a long shot and Narey knew the answer she expected, but it had to be asked. Kayleigh looked blank and when Narey described him she shook her head firmly. 'Doesn't sound like her type at all.'

It didn't. Brianna's exes seemed to be a collection of good-looking chancers and wide boys.

'This one guy, Ricky McKenzie, he was a drummer in a band. Long dyed-blonde hair, always wore a vest top to show off his muscles. Crap drummer but he looked the part. Loved himself to death. I think he got Bri into a bit of drugs, nothing heavy but enough that they were wild together. Last I heard he was living in London, playing in pubs. Probably looks like shit now.'

'Who ended it between them? Ricky or Brianna?'

A shrug. 'I don't know. Probably Brianna though. It was usually her.'

She dumped Danny, the amateur footballer, after three weeks. She dropped Jack the barman after one. She dated a computer programmer named Lee Fairley for two months before deciding he was too boring and went out with his best mate Aaron instead. She was just young though, Kayleigh insisted, nobody would have thought twice about a man doing the same.

'How did Lee Fairley take it?' Narey asked.

'Not too well? Called her every name under the sun and said he hoped she walked in front of a bus. His poor wee heart was crushed.'

Narey's skin prickled but she kept her voice even. 'Do you know where he is now?'

Another shrug. 'No idea. Probably went home and never showed his face again.'

It was an unusual enough name. She'd find him.

'What about Kevin Monteith, the man who went on trial for Brianna's murder? Tell me about him.'

Kayleigh sighed heavily. 'He lived just a few streets away from us in Shawlands. He was a couple of years older than Bri and had always been interested in her. Wasn't shy at letting her know either. He'd stand at a street corner and say "Awright, gorgeous? How you doing today, beautiful?" That kind of shit. The harder he tried, the more Brianna ignored him. Poor sod never gave up though. He must have asked her out half a dozen times and she always said no. He became properly annoying, pushy and then abusive. After Bri was – after she died – her handbag was found in Monteith's car. They were sure he'd killed her. Plenty of people told them how he'd acted with her and how she'd snubbed him.'

'Including you?'

'Well, yeah. They asked me and I told them. The cops were so sure that Monteith had killed her and I wasn't going to doubt them. I guess what we told them about Monteith just made them more certain. They were adamant they were right. Right up until they were wrong.'

'Any of the guys that Brianna dated, or any of them that knew her ... did they know Monteith? Someone framed him. It would make sense for it to be the person that killed her.'

Kayleigh's face twisted. 'Christ. I don't ... Well, Bruce Devlin would have known him. Danny Whatsisname – Danny McDaid – would have known him too. Probably. Monteith and Lee Fairley know each other for sure. They both used to drink in the same crowd in the Granary.'

'Anyone else?'

The sister tilted her head to the side and huffed. More secrets to spill. More names to make Brianna look bad.

'Bri once went out with this French guy. Martin. Although he pronounced it *Martan*. I know for a fact that Kevin Monteith knew him. They got into some kind of fight at Sweeney's one night. Bri told me about it. Said she'd hoped Martin knocked Monteith's head off.'

'Do you know Martin's second name?'

'No. Never knew it. Oh, and there was this mechanic she dated a few years ago for a couple of months. Big handsome guy called Sean. Monteith is a mechanic as well so they maybe knew each other.'

'Maybe.'

And maybe Monteith was known to Davie, the barman at Sweeney's. Or to Phil, who DJ'd at Bar Soba. Or Mick or Mike, she couldn't remember which, who Brianna met in Ibiza and was in love with until the flight home.

One thing was for sure. She was known to the man calling himself Matthew Marr.

CHAPTER 30

Narey's gaze switched between the monitors. One with the young man twitching uncontrollably, his left leg kicking out despite not being awake. She knew the medical opinion was that his heart rate was increasing, racing like a rabbit on the run. He was asleep but in overdrive.

If that was bad, the second screen was somehow worse. The green light blinking. The text from Marr creeping across the page. It sickened her but she had to talk to the man.

> How come you knew Ethan Garland's name,
> but he never knew yours?

**He told me his. I didn't tell him mine.
It's simple.**

> Okay. Why did he tell you and why didn't you
> tell him yours?

**Because of where we met, there was a choice to
be made and he made a different one from me.**

> Explain. How did you meet Garland?

Where do any two people meet these days? Online.

On a website? Chat room?

Not in the sense you mean, no. Not one you'd find or would have heard of.

Something on the dark web?

More deep than dark. And stop fishing, I'm not telling you where it was. And it doesn't matter. We got talking in a safe space and we found we had things in common.

Were you talking in a place where you were likely to have things in common?

Maybe. But some people are all talk. Ethan wasn't, neither was I. We both knew that pretty quickly.

When you say things in common, let's be clear what you're talking about.

I think you know. You just want to hear me say it? Like it's evidence? We thought similarly. Very similarly. I knew almost right away that he was someone like me.

Yet you didn't tell him who you really were?

I knew I could be open about myself. But I still wasn't stupid enough to trust him with everything. He was that stupid, that was his

choice. I protected myself with an alias. I
suspect he knew that but he never asked.
That suited us both.

> So how much more did you know about him
> than he knew about you?

Quite a bit. I told him some things that were
true and some that weren't. We knew all the
things we needed to carry out our shared
ventures. We knew each other's tastes.

The words soured her mouth before she typed them.

> In victims?

Yes.

> You chose his and he chose yours?

Within certain parameters. And we had
discretion to say no thank you.

> So, you chose this guy that's chained up?

I found him. Ethan chose to take him.

> How you could you find him? You were five
> thousand miles away.

Don't try to play me. The internet makes the
world a smaller place and you know it. The
kid knew I was a voice in the ether and that
was all he needed to know.

241

Do you know Los Angeles?

I know how to use Google. And I know stuff
Ethan taught me. It was more than enough
to bait my hook and catch me a little fishy.

So why couldn't Ethan have just done
that himself?

He could have, but that wasn't our play. We
had our own game.

Want to tell me about it?

No. You get paid to work it out. Maybe you
already have.

Maybe. So what did Ethan tell you about LA?

He hated it. Hated the traffic and the people,
hated the phonies and the freaks, the
YouTubers and the wannabe celebrities, the
hypocrites and the hippies. He hated LA
but never went anywhere else. Thing about
Ethan was he loved the Los Angeles he
grew up in. He hated change. Said change
always made things worse.

What do you mean?

Never mind. I read something once. It was
by a defence lawyer, saying that everybody
is more than the worst thing they've ever
done. That's true, right?

I can see why you'd want it to be true.

But it stands to reason, doesn't it? Everyone is better than their worst?

So, if someone once put a tenner in the poor box and helped an old lady across the road then we judge him by that rather than that he shot three people in cold blood?

Yes. It shows his best is better than his worst.

Best is better than worst. It's a dictionary definition, not a way of judging a person's character or behaviour. One decent act, even a hundred of them, is overshadowed by the worst thing a person does, if that thing is bad enough. If you have done good things in your life, and it's to be expected you have, then you're still going to be your worst thing. That's what defines you.

The silence was drawn out, but finally, fatally, punctured by his response.

What if I haven't done my worst thing yet?

Chilled, Narey's fingers rattled the keyboard.

Then you'll be judged by that.

You do know I'm aware that everything you
say, everything you ask, is about trying to
catch me out? That you're trying to trip me
up, get some info out of me.

You'd be pretty stupid not to.

I'm not stupid.

Well that's okay then. Can we continue?

You won't get anything from me.

Maybe I already have. Can we move on?

She assumed the pause was either rage or sulking but
didn't care much which.

Okay, ask me your question.

How did you know that you and Garland were
the same? What was it you said, that he was
'someone like me'?

I just knew. Things he said. The way he said
them. When I told him some of the things
I've done in my life, he didn't react the way
other people had. I'd told people before.
Online, anonymously. They freaked mostly.
Ethan didn't. He was interested. And he had
his own stories to tell.

How did you know he wasn't just full of
bullshit? Trying to impress you.

**You're not listening. It was how he said
it more than what he said. It was how he
felt. Only someone like me and him could
know that.**

You're ill, Matthew. Sick. You know that,
right? How can you even function around
normal people?

She was pushing him and didn't care that Dakers was
signalling caution.

**I'm normal. I'm my kind of normal. I live my
life and no one knows but me. I function just
the same as other people when I want to.
And I function like me when I want to too.
That's my trick.**

Your trick? That's how you think of it?

It's just a word.

It's an arrogant fucking boast, is what it is. A
trick? You think being a functioning psycho
doesn't make you a psycho? Being able to
switch emotions on and off isn't a party trick,
it's a mental illness.

**I'm not ill. They thought I was ill, but I
wasn't. Stupid bastards at Carstairs wasted
time on me. I'm not ill. I can control myself.
It's my trick.**

Carstairs was the State Hospital. Where patients were admitted because of dangerous or violent tendencies, usually by the prison service or the court.

> When were you in Carstairs?

> **Fuck you. It doesn't matter. I'm not ill. That's all you need to know. And all I need is to see this guy die.**

She'd happily have ripped his eyes out with her nails if she could. She ripped the plug on the conversation instead.

> You'll see what I let you see and don't forget
> it. Goodbye.

It maybe wasn't as much as she'd hoped for, but she'd got something from him at least. *It was her trick.*

The line flashed from LA again. 'Nice job, Rachel. You really pushed his buttons,'

From her side, Lennie Dakers nodded in approval. 'You got him angry enough to reveal more than he wanted to. I'm sure most, probably all, of what he told us was genuine.'

'Thanks. I was worried a couple of times that I was pushing him *too* far. We'll contact the State Hospital at Carstairs. See if they'll tell us about anyone that fits his profile. They only admit around thirty patients a year. Cally, I hope that his line about Garland hating change and loving the Los Angeles that he grew up in is of some use to you.'

'Already on it. We're getting closer'

They were. Just as the young man chained in some unknown location was getting closer to death.

CHAPTER 31

Igloo. Messages. Vikki, 32.

Ryan: So how long have you been on this site?
Delivered, 12.05
Read, 12.06

> **Vikki: A few weeks now. I'm ready to quit it
> to be honest. I've pretty much given up on
> thinking I'll meet anyone decent.**

I know what you mean. This place seems to be
full of crazies. Some nice people too though.

> **Yes. Some.**

I hope you don't leave though. Not yet anyway.
There are some decent guys, honestly.

> **You do seem nice. So tell me stuff about you.**

Okay. I'm a teacher. Primary kids. Love it. Been
doing that for six years now. It's tough at times
but really worth it.

Cool. Must be fun. Tell me more about you.

I'm into movies, old stuff more than new stuff
though. They make too much crap these
days. All those superhero films.

Agreed! So what's your favourite movie?

Hard to choose. But I'd say maybe Some
Like It Hot.

No way! That's MY favourite!! I love that
movie. Okay, what else?

To Kill a Mockingbird. Bringing Up Baby. And
okay, corny maybe, but It's a Wonderful Life.

Are you kidding me? I love those. I watch
Wonderful Life EVERY Christmas. Okay,
what about music?

All kinds of stuff. Soul. Pop. Blues.

Soul is cool. Name your top three.

That's tough. Nina Simone. Curtis Mayfield.
Otis Redding.

Two out of three ain't bad. I'm not crazy
about Otis. Anyone who was in the charts
after I was born?

Kendrick Lamar? Lauryn Hill?

Yes!! This is spooky. Have you stolen my
Spotify or something? You could be my
music twin.

That's got to be a good thing, right?

Maybe ☺ Okay, ask me about me.

So what do you do? And what are you doing tonight? It's Saturday after all.

Slow down, mister! One question at a time. I work in a bank. Customer service. Been there three years. Did the same thing in another bank before that.

Can I open an account?

If you keep my interest.

I plan to. How long have you been single?

Two years. You?

A bit over a year. About ready to dip a toe back in the water. With the right person.

Me too, I guess. Finding the right one is the hard bit. I'm really wary. It's easy for a guy but women have to be careful. You know? People aren't always who they say they are on here.

I guess that's true. You do have to be careful. I hope you wouldn't rule out meeting someone though.

No.

Good to hear.

       Okay, I need to go make lunch. We can talk
          again later if you'd like that.

Oh, I would. Okay, I suppose I better let you go.
Bye for now Vikki x

                 Bye Ryan x

CHAPTER 32

The decision to release two photographs of the kidnap victim was taken way above the heads of Salgado and O'Neill. Their lieutenant, Annie Burns, told them it had got as far as one of the deputy chiefs before anyone had the cojones to make a call in the time needed. Adam Berkovic was the one who finally put his on the line and said that, quite simply, they had no choice. They did it or the man died.

Few doubted that he was right, but the chaos was inevitable, immediate and sensationalist. A kidnap victim is always grist to the media mill, and they didn't waste the opportunity to scare the shit out of viewers, readers and listeners. Every news station in southern California led with it, every newspaper in the state splashed it. The photographs, poor quality but enhanced as much as technology would allow, were in front of eyes from Crescent City to San Diego.

The department had said as little as they could. They wanted the public's help in identifying the young man in the pictures. They were concerned for his welfare. It was a matter of great urgency. All calls would be treated in confidence.

It was never going to be enough and they knew it. It was like throwing a lamb to a pack of wolves and telling them they could play with it for an hour.

Who is he? Where is he? How did you get the photographs? Who set up the video? What are you doing to try to find him? Is the public in danger? When will he die? *When will he die?*

If the mainstream media were wolves then their online counterparts were dragons and vampires. Conspiracy theories were rampant and instant. The photograph was a fake; the man was already dead; it was the "real" movie star who'd been replaced by a lookalike; it was a scam by the cops to flush out patriots; the man had been kidnapped by aliens, democrats, Russians and Muslims.

Once unleashed, none of it could never be reined in again.

The photographs were two of the few shots they had of the man awake and looking at the camera. His suffering and failing health were all too obvious and they were inundated with complaints that they were too distressing and should never have been released. Many of the ardent objectors seemed more bothered about the release of the photograph than of the man.

Salgado and O'Neill were cussing the whole circus when the call came through. It had been less than an hour since the photograph was made public. A shout from the other side of the incident room, urging one of them to pick up the phone immediately. O'Neill took the call.

'LAPD, Detective—'

Salgado could hear the rapid, urgent voice leaking from the receiver. O'Neill wasn't getting a word in.

'Slow down, ma'am. Please.' She nodded at Salgado to let him know they were on. 'You're sure it's your son?'

It wasn't. In the next three hours, their kidnap victim was Paul Weiss, Aaron Hope, Bradley Jansen, Fred van der Hoorn, Jack Arnold, Ricky Lessing, Michael James Green, Cody Welsh and Justin Greenhaugh. He was also a dozen other young men whose names never got as far as Salgado and O'Neill. But they kept coming.

'LAPD, Detective Salgado speaking.'

No one spoke but Salgado knew the line was live. He could hear someone breathing nervously.

'LAPD, can I help you?'

'The photographs. On TV and online. I know who they are.'

Okay, this time. Salgado thought. *Make it this time.* The voice was female, frantic and certain.

'Okay, ma'am. Can you give me some details, please? Who do you believe the man in the photograph is?'

'I don't *believe*. I *know*. It's my son. Dylan Hansen. It's Dylan.'

She was crying, and the words were choking her.

'Okay, who am I talking to?'

'Steph Hansen. My name is Steph Hansen. My phone number is 213-637-9242. I am Dylan's mother and I *know* that's him in those photographs. But I don't understand. How can he be there? Who did this?'

'We're working on that, Mrs Hansen. I'm going to need some information from you though. Tell me about Dylan, when you last saw him, when he was reported missing.'

She was still in tears. 'He's not been reported missing. I didn't think he was missing. I'd texted him three times but when he didn't reply, I left it. Dylan drops out for a few days now and again. I didn't think that much of it. Now I . . . now I'm scared he couldn't reply.'

'Tell me about him. What does he do? What's his address? When did you last see him?'

'He's – he's a script reader. For the movies. He works for himself, reading scripts that the studios send him. He's got a major in film. He lives in Glendale, 900 East Lomita Avenue. I last saw him six days ago. I kept expecting him to call or text but he didn't. So, I texted him. Three times.'

'We're going to need a photograph of Dylan to—'

'I've emailed some. To the hotline address. You already have them. It's Dylan. I know the shirt he's wearing in the photograph. I bought it for him. *It's him.*'

Salgado cupped his hand over the phone and told O'Neill to check the email. He watched as she did so, hearing the woman sobbing on the other side of the line and not being quite sure if he wanted it to be Dylan Hansen or not.

She was telling him how it wasn't completely unusual for Dylan not to answer a text but that three was . . . He stopped listening as he saw O'Neill turn to face him, her mouth open until she composed herself enough to close it. 'I think it's him.'

An email alert popped up in front of Salgado and he clicked through it until there was a photograph filling the screen. *Shit.*

'Mrs Hansen, where are you? We're coming right over.'

CHAPTER 33

The State Hospital at Carstairs was Scotland's highest security psychiatric hospital and a byword for the highly dangerous and mentally ill.

It was probably the most feared and misunderstood institution in the country. Even its location added to its fearsome mystique, hidden away on a windswept moor and far from the public gaze. It housed those deemed too dangerous for even a high-security prison – murderers, rapists and child killers – those who needed two members of staff for every prisoner, those who needed to be sedated just to keep others around them safe.

This was the environment that, seemingly, Matthew Marr had once been held in. This was the building that housed him and let him go. Except that they hadn't had Marr, not by name at least.

Narey was there to meet Andrea Wallace, the hospital's chief executive. No promises had been made but enough encouragement had been given for her to make the forty-minute drive south-east from Glasgow. Carstairs had procedures to follow and confidences to keep, but Wallace said she'd do what she could.

The drive across the moor had been in ever-falling darkness, and the nearer Narey got the more the gloom enveloped her, and the greater the sense of foreboding. It was only when she approached the perimeter that she was able to see the razor-wire fencing and then, finally, the largely anonymous but fortified entrance. The sole sign outside said little but said everything. *The State Hospital*.

She negotiated security at the gatehouse and waited while a massive green gate slid back to let her drive inside. Perhaps surprisingly, she'd never had the need to visit, and that probably explained the first-time nerves that she was acutely aware of.

A guard escorted her to a waiting area, saying that the chief executive would be with her shortly. Wallace had finished for the day but had agreed to wait behind to meet her, given the urgency of the situation.

Narey spent the wait idly trying to remember if any of the men or women she'd helped put away had ended up in here rather in mainstream prisons. The shimmering line between the dangerous and the criminally insane was a distinction she was glad she didn't have to make.

Andrea Wallace was a short, neat woman in a black trouser suit, with blonde bobbed hair and a wide smile. She greeted Narey with a handshake and a wave of her arm for her to follow. They walked along a narrow corridor that had Narey wondering what would happen if there was someone coming the other way. Wallace seemed to read her mind.

'Your first time here?'

'Is it that obvious?'

Wallace nodded. 'There's a look. I've seen it many times. But, rest assured, the reality is different from whatever you're likely to have heard. It's a lot safer in here than it is out there.'

'That's good to know, but given how some places are out there, it might not be saying much.'

'Maybe so. But we're working on making the hospital safer all the time. We're looking to reduce the number of patients, ideally down to around one hundred from the two hundred and fifty that we currently have. We'll be moving more of them out to medium-security units, including all of the women.'

Wallace opened the door to her office and invited Narey inside. The room was neat and minimalist: white walls, a wooden desk, computer, phone and a solitary pot plant was all that was to be seen.

'I'm not going to waste either of our time by going through the issues with us helping you on this. We both know them, and they've been discussed above my head and yours. And we've taken on board how serious the situation is that you're dealing with. And a decision has been made.'

She opened a drawer to her right and produced a beige folder which she placed on the desk in front of her. She tapped it as she spoke.

'We've taken into account what you've been able to tell us in terms of his possible age, location, time parameters, and the suggestion that we didn't diagnose him as being dangerous enough to retain. I have to say, it wasn't a lot to work with.'

Narey felt her heart sink.

'We typically admit around thirty patients a year – that includes men and women. Most of those are with us for a prolonged period of time, many of them indefinitely. Those who can be readmitted to society on their own recognisance are always far fewer than we'd like. If we commit ourselves to saying a patient is safe to be released without supervision then we must be completely certain that decision won't come back to bite us on the arse and, more importantly of course, endanger the public. As a result, it doesn't happen either easily or often. So that, in this instance, has helped us narrow down the possibilities. Getting to the point, within the time period we are talking about and eliminating those who don't fit the criteria or who have been readmitted here or elsewhere, it leaves just six men who fit the profile.'

'Only six?' Narey couldn't hide the excitement in her voice.

'Yes.'

'And you can be confident about that?' She knew she was only making things difficult for herself, checking all the teeth on the gift horse that was being presented to her, but she had to be sure.

Wallace pursed her lips and didn't seem at all impressed by the question.

'I can be as confident about it as I can in the information you've given me, Inspector.'

She took the riposte on the chin, knowing she'd asked for it.

'I'm sorry. It's just more – better – than I'd hoped for. May I see the folder? I assume that's the six men you've identified.'

Wallace nodded and pushed the folder across the desk. 'It's all in there. Their histories, staff appraisals, release dates. Take it with you and please, keep in touch. If we've messed up by letting someone go who has gone on to do the things you believe he has, then we need to learn from that, and we'll need to be prepared to apologise for it.'

Narey nodded at that – there were going to have to be a lot of apologies made before they were finished. She opened the folder and pulled out the top sheet.

Derek Solomon. Colin McPake. John Paul Kepple. Fraser Anderson. Martin Geir. Ian Bryce.

Six men. Six files. Six histories. Six chances of finding the man calling himself Matthew Marr.

'You have to be aware, Inspector, that the man you're looking for may not be known by the names on these files, never mind the name you know him by. He might have invented a completely new life for himself. If he somehow convinced our staff that he should be released by hiding his true self then he's a person of some considerable guile who has also managed to hide himself from those around him. Anyone that good at hiding won't be found easily.'

Narey nodded. 'No matter how good he is at hiding, we're nearer to finding him than we were an hour ago. So thank you.' She held up the folder. 'If he's in here, he's ours.'

CHAPTER 34

Igloo. Messages. Vikki, 32.

> Hi Ryan, are you still on this site?
> *Delivered, 14.34*
> *Read, 14.34*

Hey Vikki. I was thinking about you and wondered if you might be online

> Oh were you? That's sweet. Maybe I was thinking the same

That's good to know! How was your lunch?

> It was good. So what are you doing with your afternoon?

Apart from talking to you? lol I might read for a bit. I'm in the middle of a book and loving it

> What are you reading?

Don't laugh, right?

Promise

Emile Zola. La Bete Humaine. I am not saying
this to sound intellectual or anything. I'm just a
huge fan of his books

Are you kidding me??? I LOVE Zola. I'm
not sure I've talked to anyone before who's
properly liked him

Really? Well I do. I don't usually tell people
because it just sounds wanky. But he's brilliant.
I don't read them in French or anything, just the
translations

Me too! What's your favourite?

Oh, tough question. I've read a lot. Maybe Le
Ventre de Paris. Any of the Rougon-Macquart
books really

Love them! You are full of surprises
Mr Teacher

I try :) Sorry but I'm going to have to go. I've got
a phone call. Will you be on tonight?

I might be :)

I hope so

I will be :)

CHAPTER 35

Steph Hansen was shaking when she sat opposite O'Neill and Salgado in her modest, whitewashed single-storey house on Jeffries Avenue on the southern edge of Cypress Park. Her eyes were wet and red, and she wrung her hands constantly.

She was slim and blonde, lightly freckled, make-up free, her hair tied harshly behind her. Sitting on a large green sofa built for three, she looked little and lost.

'I know this is difficult,' O'Neill led with the understatement, 'but we need you to tell us about Dylan. Anything that might help.'

Steph puffed out her cheeks and gathered enough courage to do it.

'He's a great kid. Never been any trouble, even when he was a teenager. The other moms used to say to me how lucky I was that Dylan never came home drunk or got in fights or stayed out late, never gave me any lip either. He would help around the house, especially after his father died. He's sweet. Kind and caring. He's . . . I always think he's nineteenth century meets twenty-first.'

Neither of the cops took her meaning, and shrugged.

'Dylan doesn't go out much. He gets anxious in crowds and prefers just one or two people at the most. That's why he works from his apartment. He prefers talking to people by email. Or text. Or online. He's an old-fashioned kind of guy who does most of his talking via modern technology. I know I'm biased because I'm his mom but he's a great writer, really brilliant, but you'd probably never think it talking to him because it takes so much for him to open up. He's not unsociable; like I say, he's sweet. And funny. He's just happier with one or two people at a time.

'Bob, his dad, died when Dylan was fifteen. Since then it's just been me and him. He moved out to Glendale four years ago, but he comes over at least once a week and we have dinner and hang out. But otherwise it's just him and his movie scripts, the ones that he reads and the one he's working on for himself. And his cat. Oh shit, shit. *The cat.* Kubrick will be starving to death.'

The last line fell between them like a body hitting the floor during a wake.

'We're going to his apartment from here, so we'll check on the cat,' O'Neill reassured her. 'He'll be fine.'

Steph didn't dare ask if they meant Kubrick or Dylan.

'So, does he have any friends, anyone we can talk to who might know where he was headed or who he could have confided in? A girlfriend maybe?'

There were two sharp shakes of the head. 'No. Dylan doesn't have close friends. Apart from me. He prefers it that way. He has people he speaks to online, gamer friends and such, but he isn't the confiding type. And he's never had a girlfriend, not that he's told me about anyway and I think he would have done.'

The mention of online friends had Salgado and O'Neill glancing at each other. They wouldn't ask just yet though.

'Mrs Hansen, can you talk us through the last time you spoke to Dylan? Anything he said, anywhere he said he was going, anyone he'd planned to meet.'

Steph tilted her head to her shoulder, looking above them to the ceiling. Maybe a vain attempt to keep the tears from sliding down her cheeks. Her words came out stilted and punctured with sniffles.

It had been six days and there was little remarkable about the last time they'd spoken. It hadn't even been real conversation, just Dylan's version of it. A flurry of exchanged texts studded with emojis and exclamation marks. He'd been excited because he'd read a script he loved and was recommending big time to the production company. He'd said how he wished he could write something as good as that and she'd told him not to be silly, that of course he would.

He'd had no plans other than to hunker down and make notes on the script then work on his own. She knew he could go days without resurfacing and that's why she hadn't questioned his lack of reply to her texts.

They both knew it was almost certainly a pointless question, but it had to be asked.

'Mrs Hansen, has Dylan ever mentioned a man named Ethan Garland?'

The woman looked at O'Neill then to Salgado, eyes

wide, as if she didn't know what the right answer was but was desperate to help.

'I've never heard the name. Should I have? Oh God, I'm sorry. Who is he?'

'We believe he's the man who took Dylan.'

Her mouth dropped. 'Then why haven't you arrested him?'

O'Neill laid it out for her. The whole tangled, sorry, frantic mess. How Garland had died. How they didn't have the first freaking clue where Dylan was. How she couldn't mention Garland's name to the press if she was asked. None of it eased her panic.

'What are you doing to find him?'

'Everything we can.' It sounded as trite to them as it did to her.

'Mrs Hansen, you talked about Dylan having online friends. What can you tell us about them?'

She shrugged dismissively. 'Losers. I'm sorry, that sounds terrible, but they're the kind of weird gamer freaks that live in their own little bubble and you don't know they exist until they crack completely and shoot up a school. Dylan isn't like those guys and I keep telling him he shouldn't talk with them.'

'Are there any names he mentioned, people he talked to a lot? And what sites did he use?'

She looked contrite. 'I didn't listen much when he talked about those guys, I'm sorry. Is it important? The guys he talked about didn't even have real names; they were all like they were out of *Lord of the Rings* or *Star Wars*. Let me think, oh God. Okay, okay. I think there was one guy named Grimblade and another named Warlock or Warshock, something like that. But the sites? I have no idea, none at all.'

Salgado went for it. 'Did Dylan use non-gaming sites? Maybe talk to other people online?'

'Not that I . . .' Steph looked at him suspiciously. 'What do you mean? Why are you asking that?'

'We're just trying to get a handle on what might have happened to Dylan. Any little thing might lead us to where he is. We think that Ethan Garland talked to people online before meeting them.'

'Wait, he's done this before?'

'We believe so.'

'Oh my God.'

'But we've no knowledge of him talking to gamers. Would Dylan have talked in chat rooms or maybe dating sites?'

'Dating sites? Internet dating? I . . . I don't know. He's never mentioned it but then he wouldn't – he'd be embarrassed telling me about anything like that. I guess he might have. This is what you think it is? Dating sites?'

'We're not saying he did,' Salgado tackled the fire they'd lit. 'We just think that's how Garland got his victims.'

The clumsy mention of victims plural sent Steph Hansen into a spiral. She was quickly lost to a tumult of tears, becoming inconsolable and devoid of any further useful information.

They left with promises to keep her informed of any developments, and headed for Glendale.

*

Dylan's apartment was in a three-floor modern building on Lomita, whitewash and brown, about two blocks from Maple Park. Hansen had a car registered in his name, but there was no sign of it in the spots outside the block or on the street. The landlord let Salgado and O'Neill inside then reluctantly left them to it.

They were greeted by the plaintive cries of a hungry cat – a handsome dark-striped tabby who came straight to them in search of food. He wound his way round their ankles, meowing shamelessly to be fed.

'I'll get him some food,' Salgado announced.

When he saw the amused look on O'Neill's face, he shrugged defensively. 'We won't get any peace otherwise.'

O'Neill smiled to herself as her partner changed the cat's water and filled two dishes, one with wet food and one with dry, setting them both down in front of Kubrick's eager mouth.

'Can we get on now?' she asked him.

'Sure. Let's go.'

The place was a bit of a mess; a typical young man's apartment with clothes growing in every corner and books and movie magazines stuffed under chairs and below cushions. They counted six glasses and three plates in the living room, plus a stack more in the sink.

They moved from room to room, taking photographs on their cell phones as they went, knowing that forensics would follow in their wake to do the same job properly. They tossed drawers, looked in cupboards, took notes of the numbers in and out from the phone's display records, and hunted high and low for anything that would give them an insight into Dylan's disappearance.

The bathroom still held what they took to be his toothbrush and most likely the few essential toiletries that someone like Dylan would need. If he'd been planning on being away from home, he would have taken those with him.

They'd need to get his mother over, see if she could identify what might be missing from the house or his wardrobe other than the things that they'd seen him wearing. Most probably nothing, but they'd have to check.

They returned to the first thing they saw when they entered the apartment – a large desktop computer; a few grand's worth of premium gaming hardware that dominated the main room. 'He's put this together himself. Probably spent more on components for it than that second-hand Nissan of his,' Salgado murmured. 'I think it's what they call a Hackintosh. Runs Mac OS but ain't a Mac computer. I'd guess it cost more than everything else in here put together.'

'Not that there's much to beat.'

'Nope. He certainly didn't spend it on his clothes.'

'Can we switch it on?' O'Neill asked him.

'Let's try, but I'd bet my last buck that someone who springs for this much tech doesn't shy from all the passwords he can find.'

He pushed what seemed to be the start-up button and, sure enough, the beast flickered into life. And, sure enough, a password was demanded before they could enter the beast's lair.

'We need to get Geisler in here,' O'Neill huffed. 'Get him to take this thing apart and find who Dylan was talking to.'

'We might not need to go all hi-tech,' Salgado countered. His gloved hands held up a notepad next to the laptop, indents from scribbling clear on it. 'Old school.'

'Jesus, Salgado, are you going all Columbo on me?'

'Whatever it takes.'

He took the pencil next to the pad and rubbed it across the paper until writing began to form.

Erica. Gravity Hill. 8.30.

O'Neill pushed her bottom lip out in a show of grudging admiration. 'Well, what do you know?'

'I know that we're going to Gravity Hill. Once we work out what it is. And that Erica probably wasn't the kind of girl that Dylan Hansen thought she was.'

'Not a girl at all? Do you mean a woman?'

'I mean a man and you know it. Gravity Hill mean anything to you?'

O'Neill had to think. 'Not here, no, but there's one back home in Massachusetts. In Greenfield, about a hundred miles west of Boston. Weirdest thing. You park your car, stick it in neutral, release the handbrake, and the car rolls uphill.'

'You're shitting me.'

'Nope. It's just an optical illusion. Or ghosts. People say it's ghosts.'

'Not you though, I'm betting.'

She lowered her brows and frowned at him. Of course not. She already had her phone in her hand and was googling.

'There's three in southern California. One in San Diego, one over in Ventura County and one . . .' she googled some more, 'just eleven miles away. Gravity Hill, Altadena. On Loma Alta Drive. A twenty-five-minute drive.'

'Nowhere is a twenty-five-minute drive in LA unless it's supposed to take five minutes.'

She ignored him and read aloud from the website. *Something strange happens when you put your car in neutral at Altadena's gravity hill. Instead of sliding backward, your car rolls forward, up the hill, as if pushed by an invisible pair of helping hands.*

'Helping hands?'

'Oh, it gets worse. According to this, those hands might just belong to the children in the fateful school bus accident years ago that left the driver and all the children dead. Now the children try to prevent another accident.'

'Okay. So, Dylan met the mysterious Erica at a spot where the ghosts of dead children push cars uphill? I can't help thinking he was asking for trouble.'

'Well he sure found it. Let's get over there. But we still need to get Geisler to rip up this computer. If Hansen's been on dating sites then we need to know everything we can.'

'Well, maybe we'll find some of it at Gravity Hill. With the rest of the ghosts.'

It was twilight when they reached the bend on Loma Alta that the locals called Gravity. The gloom was settling over the San Gabriels but they could still see the road sloping away from them, down the hill to one of only two houses in sight, the other just peeking out from raised land to their right.

Salgado pulled into the side of the road and looked downhill at the house, a modest beige adobe topped by wooden panelling on the extension above. He looked much longer than he needed to.

'I've been doing some googling of my own,' he told her. 'It's said that if you sprinkle baby powder on the car's bumper before you park here, not only will you get pushed up the hill, but the powder will reveal tiny fingerprints where the kids have put their hands. Apparently, hundreds of people have reported exactly this phenomenon.'

O'Neill sighed. 'I don't doubt it. The powder would reveal prints that were already there, just the same way fingerprint powder does.'

'You know how to take the fun out of everything, don't you?'

'It's a gift.'

She watched Salgado stare at the road until impatience got the better of her. 'Oh for God's sake, just get it over with.'

'What?' Salgado protested innocence.

'I know you too well. Get the car in neutral and see what it does. I know you're desperate to try it.'

He grinned. 'We kind of have to, right?'

'*You* do. Like I said, just get on with it.'

Salgado rolled down the window. 'I want to hear if there's anything going on. The buzz of a magnetic field. The chatter of ghostly schoolkids.'

She ignored him so he slipped the shift into neutral and

released the brake. Nothing happened for a moment or two, then they began to move. Slowly. Uphill.

Salgado grinned wildly and O'Neill shook her head in despair. They rolled 'up' the hill far enough that she was able to take in the view on the other side of the fence that ran the side of the road to their left.

'Stop the car.'

'You don't think this is cool?'

'Stop the car, asshole. There's a white Nissan parked over there. It looks like a Sentra to me.'

'Shit.' Salgado stopped the fooling immediately. He slid the car into drive, made for the other side of the road and parked on the gravel shoulder. He was out of the car in seconds, vaulting over the fence despite its barbed-wire topping.

He was back just a few minutes later. 'It's Hansen's. Licence plate matches. It's locked, no obvious sign of anything suspicious. I've called it in, so we can get it opened up.'

'Well, at least we know we're in the right place. We know Garland took him from here. We just need to know where the hell he took him.'

She sighed heavily and looked down – or up – the hill again, where the beige adobe stood. 'Let's go knock on the door. They've got to be our best chance of someone having seen something.'

The door was answered on the third knock and a tall, grey-haired man in his mid-fifties opened up, a friendly crossbreed dog weaving around his knees. The man's face was tanned and weather-lined but his eyes were startlingly bright blue against the leathery skin. They both sensed an instant weariness of strangers arriving on his doorstep.

'Can I help you?'

O'Neill held up her badge and saw the look on the man's face change, brows furrowing into a crease of worry.

'Detectives O'Neill and Salgado. LAPD. We're working in the area and wanted to ask householders a few questions, Mr . . .'

'Lohmann. Tommy Lohmann. What's happened?'

'There's a car parked up the hill a way, on the other side of the fence. White Nissan. Have you seen it?'

Lohmann nodded. 'Been there for nearly a week. I've been minded to call the cops but it's not in anyone's way so I haven't. Should I have?'

'Well, it might have helped. Did you see the person who'd been driving it?'

The man made an apologetic face. 'Not really. I think I saw him but didn't pay much attention. We get so many people up here trying out the hill that it gets to be a pain in the ass pretty quickly. I did see the car he got into, though.'

Salgado and O'Neill flinched in unison.

'I was taking Madden here for a walk and saw someone walk from the direction of where the Nissan is parked and get into a cherry-red Toyota SUV. I guess I knew there was something weird about it because they didn't try to roll up the hill. The car kinda rocked for a bit then drove away again. It was only the next day I saw the Nissan but didn't give it too much thought. Sorry if I should have.'

Ethan Garland drove a cherry-red Toyota 4Runner.

'Which way did the car leave, Mr Lohmann? Up hill

or ...' Salgado tried to be clearer. 'Past your house or away from it?'

'Past my place.'

'Where would he likely be heading if he went that way?'

'Pretty much anywhere. You'd head that way to get onto Lake Avenue then south to Pasadena and from there to LA. If you knew the area and were heading to San Bernardino or Ontario maybe, you'd go the other way. LA most likely, I'd say.'

LA. Big place. Big haystack.

CHAPTER 36

'Elvis has entered the building.'

The forensic tech's cheery greeting did not meet the mood within the office on West 1st Street. Instead, he was met with stony-faced silence by the two detectives to whom he'd promised news. He'd called ahead to say he had more DNA results and they were more than anxious to hear them. His face fell at their lack of reaction.

'Should I have brought doughnuts? Is that where I've gone wrong?'

O'Neill jumped in before Salgado could, eager not to let it dissolve into anything that slowed them down.

'We're just up against the clock here, Elvis. What have you got for us?'

The crime scene tech heard the tone, businesslike and urgent, and shrugged. 'I get it. We're all on the clock on this one. Okay, I have the remaining DNA results from the body parts in Garland's cellar. And I have positive IDs on three of the four. The first is one you're expecting.'

Salgado's excitement got the better of him. 'Adrian Mercado?

Elvis nodded. 'Yes. The ear proved a match to the DNA sample you got from his father. No question it's his.'

The detectives nodded at each other, soberly. They'd been sure, but now they knew.

'Okay, good.' O'Neill spoke for them both. 'What else have you got?'

Elvis whistled out air and the nervousness of his action scared them.

'Plenty. The nose is a match to a Brad Stiepermann.'

'I know that name. Tell me why.'

'His body was found in the old Griffith Park Zoo three years ago. It was thought he'd slipped and cracked his head on a rock. Wasn't found for days.'

'And by that time the local wildlife had feasted on him. Half eaten, wasn't he?'

Elvis nodded. 'More than half, according to the report I read today. His skull was largely intact, so they were able to make the diagnosis on the fall, but much of his face had been eaten by coyote or mountain lion or whatever. No surprise then that they didn't think much of a missing nose.'

'Sweet Jesus.' Salgado shook his head. 'Was there any other DNA recovered from the scene?'

'Yep, some. From Stiepermann's clothing. As far as I can see nothing much was ever done with it because they thought it was an accidental death, but at least someone had the sense to keep it just in case. I ran it against Garland's DNA and we scored. It's a partial match, maybe not enough for court but enough to let us know it was him.'

'Son of a bitch. I say we pull him from the morgue, put some make-up on him, stick him in a suit and put the sick fuck on trial anyway.'

'Oh, we will,' O'Neill assured him. 'Just without the corpse. What else do you have, Elvis?'

'I have a match to the thumb. You ready for this? Ava Houseman.'

'No fucking way.'

'Way.'

'Ava Houseman? But her father is doing life for that. Elvis, if you're shitting me, I'll kick your ass from here to the Hollywood Bowl.'

'I'm not shitting you, man. The match is a sure thing. That thumb is from Ava Houseman, one hundred per cent. And we already knew she'd lost it.'

Ava Houseman's death had made headlines across the country. She was young, just nineteen, pretty and had made herself into a celebrity among the YouTube crowd, picking up a small fortune in endorsements and advertising. She'd been known as Sizta A to her subscribers and had added a ghost-written book deal and a fashion line to her endless collection of talents, making her the face of young American vloggers from her home in Silverlake. Until she was found dead at Angels Point in Elysian Park with both her hands cut off and her tongue severed and placed beside her head.

O'Neill puffed. 'Going to be a lot of people not very happy with us, Salgado.'

'Not yet, they ain't. Nothing to be gained by opening this can until we've found Dylan Hansen. Everything else can wait. Agreed? We keep as much of this under wraps for now as we can?'

'Agreed. We've got enough to deal with without cops and prosecutors jumping on our asses. Elvis, you with us?'

He shrugged and wrestled with it. 'Well, I got a duty to report substantive developments to the investigating detectives. And I'd say this is pretty damn substantive. But I can run some more tests. Make *absolutely* sure that I have matches on every item then maybe crosscheck them against some missing persons. That could take some time.'

'Thanks, Elvis. Appreciated.'

'It's cool. Pay me in doughnuts. Anyway, I still have Garland's other trophy to get a score on. The scalp. That's going to slow me down a bit.'

'What do you have on that?'

Elvis could only shrug apologetically. 'We got nothing. There have been nearly three hundred homicides in LA this year and this isn't a match to any of them. There were two hundred fifty-nine murders in 2018 and two hundred eighty-two the year before that. It's none of them, either. So, most likely, it's someone on the missing list or the unreported missing. Some of the missing we have familial DNA samples and some we don't. It's going to take a long time to get around them all. Meantime, there's a body out there somewhere. Finding it is down to you guys.'

Elvis left the building and O'Neill closed the door, leaving just her and Salgado to soak in the consequences of the DNA results he'd delivered.

For a couple of minutes, neither of them said a

word. They took it in turns to pace around the room, exhaling noisily and scratching at their heads. Twice, Salgado stopped as if to speak then continued his silent deliberations.

Finally, it was O'Neill who spoke first. Although only just.

'Okay,' she breathed out hard. 'We are going to have to speak to Marianne Ziegler again.'

CHAPTER 37

Igloo. Messages. Vikki, 32.

> Hi Ryan, how's you tonight?
> *Delivered, 21.34*
> *Read, 21.38*

Hey Vikki. I'm good thanks. All the better for
hearing from you. How are you?

> Great ta. Good to see you online.

You too. How was the rest of your day?

> Good ta. I wasn't working so all was good.
> Nice to have the day to myself for a change.

You need lots of change in a bank
though, right?

> PMSL. Idiot. How many bank jokes have you
> got up your sleeve because I think I've heard
> them all lol

Credit where credit is due, it wasn't that bad.

Groan!!! So are you glad not to be in school?

Yes and no. I love my job. Especially when they actually learn stuff.

Nice. Must be so rewarding when they do.

It really is. I joke about it but truth is that's why I do it. It feels like you're really making a difference and the kids are better off for it.

You're such a nice guy. What is it the Americans say? Thank you for your service!

Ha. Well thanks for your thanks. You ever want kids of your own one day, Vikki?

Maybe ... You?

Yeah, definitely. With the right person and all that. Not that I'm pushing for that, don't get me wrong. We'd need to start with a coffee first lol

Are you suggesting a date Mr Schoolteacher?

I might be. What if I did?

You took me a bit by surprise. We've only chatted a couple of times. I'm not saying no, but ...

Sorry. Didn't mean to pressure you. I've just really enjoyed chatting to you and ... well ... I think you're gorgeous and really easy to talk to.

Thanks. You're pretty nice yourself. Very nice,
in fact. It's just, you know, I said. I'm wary on
here. You understand?

Of course I do. And you're quite right. You need
to keep yourself safe. But at the same time,
life's short. I know that better than most people
and I think we should grab every chance at
happiness that we can.

Well, that's true. Can I ask, what happened?
You say you know better than most
people that life's short. Don't tell me if you
don't want to.

Oh it's okay. I don't tell most people but I feel
I can talk to you. My mother died when I was
eight. She killed herself.

Oh my God. That's terrible. I'm so sorry.

It's okay. I mean, it's not okay obviously but
it was a while ago now. And thanks. You just
have to get on with life. That's why I say don't
wait, do the things you want while you can. You
never know what's around the corner.

It must have been awful. I hope you had
people looking after you.

My aunt and uncle took me in. I had all sorts,
psychologists and social workers. I saw her do
it, you see.

You saw her?

Yes. She killed herself in front of me and my
little brother.

Oh my God. I'm sorry. You must hate
talking about it.

I don't really talk about it at all. You're a good
listener and I guess that makes it easier. I was
always told it was healthier to talk about it and
not keep it locked up inside. I think I've done
okay. I've got a good job that I love, feel I'm
helping the kids. All I need is a good woman
to love lol

Well I'm sure you must have your pick. You're
very handsome. Are your photos recent?

Thank you! They're from last year. Really glad
you like them. You're so pretty. I had to come
over to talk to you when I saw your profile.

I guess that's something we have in
common then lol

We have lots in common, don't you think?
Music, movies, politics, everything really.

Yes, that's true. It's amazing.

So . . . what do you think? Carpe diem. Seize
the day. You only live once and it really is far
too short.

I don't know. It's very tempting . . .

Okay, so what would your dream first date
be, Vikki? Something traditional like a coffee
or dinner and drinks, or meet somewhere
interesting, something different?

What kind of something different are
you thinking?

Somewhere romantic. Somewhere no one else
goes for a first date. Somewhere we can tell
our kids about and they'll go ahhhh lol

Steady on lol. But I like your thinking.

Good. I don't know, I haven't thought it
through. Oh, I know. Have you ever been to the
House for an Art Lover?

Is that the Charles Rennie Mackintosh place?

Yes, the one in Bellahouston Park. It's fabulous.
Have you been?

No, never.

You have to go. It's full of amazing details, both
inside the house and in the gardens. I think
you'd love it.

It does sound good.

There's . . . actually, here's an idea . . . there's
this fantastic seat on the lawn, made of a living

willow. You can't get much more romantic than
that. In Glasgow anyway.

That is pretty damn romantic I must admit.

Meet me there? If we don't like each other then
we can politely say goodbye and nothing lost.
Life is short, remember.

Um ... Um ... oh damn it, okay! Why not. Life
is short. When?

Really? Great! How about tomorrow?

Oh God. Okay. What's the worst that
can happen?

Famous last words lol

CHAPTER 38

Marianne Ziegler looked neither particularly surprised nor pleased to see O'Neill. She also looked like she probably hadn't slept much since the ghost of Ethan Garland revisited her. Her long auburn hair hung loose, tousled and limp, while dark circles patched her green eyes.

'Detective O'Neill. No partner with you this time?'

'Detective Salgado is back in the city. We had to split up to cover everything we needed to do. May I come in, Marianne? There's some questions I'd like to ask you.'

Garland's ex-wife nodded wearily, as if incapable of summoning the energy to argue otherwise. She led O'Neill into the small front room, the crowded temple to a hippie nirvana, and offered her a seat. The same calico cat slept in the same armchair and, rather than move it, Ziegler took a spot on the floor, her legs pulled under her. O'Neill sat on the two-seater sofa under the broad blue and cream mandala that dominated the room.

'How have you been, Marianne? I'm afraid we delivered a bit of a bombshell the last time we were here.'

She looked up, surprised, and O'Neill saw the question

run through her head before she worked out the obvious answer.

'I've been okay. I guess it's been playing on my mind. What you and your partner said about Ethan. About what he might have done. You *do* think he's killed someone, don't you?'

The correct answer was that she couldn't comment. Or some well-practised play about procedure and process and an ongoing investigation. She looked at Marianne Ziegler's tired eyes and decided to take a different path.

'Yes. Yes, we do. We may be wrong, and we still have a lot of work to do, but we think it's likely that your ex-husband was directly involved in one or more homicides that we are currently investigating.'

'*One or more?*'

'Yes.'

'My God. How ... how many?'

'I really don't know. I couldn't tell you if I did but I genuinely don't know. We have a lot we still need to learn. And we need your help.'

Ziegler sat open-mouthed, tears not far away. For the first time, O'Neill noticed red scratch marks at her wrist and saw her reach for them again, left on right and right on left.

'Anything. I'll do anything I can. What do you need to know?'

'We asked you before about the place that Ethan might have spoken about near Barstow and you told us about the waterpark he used to visit as a child – Lake Dolores.'

'That was it. I knew it was a woman's name.'

'Right. That was a big help, Marianne. Really, it was. I'd like to ask you about some other places that Ethan might have had an attachment to. Do you think you might be able to pick some out if I ran them by you?'

'I guess. Maybe. He was more of a talker in our early years together. Maybe some of that will have stuck with me. Are you going to tell me what these places are, why you're asking about them?'

'I'm sorry, but no. I will when I can, I promise you.'

Marianne blew out a long, slow song of air. 'Okay. Okay. That's um, okay. Try me.'

'Thank you. How about the Vista Theater on Sunset? Do you remember Ethan ever mentioning it?'

'The Vista? Sure. We went there together quite a lot. It was his favourite movie theatre in the city. He liked a couple of others, the Orpheum on South Broadway and sometimes the Aero in Santa Monica but the Vista was easily the number one choice. He hated the new cinemas, like the ArcLights. He'd much rather have watched an old movie in an old theatre than anything new in a new one.'

O'Neill felt her pulse quicken but told herself not to get ahead. It was one place.

'That helps, Marianne. Thank you. What about the former Griffith Park Zoo? Was that somewhere that Ethan might have known well?'

Marianne's eyes narrowed in confusion. 'Yes. How do you know this?'

'I don't. We're guessing a bit. But is it right? Was the old zoo somewhere that meant something to Ethan?'

'Yes. Quite a lot. I really don't understand what's

going on here. I don't mind telling you I'm scared. This is overwhelming.'

'I'm sure it is. And I don't blame you for being scared. It's a lot for you to take in. Tell me about the zoo. Please.'

The woman's eyes were red now, but she nodded acceptance.

'Ethan said the last memory he had of both his parents together was at the old zoo. It was just before they broke up and just before the zoo closed down. I think in his head, the two things were somehow linked. Like the ends of two eras. When he was older, in his teens and even once we were married, he'd hike up to the park and wander around there for hours.'

'Did you ever go with him?'

'Once. I really didn't like it. It's such a creepy place. The old enclosures and cages are still intact and it's like a ghost town, except for animals. He knew I didn't like it and he got angry, as if I wasn't sharing in his thing. But it was weird how he liked the place and that freaked me out a bit too. We never went again but he'd go up there when he wanted to get away from things. Including me.'

'Did he ever go there with anyone else? Maybe show people around the zoo?'

Marianne shrugged. 'I think maybe, yes. *Yes, he did*. I didn't pay much attention but one time I do remember him telling me how much someone had liked the place. I've no idea now who it was. I just remember him telling me as if pointing out that I'd been wrong. That was very Ethan.'

'What about Angels Point?'

'Where?'

The very question punctured O'Neill's growing confidence that they were on to something.

'Angels Point. It's a lookout point in Elysian Park.'

Another shrug. 'I'm sorry. No. I don't think I've ever heard of it. Should I have?'

'Perhaps not. It's on a hiking trail. Was hiking a big thing for Ethan?'

'Not really. The zoo was the only place I can remember him hiking to. I'm sorry, Detective. It might have been a place he went to, but I don't remember him ever mentioning it.'

'It's a public art installation,' she persevered. 'A platform on the edge of the point? It directly overlooks Dodger Stadium.'

'The Dodgers? Well, yes, in that case I wouldn't be at all surprised. He was crazy about the Dodgers. Had been since he was a kid. A real ball team in a real ballpark, that's what he always said. These new franchises and new stadiums, he'd get all angry and say how they weren't real, just corporate America and all about the money. It didn't matter to Ethan that the Dodgers had been ripped out of Brooklyn. They were in LA when he was born and that was all that mattered.

It wasn't Angels Point at all, O'Neill realised. It was the stadium.

'So, Ethan wasn't a fan of change in the city?'

'He wasn't much of a fan of change, period. He always got very uncomfortable with it and would complain that there was no need for change, that things were better as they'd been. He used to say that Los Angeles was the centre of the world in the fifties and sixties, that it was the place that no one was from but where everyone wanted to be. But then LA kept reinventing itself, kept trying to become the thing it dreamed of without ever knowing what that was.'

'Who did he blame for that?'

'Apart from me? He blamed the chasers, that's what he called them. The people who came out here and just added another car to the road, the ones who chased a dream with minimal chance of catching it. He blamed anyone who came after he did, anyone who changed things, built anything new or said anything new or did anything new. And that's Los Angeles. It's built on being different to what it was yesterday. Ethan used to say he loved LA, but the truth was he hated it and just didn't know it. He loved something that wasn't here anymore.'

O'Neill nodded sombrely, sure the women's hostility and her answers were coming from the heart. But she wanted to be sure.

'Can I ask you about another place, Marianne? El Coyote, the Mexican restaurant on Beverly Boulevard. Was that somewhere that Ethan might have had a connection to?'

Marianne looked doubtful then apologetic. 'Well, I'm sure it's the kind of place Ethan would have approved of, being around as long as it has, but I can't say I remember him ever talking about it as if it held any special significance for him. I'm really sorry, Detective. I wish I could say differently. I'm not sure I remember him even mentioning the place.'

'That's fine, Marianne. Don't worry about it at all. It doesn't matter.'

It didn't matter at all and O'Neill felt a stab of guilt at having tried to trick the woman, but she couldn't take the chance that Marianne was simply saying yes to everything in the hope that it was what she wanted to hear.

'Okay, let me try one more. There's a hill in Altadena that the locals call Gravity Hill. Does that name mean anything to you?'

'Oh God, yes. That's the place where if you put your car in neutral on the slope it seems to roll up the hill when it's actually going down, right? It's some trick of the landscape. That's what Ethan told me. His dad took him up there in his Chrysler Valiant and pulled the trick on him. Ethan said it blew his mind, especially when his dad told him the stories about it being the ghosts of schoolkids that pushed them back up the hill. Ethan loved that, being how he was. His dad took him a bunch of times before Ethan finally figured out that it was something else at play. I had a young cousin visit from Missouri once, I think Tom was about twelve at the time, and Ethan drove him out to Altadena and showed him Gravity Hill. I thought that was a nice thing for him to do, although I wasn't happy with him filling Tom's head with the old stories of dead kids and told him so. He blew up at me, of course, raged at me for days, and told me I didn't understand kids or anything else.'

Another box was ticked, and O'Neill made it a full set. Five locations that they knew of, four dump sites and a kidnap point, and all five were places that Garland had some sentimental attachment to from his youth.

Was there a sixth place? Yes, she'd no doubt that there was. The trick was going to be finding it. For that, they were going to need all the help that Marianne Ziegler could give them.

'Marianne, you've been really helpful but I'm going to have to ask you for more. I need you to come back to the city with me tonight. Will you do that? We'll put you up somewhere near headquarters, make you comfortable, and talk to you a lot. Okay?'

She nodded, resigned to whatever it would take.

'Thanks, Marianne. I wouldn't ask if it wasn't so important. Let me ask you one more thing before we go. You said earlier how Ethan was such a big fan of the Dodgers. That he had been since he was a kid. But how did that happen? Did he ever say?'

'It was his dad. His old man used to take him when he was a kid.'

His dad. Always his dad.

CHAPTER 39

Why are you talking to me, Matthew?

What do you mean?

You must know that chatting to me is going to
get you caught.

It took a while to get an answer even though the screen showed he was writing. She guessed words being written, deleted and rewritten.

Maybe I want to get caught.

It took Narey by surprise and she turned to look at Dakers for confirmation. He pursed his lips and nodded. *Could be*. She pushed back in her chair and swore quietly before returning to the keyboard.

Well, Matthew, if you want to get caught, I can help
you with that.

No answer. She tried again.

> Why do you think you want to be caught?

**I don't. It was just a thought. I wonder why I
do things sometimes.**

Dakers leaned forward in his seat and Narey knew he was
interested.

> You feel guilty?

No.

> Never?

**Sometimes, yes. I don't know. I don't always
know what guilt feels like. Not the way I think
other people do.**

> Do you sometimes wish you hadn't done it?

**Sometimes. Afterwards. Not during.
Never during.**

She sensed he was open and took a chance.

> What about Eloise Gray? Did you feel bad
> about killing her after it?

I didn't say I killed her.

> Did you?

Long pause.

Yes.

The jump in Narey's chest was a cocktail. Anger. Satisfaction. Relief. Rage. She swallowed them down and typed.

Prove it to me. Where did you kill her?

Not the Highland Fling. Is that enough for you to know?

It was enough to know it was him, but it just begged more questions.

Tell me about Eloise. Why was she chosen?

She was careless. Made it easy. She left all this information about herself just lying around for anyone to see. He saw her on a dating site we both liked to trawl through. She seemed a likely candidate.

And what does that mean? A likely candidate.

There's something we can see. A vulnerability, a need that can be exploited. Someone too trusting, too needy. It's instinctive, maybe.

The smugness of the reply sickened her. Like he was claiming he had a superpower.

When Ethan saw that in her, he went looking
for her elsewhere and found her. He looked
at her Facebook page, her Twitter account,
her Snapchat and Instagram. Her whole life
laid out for the world to see. He took what he
needed and made use of it.

So, she could have been anyone?

His response took a while. They thought he might be
editing, but he was writing chapter and verse.

Anyone who made it that easy, yes. These people
forget that they are in a shop window. The whole
world is pressing their noses up against the
glass, but they never notice. They talk about
themselves as if no one else is listening. We're all
listening.

She could hear both his craziness and the sense in what
he said. But she still wanted to believe there was more to
it. That there was a reason, however illogical, however
fucked up.

But why Eloise?

We are predators. Predators take victims.
Eloise was a victim.

You utter piece of shit, she thought.

Do you want to know how she was
when she died?

                                       No.

She cried a lot. That was quite annoying.
I don't like that much. She cried, and she
whimpered, and she begged. Begging I
don't mind. I actually like it when they beg,
but the crying becomes a pain.

        I don't want to hear it. Where did you kill her?

I have a place I use. You'll never find it.

She wanted to kill him. She wanted to rip his throat out.
She wanted to tie him up, cut him till he bled to death.

              Did you touch her? Sexually, I mean.

No. That's not what I do.

                    So, it's not sexual for you at all?

Pause.

Yes, it is. Probably. But I don't touch them.
I just get what I get from it without doing
that. Sometimes, later, I think about it. When
I'm alone.

The image that conjured up made her skin crawl.

You don't get it, do you, Inspector? You don't understand someone like me. Don't understand someone like Ethan.

I don't have to understand you. I don't want to. And what do you think that is, 'someone like you'? You keep saying it.

A long pause. Words written and rewritten.

I'm someone you're never going to catch.

CHAPTER 40

Mike Durrant was a heavyset man of around seventy, broad shoulders and stomach hanging over his belt. His reddish beard had outlasted the hair on his head and the lines round his eyes suggested a man that laughed a lot. But not today.

When he saw Marianne Ziegler for the first time since her wedding day, he smiled warmly and took a step forward, then stopped as if unsure whether to proceed. Marianne stood and moved towards him, both offering then withdrawing a handshake, before transitioning into an awkward hug.

'It's been a long time, Marianne. You're looking good.'

'It sure has. Thanks, Mike. And you too. You haven't changed at all.'

He smiled kindly. 'Well, we both know that's not true but let's pretend it is. Are you doing okay?'

She hesitated, trying to work out if she was or not.

'Yeah. I think I am. It's been a lot to take in at once.'

It was Durrant's turn to pause. 'So, you know what's

going on? Because I sure as hell don't. I know it's got some-thing to do with Ethan, but no one's told me shit.'

Marianne turned to look helplessly at the two detec-tives. It couldn't and wouldn't be her who told him. O'Neill nodded, she'd deal with it.

'Mr Durrant, why don't you take a seat?'

'Am I going to need one?'

'Please. Just sit and we'll talk.'

And they did. And Durrant listened, often with his mouth hanging open. He leaned forward in his chair, scratched at his beard and his thinning hair, and turned to look at Marianne for confirmation. All sure signs of growing confusion and nervousness.

Through it all, he didn't say a word, letting his body language do the talking for him, until Salgado explained the reason for their urgency. The kidnap victim. The ticking clock.

'Shit.'

By now he was pale, wide-eyed and shaking. When Salgado asked if he was ready to talk and help them with anything he knew, he nodded numbly.

They started him off by going over some of the ground Durrant had already covered with the Carson City sher-iff, easing him into it. The family holidays, the tension between his father and his uncle, Ethan's relationship with his mother.

'Mike, when you met him that last time in LA, you say Ethan told you he was busy with a new partnership. Did he tell you anything else about what that partnership was all about?'

'Nope. I got the feeling he regretted even mentioning it.'

'What about you, Marianne? Would you know what he might have been talking about?'

Ziegler shook her head. 'I guess it could have been a business thing, but I don't remember anything. And I guess it could have been another woman, but I seriously doubt it.'

They doubted it too. It was Marr. It had to be.

'Mike, you told the Carson City sheriff that Ethan blamed his mom. Was that always how he talked about her?'

Durrant looked uncomfortable but nodded. 'Look, it's not an easy thing to say.' He paused and looked at Marianne. 'Or an easy thing to hear, I guess, but Ethan hated his mother. Maybe not initially but definitely as he got older, after his father left. He blamed her for Zac leaving. He blamed her for everything, including killing herself. You probably don't want to hear this, Marianne, but Ethan used to call his mother a whore. It was the word he used most often about her and, for my money, it came straight out of his father's mouth.'

Marianne nodded, sadly. 'Ethan didn't talk about his mother a lot. But when he did ... let's just say there was a ton of suppressed animosity. Sometimes not so suppressed. If he was lashing out at me then I'd get compared to her. And it wasn't pretty. Believe me, I've heard the word *whore* before.'

'Yep,' Durrant agreed. 'It was always Uncle Zac with him. Always his dad rather than his mom. The two of them were thick as thieves. They'd go on these long walks and I think Zac just talked and talked, filled Ethan's head with whatever he wanted to. If Zac said the moon was made of cheese, then Ethan would ask for a giant pack of crackers. He hated Aunt Veronica because Zac told him to.'

'He's right,' Marianne said sorrowfully. 'Ethan had memories of his father hitting his mother, slapping her around, throwing cups of hot coffee over her, verbally abusing her and constantly running her down. But all of those acts were, in Ethan's mind, the result of his mother bringing it on herself. She'd hector his father, always be on his case when he'd only been out working hard, trying to do his best for his family. That's how his dad had explained it to Ethan. No action without a reaction, that's what his father always told him. If she acted, she had to expect him to react.

'Mike's right. Ethan idolised his dad. Probably in the way that you can when the object of the worship disappears before his faults can be revealed.'

'He died in a small city outside Lansing, right?'

'Yes, when Ethan was twelve. It was all very mysterious, it seems. I don't know what Mike knows about it but Ethan's dad was supposedly found after being run over by a garbage truck while lying in the road.'

'Supposedly?' O'Neill picked up on it immediately. 'I read the report. That's what it said.'

Marianne sighed. 'There were seemingly strong hints that he was already dead when the vehicle hit him.'

'How did Ethan react to the news?' Salgado leaned closer as he asked the question.

'I think it devastated him. He rarely talked about it but if it ever came up, he'd go very dark and disappear inside himself for days. Even though his dad left, and he hadn't seen him for a few years, the impression I got was that his death floored Ethan and changed him.'

'For the worse?'

'I'd say so, wouldn't you?'

They went on and on, digging deeper into Ethan Garland's life, getting dirtier and grubbier. And getting maybe half a heartbeat closer to finding the young man that was chained somewhere in the city and dying of thirst.

CHAPTER 41

The time of day had ceased to matter. There was no start or finish, no shift pattern, no clocking on or off in either Los Angeles or Glasgow. Time difference made no difference.

It was ten at night in LA and six in the morning in Scotland. One in darkness, the other in daylight, both at work.

The folder on the six released patients from Carstairs made grim reading. There was nothing hugely off the scale in terms of what the men had done – they wouldn't have been put back on the streets if there had been – but it still held the power to shock.

Narey was huddled in an incident room along with Giannandrea and DC Kerri Wells, each of them taking a file at a time and making notes before comparing. Photographs of the six men were pinned to whiteboards and the detectives occasionally scribbled notes under them.

Derek Solomon was admitted to the State Hospital in 2012. He'd been arrested following a disturbance in a pub in Balornock. The then thirty-seven-year-old had got into an argument with two men over football, the city's most clichéd reason for a fight, and had bitten off one of the other men's ears. When police turned up, he hurled pint tumblers and tables at them, produced a knife and launched himself at the three coppers, stabbing two of them.

Colin McPake was referred to Carstairs by social workers and police after what was described as extreme antisocial behaviour. He had a habit of wandering around the streets near his Rutherglen home in bare feet and stripped to the waist, intimidating anyone who came across his path, including noising up the local dealers and calling them out by name. When he was taken in and referred for tests, he'd gone willingly, telling psychiatrists that he wanted to know what was happening in his head.

John Paul Kepple was a thirty-two-year-old electrician who walked into a Catholic church in Bishopbriggs north of Glasgow in 2005 and demanded to speak to the priest, threatening to burn the church to the ground if the priest didn't come. When Father Thomas Kiernan entered the chapel, along with two police officers, they found Kepple sitting surrounded by debris – smashed pews, broken chairs, a hacked-down pulpit, torn curtains, relics torn from the walls – and the caretaker lying face down next to him. Kepple gave himself up to the officers without saying a word, just glaring at Father Kiernan as he was led away.

Fraser Anderson was an IT consultant in the summer of 2012, a man with a flourishing career, a wife and young family. His life seemed perfect until he learned his wife Erin was having an affair with his best friend. Anderson went to the home of his friend Alastair Drummond and beat him with a baseball bat until he knocked him out. He then held Drummond hostage for eighteen hours, waking him up, hitting him again, over and over. Police were finally alerted by neighbours, who heard Drummond's moans. It transpired that his belief of Drummond's infidelity with his wife was completely delusional.

When the social work department denied him access to his children on his release two years later, Anderson orchestrated a service attack against the city council's computer system, forcing it to crash on several occasions and earning him another year inside as he completed his sentence.

Martin Geir killed cats. Dozens of them. After a year-long killing spree which captured the attention of the press, Geir was finally caught on CCTV in 2006, crushing the skull of a ginger tabby with a brick. He admitted the other killings, many of which he couldn't deny after the remains of ten cats were found buried in the garden of his Bridgeton home.

He'd poisoned some, trapped and strangled others. He never tried to justify it other than by saying that a cat had been shitting on his lawn and he was getting his own back. He'd been unable to identify the culprit so killed every cat he could find. He was ordered to serve at least part of his eighteen-month sentence at the State Hospital.

Ian Bryce had been an accountant working for Glasgow City Council. His colleagues had always identified him as a loose cannon and there had been several complaints about his workplace behaviour. In March 2011, the thirty-three-year-old got into an argument with his line manager about signing off a head of department's expenses. It started out as something routine and within minutes escalated into Bryce smashing every computer screen in the room, assaulting five people and holding two others hostage using a taser he'd bought online and hidden under his desk.

He was admitted to the State Hospital and stayed there for three months before responding well enough to treatment that he was released, initially on parole. He was last known to be working for a charity in the city centre delivering meals to the elderly.

'So, who do you like best?' Kerri Wells asked, a mischievous grin on her face.

Narey and Giannandrea knew it was a facetious question, but it was as good an opening gambit as any. Rico went first.

'Kepple. the guy who tore up the church. There's something more than sinister about what he did, and how he did it. There was a coldness, a restraint before the destruction that chimes with me for Marr.'

'I like the accountant,' Wells pitched in. 'The guy knew he was going to explode and bought a fucking taser. Smart enough to prepare, crazy enough to actually do it. He gets my vote.'

Narey nodded, seeing arguments for both. 'We've no grounds to pull them but let's pay them a visit and ask some questions.'

'What about you, boss?'

'I'm not a big fan of guessing. But maybe Anderson,

the IT consultant. Delusional but functioning. Obviously intelligent. Capable of extreme violence. The service attack on the council's computers suggests a tendency for risk and a public display of power.'

Giannandrea smiled. 'You've been spending too much time with Lennie Dakers, boss.'

'Tell me about it.'

'So, should we put our money where our mouths are?' Wells grinned. 'A test of intuition. A tenner a head?'

Narey gave her a disapproving frown but the DC was irrepressible. 'Come on, boss. Just a bit of fun and no one else need ever know. God knows we need something to lighten the mood.'

'Oh, go on then. But obviously if anyone senior hears of this then we all deny it completely. And if they can somehow prove it happened then I throw you two under a bus and keep the money anyway.'

'Goes without saying, boss.'

'Okay, okay. Let's get moving and find these guys this morning.'

CHAPTER 42

Salgado had left O'Neill with Ziegler and Durrant while he awaited the imminent arrival of Howie Kelsey. The detective had phoned ahead saying he had some information on the lead they'd given him into the Black Dahlia case.

Salgado was staring out over 1st Street, allowing himself a moment to take in the lights on the towering white walls of City Hall. Dylan Hansen was out there somewhere, one of four million, but the one that needed their help.

From behind him, he heard footsteps and knew it was Kelsey.

'You want coffee?'

Salgado turned around in time to see Kelsey make a face. 'You got LAPD coffee, or your own supply?'

'Government issue.'

'In that case, I'll pass. You got a line on your guy yet?'

Salgado sighed heavily. 'No. We're closer to understanding the guy that took him and that might get us somewhere, but right now, we have no idea where he is. But you've got something on the Dahlia case?'

'Well . . . let's see.'

Salgado caught something in the way Kelsey said it and the hairs on the back of his neck bristled.

'Okay, so there's about six thousand pieces of paper in the Elizabeth Short file. Most of it was collated following the murder but it's added to every time some nut comes forward with a theory or a confession or, occasionally, when something new turns up.'

'Like Garland owning the purse.'

'Like the purse. Maybe. The point is that there's a lot of it and I've been wading through the swamp trying to catch a break on this line through the Frankie Wynn character to Delmonico's to Ralph Asdel's report and to the Dahlia.'

'And you got something?'

'Yeah. Maybe. You tell me.'

'Go on.'

'So, I wanted to find some other mention of Frankie Wynn or of the restaurant. Sure, it might have gone nowhere but your guy that died seems to have owned some very genuine shit so why should the Dahlia purse be any different, right? So, I set out to trace back the enquiry that was made into Wynn's confession. Two detectives, Jack Mortimer and Artie Crouch, took a statement and followed through on it. Like I said, they went to Delmonico's, where Wynn said he worked, and the manager said no one of that name worked there or had ever worked there. So, I figured that if there was no Frankie Wynn then Mortimer or Crouch might have at least taken a note of people who *did* work there so they could rule this guy out.'

'And they did?' Salgado could hear the excitement in his own voice.

'They did. It took a lot of searching but I found it.'

He reached into his bag and produced a sheet of paper in an evidence bag, holding it out so Salgado could read the typed names. There were around twenty of them.

Giulio Argento, manager. Vincenzo Pacitto, assistant manager. Angelo Dionisi, mastro di cantina. Gianluca Ricci, head chef. Marco Manfredi, chef. Domenico Sciarra, waiter. Anthony Giordano, waiter. Serena Sciarra, waitress. Viola Facci, waitress. Chiara Tassinari, waitress. Louis Smith, waiter. Katherine Joyce, dishwasher. Francesca Domenici, dishwasher.

Salgado looked up from the list, seeing Kelsey looking at him expectantly. After the managers and waiters, after the waitresses and the dishwashers, there were listed three busboys.

'No fucking way.'

It was like all the clocks had stopped. Salgado needed confirmation that the world was still spinning.

Zachary Garland, busboy.

'Now,' Kelsey continued. 'Obviously, I know that your dead guy who owned the purse was named Garland. Seemed too neat to be a coincidence. And I'm guessing by the way that you have stopped breathing that it ain't.'

'It ain't,' Salgado echoed. 'Zachary Garland was our guy's father.'

When Kelsey left the office, Salgado spent some time trying to make sense of it before deciding that he couldn't. Not on his own, at least.

'Cally? You got Mike Durrant with you still? He said before how Zac Garland used aliases when he was chasing women. Ask him if he knew or remembers any of them.'

'What's this about, Salgado?'

'I'll fill you in after you've asked Durrant.'

The wait was less than a minute but seemed much longer. O'Neill's voice betrayed her surprise.

'Salgado? He remembers one name, says his dad used it to wind his uncle up. Says his old man used it in front of Zac's wife as he knew Zac couldn't call him on it.'

'The name?'

'You ready for this?'

'I think I might be.'

'Frankie Wynn. Frankie fucking Wynn.'

CHAPTER 43

The report on Bruce Devlin, the first of Brianna Holden's ex-boyfriends, was quick but largely unhelpful.

Kayleigh McGrath had been right about him joining the army. Devlin had done a tour of Helmand province in 2009 but was out and back in civvies by early 2010. The reasons were unclear but the suggestion was there had been mental health issues and a compromise had been made to get him out as quickly as possible.

He'd come back to Glasgow but, perhaps because of lasting damage from his time in Afghanistan, he couldn't get a job and ended up homeless. He got support from Glasgow's Helping Heroes, the serviceman's support organisation in Govan Cross, and they were helping him for a while before he simply stopped coming back. They looked for him, but he was nowhere to be found. They were worried about him, describing Devlin as 'extremely volatile'.

Wells got a surname for the French guy who Brianna had dated, Martin, and who'd had a fight with Kevin Monteith in Sweeney's pub on Pollokshaws Road. The incident log had him named as Martin Grenier. Neither of the men were charged, not even with good old breach of the peace, but they were both barred from the premises.

Grenier had been a student, studying English literature at Glasgow University and working part-time in a restaurant on St Vincent Street. He'd left Scotland for Lyons in 2016 and a check with authorities there confirmed he was employed as a teacher and hadn't left France in over a year.

Lee Fairley lived in a tenement in Newlands on the south side and a warrant card got Narey and Wells inside the door. The front room had barely a square foot of carpet to be seen under a sea of papers, books, shoes, cushions and dirty plates. A man living alone.

'I work from home.' He waved his arm aggressively across the room as if somehow explaining the carnage. 'What's this all about?'

'We're trying to locate a man named Matthew Marr. We thought you might be able to help us find him.'

Fairley shoved his bottom lip forward. 'Never heard of him. What makes you think I might know who he is or where he is?'

'He used to date Brianna Holden. We're talking to other people that she dated in an effort to find him.'

Fairley's eyes widened, and his lip curled in distaste. 'I wouldn't know anyone she dated. And I wouldn't want to. I've done my best to forget Brianna Holden and everything that went with her.'

'You were pretty angry back then though, weren't you? Called her every name under the sun and said you hoped she walked in front of a bus. That's what we've been told.'

The man flushed again. 'I was angry, but I wouldn't wish anyone any harm. I'm not like that.'

Wells made a show of producing her notebook. 'Your record says that you *are* like that. Two convictions for assault. It seems you've got a bad temper, Mr Fairley.'

Fairley said nothing but glared at Wells.

Wells raised her eyebrows sceptically, raising Fairley's blood pressure along with them.

'You're still working in IT?' Narey nodded at the desk and the oversized computer that took pride of place on it. 'What if I got a search warrant and came back to have tech support look through that computer?'

Fairley shrugged, his face sour. 'Well, first I'd wonder on what grounds you possibly got a warrant. Second, you'd be wasting your time. I'm a computer programmer. If I wanted to hide something on there, you'd never find it. Third? If you want to look at it, feel free. I've got nothing to hide.'

Narey nodded. 'I'm curious, Mr Fairley – not once since we've been in here have you mentioned that Brianna was murdered. But you undoubtedly know that she was. Not once have you asked if we're looking for Matthew Marr in connection with that murder.'

Fairley's temper had been boiling and now it burst.

'Get the fuck out of here. If you want to come back and talk to me then bring a warrant. Get out of my flat. Now.'

Narey was back in her car, Wells beside her, when her mobile rang. The screen showed the caller to be Kayleigh McGrath.

'Inspector, you said I should call if I remembered anything else. Or anyone else. It's about the guy whose name I couldn't remember. The one that Bri got off with one Saturday night when she was going out with Bruce Devlin? Well, his name was Andy. It came to me when I was watching the telly. There was some guy in the programme I was watching called Andy and . . . well, I just knew.'

'I don't suppose you remember a surname?'

'No, sorry. I don't think I ever knew it. I know that sounds terrible. He was older than her, I remember that much. She'd been out with pals in the Social, and was a bit pissed. I don't think she'd have gone for him otherwise, not from what she told me. She saw him two or three times after that but he wasn't her type, so she told him and finished it. She wasn't really dumping him though, as they were never really going out, if you know what I mean. Anyway, a month or so after that, she started going out with Graeme Holden and they got married about a year later. Out of the frying pan, into the fucking fire.'

Narey's head was spinning. It bothered her that their only solid leads on Marr's identity were the result of hunches and assumptions. She liked to think that both were based on solid reasoning but knew full well that both could be entirely wrong.

She thought of how Lennie Dakers had separated everything Marr had told them into three lists. *Truths.* *Deceptions.* *Question marks.* She wasn't sure they'd placed them properly, and could now see nothing but question mark after question mark.

CHAPTER 44

'So, Mike, I know you've told my partner this, but I'd like to hear it too. This fake name that your Uncle Zac would use . . .'

Mike Durrant looked tired and not a little beaten by it all. But he was still in his chair, still talking.

'Whatever you guys need. So, the name thing was like a standing joke with my dad. It was his way of getting at Zac. I guess he heard the name on the grapevine maybe, and he'd use it when Aunt Veronica was there, just to wind Zac up.'

'And the name was . . .?'

'Like I said, Frankie Wynn. My old man used to get steamed up and say "Hey, how's Frankie Wynn doing these days? Have you seen Frankie Wynn recently?". Uncle Zac would give him the stare and I'd get worried they'd fight. It would obviously make Zac mad, but he couldn't say anything when Veronica was there.'

'Okay, okay.' Salgado paced the room, dragging his hand through his hair as he thought. O'Neill let him run the play, knowing he was running on instinct and that was when he worked best. He stopped in front of Durrant and pushed him further.

'Tell us a bit about Zac Garland. You've said your father didn't think much of him.'

Durrant laughed bitterly. 'That's an understatement. My old man always said that Uncle Zac was a snake. That was the word he used. Said he'd never have left my mom alone with him if she wasn't his sister. He'd say that Zac thought he was a lady's man but that the ladies didn't always have a say in it. Once, when he was drunk, he told me how as well as using aliases, Uncle Zac used to make up glamorous jobs and tell all sorts of lies, anything to get what he wanted.'

'What kind of jobs?'

'Oh, he used to tell them he worked in the movies back in the day. That he used to date starlets. That he'd killed someone once. Dad said it was all bullshit. You see, sometimes Uncle Zac was a drinker, sometimes he was a drunk. Not one of those happy drunk uncles that ruffle your hair and give you ten bucks. He was a mean drunk. He'd go hard at my dad, he'd bitch about Aunt Veronica, he'd boast about all kinds of shit and talk in riddles. He scared people.'

Salgado processed the information and O'Neill could see his brain was in overdrive. 'So, Zac claimed he'd killed someone?'

Durrant made a face. 'All bullshit. He'd have said he'd fixed the World Series if he thought someone would have believed it.'

'Okay, okay. I know this will be a tester, Mike, but I

don't suppose you can remember what kind of car Zac Garland drove? Maybe back when you were a kid. Or even before that, if you can remember your mom or dad ever mentioning it.'

Durrant's eyebrows knitted tightly. '*What kind of car?* Man, you're talking a long time ago. I can barely remember what I drove ten years ago.'

'Maybe something old,' Salgado was wary of leading him to it. 'A classic car maybe?'

A light went on in the older man's memory and a smile spread over his face.

'A sedan. Zac had this ancient sedan in the garage – it wasn't his everyday car. Like something out of the *Keystone Cops* or *Bonnie and Clyde*. He always said how it was a classic and the kids shouldn't climb on it. Zac said it was worth a lot of money, but my dad said it was a heap of junk.'

O'Neill and Salgado swapped animated glances. Durrant saw it and was confused.

'What is it? How can Uncle Zac's old car mean anything?'

Salgado ignored the question and posed his own. 'I know it was a long time ago, Mike, but can you remember how old that sedan was? Maybe the year?'

The man shrugged. 'I was just a kid, but from what I remember of the shape, it must have easily been thirty years old even then – 1930s for sure.'

'You remember anything else about it?'

'Christ, I haven't thought of that old car in years. It had a dark paint job as I remember. It had once been some light colour, can't remember what, but Zac said he had had it painted black.'

The air was sucked out of the room. O'Neill managed to keep her features steady, but Salgado turned away and she heard him swear quietly under his breath. He turned, his face straightened again but clearly agitated.

'That's really helpful, Mike. Let me try you with something else. Was there anywhere in town that you remember Zac Garland staying when he wasn't at home? I'm thinking maybe a hotel or a motel. Somewhere your folks might have mentioned.'

When Durrant shrugged and apologised, he pushed it further.

'I'm going to suggest a few places to you. I'd rather not, but we're going back a long way. Please think before you answer. Remember – *all* the places I mention might be relevant, or none of them. Okay?'

'Okay.'

Salgado did his best to keep his voice neutral, not to favour one name over the other. He kept it slow and rhythmic.

'The Lincoln Park Motel. The Aster Motel. The Harrington Motel. The Mayflower Motel. Any of those mean anything to you?'

Durrant began to speak immediately but Salgado shushed him. 'Take your time.'

The man nodded, but after a few moment's thought he spoke up. 'Same answer. It's the Aster. Whenever Zac got kicked out or when he later came back to town to see Ethan, he stayed at the Aster Motel. I remember my dad talking about it. It was a *thing*. He'd say something like "Zac's at the Aster. That's trouble for someone." Definitely the Aster.'

O'Neill saw Salgado's jaw drop momentarily before tightening into a grimace.

'Okay, I think we should take a break, Mike. It's been a lot to handle and you're probably needing a coffee, right?'

'I'm okay,' Durrant sounded confused. 'I can carry on.'

Salgado smiled but O'Neill saw it was fake. 'Well, I need a coffee even if you don't. Let's break for a while. We'll pick it up again in thirty minutes.'

When there was a closed door between them and Garland's cousin, O'Neill turned to Salgado and demanded answers.

'You wanted a break because you need a coffee? Now, why am I not buying that?'

He sighed and eased himself slowly into a chair. 'Maybe because what I really need is a large shot of Jack Daniel's.'

'So, what was all that about the Aster? I know it was the answer you wanted. I just don't know why.'

Salgado hesitated and that freaked her slightly.

'What is it?' she pressed.

'The original investigation into Elizabeth Short's murder never identified a locus for the killing. There were a few suggested sites but one that comes up most often is a motel.'

'Oh fuck. You're shitting me.'

'Nope. The Aster Motel on South Flower Street, just outside of downtown. The owners of the Aster admitted that on the day Beth Short was murdered, one of their rooms – cabin 3 – was found to be covered in blood and faecal matter. It was spattered over the floor, the bathroom and up the sides of the walls. They had to soak the bedsheets in a pail of water before they could send them to the laundry. Nothing was ever proven, and I haven't the first idea of what's true and what ain't, but the Aster is where a lot of people think the Black Dahlia was murdered and cut up.'

O'Neill held up a hand to stop him. 'Okay, let's just . . . what the fuck have we got here, Salgado? Ethan Garland owns a piece of murderabilia said to be the Black Dahlia's purse. His father worked at Delmonico's, where the Dahlia's shoes and purse were found. Zac Garland used the alias Frankie Wynn. The same name as a man who confessed to the killing and claimed he worked at Delmonico's. He owned a light-coloured 1930s sedan and he was known to stay at the motel where the Dahlia may have been murdered. Have I missed anything?'

'I don't think so. We're going to have to take this back to Howie Kelsey. It's his case.'

She nodded but was deep in thought. 'Yeah. Maybe. But maybe not yet. It's not still there, is it?'

'The Aster? I think so. It's pretty run-down but last I heard it was still operating.' The moment the words were out his mouth, he caught her meaning. 'Let me google it.'

He fished out his phone and punched in the name. Less than thirty seconds later, he raised his head again and stared at her.

'The Aster closed down. About a year ago. It's been locked up since then.'

CHAPTER 45

There was a black and white waiting for them on South Flower Street by the time Salgado and O'Neill got to the Aster, with a paramedic truck not far behind. The low, grubby, white-walled cabins were in the lot to their left, dimly lit by the streetlights, the Harbor Freeway still roaring overhead to their right. A gaudy sign spelled out MOTEL in alternate red and yellow block letters.

Salgado turned in past the patrol car and parked up in front of cabin 3. The word seedy could have been invented for a place like this. The cheap alternative used by travellers on the thinnest of dimes or someone not caring what the bed was like as long as it had one. The whole complex looked more like a parking lot than somewhere to stay.

They took a moment to size up the dark, curtained windows of the cabin through the car's windscreen

'You think he's in there?'

O'Neill pursed her lips and shrugged before shaking her head. 'Let's find out.'

The patrol car had followed them through the green

surround fence and the two uniformed cops were getting out of their vehicle. The detectives recognised both by sight. Kate Kuhlmeyer and Mickey Bryant.

'What we got, Detective? We were told urgent but there doesn't seem to be anything going down.' Kuhlmeyer wasn't grouching, just curious.

'We need that door opened,' O'Neill told her. 'And fast. No time to find the owner or keyholder. We need it opened now.'

'Want to give us a heads-up on what's on the other side of it?' Bryant asked her.

'Maybe a body. Maybe dead, maybe alive. That's why we're in a hurry.'

The cops exchanged a quick glance. 'Okay, you got it.' Within a minute, Bryant had pulled a metal enforcer from the trunk of their car and crashed it into the lock of cabin 3. The door splintered and swung.

The detectives and the officers pulled on face masks and gloves and stepped inside the black interior of the dingy cabin. The air was fetid, thick and threatening. All four cops sensed it immediately. The stale stench of decay. The unmistakeable *feel* of death.

O'Neill flicked a switch but there was no power, forcing them to pull out their Pelican 7060 flashlights and send searing beams across the room. Their eyes searched left and right, hungry to see whatever the cabin held.

There was no body in sight.

'Bathroom,' O'Neill said firmly. 'That's where the Dahlia was supposed to be cut up.'

She caught the look that passed between Kuhlmeyer

and Bryant, wondering what the hell they were now in the middle of, and ignored it.

Salgado moved first, striding towards the white bathroom door and edging it open. He knew before it swung fully back but his eyes and his flashlight confirmed what his nose and his cop sense was telling him.

'Oh fuck.'

The body was propped up against the far wall, half sitting, half toppled towards the floor, its dark silhouette in stark contrast to the flash-lit, white-tiled wall and floor. The head was slumped forward, concealing the face. But dead, unmistakeably dead.

O'Neill was by his side, staring, trying to make sense of it. Kuhlmeyer and Bryant looked over the detectives' shoulders but then edged back, leaving them to it, not needing another stiff to fill up their week with paperwork.

The 7060s picked out the dirty, rusty spatter of old blood marking the floor and walls, as if framing the portrait. The hands were on the floor, palms upturned, as if pleading for help that never came.

The urgency had seeped suddenly from Salgado and O'Neill. No point in rushing for the dead. Instead, it demanded the care and attention of sombre, dispassionate consideration. They both knew the first thing that was obvious about the body in front of them, but she said it aloud anyway.

'Whoever it is, it's not our guy. Different clothes, not as tall. And this has been here for months. Dead for months.'

The corpse was decomposed in shades of purple and grey, held together by the clothes the man died in. They'd both seen more than enough bodies to be able to gauge it without needing CSI to do it for them.

'Not our missing guy,' Salgado agreed. 'But it's Garland's doing. Has to be.'

They both looked around the bathroom, looking for where they should step and where they shouldn't, looking for anything that might help them.

'Camera!'

O'Neill saw it first, or got the word out first, neither of them were sure. But there it was: a small wall-mounted video camera behind them, pointing directly at the man on the floor. Salgado stepped back and examined it. Cheap, mass produced, easily rigged up, and doubtless once relaying its feed straight to Ethan Garland's computer and to his partner in the UK.

She walked over and crouched by the body, professionalism overcoming anything else. The corpse was restrained by chains tying it to the radiator that it was propped up against. The set-up so similar, the end so predictable.

She began to dip her head to see if she might recognise the corpse's face, when she noticed the top of the head in more detail and stopped fast. The ripped skin, the discoloured pate, the awful patchwork of decay.

She turned to look back at her partner, easing the mask from her mouth and catching her breath.

'From the other side of the room, I thought this guy was bald,' she told him quietly. 'He isn't. It's the colours of decomp that's obscured it, but he's been scalped.'

Salgado reached out and pushed the bathroom door

closed. There was some news that didn't need to be shared too widely.

'The last piece of Garland's collection. Well ...' he hesitated as he tried to see a plus side, '... at least we have a DNA sample already typed up in Elvis's lab waiting to match to this poor sap, whoever he is.'

O'Neill shook her head at him. 'It's not the last piece. There's another whole body out there.'

CHAPTER 46

The accountant Ian Bryce worked for a charity named Meal Angels. Narey and Wells waited for him outside the warehouse on Dunn Street in Dalmarnock as he arrived to deliver meals to the elderly.

The man denied knowing the name Matthew Marr, and initially denied even being in Carstairs. He got angry and defensive, insisting that he hadn't been a patient there, that he'd only been there for 'unnecessary tests'.

They pushed him on knowing Marr. Bryce got increasingly anxious and angry but maintained he'd never heard of him.

Giannandrea traced John Paul Kepple from a rented flat above a shop on Kirkintilloch Road in Bishopbriggs to a forwarding address in Rosevale Street in Partick. The young woman who lived there had been in the flat for three years and didn't know who'd been there before her. The landlords said they'd no record of a John Paul Kepple ever renting one of their properties.

Kepple had gone off the grid.

Martin Geir, the cat killer, had seemingly disappeared

too. He wasn't on the electoral roll, wasn't receiving any benefits and wasn't paying tax. Narey put in a call to a reporter on the *East End Echo*, a weekly local paper, and prayed he'd be able to help. Gerry Grady said Geir had moved from Bridgeton to Dennistoun but had to get out of Dodge one more time when people found out who he was. That time, he did a bunk in the middle of the night and no one knew where he'd gone. Grady promised to do his best to find out on the half promise of getting a story.

Derek Solomon and Colin McPake turned out to be the easiest of the six profiles to track down and eliminate from their enquiries. Solomon was in Barlinnie and had been for the past six months. McPake was also in the Bar-L, halfway through an eighteen-month sentence for aggravated assault.

There was no sign of Fraser Anderson. Nothing on the electoral roll, no council tax listing, and no mention of him on the local crime system or the Criminal History System since his release from Carstairs. Like Kepple, like many other people with severe mental health problems, he seemed to have dropped off the grid.

His ex-wife, Erin, now lived in Paisley. She was pencil-thin with short blonde hair and gave off a nervous anger. When Narey and Giannandrea said who they were, the woman had no doubt who they wanted to talk about.

'What's he done?'

'We don't know that he's done anything,' Narey told her. 'We are just anxious to find him, and as quickly as possible.'

'I can't help you. If I could, I would, believe me. If

you find him you could maybe tell Child Maintenance. They've supposedly been looking for the bastard for three years. Although I don't think they've tried very hard.'

'You haven't heard from him?'

Her face twisted. 'The kids get a Christmas card. That's if I don't recognise the handwriting and rip the thing up before they can open it.'

'Do you know where the cards are sent from? From the postmark?'

'Glasgow. They've always been sent from Glasgow. But I know he's here. People have seen him. Every few months someone will say "Oh, I saw Fraser on Buchanan Street", or "You'll never guess who I saw on the subway". It's mostly been city centre so I've no idea if he's West End, south side, wherever. I'm told he looks shit though, so that's good news.'

'When was the last time he was seen?'

Erin reached for a packet of cigarettes and fumbled one out. 'My cousin Eleanor was in Glasgow, in the Buchanan Galleries, maybe six weeks ago. She was going up one of the escalators and he was going down the opposite one. He saw her but just looked at her, no hello, no expression, nothing.'

'Would that be usual for him? Just blanking people like that?'

'It would depend on which Fraser he was being that day. He might wake up being Mr Nice Guy, he might be a miserable bastard, he might be one thing to one person and something completely different to another. You never knew.'

'Is there anyone who might know where he is? Old friends of his, or family?'

'No, I doubt it. He never had many close friends to start with and he lost those after what he did. He doesn't have much in the way of family and never had anything to do with them anyway.'

They were getting nowhere. A last throw of the dice.

'Does the name Matthew Marr mean anything to you?'

She gave the name some thought but shook her head. 'No, doesn't mean a thing. Listen, Inspector, I don't want anyone like Fraser anywhere near my kids. So, if you do find him, get him to pay the money he owes us, then lose him again. We're better off without him.'

Derek Solomon and Colin McPake were ruled out, Martin Grenier too. Kepple, Geir, Anderson and Devlin were still places unknown. Bryce and Fairley had given nothing away. And the clock ticked.

Narey needed something and, right on cue, her mobile rang. The screen showed it was Gerry Grady.

'Hey, Gerry. You got something for me?'

'Inspector, I've got a hit on our cat killer. I know where Martin Geir is.'

'Gerry, I knew I could count on you. Where is he?'

'Well, before I tell you, I was thinking that I've been doing all the back scratching in this deal and was looking for a bit coming back my way. What's the story here, Rachel?'

'Christ, Gerry. You're really going to try to play hardball with me at this stage?'

'Yes.'

'Okay, let me tell you something. *Don't*. I have a major investigation where the shit is not so much hitting the fan as battering it to death. I have zero time for getting dicked around and I am currently considering charging you with obstructing a police investigation. You will subsequently get nothing from me and nothing from anyone else in Police Scotland but might find your car checked for bald tyres on a regular basis. Do you understand me?'

'Can't blame a man for trying, Inspector.'

'I don't have time to blame or not blame. Just fucking tell me.'

'Martin Geir is dead.'

'Shit. You're sure?'

'Pushing up daisies somewhere in the Motorway Triangle is what I'm told. He'd been driving an unlicensed taxi in Toryglen, cash in hand, calling himself Michael Johns. The firm he drove for is a front for Alec Kirkwood, the gangster. It seems that one of Kirkwood's daughters heard about Michael Johns and his backstory. The daughter is a cat lover and went mental at Kirkwood about having this guy on the books. She wanted him out, but she also wanted him sorted. The same way he'd sorted the cats. This was three months ago, Inspector. Whatever you want him for, Geir isn't your man.'

Narey had Lee Fairley watched around the clock, making sure the patrol car that made regular trips down his street was as visible as possible. If that made him nervous, then so much the better.

The neighbours had been questioned about security and seeing anything odd in the area, leading of course to questions about Fairley.

Quite a few said there had been arguments about noise late at night, about bins being overflowing, his car being parked where it shouldn't. None of that was unusual but a few spoke about the ferocity of the man's temper.

He'd left his flat for one quick walk to a local shop, a drive to a flat in King's Park where he stayed for just twenty minutes before leaving, and a longer drive over the river to Kelvingrove where he sat parked outside a block of flats for over an hour.

That was enough to have Giannandrea and Wells on his tail when he next drove down Langside Road. When he indicated right at the last moment and turned into Earlspark Avenue, they were tight enough that they had to take the next turning then wheel back round. Even so, they were pretty sure he'd clocked them. When they parked up behind Fairley's Honda, they saw that it was empty and there was no sign of him. He'd got out before they got there and probably legged it around the corner to Langside station, where he was doubtless on a train bound for the city centre.

Giannandrea was less worried that they'd lost him than the certain feeling that Fairley had done it just to show that he could.

CHAPTER 47

Narey's eyes were glued to the screen. Somewhere in the greater Los Angeles area, Dylan Hansen sat slumped against the radiator, his hair covering his face and his body motionless. She'd become used to looking for the slightest hint of movement, the smallest sign of continuing existence.

When the other monitor flickered into life, it made her jump, her mind leaping to a false conflated dawn, a vision of an ECG graph soaring to new heights. The reality of the still-motionless Dylan was a depressant.

She held it together and turned to see Cally O'Neill staring back at her.

'You watching Dylan, Rachel?'

The strain must have been showing on Narey's face and she was annoyed with herself that it did so. The only saving grace was knowing that O'Neill shared her worries.

'Yes. He hasn't moved in the fifteen minutes that I've been here.'

'Our doctors tell us he's running on empty. Organ failure is probably inevitable from here on in.'

'Are you any closer, Cally?'

O'Neill hesitated, thought long and deep before answering. 'Yes. We're closer. We're learning more about Garland all the time and we now know more about who he was and how he thought. We're closer. And that's why I'm calling. We've been working a line on Ethan Garland's father. It started out as something very left-field but we're now thinking it goes right to the heart of who Garland was and . . . well, there's things I need to know from you.'

'Okay. Go for it.'

O'Neill breathed deep and readied herself. 'Okay . . . you'll remember that among the murderabilia items we found in Garland's cellar was a purse said to belong to Elizabeth Short and tagged with the name Frankie Wynn. It was just one of several such things, so we didn't pay it any more attention than the others, but we followed process. We now know that Frankie Wynn was an alias used by Zac Garland and we have several links between Garland senior and the Short investigation. He drove a similar car to a prime suspect, he frequented a motel where many think the murder was committed, he worked at a restaurant where Short's shoes and purse were found. The links are largely circumstantial, but they keep on coming and coming.'

'You're thinking Garland's father murdered Elizabeth Short? *Really?*'

O'Neill held her gaze, thinking, deliberating. 'Yes. Maybe. It's so far from what I thought we were working on but yes, it's all pointing that way. How much do you know about the Short murder?'

'She's the one they called the Black Dahlia, right?'

337

'Right.'

Narey hesitated. 'I guess I don't know that much. I know of the case, know it was brutal, headline-making stuff and never solved. After that, I'd be guessing.'

'Okay, let me give you the Cliff's Notes. She—'

'The what?'

'The quick-study version. Elizabeth Short was twenty-two years old. Dark hair, model looks. She'd been working as a waitress, may have had aspirations to get into the movie business. Her body was found lying on an empty building lot in 1947. Cause of death was a cerebral haemorrhage. The key thing I want to talk to you about was how her body was displayed.'

'Okay ...' Narey sensed O'Neill's nervousness as she neared the business end of her explanation.

'Elizabeth Short's body had been cut in half.'

'Oh Christ ...'

'Right. So you now know why I'm making this call. Eloise Gray's body was severed too, right?'

'Right. Cut in two just below the waist. A technique called—'

'A hemicorporectomy. Rachel, you saw Eloise's body. Tell me how it was arranged.'

The inescapable sense of dread made Narey close her eyes. Behind them, she saw Eloise's body in the harsh light of the cellar of the Highland Fling, the two halves so deliberately positioned.

'She'd been placed with her arms above her head. Her elbows were bent at right angles. Her legs were spread apart in a way that I'd suggest was intended to be sexual.'

O'Neill nodded grimly. 'Exactly as Elizabeth Short was.'

Narey's gut twisted. 'Marr's done this as a copycat killing? As what, some kind of homage to Ethan Garland's father?'

'It sure looks that way.'

'Wait,' Narey pulled a hand through her hair as she thought. 'How old did you say she was? Twenty-two? Eloise was twenty-two. Does that sound like a coincidence to you?'

'Nope. None of it does. Everything either of them has done has been for a reason, however fucking sick it is.'

Narey nodded animatedly. 'Marr has been adamant with me that there was no reason that Eloise was chosen other than that she was a victim. Lennie Dakers told me Marr was lying but we couldn't call him on it or be sure there was more to it. Now we know different. What did Elizabeth Short look like?'

O'Neill was ready for the question and immediately raised a grainy black and white photograph to the screen.

Narey couldn't help but see the connection right away. While Eloise and the woman they called the Black Dahlia didn't exactly look alike, they were most definitely a similar type. The dark hair, the fresh-faced beauty, the bloom of youth. They looked enough alike that if you were searching for a stand-in for Short then Eloise would adequately fit the bill. Narey swore.

'Ethan Garland did this search, Cally. He picked someone who fitted the profile and delivered her to Marr for dispatching. Marr told me she was killed because she was a victim, nothing more, but he was lying. It suited him for me to think she was just some random, that it could have been anyone.'

'There was nothing random about it, Rachel.'

'No. They picked her out and hunted her down. And I'm going to make Marr regret it.'

CHAPTER 48

Igloo. Messages. Vikki, 32.

Ryan: Hey, how are you this morning?
Delivered, 11.05
Read, 11.08

> **Vikki: Hi! Good thanks. Just chilling at home.**

I'm just checking you're still okay for tonight. I'm really looking forward to it.

> **Yeah me too! I'm a bit nervous, first time meeting and all that. I barely know you!**

I know. I'm a bit nervous myself. Only natural, I guess. And I know we've not talked for long but it feels like we know each other. Maybe just because we've got so much in common.

> **Well that's true. But what if we don't get on in real life?**

But what if we do? :)

Lol

It could be the start of something beautiful

Oh that's cheesy dude!

Yeah sorry lol. What can I say I've got an old
romantic heart

Nothing wrong with that :)

So you'll be there?

Yeah. I'll be there

Great. I can't wait!

Lol me neither

I'll see you tonight Vikki!

CHAPTER 49

Narey and Dakers watched Dylan Hansen do nothing.

He hadn't moved in the twenty minutes they'd been there, nor in the previous hour that Wells had been in the chair.

Not a flutter of his eyelids. Not a turn of his head. Not a kick of his leg or a beat of his heart. Not a single physical sign that he was breathing, thinking, functioning. If he was alive, his body had shut down on him. If he was alive, he wasn't going to be for long.

Five thousand miles away, they knew Salgado and O'Neill were watching too. Watching nothing. Watching everything.

And somewhere just a few miles away from them, the man they knew as Matthew Marr was doing the same.

When the green light flashed, Narey's heart sank. The conversations with him were hacking away at her soul, carving slices from it every time they talked. She huffed, nodded at Dakers, and began to type.

Are you watching him, Matthew?

**Yes. Of course. But it's coming to an end.
Maybe it's already there.**

> Maybe he's already dead. Maybe you are
> waiting for an ending you'll never see.

I'll see it. I'll know it.

> How can you be so sure?

**There will be a sign. A send-off from his
body. A final, futile instinctive movement.
I'll see it.**

> And what if you don't get to see it?

What?

> You haven't given me enough, Matthew. Or
> whoever you are. You talk and you watch but
> you don't give.

**I've told you about Eloise. Told you about
Ellen Lambert. I've told you things.**

> I want more.

No.

> Yes. You give me more or I take this feed
> away from you. You know I can, and you
> know I will. You've been through all this and
> you won't see the end of the show. The one
> thing you want.

The message was read but not replied to. The green light shone but the screen remained static.

'He's trying to find a way round it,' Dakers intimated. 'He's driven by two strong, opposing instincts. He doesn't want to give you anything but knows that if he gives you nothing, he might lose what he wants. If he gives you too much, the same thing might happen. The chances of him lying at this point are high.'

Marr began to type, then stopped. He scrubbed whatever he'd written and started again. And stopped again. The hesitancy continued until he final sent the message.

I will tell you something. Not everything.
That would be stupid and I'm not stupid.

And you'll tell me the truth?

Yes.

'Keep him on a tight lead,' Dakers advised. 'If you leave this open-ended, he can tell you anything. And he will lie. Give him no room for manoeuvre.'

She paused, thought, and nodded her agreement. She had precious few favours left to call in from Marr, few bargaining chips remaining before the man would refuse to deal. She had to choose what she wanted most.

Okay, Matthew. I want information about a woman who was murdered. If you know about it, will you tell me?

If I do.

She was murdered in her home in Polmadie. She
bled to death from a puncture wound to each
wrist. Do you know who this woman is?

More hesitancy. More letters typed and deleted. Then a reply.

Yes.

Tell me.

Her name was Irene Dow. I killed her.

'Good,' Dakers chirped. 'He'd nowhere else to go.'
Narey kept at him.

You could have read about her in
the media.

You could just be telling me what you think I
want to hear.

I'm not.

Prove it. Tell me something only Irene Dow's
killer could know. Prove it now or I stop the
video feed.

The pause was long enough to convince Dakers that a
deception was coming, and he made a face to make sure
Narey knew of his doubts.

I used a screwdriver to puncture her arteries at the wrists. The holes were small. The screwdriver was quite blunt, so I had to force it in. Is that enough?

Narey sat back in her chair, suddenly tired. He'd sliced off another chunk of what remained of her soul.

'It's true,' she told Dakers. 'I've read the Dow file. It's true and it hasn't been made public.'

Yes, she typed to Marr. It's enough for me to believe you killed her. Thank you. But I want more.

No. You leave the feed on.

Let's talk about Eloise Gray.

No.

I'll turn it off. You know I will.

Silence. Anger brooding. Resentment rising.

Okay. What about her?

Why did Ethan choose her?

Her message was read. But he hesitated.

'He's thinking,' Dakers said from behind her. 'Thinking of a way to avoid it. Give him no room.'

I can't be sure. She was Ethan's choice. How can I guess his thinking?

'Equivocation,' Narey said it before Dakers did. 'He's avoiding saying a lie, avoiding saying the truth. He knows. We're right.'

She typed.

> You don't have to guess. Do you? You know.

Hesitation.

> **Do I?**

More equivocation.

> You do. You know about Ethan Garland's father. So you know why he choose Eloise. It's because she looked like her, isn't it?

Hesitation. Lots of it.

> **Like who?**

> You know who. And you tell me now or this feed goes off.

Hesitation. Words typed. Words deleted. More words typed.

> **Elizabeth Short. She was chosen because she looked like Elizabeth Short.**

Narey sat back in her chair, momentarily stunned. She turned to Dakers, who nodded encouragement. 'Go on.'

When did you learn what Garland's father
had done? Is that what brought you and
Ethan together?

I've told you enough.

I think it was. I think you met in an online
forum about murderers. Am I right? 4chan or
8chan or the like?

**I'm saying nothing. We had a deal. It will be
my turn to walk away if you don't leave it
on. I told you before, I'm not stupid.**

No, you're not. You're an intelligent man, I
know that. Setting up this messaging service
shows that. Not everyone would know
their way around a computer enough to
know that.

A pause.

**I think they would. Maybe most people would.
It's not that difficult. Even you might be able
to do it. Okay, I've done what you asked. I
don't need to talk to you anymore. Keep that
feed open.**

The green light died.

Dakers turned to her. '"I think. Maybe. Might." More
equivocation. He's hiding something.'

'Yes. And I think I might know what.'

CHAPTER 50

Narey, Giannandrea and Wells were working it hard. Every lead was being chased down, even if most of them turned into cul-de-sacs.

Lee Fairley had lain low since his disappearing act from Langside. He'd only left his flat twice, but on one of those two trips he'd again given his surveillance team the slip. He was being tailed along Merrylee Road when he entered the White Elephant bar and restaurant. When he hadn't re-emerged half an hour later, the DC following him went inside to be told the man had come in then walked straight across the restaurant and out the side door by the conservatory.

The DC went out the same door and emerged next to the car park, seeing immediately that all Fairley had had to do was step across a short wall and he was into an area of housing and away. Maybe he'd taken a shortcut, maybe he was just messing with his surveillance because he was pissed off at being watched. Either way, another hour later, he calmly returned home as if nothing had happened.

Fraser Anderson remained missing, whereabouts

unknown. By the nature of his job, he didn't need an employer as such, could work from home and never have to see another soul. Like Fairley, all he needed was a computer and an internet connection. No need for anyone to see his face or know if he was who he said he was.

They were trying to get information out of banks but that was never easy at the best of times and not in the timeframe that they were working with. Nor did it help that the chances of Anderson working under an assumed name to avoid the dark cloud associated with his service attack on the city council were pretty high.

Without being able to speak to him, all they had to go on was Erin Anderson's brief on her ex-husband's changeable character and the psychiatrist's report from Carstairs. It ticked enough boxes that Narey was most definitely interested.

Angry when challenged. Controlling. Volatile. Possible borderline personality disorder. Potentially escalating violent tendencies.

Kerri Wells dug deeper into the John Paul Kepple case, discovering the priest that Kepple demanded to see, Father Kiernan, had left the area shortly after that, got transferred to a diocese in the south of England and died five months later. He was found at the foot of the stairs in the chapel house with a broken neck. Wells spoke to the local cops and it seemed they thought there was something suspicious about it but that they'd no evidence that it was anything other than a fall. Wells and Narey thought otherwise.

Kayleigh McGrath called again, putting Narey in touch

with a friend who had some info on Andy, Brianna's unknown one-time sort-of boyfriend. Mel Campbell had been with her in the Social the night she'd met the guy and had hazy recollections of him.

Narey went to the supermarket where the woman worked and they chatted in the car park, standing under a shopping trolley shelter as the rain lashed down around them.

'Sorry, I know this isn't ideal, but I didn't want to do this in the shop,' Campbell explained. 'Too many nosy buggers in there. So, you want to know about this guy that Bri met? Kayleigh says it's important.'

'It might be. I honestly don't know yet. But anything could be hugely important, so thanks for taking the time to talk to me.'

'Sure. Of course. Well, the first thing is that we were all pretty drunk. We'd been drinking in my place before we went out, prosecco and gin, so a couple of drinks in town and we were fleeing. Plus, it was a few years ago now. So, I might not be remembering it right.'

'Just do your best.'

'Well, the reason I remember it was this guy wasn't exactly Bri's type. He was a few years older and not great looking, not the kind of "wow" guy she usually went for. But, like I said, we'd been drinking. She talked to him for ages and the rest of us thought she was taking the piss out the guy. But she came back over and said that he was really nice, and they were having a right good chat.'

'Can you remember what he looked like? And maybe his age?'

Mel huffed. 'Not really. He was maybe about five feet ten. Dark hair, collar length, kind of boring looking, a wee bit overweight. I'd say he'd be about thirty-five. Bri usually went for the flash types, pretty boys and bad boys. So, when she went off with him at the end of the night, we were all gobsmacked.'

'Do you think you might recognise the guy if you saw him again? Maybe if I showed you some photographs?'

Mel made a face. 'I don't know. Maybe. It was ages ago. But I have seen him again, maybe three years ago.'

Narey's pulse quickened. 'Where?'

'In town. It was near Central Station. It took me a minute to think where I knew him from, but it was him. Thing is, the bastard was married. He was hand in hand with this woman all happy husband and wife. He saw me and he knew I knew.'

'Are you sure?'

'Definite.'

CHAPTER 51

Salgado had grabbed some sleep but was feeling the worse for it. He was disorientated as much by the two hours he'd slept as he was by the body in the bathroom of the Aster. They had a sense of Garland now. They knew how he worked, how he was wired, but it still wasn't enough.

The Aster had *felt* right, and in some ways it was. Old LA, an old haunt of the Garlands, the Black Dahlia connection. After the visit to the Aster they had officers call on the house that now sat on the once vacant lot on South Norton where Elizabeth Short had been found, but it was a perfectly normal family home with no skeletons in any of the closets. The same went for the house on Talmadge Street in Loz Feliz where Ethan had grown up. All hunches. All wrong.

Dylan Hansen hadn't moved, hadn't seemingly breathed, in the time Salgado had slept or in the half hour he'd been awake again. Opinions were spilt between what they could see and what they could believe. Cold realism versus hope. Salgado continued to cling to hope.

'You awake in there, Detective?'

He looked up from his desk to see Howie Kelsey walking in slowly, like a man bearing bad news.

'Hey, Howie. What's up? You been made lieutenant yet?'

Kelsey grimaced. 'I think that's going to have to wait a while.'

Salgado tried to read the man's mood. 'You got news?'

Kelsey advanced his right hand and tilted it side to side. Maybe yes, maybe no.

'I don't want any bad news, Kelsey. We don't have time for any of that.'

The tall man looked mournful and in no mood for jokes. 'So, let me tell you what I've got. I managed to get three detectives on this, used your kidnap guy to convince my boss it was urgent. We tried to track down all the employees from Delmonico's who appeared on the witness statement that Mortimer and Crouch took in 1947. It was a long shot but three of them are still alive and still living in LA.'

'Jesus, how old are they?'

'Viola Facci is eighty-nine. Domenico Sciarra is ninety-five. And Tony Giordano is ninety.'

'Giordano is the guy who owned the sedan?'

'Right. So, first of all, Sciarra is alive but has dementia. His doctor says he's as happy as Larry but couldn't tell us what he had for breakfast never mind what happened seventy years ago. But Viola and Tony are sharp as tacks.

'Viola is in a retirement home in Westlake. Chirpy and chatty and remembers Delmonico's as if it were yesterday. And she remembers Zac Garland very well. Want to know the first thing she said when we told her we were cops and wanted to talk to her about Zachary Garland? "I'll bet this is about the Black Dahlia".'

'Whoa . . .'

Kelsey held up a hand in warning.

'No, hold on. Don't get too excited. It's all about *why* she remembers him and the Dahlia. Viola said, and I quote, "Zachary Garland was full of shit." She said he was a born liar, always making things up to try to impress people. Particularly women. She said she wouldn't believe that guy if he told her the sun came up in the morning.

'Viola said that probably most people in Los Angeles were talking about the Black Dahlia murder but that *everyone* in Delmonico's was talking about it. The cops found the shoes and the purse nearby, that was the first thing. But the staff just assumed they'd been dumped there and that was that. But then cops came looking for a guy named Frankie Wynn who'd said he worked there. Of course, there was no Wynn there but it had them all scared and excited and talking, talking, talking.

'She said it was maybe a month after that when Zac Garland began telling people he was Frankie Wynn. He'd tell one or two, like a confession, and then let them tell other people. At which point he'd deny it. She said, and again I quote, that "he started to wear the name like a coat." She said he was always this weird kid who wanted to be more interesting than he was. Said he was dating starlets when he wasn't. That he'd got into fights when he hadn't. Killed someone when he hadn't.'

'She was sure?'

'She was certain. She remembers one of the waiters

saying he was out on the town with Zac, hitting a few bars and hitting on a few girls. Says the first thing Garland did was introduce himself to the girls as Frankie. But no one had ever heard him use the name before the cops came calling.

'Viola says Garland hit on her, told her all kinds of stories, but she knew they were bullshit, knew Zac was full of it. I asked her if there was any chance he'd killed the Black Dahlia and she nearly died laughing.'

'Wait. But what about the car?' Salgado was reaching. 'Zac Garland owned the sedan that was seen on Norton, right? Durrant had no doubt about the age, the shape, the paint job.'

Kelsey shook his head. 'He owned a sedan, that much was true. But remember, we don't even know if Ralph Asdell's sighting on Norton was the guy who killed Beth Short. And, anyway, that brings us to Tony Giordano.

'So Tony is in a home in Montecito Heights, a very dapper OG, shirt and tie every day. Likes to chat to the ladies. Got all his marbles, maybe just a bit slower than he was. He had to think a bit more before things came to him, but he got there. Tony, like you say, owned a 1935 sedan. But he was working the night Elizabeth Short was murdered, went straight home to his wife and was there all night. Checked and confirmed by our guys at the time. Completely in the clear. He got a paint job done on his car, simple as that, but it was enough to draw cops to the restaurant.

'So, I ask him about Zac Garland and got nothing until I prompted him about his sedan. And then he was like, "Yeah, Garland. I remember that son of a bitch. He bought a sedan, same as mine. Even got a black paint job on it, same as mine. He was one crazy son of a bitch."

'Bottom line is, Tony Giordano has zero doubt that Zac Garland bought the sedan way after the Dahlia murder. He bought it because he was obsessed with the Short killing. Because of Giordano, he knew the cops thought a guy with a '35 sedan was the killer, so he bought one to make people think it was him. Crazy fuck. Giordano says the staff all called him the Dahlia killer. Like it was one big joke.

'I'm sorry to say it, Salgado, but Zac Garland was a fantasist. A dangerous fantasist going by the rest of the stuff you told me, but there's nothing to think he had anything at all to do with the Dahlia murder. Any bad shit he got into was after that, and yeah, maybe because of it. But he didn't murder Elizabeth Short.'

Salgado sat with his head in his hands, trying to make sense of the news, wondering what it changed and what it didn't. Had they been wasting time chasing the Dahlia angle?

'Don't write this off just as bad news, man,' Kelsey encouraged him. 'So Zac Garland didn't murder Elizabeth Short, neither did a million other guys in 1947. But from what you told me, your guy Ethan *believed* his father did. And that was the thing that mattered. He believed he was the son of the Dahlia killer. You got to think that had a whole lot to do with him turning out the way he did. You got motivation, you got an insight into his thinking. Use it.'

Salgado nodded grimly. 'We know who he is now. He's who he wanted to be. A man gets told often enough that he's born to be something, then he's going to believe it. If he's told he's going to be a star, then he reaches for the sky. If he's told he's the son of a famous murderer, then he's either going to live up to it or never live it down. Ethan Garland made his choice.'

CHAPTER 52

Marianne Ziegler was tired.

It was barely nine in the morning and she'd already been interrogated for another two hours. All the things she'd done her best to forget were now being dredged out of her. The man who'd tried to kill her, the man who'd ruined her life, her self-respect and confidence, had returned to haunt her. She didn't have much left.

Salgado and O'Neill had fuelled her with gallons of coffee and thrown memory prompts at her until she was sick of it. They knew they should have gone easier on her but there wasn't time for niceties.

They asked again about Garland's childhood, his schooling, his favourite haunts. They asked about things that he obsessed with, about favourite TV shows, parks, streets, anything and everything. And they asked about his father, again.

'We think that maybe Ethan was obsessed with the Black Dahlia murder from 1947. Would you agree with that, Marianne?'

'I . . . well, yes. I never really thought about it that way before but . . .' Garland's ex-wife faltered. 'Maybe I never wanted to think about it that way. He had books on that killing, quite a few of them, and he'd read them a lot. I thought it was a bit weird but lots of people are into true crime. It doesn't mean anything, right? That's what I thought at the time, but now, now it looks very different.'

'Did he ever mention places connected to the Dahlia murder? Anything at all that you can remember?'

Marianne raised her hands in exasperation. 'He used to walk over there. Leimert Park, wasn't it? It was one of his regular walks and now I guess I know why. But nothing else. Nothing that I can think of.'

'Okay, what about other murder cases?' O'Neill could hear the desperation in her voice. 'If Ethan was into true crime, can you remember other murders that he had a particular interest in?'

'This was a long time ago. I can't remember every strange thing that Ethan was into. You'll have seen the books in the house. He watched lots of documentaries. That was his go-to thing on cable. I should have seen this, right? Is that what you're telling me? That I should have known?'

'No,' O'Neill reassured her. 'We're not saying that at all. People like Ethan are remarkably skilled at hiding the side of themselves that they exhibit when they carry out horrific crimes. Even those near to them don't get to see it. Except when it's unleashed on them. Most people who are into true crime just binge on it, they don't get affected by it, or act on it. Don't blame yourself for not seeing that.'

'Cally is right, Marianne. This wasn't down to you to

notice. But we have to keep at it. We need to keep look-ing. All the places that we know of that Ethan used were associated with his youth, a better time, maybe. So, school seems to be an obvious place. Maybe places he hung out after school?'

Nothing.

'What about elsewhere in the city? Where else did he talk about? Maybe somewhere that he spent a lot of time, maybe still visited when you were married.'

'I don't know.'

'Maybe somewhere old,' Salgado kept at her. 'An aban-doned property or a derelict building. Somewhere nobody would go.'

'I don't know.'

'What about an old house they lived in? A place he went for sports or music? There must be somewhere.'

'I don't know. Look, we've gone over this—'

She stopped abruptly. She raised her head and looked up at the two detectives, saying nothing but with her brows furrowed in thought. They saw the look and their blue sense tingled.

'There is something else. It might be nothing and I haven't thought of it in years until now. It was something you said a few moments ago, Detective Salgado. About thinking of somewhere that had been abandoned. That's not a very common thing in LA with house prices being what they are. And about another murder.'

Salgado and O'Neill looked at each other, neither quite sure if they were sensing or hoping for a breakthrough in whatever he'd triggered in Marianne's memory bank.

'There *is* a place Ethan used to talk about. And he used to go visit it with his dad.'

They were most definitely interested now.

'Have you heard of the Los Feliz Murder House? The Perelson family, I think the name was. Yes, Perelson, that's it.'

'I have,' Salgado confirmed as O'Neill looked confused. 'A doctor clubbed his wife to death, tried to kill his oldest daughter, took an overdose in front of his younger kids and died next to his wife's body on their bed. They lived in some big villa near Griffith Park, right? Glendower Place, I think. Garland had an interest in that place?'

'Oh yes. It was all a bit strange. His father would take him up there and show him the house, try to scare him a bit, I think. Of course, Ethan being Ethan, he loved it. He often talked about it later.'

'Tell us more.' Salgado's tone had changed and O'Neill couldn't miss it.

'According to Ethan, his dad would march him up the hill to the Perelson house on Glendower Place and fill him up full of tales that little boys shouldn't be told. He'd tell him about mad Dr Perelson and his machinist's hammer. Ethan lapped it up – by the time they got to the house, he would be fit to burst with excitement, desperate to look in the windows and see where Mrs Perelson was hit, to look at the old furniture and the dolls and the half-made beds.

'He said himself he was a strange kid – loved gore and horror. He couldn't remember if he got like that because of the stories his dad told him or if he was like that anyway and that's why his father told him the things he did.'

'Do you remember him ever saying he'd gone back there as an adult?'

'Yes. I'd forgotten all about it, or more likely just didn't give it much thought at the time. When he was in a dark mood, he'd go walking around the neighbourhood. Sometimes he'd tell me where, most often he wouldn't. But I do remember him saying a few times that he'd walked up North Vermont to Glendower to look at that house and peer in the windows. I thought it was strange, but it was Ethan, and Ethan was strange.'

Salgado sprung up out of his chair. 'Marianne, we've got to go. You've been a big help, I mean it. Cally, let's move. And call a paramedic, get them to Glendower Place in Los Feliz.'

'Wait a minute. I'm still not sure I'm getting this. Salgado, I can tell you're hot for this house, but what makes you so sure it's right?'

He was already on his way to the door, beckoning her to follow him.

'The Perelson murder took place in the late 1950s. The reason it's known as the Los Feliz Murder House is that it's been unoccupied ever since. Another family bought it right after the murder, but only used it for storage. They didn't even clear it! Old radiators, old carpets, old curtains – all left from the day that nut killed his wife.'

She was through the office door before he could say another word or take another step.

CHAPTER 53

'Why have I never heard of this murder house?' O'Neill demanded as they lurched onto the street and past the gleaming white tower of City Hall with Salgado at the wheel of his Lexus.

'Because you're not an Angelino. You're some strange, East-Coast bird flown in on the wind. A lot of people in the city would know about it, mainly because it's prime real estate but has stood empty and untouched for so long. The murder itself was horrific, but the house virtually became a tourist attraction.'

'People are sick. Wait, which way are you going?'

'The 101.'

'Are you crazy, Salgado? You really want to take that chance? If it's snarled up, and it will be, then we'd be quicker walking, siren or no siren. Go under the 101 to Sunset, go west on Sunset until we hit Vermont and then it's a straight shot north from there. I might be a strange East-Coast bird, but I know how to get to fucking Los Feliz in a hurry.'

The freeway roared below them as Salgado sped over

it on North Main Street, then hauled a left onto Arcadia, running parallel to the blasting horns of the 101.

'So it was December 1959, the middle of the night. Dr Harold Perelson smashes the back of his wife's head with a hammer while she's sleeping. She dies instantly, suffocated in her own blood, enough that the whites of her eyes turned red. He tries to do the same to their eldest daughter but misses, and just injures her. She runs screaming into the street, waking neighbours by banging on their windows.'

Salgado turned right onto North Broadway, cursing as he saw traffic stacking up in front of them. The road was narrowed with construction, creating yet another bottleneck.

'Perelson walks past the two younger kids in the hallway, mixes himself up some Nembutal and tranquiliser pills and downs the lot. The crazy fuck then goes back into the bedroom and lies down beside his wife, still holding the freaking hammer. He's dead before paramedics can get there.'

He threw the light on top of the car and swung onto the other side of Broadway to get past the line of cars, just narrowly avoiding the oncoming traffic.

'So, the house on Glendower was sold but the new owners never moved in. Who wants to move into that, right? And it sits, and it sits, and it sits. For sixty years. The longer it goes on, the creepier the house gets. It gathers dust, it becomes like a museum of horror, everything just like it was the day the doc went loco. Like Pompeii after the volcano. People climb the hill and peer in the windows, like that's normal. It's a few million dollars' worth of freak show.'

'How sure are you that it's this house?'

'It just fits with what we've seen from the video feed. The radiator. The drapes, the carpet. Old. It feels right, *right*?'

They pushed west and north and west again. Past impossibly tall and slender palm trees, past purple cherry blossoms and tattoo parlours, along part of the old Route 66, racing by laundries, auto services and psychics. The hills were visible in the distance now and Salgado pressed on the gas.

At North Vermont they swung right and charged straight for the Hollywood Hills. They had to slow as they passed the chic boutiques and restaurants around the Dresden and Figaro, Skylight Books and the Vintage, but that suited them fine. They had to gather breath, hush their arrival, and wonder what the hell awaited them.

They were soon on Glendower Avenue, narrow and crowded with palms and multi million-dollar homes. And there, suddenly, a swing to the right and they were on Glendower Place and the villa was on the hill in front of them. The Murder House.

CHAPTER 54

Whitewashed walls and a terracotta roof; tall arched windows and a large balcony with sweeping views of the city; a tousled stretch of dry, sloping gardens running the entire width of the building. The Spanish Revival-style house looked like just another overpriced dream mansion, high above the City of Angels.

But it was different. Very different.

There was already a paramedic truck and a patrol car parked outside and a couple of neighbours who'd emerged into the heat of the day to see what the fuss was.

Salgado and O'Neill charged past them without explanation, waving at the cops to follow. The narrow concrete steps up to the villa led from an overflowing mailbox through an overgrown expanse of tall weeds that choked the dry earth.

The tall front door to the mansion was shielded by a massive concrete arch, its wood faded by decades of staring into the blistering heat of a southern Californian sun. The lead cop readied his battering ram, swung, and the wood grunted, splintered and gave way, swinging back uneasily on its rusted hinges with a groan of protest.

The cops stepped out of the heat and into the gloom and cool of the murder house. Slowly, looking around, guns poised just in case, they all sensed it. The house had an intense energy of its own that all of them had known before.

'They say you used to be able to peer through the windows,' Salgado spoke more in a whisper than he'd intended, 'and still see the Christmas tree with presents underneath it. Decades after the murder.'

Low mustard-coloured chairs with short wooden legs sat on a thick beige carpet studded with purple floral motifs. Vinyl 45s and albums sat stacked next to an old-time gramophone. Children's dolls, freaky enough at the best of times, had extra menace with a layer of dust and decay. They moved on, emerging into a tiled hallway with stairs leading both up and down, rooms beyond through open archways, and a frieze along one wall.

'Up or down?' O'Neill asked. 'You're the one with intuition.'

He lifted his shoulders in response. 'Let's split. I'll try up.'

They both knew that up meant the master bedroom where Harold Perelson had battered his wife's brains in – it seemed the kind of room that Ethan Garland would use if he could.

On the upper level, Salgado and one of the uniform cops passed high windows, ignoring the views of LA as they turned into a large corner room with more near floor-to-ceiling windows on three sides and a bathroom off the corner. No video camera, no Dylan Hansen.

O'Neill finished scoping out the ground floor and then took the stairs down. The decay was worse, wallpaper faded and peeling, and a smell that bothered her nose. The lower level was dimly lit and foreboding.

She traced her way down by holding the rail, suddenly flinching and taking a hurried step back as she felt a spider scurry up her arm. She flailed at it, swiping it onto the floor and turning in time to catch an amused grin on the face of the officer behind her. O'Neill glared at him till the smile disappeared.

At the bottom of the stairs, the light was even poorer. The wall coverings were so thick with mould that she wasn't sure what they'd been. The ceiling was blistered, peeling apart and sinking worryingly. Two short chains hung from a ceiling rose, one with a light bulb and one without. The smell was worse.

Something scurried. She hoped it was mice.

She began to turn the corner, then stopped in her tracks. The wallpaper. The curtains. She knew before she saw anything else.

'Salgado!'

Her shout went through the house and she repeated it. 'Salgado! Down here. Officer, get him. Get the paramedic too. Now!'

There he was. Slumped against the far wall. The radiator at his back. No signs of movement at all. The smell was coming from him.

She heard the clatter of Salgado's shoes on the stairs

before she got to the other side of the room. Others followed him, all charging, all hurrying.

Dylan Hansen didn't move. Didn't breathe.

The kid's flesh was discoloured and cold to the touch. His skin was dry and blotchy. He stank. She eased back an eyelid and saw nothing but lifelessness.

She reached for his wrist and felt for a pulse. Nothing. She tried again, willing it to be there, before looking up at Salgado and shaking her head.

'He's dead.'

'Fuck. *Fuck!*'

O'Neill looked beyond her partner, to where the camera blinked on the wall, and exploded in rage. She pulled her jacket off and placed it over Dylan Hansen's head.

'He doesn't get to see any more of this!' she shouted.

She stood and rushed past Salgado, heading straight for the camera and screaming into it.

'You're done, you sick fuck. Game over.'

She grabbed the camera and wrenched it from the wall, hurling it to the ground where it smashed in a shriek of wires, plastic and glass. She stood with her head in her hands as the last shards of it rattled and spun on the floor and finally came to a stop.

CHAPTER 55

Narey watched the drama unfold as it happened, her heart in her mouth. The pictures from the house on Glendower Place filling the screen to her right.

It felt distinctly odd being so remote from it and yet having a ringside seat. Hearing voices off camera, recognising one as being O'Neill and being aware of it getting quickly closer over the footsteps and the pounding of her own heart.

Seeing her crouch by Hansen. Hoping for the best. Expecting the worst. Hearing the worst.

Giannandrea was at her shoulder, both staring at the monitor, numbly. Their case. Not their case. Helpless voyeurs. Watching him die. Watching him. Already dead.

There had been silence in the dark of the room in Dalmarnock as they looked on from afar. Now, without the sounds from Los Angeles, that same silence grew larger and swamped them.

You're done, you sick fuck. Game over.

The last words they heard. The last picture that of O'Neill looming large and furious in the frame, the camera shifting quickly to the side, the room panning through the shot, then blackness.

Neither of them said anything. Nothing to be said. Helpless.

Giannandrea nudged her and she turned her head to the left just enough to see the green glimmer of the connection being made. The light that signalled Marr was online. Her gut twisted.

'No. Not now. Not this bastard.'

But, of course, it was now. Of course, it was him. He'd been watching as they had, that was as obvious as it was inevitable. And here he was to gloat, to crow, to deliver some misplaced, fucked-up eulogy. She wouldn't need Lennie Dakers to get a psychological understanding of what was going to be said.

Nor could she ignore it, much as she'd like to. She hit the switch and they were connected.

**Game over. Like that bitch said. Now
it's game on.**

Is it? Garland is dead too, remember. Your
little game with him finding your victims for
you is over.

**So, I'll play a different game. I've learned
lots from this one.**

Like what?

**How to do it. How to talk to them. How to
draw them to the spider's web like good little
flies. All so desperate to be caught.**

> Why don't you just stop? Stop before you're
>> the one that's caught.

But you want to catch me.

> Of course I do. But I also want you to stop.
> There's no need for anyone else to die.

There was a long enough pause that she allowed herself to think that maybe he was considering the sense in what she said. That didn't last.

**No. This wasn't enough. The American kid was
pathetic. Barely a struggle. I'm going after one
who will put up more of a fight.**

She hated herself for asking. Hated herself for giving him the platform to tell her. But she had no choice.

> What are you going to do?

I'm going hunting.

CHAPTER 56

Igloo. Messages. Vikki, 32.

> Ryan: Hi Vikki. I've got stuck with some
> weekend work. One of the kids has issues and
> I've had to help out. Can we make it a bit later
> than planned? Sorry!!
> Delivered, 15.22
> Read, 15.26

> > Vikki: Hi! No, that's fine. These things happen.
> > So when do you think you'll get there?

> Should we say 7.30 to be on the safe side? I
> don't want you to have to be waiting.

> > Oh okay. Won't the house be closed by then?
> > And it will be getting dark!

> Yeah, it will. But we can still visit the gardens.
> And the living willow love seat! It will be dusk but
> all the more romantic for that :)

> > Yeah I guess so :) Okay, see you at 7.30!

CHAPTER 57

She drove north along Dumbreck Road with a flutter in her heart and her pulse beating faster than it should. It was crazy, she knew that. It made no sense at all to meet a person she didn't know in a place so far out of people's view.

She'd had a message from him saying he'd been held up at work and would be a bit late. That meant it was going to be dusk when she got there and the House for an Art Lover would be closed. That either made this a great idea or a terrible one. Maybe he wouldn't even turn up. That would really ruin her night. She was sure he would, though. Sure of it.

She was also sure he was the one. Ryan.

Ryan. Ryan. Ryan. So many things made sense, even if meeting him in the near dark was maybe not the most sensible way of doing it.

His messages had made her sure of it. He was so like her in so many ways, liked the things she did, disliked the things she did. They had so much in common that it had to be right.

Even the place he'd suggested they meet was so spot on. Public and well known but also private and secluded. She was pretty sure her mother would have had something to say about it, but this was her choice, her decision.

She took a deep breath, nerves jangling, signalled and took a left off Dumbreck Road. She wound her way past the Victorian walled gardens until she got to the deserted car park. No sign of him, but she was early and hadn't really expected him to be there yet. She parked up and walked to the house on foot in search of the seat made of the living willow. It was a beautiful evening and he'd been right, the house looked magnificent and romantic lit up in the gloom of a dark September sky.

She stood still for a moment, realising what little noise she could hear. There was a distant rumble from the main road, but it was no more than a hum. The wind rustled lightly through the trees and whispered across the lawn. A lone bird was on the wing and its flap beat the drum slowly.

As she walked, she heard her own feet and her breathing. And the pounding of her heart.

It took a few minutes to find the willow seat in the gloom. It was a beautiful thing, so Mackintosh and yet so natural. The base was dark and broad, and the arched lattice back was tall and graceful. She settled into the seat and waited. And waited.

By a few minutes after the hour she began to fret that he might not show. She got to her feet and wandered around the half-hidden lawn, as if that would make time slip past faster. Then she heard a crunch on gravel followed by soft footsteps on grass and knew he was there. Ryan. Her man of mystery. Her heart missed a beat and she had to tell herself to calm down.

He was behind her but she didn't turn, played along with the game and the romance of the setting.

'Ryan?'

She heard his voice for the first time. Low and firm, slightly muffled. Confident but perhaps a hint of nerves.

'Don't turn around.'

The instruction made her wary, but it excited her too. She stood still, letting him approach, her head telling her one thing and her adrenalin another. A triumph for exhilaration over sense.

She heard him take a step closer, felt his breath on the back of her neck, and just before he reached her, felt a chill run down her spine. She started to take a step away, an instinctive survival motion that kicked in a split second too late.

The hand on her mouth came as a shock.

Not just a hand – material between the hand and her mouth. A cloth of some kind. It was gripped tight to her and she could smell something on it. It stung her nostrils and she tried to pull away, but he was tight behind her and the hand was clamped firmly across her mouth.

His voice was in her ear, husky and breathless, laced with naked menace.

'You're going to die, bitch. Accept it.'

Her head was starting to spin, and she could feel her senses scramble. Darkness was coming.

'Give in to it. Fighting's no good.'

She raised her right knee to waist height, held it for

just a second, then crashed her foot down onto his shin with every bit of strength she had. His grip on her mouth weakened and he cried out in pain. She repeated the move, stamping her foot hard and fast onto the already damaged shin. He screamed in agony, and shoved her away from him, a gentle thud as something fell to the grass.

She spun, head still woozy but adrenalin washing the effects way. He was dressed in black with a balaclava masking his face. A knife lay on the lawn near his feet. She grabbed his wrist, twisting hard till his arm was wrenched behind his back in one slick, practised move, making him squeal and beg. She reached up with her left hand and ripped the balaclava off his head.

'Stop. Don't. Please.'

She twisted his arm further, knowing it was close to breaking and not caring.

'*Please!*'

'I actually like it when they beg.'

She saw his head half turn towards her in confusion.

'Do you remember saying that? *I like it when they beg, but the crying becomes a pain.* So don't cry, whatever you do.'

His head twisted round, seeing her face properly for the first time. Confusion and rage contorting his features. She wrenched his arm tighter.

'Why don't you beg some more, huh? Go on!'

The voice emerged from the side of the building. Urgent. 'That's enough, Rachel. Rachel, let him go. We've got it from here.'

Narey turned to face Giannandrea, impassively returning his stare. Without looking at the man she held, she twisted his arm fiercely one more time and waited till the two uniformed cops had hands on him before releasing her grip. They took an arm each and lifted the man near clear off his feet so that he was facing her.

'Fraser Anderson, I am arresting you on suspicion of the murder of Eloise Gray on or around April 12 2019 at an unknown locus, as a result of electronic communications evidence. You do not need to say anything but anything you do say will be noted and may be used in evidence. Do you understand?'

Anderson grinned wildly before throwing his head back and laughing. The sound filled the air, echoing off the walls of the house.

Narey stared at the former IT consultant, itching to slap the laughter off his face. Instead, she nodded at the firearms cops and they wheeled him away as he spewed invective at anyone who would listen.

Giannandrea was at her shoulder, joining her in watching the constables load the man into the back of a newly arrived van to take him to the station.

'You're okay, right?'

'I'm fine, don't worry. It was just a bit of chloroform. Not enough to knock me out in that time.'

'Respectfully, Rachel? If I may?'

'Go on, Rico. Just say what you've got to say.'

'It was a really stupid fucking idea. What if he'd come behind you with a knife rather than a soaked cloth?'

'I'm wearing a stab-proof vest. You know that.'

'Not round your neck you aren't.'

'Then we'd have had a cast-iron case and Tony and Alanna would have done very well out of the insurance and the compensation.'

'That's not fucking funny, Rachel.'

'Oh come on, Rico, you had eyes on me at all times. The uniforms were ready to move. It was our best shot and I wasn't going to put anyone else in the position of doing it. And I wanted to do it. More to the point, we've got him.'

'Did you know it was Anderson, before you turned around? That he was Marr?'

'No. But he seemed most likely. He ticked all the psychological boxes, he had the ability to be different things to different people, he had the IT knowledge. And he was violent. He fitted the description of the guy dumped by Brianna Holden. Andy, the married guy who probably didn't tell her his real name and shortened his surname instead. Thing was, it didn't matter. Whoever was standing behind me was the person who murdered Eloise and the others. That's all I needed to know.'

Two hours later, Narey and Giannandrea sat at one side of a desk in the custody suite at Dalmarnock. On the other sat a clearly manic Fraser Anderson and a dour duty solicitor named Eric Rennie.

Anderson had replied with a firm 'no comment' to each of her opening questions, but she knew it wouldn't last. His temperament was like a beach ball being held under water and would soon erupt. She'd make sure it did.

'Are you going to beg, Fraser? I know you hate it when they beg.'

His eyes flared and she knew she'd got to him. No time to delete and retype, no time to consider or hide his reaction.

'Luck,' he blurted out. 'It was just luck. Nothing else.'

Rennie glared at his client, urging silence. Narey pressed.

'What was luck?'

'No comment.'

'I always believe you make your own luck. You contacted Vikki on that website but you could have contacted any of fifty women on that site and it would have been me you got. We put every one of those profiles up in the hope you'd come after one of them. And we left enough info lying around on social media pages we constructed to let you find what you needed to carry out your pathetic little seduction charade.'

'No. I don't believe it.'

'I bet you don't, but it's true. And I suppose you won't believe that we chose photographs of young women who all bore a resemblance to Brianna Holden. Just the way you like it.'

'That's not why I picked her. Not why I messaged her.'

She leaned across the desk and laughed in his face. 'Sure, you keep telling yourself that.'

He exploded, words tumbling out of his mouth, every other one a fuck, barely coherent as they were strangled by his anger. Spitting words at her like arrows.

His crazed laughter was replaced by fury. The rage of the entitled who don't get their own way. In that moment, his eyes burning, face twisted, hands forming claws, she saw what Eloise must have seen. What Brianna Holden must have seen. Ellen Lambert. Stuart McLennan. Kris Perera. Chrissie Ramsay. Irene Dow.

She saw a homicidal madman.

And she saw her chance.

'Is this how you were when you killed Eloise and the others? So riled up with rage that you couldn't control yourself?'

'I was in control. I killed that stupid bitch the way I wanted because I wanted to. Don't think you know me. Don't think you have any idea how I think or why I do anything. I made all that happen. I'm in control. I'm in control!'

'Yes. Sounds like it. You've admitted to killing Eloise Gray, why stop there? Keep going, Fraser. Keep going.'

Later, Narey and Giannandrea stood in the corridor outside the custody suite, a quiet calm finally enveloping them. It lasted all of thirty seconds before being crashed by a chirpy voice floating towards them.

'Great work, boss. I loved the sound of that bastard squealing as you took him out on the lawn.'

Kerri Wells was walking with a ten-pound note held out in front of her and a wide smile on her face.

'Don't say I don't honour my debts. Ten pounds for the winner of the Matthew Marr Sweepstake Challenge.'

Narey managed a laugh. 'Put that away before some-one sees it. You'll have me up in front of the chief. I'm not actually going to take money for a lucky guess on a murder suspect.' She stopped and hesitated, looking at them both. 'Oh fuck it. You know what? Yeah, pay up. A tenner each.'

Wells grinned and Giannandrea shook his head as he too handed over his ten pounds.

'Okay, come on. Let's go see what we can buy in the Station Bar for twenty quid. I think we could all do with a drink.'

CHAPTER 58

It was four in the afternoon in LA, midnight in Glasgow. Just as it always seemed to be.

Maybe it should have been too late for wine for one and too early for the other, but Narey and O'Neill were enjoying a glass together an ocean apart thanks to the wonders of modern communication.

Celebrating wasn't the right word. Job done was more like it. Relief for sure. Tired for certain. There was undoubtedly an element of personal satisfaction, but people were still dead, people were still grieving. It wasn't a time to have a party, not a public one anyway.

The two cops were separated by five thousand miles but connected by the devices in front of them and everything they'd been through. It took one to know one.

Rachel was the only person still up in the house on Belhaven Terrace, her husband and daughter asleep after they'd properly enjoyed each other's company as a family for the first time in what seemed an age but was only a week. She was curled up on the sofa, legs tucked underneath her, wind rattling at the windows, glass in hand and O'Neill a few feet away on the screen.

Cally was in her apartment in Willowbrook, blinds closed to keep out the fierce late-afternoon sun. The next few days were going to be filled with endless interviews, forms, lawyers and unhappy cops. She and Salgado now had more cases than days in the week so when her lieutenant offered her the chance to go home early before the onslaught began, she jumped at it.

A glass of red was raised in Glasgow. It was matched with a chilled white in LA. They sipped, and breathed, nodding at each other without the need for words. Rachel was first to break the contented silence.

'So how is Dylan Hansen doing?'

O'Neill closed her eyes and exhaled hard. 'He's going to make it.'

'Thank God. You really had me worried.'

'Yeah. Sorry for scaring the shit out of you when we found him.'

'Ha. It's cool. The strange thing was, even though we knew you were going to say he was dead whether he was or not, I still couldn't tell if you were faking it. It was because we'd no idea what you'd find. You did too good a job of acting.'

O'Neill grinned. 'I was only partly acting. When I found a pulse, it was actually easier to be mad at that bastard on the other side of the camera. My rage was real.'

'When you came up with the plan, I wasn't sure about it, but it certainly worked. It convinced Marr . . .

Anderson, I mean . . . that Dylan was dead and it was his turn. It flushed him out.'

'Yeah, well, it was risky. Especially when you were putting yourself on the line. And without a gun. I don't know how you guys do that.'

Narey shook her head. 'And I don't know how you guys can carry one. I've been doing this job for years and I've never felt the need for a gun. It would scare the shit out of me to have one, and to think that the bad guy had one too. Is Hansen able to talk?'

'Not yet. All he's been able to do is nod, but he's let us know he's aware he was held hostage, doesn't know where, didn't see the face of the person who took him. We've shown him a photograph of Garland, but it meant nothing to him. He's taking liquids intravenously, but the docs are hopeful he'll be feeding himself in a week or so. He's very disorientated and we haven't told him the full story yet.'

'He'll make a full recovery?'

'Hopefully. In time. The docs were very worried about brain damage, but he's come through the tests they gave him and they're much more optimistic. What it will do to him emotionally is another matter, but they're going to be working on that from the start, so he'll have the best chance of recovery.

'He suffered kidney failure and they're worried about his heart and liver. They all took a severe pounding. He's looking at dialysis or a transplant for the kidneys. But it could have been much worse. One of the specialists said that if we'd been as little as six hours later, then brain damage might have been irreparable. If we'd been twelve hours later, he'd have been dead. We got lucky.'

Narey disagreed with her. 'Like I told someone yesterday, you make your own luck. You got that info from Garland's ex-wife because you put the work in, you asked the right questions and eventually you got the right answers. It had nothing to do with luck.'

O'Neill smiled. 'Yeah, you're right. And if you want to email my captain and tell her that then I won't stop you. So, do you think it was luck – good or bad – that Garland and your man Anderson found each other?'

Narey sighed and tipped her glass towards the screen. 'That's a big question for a second glass of wine. You can believe it was fate or just the simple practicalities of two psychopaths inevitably going to the same twisted forum on the same twisted subject. But given that Garland was convinced his father was Elizabeth Short's murderer, it makes most sense that their mutual interest in the Black Dahlia brought them together. But I'll get it out of Anderson.'

'Garland was convinced of it because his father claimed it himself. Zac was happy for other people to think he was the Dahlia killer, but he was determined to have Ethan believe it. It's one way to make your kid proud of you.'

'The psych that's been working with me, Lennie Dakers, has no doubt that's what did the damage to Garland – the effect of believing that his father was a notorious killer, the man responsible for one the highest profile murders in the US. And crucially, he says, a murderer that was never caught. The power imbued by that knowledge left him feeling invincible, uncatchable, smarter than all of us. Nurture and nature at work, getting the worst kind of nurturing from the man that also gave him his DNA. For Ethan to be how he was, it didn't matter that Zac hadn't killed Elizabeth Short, it only mattered that he believed it.'

'Rachel, I don't mean to be rude but you're a bit harder to understand when we've both had a couple of drinks.'

'That's funny. I was thinking you're easier to understand.'

O'Neill laughed. 'Touché. What's Glasgow like, Rachel? I've always wanted to go to Scotland but never been. I guess like most Americans I've got an idea in my head that's probably completely wrong.'

'Well, you should come.'

'I'd love to!'

'Then do it. You can stay with us and I'll show you around. Listen, if the idea about Scotland in your head is *Brigadoon* then yes, you're completely wrong. And if you're thinking it's like *Trainspotting* then you're still completely wrong. The truth is maybe somewhere between the two. Scotland is a small country but manages to squeeze in a whole load of very different places. Different cities, different islands, scores of different accents. Glasgow isn't Scotland but it might be the best and worst of it. You'll find out.'

'I can't wait to. If you're serious, I'm booking a flight.'

'I'm serious.'

'Cool. Now what about Anderson? Have you got anything out of him?'

'He's admitted to four murders and denied any memory

of another three. He's lying, and he knows we know he's lying. He's playing games simply because he's irritated at being fooled. He's trying to take back control.

'But what really gets to me is how matter-of-factly he describes what he did. No emotion, no remorse, as if he was telling us how he changed a tyre on his car. He will describe the most terrible thing and be genuinely surprised if we find it shocking or dreadful. He thinks it's the most natural thing in the world that he and Garland operated together. To him, it makes complete sense.'

'I think it would have done to Garland too. I really regret we never got the chance to do the same with him as you can with Anderson. It's going to leave a lot of unanswered questions. And a lot of families not knowing what happened to their loved ones, or why. Of course, if he hadn't died from that heart attack then we might never have known about any of this.'

'You'd have got him eventually.'

'Maybe. Maybe not. That's the thing. It scares me how many of them are out there. Unknown serial killers. Murders that we don't even know are connected. It scares me how many men are like Garland, like Anderson – emotionless, pathological, compulsive killers. Little or no reason to what they're doing and therefore so much harder to catch.'

'No point in it scaring you. They're there whether we're scared or not. Our job is to catch the fuckers.'

'It doesn't really scare me. Scared is for other people. It's our job.'

'I know.'

'I know you know.'

They both laughed and took gulps at their wine.

'Why do you do it, Rachel? Why do you put it all on the line, time after time? Go after people like Garland and Anderson?'

'Obviously I could ask you the same question.'

'Well, obviously, but I asked you first.'

'Fair enough. I guess I've thought about this before. First, my dad was a cop, so it was in the blood. I grew up taking it for granted that the good guys went after the bad guys. For a long time, I thought my dad was a super-hero – and he was, to me – but then I came to realise that he was just an ordinary man doing extraordinary things. The bottom line is, someone's got to do it. And I want it to be me. It's my job.'

O'Neill raised her glass in salute before sipping from it.

'Okay, Cally, your turn.'

'Oh, much the same. You know the quote about how all it takes for evil to triumph is for good men – always men of course, not women – to do nothing?'

'Supposedly by Edmund Burke, but he never said it.'

'Right. Well that. Whoever said it first, it's right. I think people have three choices. Be the bad guy, be the good guy, or do nothing and hide your head in the sand. I don't like sand in my face.'

'Nor me. I guess that's why we have to do it, because no one else will. It has to be someone like us.'

'Someone like you. Someone like me.'

ACKNOWLEDGEMENTS

This book took far longer to complete than it should have done but would have taken even longer without the help, creativity and dedication of my editors at Simon & Schuster, Jo Dickinson and Bethan Jones, and my agent Mark 'Stan' Stanton. My gratitude goes to all three.

I owe a huge debt to Katherine Ramsland, Professor of Forensic Psychology at DeSales University in Pennsylvania. She is possibly the world's foremost expert on the minds of serial killers and was kind enough to school me on Matthew Marr and how best to interview him.

I'm equally grateful to Aileen Sloan, recently retired inspector at Police Scotland, whose diligent checking of my police procedure saved me from too many embarrassing errors.

Above all, I owe all the thanks and all the love to Alexandra Sokoloff – wife, lover, friend, muse, sounding board, and bestselling novelist.

Craig Robertson

The Photographer

A dawn raid on the home of a suspected rapist leads to the chilling discovery of a disturbing collection hidden under floorboards. **DI Rachel Narey** is terrified at the potential scale of what they've found and of what brutalities it may signal.

When the photographs are ruled inadmissible as evidence and the man walks free from court, Narey knows she's let down the victim she'd promised to protect and a monster is back on the streets.

Meanwhile, **Tony Winter**'s young family is under threat from internet trolls and he is determined to protect them whatever the cost. **He and Narey are in a race against time to find the unknown victims of the photographer's lens – before he strikes again.**

Available in print and eBook

Turn the page to read an extract now ...

SIMON & SCHUSTER

PROLOGUE

Lainey Henderson drew down hard on her cigarette with one eye on the clock, her free hand working continually to waft the smoke out of the window. Less than thirty seconds to go, her cheeks sucking the life out of the death stick.

The nerves were to blame but she thought of them as a good thing. What kind of person would she be if she wasn't nervous on behalf of the woman who was about to walk through that door? The woman expecting Lainey to make everything all right when nothing could possibly do that.

It was an ISS, an Initial Support Session. They were the worst and the best.

The worst because you got it all in the raw. The open wound of a victim talking, often for the first time, about their worst nightmare. They might be calm or hysterical, might talk or might not, might lash out at you because there was no one else there or they might cling on for dear life. They might just break down and cry in a way that ripped at your emotions and left you feeling worthless. That happened a lot. An ISS could break your heart.

But it could be the best too, because if you managed to take away even an inch of their pain then it would all be worth it.

The knock at the door was quiet, almost apologetic.

'Just a minute.' Lainey encouraged the final swirls of smoke out the window and pinged the butt out after it. She leaned far enough out that she could see a couple of dozen pieces of evidence of previous guilt and swore under her breath, making a mental note to clear them up before she got fired. The cigarette packet went in her pocket – she liked to have it at hand even when she couldn't smoke. 'Come in.'

The door slid open barely enough to let the girl slip through the gap. Lainey knew she was supposed to say, and think, *woman* rather than *girl*, but the ghost of a teenager who was gliding over the carpet made Lainey want to sweep her up in her arms and mother her. But she wouldn't. Or she'd try not to.

An ISS had rules. The idea was to make the client feel welcome, to assess them and find out what they wanted from the service. The case worker wasn't to ask a lot of questions or offer advice. Lainey had never been one for rules though.

The girl was a shade over five feet tall, dressed in baggy black from top to toe, pale as the moon with dark auburn hair that had been brushed with her eyes closed.

She glanced nervously round the room, looking for the monsters that Lainey had seen others search for.

'Jennifer? I'm Lainey. Do you want to take a seat? Coffee, tea, water?'

'No. No thanks. Well yes, water would be good. Thank you.'

Lainey poured her a glass from the bottle, taking the chance to gently touch the back of the girl's hand as she passed it to her. Jennifer flinched, but only slightly. It was a good sign.

Their chairs were just a few feet apart, facing each other. Lainey would rather have moved them till they were touching but she knew better or, more accurately, had been told better. She sat back and gave Jennifer the chance to speak first but soon realised it would be a long wait. The girl studied the walls even though there was precious little to see, just a couple of cheap, bland prints and a shelf studded with leaflets. When she finally returned her gaze to Lainey, Jennifer's eyes were wet with pleading. *Please talk. Ask me something. Say something.* So she did.

'The first time I came here, I had no idea what to expect. No idea what to say. Or even what to think. I might have sat here all day with my mouth shut and a million ideas running riot in my head if someone hadn't finally saved me from it. She told me that it was always scarier in your head than it was when said out loud. It's tempting to think if we don't say it then it's not real, it didn't really happen. That doesn't work though. If we leave them inside, they just get bigger and bigger. Let them out and they get small.'

Jennifer bobbed her head, although still not entirely

convinced. 'Have you ... Do you know what I'm going through?' There was a second question in there, unasked but unmissable.

'I do. Maybe not exactly because cases are different. But yes, I know.'

A little noise escaped from the girl. Relief of sorts. She swallowed and nodded and readied herself.

'I was raped. A man broke into my flat and raped me.'

Lainey just nodded to let her know she'd heard and understood. The words were unnecessary but important for Jennifer to say. The evidence of it was all over her, it was why they were here. The stomach-churning damage to her face was proof, too, that the rape had been accompanied with a fearful beating.

'Was it someone you knew?'

'No. I don't think so. He wore a mask. A balaclava.'

Anger twisted in Lainey's gut, something more too, and she had to wear a mask of her own to hide it. It wasn't going to do either of them any good if she had a meltdown. Her cigarette packet found its way into her hand and she began tapping on the top of it the way she always did when she was in desperate need of a fag.

'We're here to help in any way we can, Jennifer. Whatever you want from us.' The words sounded trite, meaningless, and they were. She wanted to be able to say she'd hunt the bastard down and cut his balls off with rusty shears.

'He kept calling me a slag. Like he knew me and it was my fault. He called me a slag every time he punched me in the face.'

Lainey felt like she'd been punched too. Sudden and hard. She looked at Jennifer, unable to say anything. Transfixed by her words and suddenly, though she'd tried not to be, by her face.

'He just kept thumping me. Pounding his fist into my nose and my cheek. Slag. Slag. Slag. Punch. Punch. Punch. I couldn't see. Just heard the noise. Heard my nose breaking. My cheek being smashed.'

Lainey's heart had stopped, her throat closed over.

'He had me pinned down. His knees on my chest and arms. I tried to fight but I couldn't move. He hit me till I passed out. Then he . . . he . . .'

Lainey managed to nod to save Jennifer from saying the rest. There was no need. She knew.

The girl's nose was almost at forty- five degrees to her pretty face, like a rugby player's or a boxer's. Both eyes were blackened and one was barely open at all. Her ashen skin was a canvas for violent patches of purple and red. Her lips were twice the size they should be.

Lainey had to resist the temptation to put her hand to her own face, mimic the places, feel where her own wounds used to be. There was a burning she wanted to cool with her touch.

Jennifer talked on, about waking to find herself naked, a searing pain between her legs, the bed sheets bloodied, her flat empty again. She saw herself in the mirror and screamed at the sight. She called a friend who called an ambulance.

Lainey knew the rules and the reasons for them. Jennifer had been raped, any semblance of control wrenched from her. It was Lainey's role to empower her as a survivor, not to reinforce the trauma by offering unwanted touching. If she sensed that the touch, the consoling hug that burst to be released from within her, was wanted then she had to ask permission to do so. Rapists never asked permission so counsellors had to.

Her gut told her Jennifer wanted and needed it. She could see it in the girl's eyes. Lainey teetered on the edge of asking and hugging and holding. And couldn't do it.

The words came out of her mouth by rote.

'What happens now is I need to ask if you want to proceed, then we put you on the waiting list and when you get to the top, your new worker will give you a call to arrange your first session.'

'New worker? It won't be you?'

'It might be me,' Lainey blurted out. 'But not necessarily.' It wouldn't be her.

'Oh. Okay.'

They said goodbye and Jennifer slipped out the door as quietly as she'd come in. Lainey waited as long as she dared to make sure the girl had gone then rushed to the corner of the desk, picked up the waste-paper basket and vomited into it.

Craig Robertson

Murderabilia

The first commuter train of the morning slowly rumbles away from platform seven of Queen St station. And then, as the train emerges from a tunnel, the screaming starts. Hanging from the bridge ahead of them is a body. Placed neatly on the ground below him are the victim's clothes.

Why?

Detective Inspector Rachel Narey is assigned the case and then just as quickly taken off it again. **Tony Winter**, now a journalist, must pursue the case for her. The line of questioning centres around the victim's clothes – why leave them in full view? And what did the killer not leave, and where might it appear again?

Everyone has a hobby. Some people collect death. To find this evil, **Narey** must go on to the dark web, and into immense danger . . .

Available in print and eBook

**SIMON &
SCHUSTER**

Craig Robertson

In Place of Death

**A tense and gripping crime novel set in
the dark underbelly of Glasgow ...**

A young man enters the culverted remains of an ancient
Glasgow stream, looking for thrills. Deep below the
city, it is decaying and claustrophobic and gets more so
with every step. As the ceiling lowers to no more than a
couple of feet above the ground, the man finds his path
blocked by another person. Someone with his throat cut.

As **DS Rachel Narey** leads the official investigation,
photographer **Tony Winter** follows a lead of his own,
through the shadowy world of urbexers, people
who pursue a dangerous and illegal hobby, a world
that Winter knows more about than he lets on.

And it soon becomes clear that the murderer has killed
before, and has no qualms about doing so again.

Available in print and eBook

SIMON &
SCHUSTER

Craig Robertson

The Last Refuge

John Callum is fleeing his past, but
has run straight into danger.

When **John Callum** arrives on the wild and desolate
Faroe Islands, he vows to sever all ties with his
previous life. He desperately wants to make a
new start, and is surprised by how quickly he is
welcomed into the close-knit community. But still, the
terrifying, debilitating nightmares just won't stop.

Then the solitude is shattered by an almost unheard-
of crime on the islands: murder. A specialist team of
detectives arrives from Denmark to help the local police,
who seem completely ill-equipped for an investigation of
this scale. But as tensions rise, and the community closes
rank to protect its own, John has to watch his back.

But far more disquieting than that, John's nightmares
have taken an even more disturbing turn, and he
can't be certain about the one thing he needs to
know above all else. Whether he is the killer . . .

Available in print and eBook

**SIMON &
SCHUSTER**

Craig Robertson

Witness the Dead

Red Silk is back . . .

Scotland 1972. Glasgow is haunted by a murderer
nicknamed Red Silk – a feared serial killer who
selects his victims in the city's nightclubs. The case
remains unsolved but Archibald Atto, later imprisoned
for other murders, is thought to be Red Silk.

In modern-day Glasgow, **DS Rachel Narey** is called to a
gruesome crime scene at the city's Necropolis. The body
of a young woman lies stretched out over a tomb. Her
body bears a three-letter message from her killer.

Now retired, former detective Danny Neilson spots a link
between the new murder and those he investigated in 1972 –
details that no copycat killer could have known about. But
Atto is still behind bars. Must Danny face up to his fears that
they never caught their man? Determined finally to crack the
case, Danny, along with his nephew, police photographer
Tony Winter, pays Atto a visit. But they soon discover that
they are going to need the combined efforts of police forces
past and present to bring a twisted killer to justice.

Available in print and eBook

**SIMON &
SCHUSTER**

Craig Robertson

Cold Grave

A murder investigation frozen in time is beginning to melt.

November 1993. Scotland is in the grip of an ice-cold winter and the Lake of Menteith is frozen over. A young man and woman walk across the ice to the historic island of Inchmahome which lies in the middle of the lake. Only the man returns.

In the spring, as staff prepare the abbey ruins for summer visitors, they discover the body of a girl, her skull violently crushed.

Present day. Retired detective Alan Narey is still haunted by the unsolved crime. Desperate to relieve her ailing father's conscience, **DS Rachel Narey** risks her job and reputation by returning to the Lake of Menteith and unofficially reopening the cold case.

With the help of police photographer **Tony Winter**, Rachel prepares a dangerous gambit to uncover the killer's identity – little knowing who that truly is. Despite the freezing temperatures the ice-cold case begins to thaw, and with it a tide of secrets long frozen in time are suddenly and shockingly unleashed.

Available in print and eBook

**SIMON &
SCHUSTER**

Craig Robertson

Snapshot

A series of high-profile shootings by a lone sniper leaves Glasgow terrorised and police photographer **Tony Winter** – a man with a tragic hidden past – mystified.

Who is behind the executions of some of the most notorious drug lords in the city? As more shootings occur – including those of police officers – the authorities realise they have a vigilante on their hands.

Meanwhile, Tony investigates a link between the victims and a schoolboy who has been badly beaten. Seemingly unconnected, they share a strange link. As Tony delves deeper, his quest for the truth and his search for the killer lead him down dark and dangerous paths.

Available in print and eBook

**SIMON &
SCHUSTER**

Craig Robertson

Random

Glasgow is being terrorised by a serial killer the media have nicknamed The Cutter. The murders have left the police baffled.

There seems to be neither rhyme nor reason behind the killings; no kind of pattern or motive; an entirely different method of murder each time, and nothing that connects the victims except for the fact that the little fingers of their right hands have been severed.

If **DS Rachel Narey** could only work out the key to the seemingly random murders, how and why the killer selects his victims, she would be well on her way to catching him. But as the police, the press and a threatening figure from Glasgow's underworld begin to close in on The Cutter, his carefully laid plans threaten to unravel – with horrifying consequences.

Available in print and eBook

SIMON &
SCHUSTER